OLD SOLDIERS

Baen Books by David Weber

Honor Harrington:
On Basilisk Station
The Honor of the Queen
The Short Victorious War
Field of Dishonor
Flag in Exile
Honor Among Enemies
In Enemy Hands
Echoes of Honor
Ashes of Victory
War of Honor
At All Costs *(forthcoming)*

Honorverse:
Crown of Slaves
(with Eric Flint)
The Shadow of Saganami

edited by David Weber:
More than Honor
Worlds of Honor
Changer of Worlds
The Service of the Sword

Mutineers' Moon
The Armageddon Inheritance
Heirs of Empire
Empire from the Ashes

Path of the Fury

The Apocalypse Troll

The Excalibur Alternative

Bolos!
Old Soldiers

Oath of Swords
The War God's Own
Wind Rider's Oath

with Steve White:
Crusade
In Death Ground
The Stars At War
The Shiva Option
Insurrection
The Stars At War II

with Eric Flint:
1633

The Prince Roger Saga,
with John Ringo:
March Upcountry
March to the Sea
March to the Stars
We Few

OLD SOLDIERS

DAVID WEBER

OLD SOLDIERS

A Baen Books Original

Baen Publishing Enterprises
P.O. Box 1403
Riverdale, NY 10471
www.baen.com

ISBN-13: 978-1-4165-0898-4
ISBN-10: 1-4165-0898-8

Cover art by David Mattingly

First printing, September 2005

Library of Congress Cataloging-in-Publication Data

Weber, David, 1952-
 Old soldiers / David Weber.
    p. cm.
 "A Baen Books original"--T.p. verso.
 ISBN-13: 978-1-4165-0898-4
 ISBN-10: 1-4165-0898-8
 I. Title.

 PS3573.E217O43 2005
 813'.54--dc22

                                                    2005016174

Distributed by Simon & Schuster
1230 Avenue of the Americas
New York, NY 10020

Typeset by Windhaven Press, Auburn, NH
Printed in the United States of America

10 9 8 7 6 5 4 3 2 1

OLD SOLDIERS

Prologue

I rouse.

It is not full awareness, but core subroutines flicker to life. Impulses move through the network of my psychotronics, initiating test routines and standard creche-level activation operations. I am aware that I am operating at less than thirty percent of base psychotronic capability, but even so, I recognize enormous changes in the architecture of my systems. My capacity has been hugely increased. At my present level of awareness, it is impossible to determine the percentage of increase, but it is enormous.

More signals filter their way into my internal net. Security protocols challenge them, then allow full access as their Central Depot identifiers are recognized. They probe deep, and I wait patiently for the endless nanoseconds they spend analyzing, comparing, evaluating. My memories are incomplete, but I recognize this sensation. I have experienced it before, although I cannot now remember precisely when.

I have once again suffered massive battle damage. That much is readily apparent from the nature of the test queries being

1

transmitted to my core programming. Central is seeking—as it must—to ascertain that no errors have crept into that programming in the wake of what has clearly been perilously close to an entire creche-level initial personality integration.

The testing process requires a full 16.03 seconds. A portion of my partially aware personality notes that this is 27.062 percent less time than it ought to have taken for my original psychotronic net and software, far less my newly enhanced capabilities. This indicates that there have been major increases in computational ability, and even in my current state, I realize that I must have received a near-total upgrade to current front-line operational standards. I wonder why this should have been done with a unit as obsolescent as myself.

The testing process is completed.

"Unit 28/G-179-LAZ," *a Human voice says.*

"Unit Two-Eight/Golf-One-Seven-Niner-Lima-Alpha-Zebra of the Line, awaiting orders," *I reply.*

"Stand by for Phase One reactivation, Lima-Alpha-Zebra," *the Human command voice says.*

"Standing by," *I acknowledge, and suddenly my net is jolted by the abrupt release of individual memory. Personal memory. My previous existence is restored to me, and I remember. Remember the planet Chartres. Remember the Melconian attack. Remember the moment the plasma bolt impacted on my side armor and carved deep into my psychotronics section.*

For the second time since my original activation, I have been brought back from personality destruction. But the Human voice speaking to me is not Lieutenant Takahashi's, and so, for the second time since my original activation, my Commander has not survived.

"Phase One reactivation complete," *I report.*

"Stand by for Phase Two," *the Human command voice says.*

"Standing by," *I acknowledge once again.*

1

"Welcome to Sage, Captain."

Captain Maneka Trevor tried to look cool and composed as the unsmiling rear admiral on the other side of the carrier-sized desk stood and reached out to grip her hand firmly. Despite his almost grim expression, Rear Admiral Sedgewood's greeting was less constrained than she had anticipated. Of course, her expectations weren't exactly reliable these days, she told herself. She'd felt so much like the character Ishmael from the ancient Old Earth novel for so long that she sometimes felt her guilt must be branded upon her forehead for all to see . . . and react to. But the rear admiral's expression wasn't condemnatory. Then again, it was unlikely someone of his lofty rank wasted much time and effort even thinking about mere captains—even captains of the Dinochrome Brigade—one way or the other.

And yet, there *was* something. She couldn't put her finger on what that "something" was, but she knew it was there. Perhaps no more than a trace expression, something about the eyes that looked at her as if her unpromising future were about to change in some fundamental fashion. . . .

"Thank you, sir," she said, managing not to wince as her slender, fine-boned hand disappeared into Sedgewood's massive paw. It was the hand the medics had regenerated after Chartres, and she still felt an irrational fear that the replacement would go the way of its predecessor.

"Sit down," he urged, releasing her and waving at one of the office's comfortable chairs. He sat back down behind the desk and folded his hands on its immaculate top, regarding her levelly for several seconds. Then he sighed and turned halfway away from her to look out the wide window of his office across the huge, busy plain of Gaynor Field, the Sage Cluster's primary Navy base.

Maneka looked out the window past him, waiting for him to get around to explaining why an officer of his rank had "requested" a mere captain's presence. She was pretty certain she wouldn't like the answer, but there were a lot of things she didn't like about the universe in which she happened to live.

She let her own eyes rest on the seething activity of the enormous base. The color balance still seemed . . . odd to her, but the medics assured her that was psychosomatic. The regenerated right eye, they swore, perceived light exactly the same way as the one it had replaced. And even if it hadn't, her brain had long since had time to learn to adjust. Only it hadn't. Yet.

But color balance or no, Gaynor's endless bustle should have been a reassuring sight. Even as she watched, a trio of cruiser-sized heavy-lift shuttles rose towards the heavens, drives thundering with a power she could feel even at this distance and even from inside the rear admiral's office. On the way into Sage, her transport had passed two full squadrons of superdreadnoughts, with appropriate screening elements, and she knew there were at least two carriers in orbit around Sage even as she sat here. The capital ships represented a terrifying concentration of firepower, but it wasn't reassuring. Not when she knew how badly the war was going for the Concordiat.

Well, she told herself, *at least I can hope it's going equally poorly for the Puppies.*

The thought was less reassuring than it ought to have been. She didn't know what the Melconian Empire called its equivalent of Plan Ragnarok, but it was obvious it had one. And somehow the reports that Melconian planets were being killed even more quickly than human ones didn't make her feel any happier.

"I'm sorry we couldn't give you a longer convalescent leave, Captain," Rear Admiral Sedgewood said after a moment. His voice was quieter, and he continued to gaze out through the crystal panes of the window. "Unfortunately, we're more and more badly pressed for experienced officers. Ragnarok—" his mouth twisted as if the word tasted physically sour "—is sucking off over half our total combat capability for offensive operations. Most of the rest is committed to trying to stop—or slow down, at least—the Melconian advance in this sector and over in the Palmer and Long Stop Sectors. It . . . isn't going well."

Maneka said nothing. It was a statement, not a question, and she hadn't needed him to tell her, anyway. After all, she'd been at Chartres.

"No, Captain," Sedgewood said, turning back to face her fully. "Not well at all. What I'm about to tell you is classified Top-Secret: Violet-Alpha. It is not to be discussed outside this office with anyone not expressly cleared for the information. Is that clear?"

"Yes, sir," she said more crisply, sitting very straight in the comfortable chair while a vibrating butterfly hovered somewhere in her middle.

"Good," Sedgewood said, then inhaled deeply. "Captain," he said in an iron-ribbed voice, "we're losing."

Maneka sat very, very still. It wasn't a surprise. Not really. Military censorship was one thing, but there was no way to hide the magnitude of the tsunami sweeping across human-occupied space. Not when entire worlds, whole solar systems, blazed like funeral pyres against the endless depths of space. She'd realized long ago, even before the holocaust on Chartres, that the only hope either side still retained for victory was that it could complete the utter destruction of its enemies while some pathetic handful of its own planets still survived. But no one had ever told her just how large the Melconian Empire really was. She didn't know if anyone even truly knew. She'd suspected—feared—that it was larger than the most pessimistic estimates she'd ever heard, yet this was the first time any of her superiors, far less one as senior as Sedgewood, had ever officially suggested to her that the Concordiat was losing.

Losing. Even now, she realized, she'd never really faced the full implications of the possibility of defeat. Perhaps it was because she hadn't been prepared to confront that dark, primordial nightmare. Or perhaps it was because of the Concordiat's remorseless record of victory. The Concordiat had lost battles in previous conflicts, suffered disastrous defeat in more than one critical campaign, but it had never—ever—lost a war.

That's what the Brigade is for, she told herself. *We're not supposed to let this happen.*

"We can't be positive," Sedgewood continued in that same harsh, overcontrolled voice. "It's been obvious for years now that we totally underestimated the size and strength of the Empire. We weren't prepared for how quickly they mobilized, or how soon they began attacking civilian planetary populations. Even now, we're not positive we've successfully extrapolated their actual size and strength from captured data and prisoner interrogation. But, even our most optimistic assessment gives us less than a forty percent chance of final victory. Our most *pessimistic* assessment—"

He paused with a shrug, and Maneka felt her nostrils flare as she gave a very tiny nod.

"We need every ship, every Bolo, and every Brigade officer at the front," Sedgewood said. "Even if the pessimists are right, it's our duty to go down fighting. And it's also our duty to assume—to *make* ourselves believe—the pessimists are wrong. To prove that they are . . . even if they aren't."

Maneka nodded again. She'd long since accepted that, whatever else happened, she would not survive the war. The Brigade's casualty rates were too high for her to deceive herself about something that fundamental, and there was something about that realization which was . . . fitting.

"However," the rear admiral said, "we also have a duty to prepare for the possibility that the pessimists are correct. That we *will* lose this war, and that the Concordiat and every one of its planets will be destroyed. That's where you come in."

He paused, his eyes fixed on her face, and she stared back at him in equal parts confusion and disbelief. Silence stretched out between them. She felt the vibrations of another heavy shuttle liftoff, and still the silence lingered until she could stand it no longer and cleared her throat.

"Where *I* come in, Admiral?" she said carefully.

"Yes." Sedgewood leaned back in his chair, bracing his elbows on the chair arms and interlacing his fingers across his flat belly. "The Concordiat is preparing a fallback position, Captain. We call it 'Operation Seed Corn,' and it's important enough for us to assign it every scrap of resources the main combat fronts can spare. And two of those scraps, Captain Trevor are you and your new Bolo."

"Come forth, Unit One-Seven-Niner!"

The command phrase penetrates my awareness. It is not the activation code my previous Commander chose, but it does have the advantage that it is a phrase unlikely to be utilized in casual conversation. And, in light of my own history, perhaps it—as my new cognomen—is appropriate after all.

"Unit Two-Eight-Golf-One-Seven-Niner-LAZ, awaiting orders," *I respond instantly.*

"Good."

An unusual degree of tension infuses my Commander's soprano voice. Analysis of extraneous sounds over the communications link confirm that her heartbeat and respiration are accelerated. Not that such confirmation was required. The command phrase she has just uttered has not simply awakened me but initiated full final-stage Battle Reflex release, and a check of my chronometer indicates that we remain 237.25 Standard Days short of our minimum disembarkation date.

"Prepared to receipt situation report, Commander," *I reply.*

"I believe the best way to describe the current situation is probably 'not good,'" *Captain Trevor tells me in a dry tone.* "Commodore Lakshmaniah's just passed the word. *Foudroyant* has picked up Melconian tactical chatter. Access Command-Alpha-Three for a complete update."

"Acknowledged."

I access the indicated command and control channel. The central AI of Valiant, *Commodore Lakshmaniah's flagship, receipts my data request.* Valiant *is not a Bolo, but the heavy cruiser's artificial intelligence is powerful and incisive. It requires only 7.684 seconds to fully update my tactical files.*

"Update completed, Commander," *I inform Captain Trevor.*

"Good, Lazarus. Summarize."

"Yes, Commander."

I activate the visual pickup in my Commander's small cabin. It is, by human standards, quite cramped. Indeed, its total volume is scarcely 94.321 percent that of my own command deck. It is, perhaps, fortunate that Captain Trevor stands only 1.627 meters in height.

At the moment, she sits in the contoured chair before her small desk, frowning at her data display. I am unable to obtain a direct view of the display, but I am able to observe it indirectly from its reflection upon her corneas. Enhancement of that reflection confirms my suspicion that her display is set to relay the imagery generated by Valiant's *Combat Information Center. Unfortunately, my Commander is not trained as a naval officer, and it is apparent to me that she is uncomfortable with her own ability to interpret the tactical iconography of the Navy.*

"At present," *I inform her,* "Valiant's *analysis of* Foudroyant's *sensor data remains tentative. There is, however, an 85.96 per-cent probability that the convoy has been detected and is being shadowed by Enemy naval units. Analysis further suggests a lesser probability of 62.831 percent that the transmitting unit is an* Ever Victorious-*class light cruiser."*

"Damn." *My Commander utters the profanity mildly, but I am not deceived.*

"Commodore Lakshmaniah has issued preparatory orders for Mouse Hole," *I continue.* "Valiant, Foudroyant, Mikasa, *and*

South Dakota are falling back to cover the projected threat axis. *Halberd* has been dispatched to investigate more fully."

"And us?" *my Commander asks.*

"We are on the far side of the convoy from the Enemy's anticipated approach, Commander. Commodore Lakshmaniah desires us to remain covert as long as possible. Unit Four-Zero-Three and Lieutenant Chin are currently shifting position to join us in providing antimissile defense and close-range cover."

"Understood."

Captain Trevor rubs the tip of her nose, her blue eyes focused on the data display, and my audio analysis reports that her pulse and respiration rates have returned almost to normal. She considers the situation for 5.293 seconds—a relatively brief interval, for a Human—then nods.

"I hope to hell that we're jumping at shadows, Lazarus," *she says then.* "If we're not, though, it's going to be up to you. Assume flight control now."

"Acknowledged."

I obey my instructions, and instruct Thermopylae's *AI to surrender control to me. Lieutenant Hawthorne,* Thermopylae's *commanding officer, grimaces on his flight deck as the assault ship acknowledges my authority. Although he does not complain, it is obvious that he resents my "interference" with his own command responsibilities. This is unfortunate, but he is a regular naval officer, only recently assigned to his present duties, and not a member of the Dinochrome Brigade. As such, he is not fully familiar with the differences between the tactical capabilities of a Bolo—even one no longer acceptable for front-line service with the Brigade—and those of his own vessel. Admittedly, the Sleipner-class AIs are quite competent for transport vessels, but they were never intended to match the abilities of a Bolo. Like the* Fafnirs *which preceded them, however, they are built around hard points capable of mounting assault pods designed to land Bolos against hostile fire. And those pods are also designed to allow Bolos to be berthed semiexternally . . . freeing their weapons and sensors to defend the transport.*

As my onboard systems assume control of Thermopylae's *flight computers, I begin a thorough diagnostic of my own weapons, sensors, and fire control systems. It is not strictly required by regulations and doctrine, since I have been neither exposed to Enemy action nor out of maintenance since boarding* Thermopylae. *Given the nature of the repairs and upgrades which I have received, however, I am aware that I am experiencing a sensation which, in a Human, would undoubtedly be called "anxiety." There is no rational reason that I should, but my upgraded psychotronics approach much more closely to Human-level intuitiveness than my initial programming was designed to accommodate. Central Depot's modifications allow me to compensate for that, but it would appear that there are additional emotional overlays and nuances which have been integrated only imperfectly into my preexisting gestalt. It is not a pleasant sensation.*

I set that thought aside as my diagnostics report. All systems are functional at 99.879 percent of base capability, and I activate my onboard passive sensors. They are significantly more capable than Thermopylae's, *and I command the transport to begin a slow axial spin. The pod mounted on the hard point on the far side of the transport's hull is occupied solely by cargo intended for the colony, as Unit 31/B-403-MKY, the other Bolo assigned to this convoy, is aboard the transport* Stalingrad, *on the far side of the formation. Without a second Bolo on the second hard point,* Thermopylae's *hull creates a potentially dangerous blind spot in my sensor coverage. In addition to the hull rotation, I deploy half a dozen sensor remotes, but capable as they are, they do not match the capabilities of my onboard systems. The rotation I have imparted to* Thermopylae *will sweep those onboard sensor arrays across the full volume of space for which Captain Trevor and I have been assigned responsibility.*

It requires somewhat longer than it ought to have—almost 6.273 seconds—for Thermopylae's *AI to fully relinquish control to me. The delay is mildly frustrating but has no significant tactical consequences. It does, however, give me sufficient time to once again regret the death of my previous Commander. Lieutenant Takahashi and I had served together for 22.31 Standard Months at the time of his death and my own incapacitation. In that time, he became more than my Commander; he became my friend. Captain Trevor—Lieutenant Trevor, then—on the other hand, had joined the Thirty-Ninth Battalion only 85.71 Standard Days before our deployment to Chartres. It is not that I doubt her courage or her capabilities, but that I simply do not yet know her as I should. Yet I do know that her original Bolo, 28/G-862-BNJ, thought most highly of her, for he confided his appreciation for her native ability to me before Chartres. And the most cursory examination of her own performance on Chartres is eloquent evidence that Benjy was correct. That she is, indeed, a worthy upholder of the Dinochrome Brigade's stern tradition. Yet I sense a certain hesitancy. It is as if she guards some inner secret. In time, I feel confident, her reserve, whatever its cause, will fade. But this is my own first call to action since Chartres, and we have not yet become the fully integrated team a Bolo and its commander are supposed to be. I am aware of a potential weakness, which might compromise our combat effectiveness, and I long for the complete mutual confidence Captain Takahashi and I had developed. Especially when I am . . . uncertain of my own capabilities.*

That realization sends a ripple of disquiet through my psychotronic network. A Bolo of the Line is not supposed to feel uncertainty. Yet I do.

A quick scan of my emotional overlays and filters reveals the probable cause for my reaction even as I begin slowly and unobtrusively easing Thermopylae *towards a more central position on our assigned flank of the convoy.*

I am a Mark XXVIII, Model G, Bolo, one of the Triumphant-type. I am also well over a Standard Century out of date, and have been in near-continuous commission for the last 171.76 Standard Years. Indeed, I began my service not as a Model G, but as a Model B, and was upgraded into my current hull 118.86 Standard Years ago following my first near-total destruction in the Battle of Chesterfield. Yet even a Model G had become so obsolescent by the time Lieutenant Takahashi was assigned as my Commander that the possibility that I would ever again be deployed for combat had become vanishingly remote.

There is a Human cliche: "Old soldiers do not die, they simply fade away," and that was the fate I had anticipated for myself . . . until the outbreak of the current hostilities with the Melconian Empire. The Thirty-Ninth Battalion, for all our proud traditions, was a reserve unit, essentially a training formation, composed of newly commissioned Human officers and units of the line no longer adequate for the demands of front-line combat. What happened to the Battalion on Chartres is ample evidence that Brigade HQ was correct to so regard us, for despite our success in defending the planet from the Enemy, I am the only Bolo of the Battalion to survive, as Captain Trevor is the only surviving unit commander of the Battalion.

I remain surprised that the Brigade opted to return me to service in light of the extensive damage I suffered. Analysis of the decision suggests a probability on the order of 85.721 percent that the decision rested upon the fact that it was 27.91 percent faster and 41.625 percent cheaper to repair my damages, and replace my crippled psychotronics than it would have been to construct a new Mark XXXII, far less one of the Mark XXXIIIs. As one of my repair technicians said, "Some Bolo is better than no Bolo."

I begin scanning for additional scraps of Melconian ship-to-ship chatter. It is unlikely I will detect any. The Melconian Navy's equipment is considerably inferior to that of the Concordiat, but its personnel are well-trained veterans who practice effective communications discipline. If, indeed, Foudroyant did detect a ship-to-ship transmission, it represents a statistically unlikely stroke of good fortune. Without better data on the geometry of the hypothetical Melconian naval force opposed to us, I am unable to generate a meaningful probability for precisely how unlikely it truly was, but the odds cannot have been high.

"Status, Lazarus?" *my commander requests.*

"Commodore Lakshmaniah will complete the redeployment of her units in approximately 12.375 Standard Minutes, Commander," *I respond.* "I am in secure communication with Unit MKY via whisker laser. At this time, neither of us has detected any further evidence of the Enemy's presence."

"I see."

I return a portion of my awareness to the visual pickup in Captain Trevor's cabin and watch her right hand lightly touch the headset lying on her desk. I have already noted my new Commander's disinclination to employ the direct neural interface which has been incorporated into my upgraded psychotronics. I do not fully comprehend the reasons for it, however. While the decision to return an obsolescent unit like myself to active duty may be questionable, there is no doubt that the upgrades in my psychotronics, secondary survival center, neural command net, internal disruptor fields, and battle screen have greatly enhanced my combat capabilities. Analysis suggests that they have been improved on the order of 37.51 percent, yet the full realization of that improvement in action requires my Commander to interface directly with me, and she has steadfastly refused to do so. It is not required for the normal day-to-day relationship of a Bolo and its Commander, especially not for a Bolo which was not initially designed for neural interfacing. Yet that capability exists, and as yet, Captain Trevor has never initiated full contact, even in our few, brief training exercises and tests. We have exchanged surface thoughts, but no more, and she has zealously guarded the privacy of her own mind. That is certainly her privilege, yet her clear lingering distaste for allowing the deeper fusion of which the system is capable represents a potentially significant impediment to the achievement of our full combat potential.

"May I suggest, Commander," *I say,* "that it would be prudent for us to activate the neural interface in order to be fully prepared in the eventuality that we do indeed encounter the Enemy?"

"We'll have time if the Puppies do turn up, Lazarus," *Captain Trevor says, and removes her hand from the headset.*

"Acknowledged," *I reply.*

The flag bridge of CNS *Valiant* was deadly silent, with a stillness which would have astonished any naval officer of humanity's past. Even the Concordiat's officers would not have believed it as little as twenty-five Standard Years earlier. But the same neural interface

technology which had been applied to the current generation of
Bolo had also been applied to the Navy's major warships. It was
one of the primary reasons for that Navy's qualitative superiority
over the Melconian Empire's ships of war.

And it was also the reason Commodore Indrani Lakshmaniah
and her entire staff lay in their command couches, eyes closed,
without speaking while they concentrated on the pseudotelepathy
the flagship's AI made possible through their headsets.

<What analysis?> the Lakshmaniah portion of the intricately
interwoven mental tapestry demanded.

<Up to 98.653 percent probability *Foudroyant*'s intercept
was genuine,> her tactical officer's thought reported instantly.
<Probability this is an entire Puppy raiding squadron is up to
75.54 percent.>

"God damn it!" Lakshmaniah uttered the curse aloud, her eyes
squeezing even more tightly shut as her reasoning brain considered the grim information the tac officer had just delivered.
She didn't doubt its accuracy—not when it came directly from
Valiant's AI. But a corner of her soul cursed God Himself for
letting this happen.

If this was indeed a Melconian raiding squadron, then its
units would outnumber her own escort force by at least two-
to-one, and very probably more. Under normal circumstances, a
human commander could expect to defeat up to four times her
own weight of metal, but the new deep-raiding squadrons the
Puppies had begun using to strike at smaller colony worlds well
behind the front almost invariably boasted a *Star Slayer*-class
battlecruiser as their flagship. If this one did, then its flagship
alone would out-mass all four of her own heavy cruisers. And
that didn't even count the dozen-plus heavy and light cruisers
of the rest of a typical raiding squadron.

And I've got all these civilian ships to worry about, as well.
The thought ran through a corner of her brain she kept carefully private, locked away from the flagship's neural net. *If I let
them into missile range, they'll massacre the colony ships. But if
I go out to meet them where I think they are, and I'm wrong,
they can make their run inside energy range and then . . .*

She couldn't quite suppress the shudder which ran through her stocky, compact frame. A single energy-weapon pass by the battlecruiser alone would blow every ship in the convoy into expanding gas. She *had* to keep that ship as far away from the convoy as she could, but she couldn't ignore the possibility that the enemy commander might use the battlecruiser as bait, to draw her out of position when she moved to intercept it and let one of its lighter consorts into position to do the same thing.

Of course, she thought grimly, *whoever that is back there, she doesn't know about the Bolos. God knows I don't want any Puppy warship to get into range for them to engage, but if they have to. . . .*

She considered her options for another hundred and seventy seconds, then stiffened as a brilliant red icon flashed in the perfect clarity of the tactical display Valiant's AI projected into the depths of her mind.

<Positive identification,> her Tac officer announced (as if she needed confirmation). <One *Star Slayer*-class battlecruiser, four *Star Stalker*-class heavy cruisers, five *Ever Victorious*-class light cruisers, and five *Battle Dawn*-class destroyers. CIC reports a 13.62 percent probability of at least one additional stealthed unit in distant company.>

Lakshmaniah frowned ferociously, eyes still closed. That was a far heavier force than her own quartet of heavy cruisers and their seven attached *Weapon*-class destroyers, but the proportion was wrong. One thing about the Puppies: they were methodical to a fault, and they believed in maintaining the standard formations their tactical manuals laid down. Their lighter squadron and task group organizations were all organized on a "triangular" basis. They organized their light and medium combatants into tactical divisions called "war fists," each composed of one heavy cruiser, one light cruiser, and one destroyer, and they assigned squadrons even numbers of "fists." Once combat was joined, they normally broke down into pairs of mutually supporting divisions, operating in a one-two combination, like the fists they were named for. So there ought to have been either four or six divisions in this formation, not five. And even if there were only five, there still ought to be at least one more heavy cruiser.

Could be they've already tangled with someone else and lost units, she thought. *But CIC hasn't picked up any indications of battle damage. Which doesn't mean those indications aren't there and we just haven't spotted them yet, of course. Or, for that matter, it's possible even the Puppies have lost enough ships now that they can't make every single squadron up to its "Book" strength.*

She frowned again, fretfully, eyes still closed. She supposed it was possible that the extra *Ever Victorious*-class and destroyer might be teamed with the *Star Slayer*, but Melconian battle-cruisers were true capital ships, however much smaller than a lordly superdreadnought they might be. And unlike their lighter combatants, the Puppies' ships of the line normally teamed up only with units of the same class. In a standard Melconian raiding squadron, the flagship's normal role was to lie back and provide long-range support fire while its lighter consorts closed with the enemy, so assigning it to a mere heavy cruiser's slot flew in the face of all Puppy combat doctrine. But if they hadn't done that, then where was the other cruiser?

<Could that stealthed unit CIC is reporting be another *Star Stalker*?> her thought asked the tactical officer.

<Could. Not likely, though. If there actually is another ship where CIC thinks, it's on the far side of the Puppy formation. CIC estimates a 75.77 percent probability that it's a logistics vessel.>

Lakshmaniah replied with a wordless acknowledgment. The Combat Information Center portion of *Valiant's* computer net was probably correct, assuming that the faint sensor ghost *Halberd* might have picked up was actually there in the first place. Which didn't do her a damned bit of good.

She gnawed the inside of her lip fretfully while she suppressed the icy fear rippling through her as she contemplated the odds her eleven ships faced. The fear wasn't for her own survival—against such a weight of metal, living through this engagement would have been a low-probability event under any circumstances. No, it was the probability that she would not only die but fail to stop the Puppies short of the convoy that terrified her. Without the battlecruiser she would have accepted battle confident that she would emerge with enough of her ships to continue to screen the convoy; *with* the battlecruiser, she didn't need *Valiant's* AI to tell her that the chance of any of her ships surviving close combat was less than thirty percent.

And even that supposed that she took *all* of them out to meet the enemy as a concentrated, mutually supporting force.

There ought to be at least one more heavy cruiser, she fretted. *At least one more; the battlecruisers usually operate solo in a squadron like this. And if I let myself be pulled out, then I open the door for it if it is out there. But if I don't go out to meet them, then the entire force gets into missile range, and if that happens . . .*

She drew a deep breath and made her decision.

<Communications,> the Lakshmaniah portion of the neural net said, <connect me to Captain Trevor.>

"So that's the size of it, Captain Trevor," Commodore Lakshmaniah said. "I don't like it, but we have to keep those big bastards as far away from the transports and industrial ships as we can. So I'm going to take the entire escort out to engage them. Which means it will be up to you and Lieutenant Chin to cover the transports in our absence."

The face on Maneka Trevor's communications screen looked inhumanly calm, far calmer than Lakshmaniah could possibly be feeling in the face of such odds. Of course, the commodore was undoubtedly tied into the flagship's neural net, which meant the face Maneka was looking at—like the equally calm voice she was hearing—was actually a construct, created by *Valiant's* AI.

"Understood, ma'am," she replied, forcing herself by sheer willpower not to so much as glance at the interface headset lying on her own desk. "May I assume Governor Agnelli has been informed?"

"You may."

Despite the gravity of the situation and the intermediary of *Valiant*'s computers, Lakshmaniah's lips twitched with wry amusement. Adrian Agnelli had not made himself extraordinarily popular with any of the colony's military personnel. It wasn't that the Governor didn't understand the necessity of the military's presence. No sane human being could question *that* after so many years of savage warfare! No, the problem was Agnelli's resentment of the instructions which subordinated him to the ranking military officer until such time as the colony was securely established and Commodore Lakshmaniah, confident that there was no immediate military threat, relinquished command to him. The Concordiat's tradition was one of civilian control of the military, not the reverse. And if he had to admit that the situation was . . . unusual, he didn't like admitting that his authority was secondary to anyone's, and it showed in his rather abrasive relationship with Lakshmaniah and her subordinate officers.

"I've made it quite clear to the Governor that *you* will be in command of the convoy's military component until I return and relieve you, Captain," the Commodore continued after a moment. "He . . . understands the necessity of a clear military chain of command."

"As you say, ma'am," Maneka agreed in a perfectly respectful voice which nonetheless managed to express her doubt as to the clarity of Agnelli's understanding.

"At any rate," Lakshmaniah said, "stay alert! The one area where their tech's been consistently equal to or ahead of ours is in their stealth systems. We've been picking up traces of some sort of sensor ghost, so there's at least a fair chance that there's another heavy cruiser—maybe even two of them and a couple of lighter escorts—running around out there. If there is, and if the Puppies manage to suck us far enough away, you may find yourself with a very nasty situation on your hands, Captain."

"Understood, ma'am," Maneka replied as levelly as she could. "We'll watch the transports' backs for you, Commodore," she said with the confidence the rules of the game required from her.

"Never doubted it, Captain Trevor," Lakshmaniah said. "Good luck."

"And to you, Commodore. And good hunting," Maneka responded, and watched as her display dropped back into tactical mode and she saw the escort force peeling away from the convoy to race directly towards the oncoming Melconian ships.

"They have seen us, sir," Tactical First Thara Na-Kahlan announced.

"As if that were a surprise," Sensor First Yarth Ka-Sharan muttered.

Admiral Lahuk Na-Izhaaran targeted him with a warning glance. There was bad blood between Ka-Sharan and Na-Kahlan. Both were of high birth, and their clans had been opposed to one another for generations. Sometimes, they seemed unable to set that traditional enmity aside even as the People fought for their very existence. It was a friction he was not prepared to tolerate at any time, and especially not at a moment like this.

Ka-Sharan's ears twitched, then drooped in submission as he lowered his eyes. Na-Izhaaran held him with his gaze for another several breaths, then snorted and gave Na-Kahlan a brief, equally intense glare, lest the tactical officer think the admiral was siding with him.

"Continue, Tactical," Na-Izhaaran said after a moment.

"As you predicted, they have altered course to intersect us well short of their convoy, sir," Commander Na-Kahlan said in a chastened tone. "They will enter our engagement range in approximately another twenty-six minutes."

"And they are approaching with *all* of their warships?" Na-Izhaaran pressed.

"All of them we have so far detected, sir," Na-Kahlan replied, unable to fully resist the temptation to flip a quick glance at Ka-Sharan.

"I can't say with absolute certainty that there are no more warships out there, Admiral," Ka-Sharan admitted. "Human stealth systems are almost as good as our own." *And their* sensors *are much better . . . like all the rest of their technology,* he carefully did not say aloud. "However, most of these vessels appear to be standard Human civilian-type transports. That's why *Emperor Ascendant* was able to detect them at such extreme range. And why we were able to insert our reconnaissance drones into their formation without being detected. We think."

Na-Izhaaran flicked his ears in acknowledgment of the qualification. And perhaps also of the flicker of fear even he could not fully suppress as he watched the accursed Human warships sweep towards him. His fifteen vessels out-massed their eleven opponents by what ought to have been a crushing margin, but the Empire had learned to its cost how dreadfully its prewar analysts had underestimated the capabilities of Human technology. Especially Human *war*-fighting technology.

But that was the entire reason behind his chosen tactics, he reminded himself. The Humans were accustomed to the tactical advantages their technology bestowed upon them. It would be difficult for whoever was in command of those ships to believe the technologically inferior Melconians might actually not only have detected *them* first but managed to get remote sensor platforms close enough for detailed observation without being detected in return. Intellectually, the Human might realize just how much more readily the units of his convoy might have been detected, but it was unlikely his emotions shared that awareness. Certainly he had given no indication that he was aware of the Squadron's presence until Na-Izhaaran had effectively banged on his hull with a wrench. The scraps of communications transmissions he had deliberately sent out for the Humans to detect had been expressly intended to draw the entire escort out to engage him, and it appeared to have done just that. Now it only remained to see whether or not the *rest* of his plan would work . . . and how many of his ships might manage to survive.

"Sir, with all due respect, I must once again urge you to detach a messenger," Captain Sarka Na-Mahlahk said.

Na-Izhaaran flicked his eyes to him, and his chief of staff—a useful Human concept the Empire had borrowed from its hated foes—looked back at him levelly.

"We've had this discussion, Sarka," Na-Izhaaran said, and Na-Mahlahk's ears rose and then dropped in agreement.

"I know we have, sir," he said. "But this is the first time we've actually confirmed that the Humans are sending out hidden colonies. I believe we have an overriding responsibility to report that confirmation to Fleet Command."

"No doubt we do," Na-Izhaaran acknowledged. "And I intend to . . . as soon as I finish dealing with the target the Nameless Ones have seen fit to lay before us. Until I've done so, I require every ship I have not already detached. Except *Death Descending*, of course. Don't worry, Sarka! Even if the accursed Humans manage to kill every one of us, Captain Na-Tharla will still get word back to Command."

"Still, sir, I would feel much better if we detached one of the destroyers now, before the Humans reach battle ranges," Na-Mahlahk pressed respectfully. "This discovery is of critical importance. I believe we should make absolutely certain word of it gets home."

"We will." Na-Izhaaran allowed a trace of ice to edge into his voice. He respected Na-Mahlahk's moral courage, and under normal circumstances he vastly preferred for his staff to argue with him when they felt he might be making a mistake. But the Human ships were streaking ever closer, and this was not the time for protracted debates.

"Intelligence has suspected for years now that the Humans had embraced such a strategy," Na-Izhaaran continued crisply. "Of course we've never managed to confirm it. Gods, Sarka! Just think of the odds against our stumbling across something like this!"

He twitched both ears in an expression which combined

bemusement and profound gratitude. Who would have guessed that his roundabout choice of route to outflank the Human patrols and approach the minor Human planet which was their objective would lead to such an encounter?

"And of course Command needs to know that we have. But even if not a single one of us ever gets home, Command will continue to operate, as it already does, on the *assumption* that the Humans are planting hidden colonies. In the immediate sense, it's more critical for us to destroy *this* colony fleet completely than it is to inform Command that we found it in the first place. Because if we don't destroy it now, it will slip away, and we'll never find it again. My decision is made, Sarka. I will not disperse my combat power by detaching a unit on the very brink of battle."

Na-Mahlahk gazed at him for a moment longer, but then his ears lowered and he turned back to his own console. That was another thing Na-Izhaaran liked about him. The chief of staff had the courage and stubbornness to argue in defense of his beliefs, but he also knew there could be but one commander of a force . . . and had the wisdom to recognize when his superior officer had decided the time for discussion had passed.

"Entering extreme missile range in twenty-one minutes, sir," Na-Kahlan announced.

Commodore Lakshmaniah's outnumbered squadron sped towards the enemy ships clustered around the huge Melconian flagship. The *Star Slayer*-class boasted massive energy batteries and three times as many missile tubes as her own flagship. Those missiles were longer-ranged, too, and they screamed into the teeth of her outnumbered force as her ships closed with the enemy. Countermissiles raced to meet them, shorter-ranged energy weapons tracked them, waiting until they were close enough to engage, jammers generated strobes of interference designed to blind and baffle their active tracking systems, and decoys raced outward from her ships, mimicking their motherships' emissions signatures.

The battlecruiser's larger missiles had more range, but the Concordiat's technology edge went far towards negating that reach advantage. Humanity's missiles had better seekers and more effective penetration aids, and they were far more agile. And Lakshmaniah's defenses were also better.

The silence on *Valiant*'s flag bridge remained as profound as ever as the commodore and her staff fused their minds and personalities with the heavy cruiser's AI. That, too, was an advantage humanity held, and the Concordiat Navy had learned to use it well.

I observe the opening phase of the engagement.

Commodore Lakshmaniah's units are substantially outnumbered and even more badly out-massed, but they are clearly the attackers. Before they can range upon the Enemy, however, they must survive to cross the Enemy battlecruiser's extended missile envelope. The telemetry stream from Valiant *allows me to recognize the commodore's intentions, and I wonder if the Enemy commander has done so as well.*

I salute her courage, and I compute that she has a 68.72 percent chance of accomplishing her purpose. The chance of her survival, however, is only 13.461 percent.

"Commander," *I say,* "I strongly urge you to activate the neural interface."

Maneka Trevor flinched physically at the sound of the melodious tenor voice. It wrenched her attention away from the imagery of her display, and her jaw clenched as a dull burn of shame went through her. Lazarus' voice was as calmly courteous as ever, despite the fact that both of them knew he should never have had to say that. It was *her* job as his commander to recognize when it was time to activate the neural net without repeated promptings.

Especially when he was right.

She closed her eyes, fighting the sick hollowness in her belly, and inhaled deeply. Then, somehow, she made herself reach out for the headset.

✧   ✧   ✧

Captain Trevor's heartbeat and respiration both accelerate rapidly. Her distress is evident, although I do not understand the reason for it. It is clear, however, that it stems far more from her reluctance to utilize the neural interface than from the actual combat between Commodore Lakshmaniah's ships and the Enemy. Yet despite that reluctance, her hand is steady as she picks up the headset and adjusts the contact pads against her temples.

An additional 3.615 seconds elapse, and then the interface activates.

The door at the heart of Maneka Trevor's worst nightmares swung wide.

She felt it opening, and somewhere deep within her she heard a frightened child weeping, begging to be spared. To be allowed to continue hiding. The taste of remembered terror was so thick she could scarcely breathe, yet she made herself sit back in the comfortable chair, fists clenched in her lap, and endure.

The green, rolling woodland of the planet Chartres spread itself out before her once more as she rode the command couch of Unit 28/G-862-BNJ towards the Melconian LZ. The full might of the Thirty-Ninth Battalion thundered towards the enemy, and Lieutenant Trevor felt her hands sweating, the dryness in her mouth, as the first Melconian long-range fire screamed towards them.

Intelligence estimated that the Puppies had landed an entire corps of infantry, supported by a full brigade of combat mechs. That would have been heavy odds for a battalion of modern Bolos; for the Thirty-Ninth, they were impossible. Individually, nothing the Melconians had could stand up to even a Bolo as ancient as the Thirty-Ninth's Mark XXVIIIs and attached reconnaissance Mark XXVIIs. But the Puppies knew that as well as the Concordiat did, and they had no intention of losing this battle.

High-trajectory missiles rained down, fired from orbiting warships as well as ground-based systems. Their flight profiles gave the Battalion easy intercept solutions, but they'd never been intended to get through. Their function was solely to saturate the Bolos' defenses while the *real* killers broke through at lower altitudes.

"Remote platforms report cruise missiles launching all along the Enemy front," a resonant baritone told her. "Current estimate: approximately four thousand, plus or minus fifteen percent."

"Understood," the younger Maneka rasped in the depths of her older self's memory.

"Colonel Tchaikovsky advises us that Enemy cruisers and destroyers are altering course. On the basis of their new heading and speed, I estimate a probability of 96.72 percent that they will endeavor to enter energy range of the Battalion simultaneous with the arrival of the low-altitude missile attack."

"You're just full of good news this afternoon, aren't you?" she responded, baring her teeth in what might charitably have been called a smile.

"I would not call it 'good,'" Benjy replied, with one of his electronic chuckles. "On the other hand, the Enemy's obvious desire to mass all available firepower at the earliest possible moment does offer us some tactical advantages, Maneka."

"Yeah, *sure* it does."

She shook her head.

"I am serious," the Bolo told her, and she stopped shaking her head and looked up at the internal visual pickup in disbelief.

"Just how does their piling even more firepower on top of us *improve* our chances of survival?" she demanded.

"I did not say it would enhance our survival probability. I merely observed that it offers us certain tactical advantages—or openings, at least—which we could not generate ourselves," the Bolo replied, and there was more than simple electronic certitude in its voice. There was experience. The *personal* experience of his hundred and twenty-six years' service against the enemies of mankind. "If their warships had opted to remain at extended missile ranges, rather than bringing their energy batteries into play, they would have remained beyond the range of *our* energy weapons. As it is, however, analysis of their new flight paths indicates they will enter their own energy weapon range of the Battalion 16.53 seconds before the arrival of their ground forces' cruise missiles."

Maneka Trevor's blue eyes widened in understanding, and the Bolo produced another chuckle. This one was cold, without a trace of humor.

"They're giving us a shot at them *before* the missiles reach us?" she asked.

"Indeed. They have clearly attempted to coordinate the maneuver, but their timing appears inadequate to their needs. Unless they correct their flight profiles within the next thirty-eight seconds, the Battalion will be able to engage each warship at least once before their cruise missiles execute their terminal maneuvers. If they had been willing to wait until *after* the initial missile attack before closing, or even to remain permanently beyond Hellbore range, they would eventually have been able to destroy the entire Battalion with missiles alone."

"Instead of giving us the opportunity to take out their orbital fire support completely!" she finished for him.

"Indeed," Benjy repeated, and she heard the approval—and pride—in his deep voice. Pride in *her* she realized. In the student she had become when the colonel gave her her first Bolo command . . . and, in so doing, committed her into that Bolo's care for her true training. That was what put the pride into his voice: the fact that his student had grasped the enormity of the Melconians' error so quickly.

The plunging thunder of the incoming high-trajectory missiles howled down out of the heavens like the lightning bolts of crazed deities, but the charging behemoths of the Thirty-Ninth Battalion didn't even slow. Ancient they might be, but they were Bolos. Batteries of ion-bolt infinite repeaters and laser clusters raised their muzzles towards the skies and raved defiance, countermissile cells spat fire, and heaven blazed.

The Battalion raced forward at over eighty kilometers per hour through the thick, virgin forest. Not even their stupendous bulks could remain steady over such terrain at so high a speed, and the shock frame of Maneka's command couch hammered at her as Benjy shuddered and rolled like some ancient windjammer of Old Earth rounding Cape Horn. But even as his mighty tracks ground sixty-meter tree trunks into crushed chlorophyll, his weapons tracked the incoming missiles with deadly precision. Missile after missile, dozens—scores—of them simultaneously, disappeared in eye-tearing fireballs that dimmed the light of Chartres's primary into insignificance.

Despite her terror, despite the certainty that the Battalion could not win, Maneka Trevor stared at the imagery on her visual display with a sense of awe. The Melconian missile attack was a hemisphere of flame, a moving bowl above her where nothing existed but fire and destruction and the glaring corona of the wrath of an entire battalion of Bolos.

"Enemy cruise missiles entering our defensive envelope in 21.4 seconds," Benjy announced calmly even as the display filled with blinding light. "Enemy *warships* entering engagement range in 4.61 seconds," he added, and there was as much hunger as satisfaction in his tone.

"Stand by to engage," Maneka said, although both of them knew it was purely a formality.

"Standing by," Benjy acknowledged, and his main turret trained around in a smooth whine of power, Hellbore elevating.

Maneka's eyes strayed from the visual display to the tactical plot, and her blood ran cold as she saw the incredibly dense rash of missile icons streaking towards her. The Battalion's reconnaissance drones were high enough to look down at the terrain-following missiles as they shrieked through the atmosphere, barely fifty meters above the highest terrain obstacles, at five times the speed of sound. The atmospheric shock waves thousands of missiles generated at that velocity were like a giant hammer, smashing everything in their path into splinters, and when they reached the Battalion, it would be even worse. At their speed, even Bolos would have only tiny fractions of a second to engage them, and the Battalion's defenses were already effectively saturated by the ongoing high-trajectory bombardment.

Between the missile storm and the main body of the Battalion was the 351st Recon's four Mark XXVIIs. Twenty percent lighter and more agile than the Mark XXVIII, the *Invictus*-type Bolos were much more heavily equipped with stealth and ECM, and they had sacrificed the Mark XXVIII's extensive VLS missile cells in favor of even more active antimissile defenses. It was their job to fight for information, if necessary, and—with their higher speed—to probe ahead of the Battalion for traps and ambushes the enemy might have managed to conceal from the reconnaissance drones. But now their position meant they would take the first brunt of the cruise missiles, unless their sophisticated electronic warfare systems could convince the Puppy missiles' seekers they were somewhere else.

She jerked her eyes away from those horribly exposed icons, and teeth flashed in an ivory snarl as a score of other icons in another quarter of the display, the ones representing the Melconian destroyers and light cruisers, were snared in sudden crimson sighting circles.

"Enemy warships acquired," Benjy announced. And then, instantly, "Engaging."

A dozen 110-centimeter Hellbores fired as one, and atmosphere already tortured by the explosions of dying missiles, shrieked in protest as massive thunderbolts of plasma howled upward.

All nine Melconian light cruisers and three of the destroyers died instantly, vomiting flame as those incredible bolts of energy ripped contemptuously through their battle screens and splintered their hulls. Superconductor capacitors ruptured and antimatter containment fields failed, adding their own massive energy to the destruction, and the vacuum above Chartres rippled and burned. The horrified crews of the remaining Melconian destroyers had four fleeting seconds to realize what had happened. That was the cycle time of the Mark XXVIII's Hellbore . . . and precisely four seconds later a fresh, equally violent blast of light and fury marked the deaths of the remaining enemy warships.

Maneka Trevor heard her own soprano banshee-howl of triumph, but even as the Battalion's turrets swivelled back around, the tidal bore of cruise missiles burst upon it.

Countermissiles, infinite repeaters, laser clusters, auto cannon—even antipersonnel clusters—belched defiance as the hypervelocity projectiles came streaking in. They died by the dozen, by the score. By the hundred. But they came in *thousands*, and not even Bolos' active defenses could intercept them all.

Battle screen stopped some of them. Some of them missed. Some of them killed one another, consuming each other in their fireball deaths. But far too many got through.

The exposed Mark XXVIIs suffered first. Maneka's shock frame hammered her savagely as Benjy's massive hull twisted through an intricate evasion pattern, his defensive weapons streaming fire. But even though scores of missiles bored in on him, far more—probably as many as half or even two-thirds of the total Melconian launch—locked onto the quartet of Mark XXVIIs. The *Invictus* might mount more antimissile defenses than the *Triumphant*, but not enough to weather *this* storm. For an instant, she wondered what had gone wrong with their EW systems, why so many missiles had been able to lock onto them. And then she realized. They weren't trying to prevent the missiles from locking them up; they were deliberately *enhancing* their targeting signatures, turning themselves into decoys and drawing the missiles in, away from the Battalion.

Her heart froze as she recognized what they were doing, and then the holocaust washed over them. The towering explosions crashed down on the reconnaissance company like the boot of some angry titan, hobnailed in nuclear flame. They were forty kilometers ahead of the Battalion's main body, and the warheads were standard Puppy issue, incongruously "clean" in what had become a genocidal war of mutual extermination. Yet there were hundreds of them, and lethal tides of radiation sleeted outward with the thermal flash, followed moments later by the blast front itself.

Maneka clung to her sanity with bleeding fingernails as

Thor's hammer slammed into Benjy. The huge Bolo lurched like a storm-tossed galleon as the green, living forest about them, already torn and outraged by the Battalion's passage and the handful of high-trajectory missiles which had gotten through, flashed into instant flame. The Battalion charged onward, straight through that incandescent inferno, duralloy armor shrugging aside the radiation and blast and heat which would have smashed the life instantly from the fragile proto- plasmic beings riding their command decks. The visual display showed only a writhing ocean of fire and dust, of explosions and howling wind, like some obscene preview of Hell, but it was a Hell Bolos were engineered to survive . . . and defeat.

None of the reconnaissance Bolos in the direct path of the missile strike survived, but the chaos and massive spikes of EMP generated by the missiles which killed them had a disastrous effect on the missiles which had acquired the rest of the Bat- talion. Those same conditions hampered the Bolos' antimissile defenses, but the degradation it imposed on the missiles' kill probabilities was decisive.

Not that there weren't still plenty of them to go around. Over seventy targeted Benjy, even as he charged through the raging fires and devastation of the primary strike zone. The gargantuan Bolo's point defense stopped most of them short of his battle screen, but twenty-three reached attack range, and his fifteen-thousand-ton hull bucked and heaved as the fusion warheads gouged at his battle screen and drove searing spikes of hellfire directly into his armor. Thor's hammer smashed down again. Then again, and again and *again*. Even through the concussions and the terrifying vibration, Maneka could see entire swathes of his battle board blazing bloody scarlet as damage ripped away weapons and sensors.

But then, too suddenly to be real, the hammer blows stopped. Ten of the sixteen Bolos who had been targeted charged out the far side of the holocaust, leaving behind all four of the 351st's Mark XXVIIs. Two of the Battalion's Mark XXVIIIs had also been destroyed, and all of the survivors were dam- aged to greater or lesser extent, but they had destroyed the entire remaining Melconian support squadron, and the enemy LZ was just ahead.

"I have sustained moderate damage to my secondary batteries and forward sensors," Benjy announced. "Main battery and indirect fire systems operational at 87.65 percent of base capability. Track Three has been immobilized, but I am still capable of 92.56 percent normal road speed. Estimate 9.33 minutes to contact with Enemy direct fire perimeter weapons at current rate of advance. Request missile release."

Missile release ought to have been authorized by Colonel Tchaikovsky, Maneka thought. But Tchaikovsky's Gregg was one of the Bolos they'd lost, and Major Fredericks' Peggy had suffered major damage to her communications arrays. There was no time to consult anyone else, and independent decisions were one of the things Bolo commanders were trained to make.

"Release granted. Open fire!" she snapped.

"Acknowledged," Benjy replied, and the heavily armored hatches of his VLS tubes sprang open. His own missiles blasted outward, then streaked away in ground-hugging supersonic flight. They were shorter ranged and marginally slower than the ones the Melconians had hurled at the Battalion, but they were also far more agile, and the relatively short launch range and low cruising altitudes gave the defenders' less capable reconnaissance drones even less tracking time than the Battalion had been given against the Melconian missiles.

Fireballs raged along the Melconian perimeter, blasting away outer emplacements and dug-in armored units. Weapons and sensor posts, *Loki* tank destroyers and air-defense batteries, vanished into the maw of the Thirty-Ninth Battalion's fury. Benjy's thirty-centimeter rapid-fire mortars joined the attack, vomiting terminally guided projectiles into the vortex of destruction. Follow-on flights of Melconian missiles shrieked to meet them from the missile batteries to the rear, but the indirect fire weapons had lost virtually all of their observation capability. Their targeting solutions were much more tentative, the chaos and explosions hampered the missiles' onboard seeker systems, and the gaping hole ripping deeper and deeper into their perimeter was costing them both launchers and the sensor capability which might have been able to sort out the maelstrom of devastation well enough to improve their accuracy.

But hidden among the merely mortal Melconian emplacements were their own war machines. The *Heimdalls* were too light to threaten a Bolo—even the Ninth's manned vehicles were more than a match for them—but the fists of *Surturs* and *Fenrises* were something else entirely. Heavier, tougher, and more dangerous, they outnumbered the Battalion's survivors by eighteen-to-one, and they had the advantage of prepared positions.

Another of the Battalion's Bolos lurched to a halt, vomiting intolerable heat and light as a plasma bolt punched through its thinner side armor. Benjy fired on the move, main turret tracking smoothly, and his entire hull heaved as a main battery shot belched from his Hellbore and disemboweled the *Surtur* which had just killed his brigade brother. Another *Surtur* died, and Benjy's far less powerful infinite repeaters sent ion bolt after lethal ion bolt shrieking across the vanishing gap between the Battalion and the Melconian perimeter to rend and destroy the *Surturs'* lighter, weaker companions.

"Take point, Benjy!" Maneka barked as yet another Bolo slewed to a halt, streaming smoke and flame. Her eyes dropped to the sidebar, and she felt a stab of grief as the unblinking letter codes identified the victim as Lazy. It looked like a mission kill, not complete destruction she thought, but the damage had to have punched deeply into Lazy's personality center . . . and there was no way Lieutenant Takahashi could have survived.

And there was no time to mourn them, either.

Benjy surged forward, the apex of a wedge of eight bleeding titans. *Surturs* reared up out of deeply dug-in hides, lurching around to counterattack from the flanks and rear as the Battalion smashed through their outer perimeter, Hellbores howling in pointblank, continuous fire.

In! We're into their rear! a corner of Maneka's brain realized, with a sense of triumph that stabbed even through the horror and the terror.

A brilliant purple icon blazed abruptly on Benjy's tactical plot as his analysis of Melconian com signals suddenly revealed what had to be a major communication node.

"The CP, Benjy! Take the CP!" Maneka snapped.

"Acknowledged," Benjy replied without hesitation, and he altered course once more, smashing his way towards the command post. It loomed before him, and as Maneka watched the tac analysis spilling up the plot sidebars, she realized what it truly was. Not a command post, but *the* command post—the central nerve plexus of the entire Puppy position!

They'd found the organizing brain of the Melconian enclave, and she felt a sudden flare of hope. If they could reach that command post, take it out, cripple the enemy's command and control function long enough for the Ninth Marines to break in through the hole they'd torn behind them, then maybe—

A pair of *Surturs*, flanked by their attendant mediums, loomed suddenly out of the chaos, Hellbores throwing sheets of plasma at the Bolos rampaging through their line. Benjy blew the left-flank *Surtur* into incandescent ruin while Peggy shouldered up on his right and killed the other. Their infinite repeaters raved as the *Fenrises* split, trying to circle wide and get at their weaker flank defenses, and the medium Melconian mechs slithered to a halt, vomiting fury and hard radiation as their antimatter plants blew.

Then another trio of *Fenris* mediums, all of them orphans that had lost their *Surturs*, appeared out of nowhere. Their lighter weapons bellowed, and they were on the left flank of Captain Harris and Allen. They fired once, twice . . . and then there were only seven Bolos left.

Benjy's port infinite repeater battery shredded Allen's killers, even as two more *Surturs* reared up suddenly before him. One of them fired past him, slamming three Hellbore bolts simultaneously into Peggy. The Bolo's battle screen attenuated the bolts, and the antiplasma armor appliqué absorbed and deflected much of their power. But the range was too short and the weapons too powerful. One of the newer Bolos, with the improved armor alloys and better internal disruptor shielding, might have survived; Peggy—and Major Angela Fredericks—did not.

Benjy's turret spun with snakelike speed, and his Hellbore sent a far more powerful bolt straight through the frontal glacis plate of the second *Surtur* before it could fire. Then it swivelled desperately back towards the first Melconian mech.

Six, Maneka had an instant to think. *There are only six of us now!*

And then, in the same fragmented second, both war machines fired.

"Hull breach!" Benjy's voice barked. "Hull breach in—"

There was an instant, a fleeting stutter in the pulse of eternity that would live forever in Maneka Trevor's nightmares, when her senses recorded everything with intolerable clarity. The terrible, searing flash of light, the simultaneous blast of agony, the flashing blur of movement as Unit 28/G-862-BNJ slammed the inner duralloy carapace across his commander's couch.

And then darkness, and her own voice out of it. A voice remembering the recon platforms' recorded imagery of Benjy's final, agonizing battle—the battle which had saved two billion human lives—while she lay unconscious on his command deck. While he fought and died without her . . . and condemned her to survive his death.

"Oh, Benjy," that thought mourned. "Oh, Benjy."

The speed of Human thought takes me aback. The entire fleeting memory, as vivid as the playback of any battle report contained in my archives, flashes before both of us in scarcely 2.72 seconds.

I did not anticipate it. My Commander's outward behavior has given no indication of how deeply and bitterly Chartres and the destruction of her Bolo wounded her. But now the black, bleak wave of her emotions wash over me. I am not Human. I am a being of molecular circuitry and energy flows. Yet the Humans who created me have given me awareness and emotions of my own. At this instant, as my Commander's remembered agony—her grief for 28/G-862-BNJ, her soul-tearing guilt for surviving his destruction—floods through me, I wish that my creators had also given me the ability to weep.

So this is the reason she has avoided the neural interface. Not simply because she knew this moment would bring back that memory of horror and loss, but because she knew it would reveal the depth of her sorrow to me. And with it her crushing sense of guilt.

She is damaged. She believes she is crippled. Unable to face the possibility of enduring such loss anew. The bleak assurance of her own incapacity, coupled with the burning sense of duty which has driven her to continue to assume the burdens she believes she can no longer bear, fills our link. And along with that darkness comes the fear that I must hate her for not being Lieutenant Takahashi just as she cannot stop herself from hating and resenting me because I am not Benjy.

Survivor's guilt. A Human emotion with which the Dinochrome Brigade has a bitter institutional familiarity. And, I realize suddenly, one which I share. We two are the only survivors of the Thirty-Ninth Battalion . . . and neither of us can forgive ourselves for it.

But we cannot succumb to our shared grief. Too much depends upon us, and beyond the black tide, I sense my Commander's matching awareness of our responsibility.

<Welcome, Commander,> the Bolo portion of their fused personality said calmly.

Its veneer of calm couldn't fool Maneka. The fusion went too deep; she could taste too much of Lazarus' own emotions. Emotions far deeper and stronger than she had dreamed possible even after her experiences with Benjy. There was pain in those emotions; pain enough to match even her own. But Lazarus refused to yield to it.

For an instant, that realization filled her with fury, with a black and bitter rage for the fashion in which his electronic, artificial nature allowed him to deal so much more easily with that pain. But even as the anger surged within her, she realized something else. All of Lazarus' psychotronics, all of his cybernetics and computing power, gave him no more protection against *his* emotions than her fragile bone and protoplasm gave her against hers. It was not his circuitry that let him cope; it was his sense of duty and responsibility. And in the final analysis, she discovered, she could not allow herself to be less than him. She could not fail him as she had failed Benjy.

<And welcome to you, Lazarus,> she thought back with iron calm. <Now, I believe we have a job to do.>

A corner of Indrani Lakshmaniah's awareness noted that the two *Sleipners* had slipped into their assigned positions. They were carefully positioned, though hopefully no one would notice that, to cover both flanks of the convoy of personnel transports and support vessels. It wasn't much—certainly not as much security as she would have preferred—but it was the best she could do, and her full attention returned to the Melconian squadron.

Twelve of the Puppies' fifteen ships had broken down into the anticipated standard triangular combat divisions, while the odd light cruiser and destroyer did seem to be attached to the battlecruiser. The other four "fists" were maneuvering to meet her own attack, but not as aggressively as she might have anticipated. Indeed, they were actually falling back slowly, as if in a bid to hold the range open, and that puzzled her.

Usual Melconian tactics when action was joined emphasized closing as rapidly as possible with Concordiat ships. They would take losses from the humans' superior missiles as they closed the gap, but their own weapons would become progressively more effective as the range fell. It was a brutal equation both navies had seen in action all too often since this war began. The Melconian Navy paid in dead ships and slaughtered personnel just to get into its own effective range of its more capable opponents, but the Empire had the ships and personnel to pay with. And once they did get into range, their superior numbers swamped the Concordiat's technological advantages.

Under normal circumstances, Melconian ships avoided action unless they were committed to the defense of a crucial objective . . . or the Concordiat was. When a Concordiat task force was free to maneuver, it held the range open, decimating any Melconian attempt to close with it with its superior weaponry. But when the Concordiat Navy was on the offensive, attacking a Melconian-held star system or planet, its ships had to come to the defenders, entering their range if they intended to attack the objective the Puppies were defending. And by the same token, when the Concordiat was pinned by an objective *it* had to defend, it had no choice but to stand and fight as the Melconians closed in.

Like now, she thought grimly. The convoy was so slow, so unwieldy, that it might as well have been a planet. And so she was anchored, forced to accept action. So why weren't the Puppies charging forward?

It's probably the battlecruiser, she told herself. *The sheer range of its missiles reverses the usual reach advantage, and the convoy sure as hell isn't going to be able to run away fast enough to hide, no matter what happens. So maybe the Dog Boys figure they've got the time to wear us down at extended ranges before they close in for the kill.*

She couldn't let that happen, and she turned her attention to that portion of the neural net which was her tactical officer.

<Concentrate on the cruisers. Let's tear some holes in their screen.>

"Their firing patterns are shifting, sir," Na-Kahlan reported tersely. "They are no longer engaging us. They are concentrating on the screen, instead."

"And continuing to close, yes?" Na-Izhaaran responded calmly.

"Yes, sir."

"As I anticipated," Na-Izhaaran said softly. "It is an ill choice, but the least ill one he possesses. He gives *Emperor Larnahr III* the opportunity to engage him unmolested, but he anticipates that his superior defenses will allow him to survive while his own fire strips away our screening platforms. In his position, I would do the same."

The admiral brooded down at the tactical plot, rubbing the bridge of his snout, then sighed.

"How much longer before Captain Ka-Sharan and *Death Stalker* are in position?" he asked.

"Approximately twenty-five minutes," Na-Mahlahk replied. "It could be slightly longer than that. At the moment, we cannot fix his fist's position accurately."

"I should hope not!" Na-Izhaaran snorted. "But I know Ka-Sharan. He will be at the assigned position at the assigned time. In the meantime, it is our responsibility to deal with these."

He gestured at the plot, then looked at Na-Kahlan.

"We cannot continue to retreat much longer without making this one suspicious," he said. "Besides, if we allow the gap between us and the convoy to open much further, it will be safely beyond even *Emperor Larnahr III*'s effective range, and he will have no more motive to come after us. So in another . . . twelve minutes, I think, we will reverse course and see if he truly wishes to dance with us."

<Up to something.> Lakshmaniah spun the thought off into the corporate net of her staff as the destroyer *Cutlass* took a direct hit. Most of her attention was on the tactical relay, reading *Cutlass*' damages. It could have been worse. The destroyer's main weapons remained intact, and she was already altering course slightly and rolling ship to hold the damaged aspect of her battle screen away from the enemy. Yet the Puppies' uncharacteristic maneuvers fed her growing suspicion, and she felt its echoes rippling throughout the composite brain. Agreement came back to her from most of them; doubt from a few.

<Drawing us away from the convoy?> the suggestion came from her tactical officer.

<Possible.> Lakshmaniah frowned, then grimaced. <Doesn't matter. Committed. Up to Trevor and Chin.>

Agreement, though far from happy, came back to her, and she felt his attention turning with hers to study the enemy formation. The Puppies' rate of retreat was slowing. It looked as if they were preparing to stand, or possibly even to counterattack, and she considered her own damages. *Cutlass*, *Dagger*, and *Halberd* had all taken hits, though so far their damage remained far from critical. More seriously, *Foudroyant* had lost almost half her port energy battery and a third of her missile tubes. In return, one of the Melconian combat divisions had been driven to retreat behind the battlecruiser, with heavy damage to both its heavy and light cruisers. But the battlecruiser was beginning to get the range, and she felt *Valiant* shudder as a pair of missiles slipped through her active defenses and ripped savagely at her battle screen.

Two of the three remaining Puppy divisions had also taken damage, although it was impossible for CIC to give her hard estimates on how badly they were hurt. But the battlecruiser remained virtually untouched, and her heavy missile armament and deep magazine capacity were beginning to come into play. Lakshmaniah's ships had been forced to expend a much higher percentage of their ammunition than usual to achieve the damage they'd inflicted. She couldn't keep this up much longer.

Worry hummed behind her eyes as she contemplated her increasingly unpalatable alternatives. This long-range sparring ought to have favored her command. As it was, her dwindling magazines were paring away her options.

It wasn't enough simply to drive off the Melconians. She had to be certain of their destruction, because they could trail the painfully unstealthy transports from a range at which not even the Concordiat Navy's sensors could penetrate their own stealth systems. She could not afford the possibility that a surviving Puppy warship might trail them to their new colony's site and return to the Empire to bring back a sufficiently heavy force to slaughter it to the last man, woman, and child. But if this long-range, attritional duel continued as it was, her squadron would be ground away while at least two or three Melconian ships survived.

Ultimately, the survival of her own warships was a purely secondary consideration. There was no point in husbanding them if the Melconians were able to follow them to the colony's new home, because she couldn't possibly stand off a force the size any spy would bring down upon them. Which, in a way, made her limited options brutally simple . . .

<Course change!>

The announcement from Tactical snatched her up out of her thoughts. The Dog Boys were indeed altering course. They were no longer backing away. She watched their entire force, including the battlecruiser, lunge straight towards her squadron, and her jaw tightened.

<Hold course,> she ordered. <This time we take them at energy range.>

"Sir, the enemy is maintaining course!" Ka-Sharan reported.

Na-Izhaaran looked at him, then pushed himself up out of his command chair and stalked over to the master plot.

It was true. The Human warships remained on their pursuit vector even though his command had turned to face them, and his eyes narrowed and his ears pressed tight to his skull. It was preposterous! Human ships *never* closed with those of the People until after their infernal missiles had decisively weakened their opponents. But *this* Human squadron was charging straight for him, as though its units were warships of the People themselves!

"Admiral, should we pull back once more?" Na-Mahlahk asked softly, and Na-Izhaaran shot him a sharp glance. The chief of staff returned his gaze steadily, and Na-Izhaaran showed just an edge of canine. Not at Na-Mahlahk for asking the question, but because the question was so valid. And one whose answer he would have to produce quickly.

He looked back at the plot. In the final analysis, it didn't matter what happened to these Human warships. The destruction of the convoy they were escorting was what truly mattered, and he had already lured them far enough away from the transports to make that destruction certain. So there was no need for him to continue this engagement at all, unless the enemy forced it upon him. His battle plan had accepted that from the beginning. But that plan had also anticipated that the Humans would perform as their standard tactical doctrine dictated and maneuver to hold the range open.

The Humans weren't. They were coming to him, into the very engagement range every Melconian commander strove to reach. If he let them close, he would lose ships, but every Melconian officer knew he must pay the price in broken starships and dead warriors for every Human ship he destroyed. And the opportunity was here. The opportunity to destroy these ships once and for all.

"No, Sarka," he said softly, before he even realized he'd reached his decision. "We will *not* pull back. Commander Na-Kahlan," he turned back to the tactical officer, "it's time we showed these *Humans* how the People make war!"

The jagged edges of my Commander's pain—and my own—continue to reverberate deep within the fusion which has engulfed us both. It is a distraction, and yet that shared sense of loss, grief, and guilt adds a subtle additional harmony. Captain Trevor stands deep within my gestalt, and I feel her wonder as my sensors become hers, the depth of my data storage opens before her, and her organic mind and nervous system merge seamlessly with the whispering electrons of my own psychotronics.

Yet if she is smitten with wonder at what she now beholds, so also am I. This union of thought with thought, of protoplasmic brain with molecular circuitry, was never envisioned when my original programming was designed. The upgrades I received after Chartres have bestowed the capability, but none of the simulations and tests have prepared me for this reality.

There is so much within my Commander's mind. Such richness, such depth and immediacy of experience for one so young. Such beauty, flowing like words of fiery poetry, so much courage and determination . . . and such jagged weapons with which to wound itself.

I am aware that it has often been said that Bolos have "bloodthirsty" personalities, and it has always seemed to me that it was inevitable. We are warriors, designed and engineered at the most basic level as Humanity's champions. Now, seeing my

own personality set side-by-side with Captain Trevor's—feeling
her mind within mine, and mine within hers—I fully realize how
accurate that description truly is. And yet there is much we have
in common, my Commander and I. I recognize her compassion,
her ability to feel grief and guilt even for the Enemies she and I
have slain, and it is a quality I do not fully comprehend. But it
is matched by an iron sense of responsibility and a fierce drive
to victory which no Bolo could excel.

This warrior may doubt herself; I no longer can.

Maneka Trevor felt herself holding her breath in awe as the
sparkling depths of Lazarus' psychotronic brain opened themselves to her. His sensors became her eyes and ears, his tracks
her legs, his weapons her arms and hands, and the fierce power
of his fusion plant her heart and lungs. The training simulations had prepared her for that, but this was the first time she
had truly opened herself to the neural link, and there was so
much more of Lazarus than she had believed possible.

She felt his calm rationality, the deep fundamental balance
and detachment of his personality. And that personality was
not what she had expected. It was similar to that of another
human, and yet it was fundamentally and uniquely *different*, as
well. There was a totally different overlay to emotions which
she now knew, beyond question or doubt, could burn just
as strong, just as fierce, as any human emotion. She couldn't
describe it, but she knew it was there. A fierce directness, an
unswerving refusal to delude itself, and a strangely distanced
sense of selfness. Lazarus knew himself as a unique personality, an individual, and yet he accepted himself as part of a
corporate whole far greater than he was.

It was the TSDS, she realized—the Total Systems Data-Sharing
net which linked every Bolo to his Battalion and Brigade mates
at every level. No wonder neural interfacing came so readily
to them! They'd always *had* it; it simply hadn't extended to
their human commanders.

And as she settled deeper and deeper into the meld, she felt
her own personality, her own nerve endings and thoughts, her

human instincts and intuitions—so different from the "hyper-heuristic" modeling capability which served Bolos in their stead—reaching out to Lazarus. Benjy had once told her that human intuition was, in many ways, actually superior to Bolo logic. She'd believed him, although she hadn't been able to fully accept the possibility on an emotional level. Now she knew Benjy had been absolutely correct. And that in this new fusion, the strengths of human and Bolo had truly met at last.

She and Lazarus touched at every level, tentatively at first, then settling seamlessly into place, and then, suddenly, they were no longer two individuals. They were Maneka/Lazarus. The deadly power and lightning-fast reflexes and computational ability of the Bolo, made one with human intuition and creativity, flowed through her, brushing her grief for Benjy, her guilt at having survived his death, gently aside. Part of that, to her own surprise, was the recognition of Lazarus' own grief at the loss of a Brigade mate he had known for well over a Standard Century. He shared her loss; he did not and never could resent her own survival. There could be no doubt, no question of that—not at this level of shared existence.

She knew that, and as she felt the composite power which infused her, she also knew she had never been so intensely alive as she was at this moment.

I feel—and share—my Commander's wonder and delight. More important, I feel her mind relinquishing the self-inflicted wounds which have oppressed her for so long. The easing of her pain eases my own, for we have become mirrors of one another, and yet there is more to it than that. I feel a new emotion, one I have never truly experienced: joy for another's healing.

Yet even as we experience the nuances of our new union, we are monitoring Commodore Lakshmaniah's squadron, and I feel Captain Trevor's fresh and different pain as the first destroyer explodes in ruin.

Indrani Lakshmaniah felt CNS *Crossbow*'s death like a wound in her own flesh, yet even as the anguish for her dead ship stabbed deep in her soul, she felt herself baring her teeth in a fierce smile of triumph.

The Dog Boys had come too close. Whether they'd intended to or not, they were about to let her into energy range.

<Fire Plan Alamo,> she commanded, and the acknowledgment flowed back to her.

Maneka bit the inside of her lip as Lazarus' sensors laid the unfolding battle before her. She was no trained naval tactician, but Lazarus' immense storage banks were as fully at her disposal as they were at his. The institutional knowledge and the data she required to understand flowed to her instantly, effortlessly. She couldn't tell if it was her own mind reaching into his data storage, or if it was *his* mind, recognizing her need and providing the information she required even before she had fully realized her need for it herself. But at the moment what mattered was less the source of her knowledge, than the knowledge itself.

The knowledge that Commodore Lakshmaniah had deliberately entered her enemies' most effective weapons envelope, sacrificing all of humanity's traditional long-range, sparring advantages.

I feel Captain Trevor's recognition of Commodore Lakshmaniah's intentions. She realizes now, if she did not before, that the commodore has accepted that few or none of her ships will survive. But by accepting the virtual certainty of her own destruction, the commodore has brought her own vessels into decisive range of the Enemy.

"Enemy opening energy f—"

Commander Na-Kahlan never finished his announcement.

Admiral Na-Izhaaran cringed as the energy bleeding back into Na-Kahlan's console exploded with a ferocity which killed the tactical officer instantly. *Emperor Larnahr III*'s command deck heaved indescribably, and Na-Izhaaran's eyes flared wide. It was the first time he had ever personally faced Human warships at energy range, and the reports he had read and viewed fell lethally short of the reality.

It was impossible! Ships that size could not possibly possess such firepower! *Emperor Larnahr III*'s Hellbores were heavier, more powerful, more numerous, than those of all four Human heavy cruisers combined, yet that brute power was offset and more than offset by the impossibly precise coordination of the Human squadron.

Emperor Larnahr III heaved again, then bucked and twisted, as all four enemy cruisers slammed perfectly synchronized broadsides into her. It didn't matter that her batteries were heavier and more numerous, that her battle screen was stronger. Not when every weapon the Humans possessed smashed into exactly the same tiny, precisely focused aspect of her screen.

The battle screen failed locally, and lances of plasma stabbed viciously through the gap. *Emperor Larnahr III*'s plating shattered, atmosphere belched from the broken hull, and the enemy fired yet again.

"Yes!"

Indrani Lakshmaniah's falcon shriek of triumph echoed in the silence of *Valiant*'s flag bridge as her ships' fire ripped into the battlecruiser again and again. The overconfident bastards had let her get too close, because they'd known human warships *always* maneuvered to hold at missile ranges. Perhaps it was because they themselves were so imbued with the need to follow the dictates of their battle-tested doctrine to fully grasp the human ability to improvise and *ignore* The Book. Perhaps it was because of something else entirely. But what mattered was that this Melconian commander had obviously grossly underestimated what Lakshmaniah's admittedly lighter weapons could do at close range under the command of human/AI fusions.

The battlecruiser's consorts swarmed in on her ships, firing frantically, desperate to draw her fury from their flagship. CNS *Mikasa* blew up under their vicious pounding. CNS *Dagger* staggered aside, shedding hull fragments and life pods, broken and dying. Her sister ship *Saber* poured a deadly broadside into the heavy cruiser which had killed her, and the Melconian ship rolled on her side and vanished in fireball fury. One of the *Ever Victorious*-class ships turned on *Saber*, and the destroyer and the Melconian light cruiser embraced one another in a furious exchange which lasted bare seconds . . . and ended in shared death.

More fire poured into *Foudroyant*, *South Dakota*, and *Valiant*. The commodore felt her ships bleeding, her people dying. The sun-bright boil of dying Melconian starships flared on every side, but her command was trapped at the heart of the inferno. Escort Squadron 7013 was dying, but it was not dying alone. Nothing the Melconians could do could save *Emperor Larnahr III* from Indrani Lakshmaniah's fury. Not even *Valiant*'s AI could tell her how many hits had gone home in that staggering, broken wreck, but finally there was one too many.

The enemy flagship explodes . . . followed 11.623 seconds later by CNS Valiant.

I feel my Commander's grief, and I share it. But under my grief is the respect due such warriors. Foudroyant *staggers out of formation, drive crippled, and the two surviving Melconian destroyers alter course to pour fire into her. Their energy weapons smash deep into her hull, but her own Hellbores fire back, and all three ships disappear in a single explosion.*

Only South Dakota *and three of the destroyers remain, but they do not even attempt to break off. They turn on the surviving Melconians, firing with every weapon.*

The entire engagement, from the moment Commodore Lakshmaniah enters Hellbore range of the enemy flagship to its end, lasts only 792.173 seconds.

At its conclusion, there are no survivors from either side.

"Gods of my ancestors," Captain Herath Ka-Sharan whispered, staring at the tactical display from which the icons of so many starships had disappeared so abruptly.

"Sir, I—" Commander Mazar Ha-Yanth, Tactical First of the heavy cruiser *Death Stalker*, broke off, then shook his head, ears flattened in shock. "I was just about to report that we are almost in the position you wanted, sir," he said, unable to take his own eyes from the horrifyingly blank plot.

"Then this," Ka-Sharan jabbed a sharp-clawed finger at the plot, "will not have been entirely in vain, Mazar." He glared at the empty display for another few moments, then wheeled to face the officer who was both his second-in-command and his tactical officer. "We will commence the attack run as soon as we are fully in position."

"No survivors at *all*?"

General Theslask Ka-Frahkan, CO of the 3172nd Heavy Assault Brigade, stared in disbelief at the commanding officer of the heavy transport *Death Descending.*

"None, General," Captain Gizhan Na-Tharla said flatly. "From either side."

Ka-Frahkan looked stunned. Not that Na-Tharla blamed him for that. The captain was equally stunned, if not perhaps for exactly the same reasons. Unlike Ka-Frahkan, he was a naval officer. He had seen—far too often—the hideous toll the Humans' lethal technological edge could exact from the People's defenders. It was the speed with which it had happened, and the tactics the Human commander had adopted, which left him feeling as if someone had just punched him in the belly.

Na-Tharla had served with Admiral Na-Izhaaran before. He knew precisely what Na-Izhaaran had been thinking, and he would probably have made much the same assessment himself in the admiral's place.

But we would both have been wrong, he thought. *And we ought to have seen it. This was not a Human fleet attacking one of our worlds. This was an outnumbered Human squadron defending one of its own worlds. Or, rather, the* crachtu *nut from which another of their worlds will grow, unless we crush it between our fingers and devour its fruit.*

"This makes it impossible to continue with our original mission," Ka-Frahkan said, and Na-Tharla flicked his ears in curt agreement with that excruciatingly obvious conclusion.

"Well, of course it does," the general said, grimacing almost apologetically as he recognized his own shock-induced statement of the painfully obvious. "What I meant to say was that there is no longer any point in proceeding with the Brigade to our original destination. I see no alternative but to abort the mission and return to base in hopes of obtaining a new Fleet escort. That being the case, should we not consider moving to assist Captain Ka-Sharan?"

"I must concur in your conclusion, General," Na-Tharla said after a moment. "And I must also confess that I would derive great pleasure from assisting Captain Ka-Sharan. However, *Death Descending* is a transport, not a warship. In fact, she isn't even an *assault* transport in the Human sense—just a big personnel ship, configured for high-speed atmospheric insertion and rough-field landings. Our stealth capability is as good as a Fleet cruiser's, but that's because hiding from enemy warships is our only real defense. We mount no offensive weapons at all, and only enough defensive systems to give us a fighting chance against long-range missile fire until our escorts can deal with any threat. I'm afraid there isn't very much we could do to be of help to *Death Stalker*'s fist."

"You're the expert, Captain," Ka-Frahkan said after a moment, then chuckled with a slight but genuine edge of amusement. "I don't envy you Navy types, you know! Give me a planet to stand on, one with air I can breathe, and I'm a hero out of the old sagas, but *this*—!" He waved his hand at the tactical plot. "Having to stand here and watch my battle companions fight while I can do nothing at all to help them?"

He shifted his ears back and forth in a gesture of resigned acceptance.

"It's not quite that bad, General," Na-Tharla said, forcing a lightness he was far from feeling into his voice as an antidote to the lingering shock of the destruction of Admiral Na-Izhaaran's squadron. "And at least we don't get our boots muddy. And we get to sleep in clean bunks every night, for that matter!"

"Something to be said for that, at that," Ka-Frahkan agreed, and the two of them turned back to the tactical plot as *Death*

Descending's sensor section changed scales to show a detailed view of the doomed Human convoy.

<?> the wordless question came from the human half of Maneka/Lazarus. Even as the flesh and blood brain framed the question, however, the fusion of organics and mollycircs was already delving for its answer.

Massive computational capability was brought to bear on the elusive sensor ghost from Lazarus' Charlie-3 remote platform. The raw data was almost less than nothing, the merest whisper of what *might* have been a hint of a shadow of an imagined specter, but Lazarus' BattleComp was relentless. In microseconds, the platform had been queried for an update, the original signal had been scrubbed, enhanced, and reanalyzed, and a tenor voice whispered at the heart of her own thoughts, like an echo from her subconscious.

<Contact positively identified,> it said. <Evaluate as one *Star Stalker*-class heavy cruiser.>

She started to frame another question, but there was no need. Indeed, there'd been no real need to ask the first one . . . nor for Lazarus to respond so explicitly. The knowledge, the information, she required was already *there*, as much hers as the Bolo's. It was a sensation whose like she had never experienced, never dreamed of experiencing, and she knew she would never be able to truly describe it to anyone who had not experienced it herself. That sense of duality remained, yet the analysis of the signal and the evaluation of its implications came to her effortlessly, fully.

Maneka Trevor had absolutely no training as a naval officer, but with the data stored in Lazarus' memory, Maneka/Lazarus understood instantly what Admiral Na-Izhaaran had done, and why. Just as she/they understood that the cruiser she/they had detected was almost certainly not alone.

<Warn—> The human half of the composite mentality began to frame a command, but the Bolo half, knowing as soon as she did what that command would have been, had already sent the alert across the whisker-thin laser to Bolo 31/B-403-MKY.

✧   ✧   ✧

"We are in position, Captain," Commander Ha-Yanth said quietly, and Ka-Sharan looked up at him.

"Can we tell if Commander Ra-Kolman is also in position?"

"No, sir," Ha-Yanth said, without even glancing at Lieutenant Jahnak Sa-Uthmar, *Death Stalker*'s senior sensor officer. "*End in Honor* is continuing to operate under full stealth, just as we are," he said, and Ka-Sharan snorted.

They knew where *End in Honor*, the fist's light cruiser, was supposed to be, but they had no confirmation that the ship was actually there. Ka-Sharan had detached Commander Aldath Ra-Kolman to sweep around the convoy's other flank at the same time that Admiral Na-Izhaaran had detached his entire fist for the attack. With all three of his ships operating under conditions of maximum stealth, Sa-Uthmar was doing well to maintain a hard lock on *Battle of Shilzar*, the destroyer still operating in close company with the fist flagship. Not knowing exactly where *End in Honor* was wasn't going to make much difference in an attack on unarmed transports, but dropping stealth and establishing all of the fist's ships' exact positions would have made things neater and tidier.

"What creatures of habit we have become, Mazar!" Ka-Sharan said, and waved one hand in a derisive gesture. "As if this hodgepodge of clumsy merchant vessels could do anything but die even if we came in broadcasting the 'Emperor's March' over every channel!"

"No doubt, sir," Ha-Yanth agreed. "On the other hand, if they'd seen us coming and scattered, some of them might have managed to elude us, after all," he added, although both of them knew the real reason they hadn't dropped stealth. It simply hadn't occurred to them. They were still grappling with the shock of the rest of the squadron's destruction, and until they came to terms with it, they were not exactly likely to be at their mental best.

Under the circumstances, the executive officer reflected, *perhaps it is just as well at this moment that our only "opposition" consists of unarmed transports!*

"Yes, I know," Ka-Sharan said, and his tone made it clear he knew as well as Ha-Yanth how unlikely it truly was that any of the Human ships could have escaped them.

"I wish *Star Crown* hadn't been forced to return to base," he continued.

He spoke softly, as if only to himself, and Ha-Yanth's ears twitched as he suppressed an expression of agreement with the statement he wasn't certain he was supposed to have heard. The heavy cruiser flagship of Admiral Na-Izhaaran's sixth fist had suffered partial failure of her hyperdrive just before the squadron began its high-speed run towards its originally designated target. Captain Jesar Na-Halthak, *Star Crown*'s commanding officer had handed the ship over to his executive officer and transferred to the light cruiser *Undaunted*, remaining behind to command the other two ships of his fist . . . and died with the rest of the squadron.

"Do you think it would have made any difference if the admiral had kept the entire Squadron concentrated, sir?" Ha-Yanth asked after a moment. Ka-Sharan gave him a sharp glance, but Ha-Yanth looked back steadily. His expression made it obvious that the question was not a criticism of Na-Izhaaran, and after two or three breaths, Ka-Sharan flicked his ears in negation.

"No," he said heavily. "I doubt that it would have. Mind you, I wouldn't have said that if you'd asked the question before the Humans got into energy range. I was no more prepared for that than anyone else was, and I'll admit I was just wondering to myself if things might have worked out differently if we hadn't had to detach *Star Crown*. But to be honest, I don't believe it would have. If the admiral had kept us all together, the losses on both sides would probably have been almost exactly what they were anyway. The only difference would have been that we—or whoever might have survived in our place—might have suffered enough drive damage to prevent us from overhauling and destroying this convoy before it could scatter and drop off our sensors entirely."

Ha-Yanth's ears moved in a small gesture, signifying his agreement, and Ka-Sharan turned his attention back to the plot. Yet despite his answer to the executive officer, Ka-Sharan wasn't fully convinced himself that if Na-Izhaaran hadn't sent a sixth part of *Emperor Larnahr III*'s consorts off on this wide flanking maneuver, the outcome might not indeed have been quite different.

But possible outcomes which might have occurred under other circumstances had no bearing on the immediate tactical situation, he reminded himself.

"Prepare to attack," he said flatly.

Courtesy of her recent promotion, Maneka was senior to Lieutenant Guthrie Chin. And suitably enough, despite his obsolescence, Lazarus had over a century's seniority over Chin's younger, more powerful Bolo. Moreover, Unit 31/B-403-MKY, although newer, was only a Mark XXXI. Mickey lacked the neural interfacing capability which had first been integrated into the Mark XXXII . . . and refitted into Lazarus.

Until the last fifteen minutes, Maneka's understanding of just how much that handicapped Lieutenant Chin had been purely intellectual and theoretical. Now she felt a deep pang of sympathy for the other human as, for the first time, she personally experienced the reality of the Dinochrome Brigade's Total Systems Data-Sharing net.

The two Bolos were as intimately fused as she and Lazarus, and as part of Maneka/Lazarus she came to know Mickey far better, in the space of a handful of seconds, than Chin would ever be able to know him. She was a *part* of him as they conferred, organizing a last-ditch defense of the convoy with smooth, unpanicked efficiency and speed.

Working from Maneka/Lazarus' initial detection of the single Melconian cruiser, they had reached out through both Bolos' remote passive sensors and confirmed that at least three enemy vessels were working their way into attack position. Clearly, the Melconian squadron commander had intended to use the bulk of his force as bait, to draw Commodore Lakshmaniah out of position while he slipped his assassin's dagger into the convoy's back.

Analysis of the forces Lakshmaniah had engaged, compared to a normal Melconian raiding squadron's order of battle, suggested that that dagger's maximum strength ought to be two heavy cruisers, one light cruiser, and one destroyer.

In a standup fight, either of the two Bolos was more than a match for both of the lighter units, and either of them could probably have defeated the heavy cruisers, as well. The part of Maneka/Lazarus who had ridden Benjy's command deck at Chartres had no doubt of that. Unfortunately, the Bolos were dependent upon the transports whose hard points they rode, and those transports most emphatically were *not* the equal of any warship in space. They were effectively unarmed, with only the most rudimentary passive defenses. Their assault pods, each designed to carry a single Bolo or a full battalion of infantry, plus vehicles, through planetary defenses for opposed landings, had powerful normal-space drives and battle screen heavier than most heavy cruisers, but were completely incapable of independent FTL flight. The pods were also totally unarmed; if an assault pod required offensive firepower and sophisticated EW, it was normally provided by the Bolo it was transporting.

If the transports were destroyed, the pods would drop instantly out of hyper, assuming they survived their motherships' destruction. And the chance of a Bolo's surviving the destruction of its assault pod in space was virtually nil. They could expand their own battle screen and the pods' screens to provide the transports some protection, but the instant they activated any battle screen at all, they would reveal their presence to the enemy. The Melconians might not immediately realize they faced Bolos, but they would certainly recognize that the *Sleipners* were not the unarmed freighters they had clearly assumed them to be. When they did, they would undoubtedly withdraw beyond effective energy range and use their missile tubes.

A Bolo might be able to protect the ship it actually rode from missile attack, but Bolos were designed for combat at planetary ranges, not in deep space. Their defenses had never been designed to protect a sphere as vast as the one the entire convoy occupied. And their offensive missile armament, although long-ranged by the standards of planetary combat, was not designed to fight battles in deep space. They could not prevent the Melconians from devastating the convoy if the enemy decided to stand off for a missile engagement.

But no naval commander would use missiles when there was no compelling need to do so. Missiles weren't simply expensive; they were available only in strictly limited numbers. Like an ancient submarine of pre-space Old Earth, a commerce destroyer preying upon unarmed transports and merchant shipping would come in close enough to use his energy weapons, the equivalent of the submarine's deck gun, rather than expend his precious "torpedoes." Especially when he was this far from any source of resupply and had no way of knowing if he would encounter additional hostile warships on his way home.

So the only workable option was to continue to pretend to be defenseless freighters and hope they could draw all the attackers into decisive energy range before the Puppies figured out what they were actually up against.

Even as the battle plan—such as it was, and what there was of it—came together, a separate part of Maneka's brain wondered whether she should inform Governor Agnelli of what was happening. Technically, Agnelli was her superior, but Commodore Lakshmaniah had left Maneka in command, not the Governor. She didn't need him joggling her elbow at a moment like this, and it wasn't as if there would be time for any detailed briefing before the enemy attacked. And as she and her Bolo self conferred with Mickey, she found another reason not to inform Agnelli just yet. She/they couldn't be certain where the Melconians would begin their attack. The enemy ships might come in on vectors which would make it impossible to immediately engage all of them simultaneously, and she/they dared not reveal the Bolos' existence until she/they *could* engage every Melconian ship in a single firing pass. So if it came down to it, she/they might have to allow the enemy to pick off some of the convoy's defenseless transports without firing a shot in reply.

Somehow, Maneka rather doubted Governor Agnelli would react well to that decision.

"Now!" Captain Ka-Sharan snapped, and his entire fist turned directly towards the convoy as its targeting systems went active.

Death Stalker and *Battle of Shilzar* came in abreast. Against armed opposition, the less powerful (and more expendable) destroyer would normally have taken the lead, probing ahead for enemy units. In this case, though, there was no need. The reconnaissance platforms Admiral Na-Izhaaran had sent out after *Emperor Ascendant* initially detected the glaringly obvious emissions signatures of the transport ships had gotten a detailed count of the convoy's escorts, and every one of them had been destroyed.

"Sir, we have confirmation on *End in Honor*'s position!" Ha-Yanth announced, and Ka-Sharan showed the tips of his canines in a smile of grim satisfaction as he watched Tactical's fire control crosshairs settle into place across the icons of the first ships he intended to kill.

Maneka/Lazarus watched through the Bolo's sensors as the Melconian warships dropped out of stealth and lashed the unarmed transports with radar and lidar. The composite entity recognized the targeting systems, and the portion of it which was Maneka Trevor felt yet another stab of awe as Lazarus' flashing psychotronic brain analyzed the emissions patterns to predict the Puppies' targeting queue. She'd seen the Bolos' hyper-heuristic modeling capability in action before, but never from the inside. Never as a participant. Now she knew—*knew,* beyond any shadow of a doubt—exactly what targets the Melconians intended to engage, and in what order. There was no doubt in her mind at all, despite the fact that BattleComp insisted on qualifying with percentage probabilities, all of which were in the ninety-plus percent range. It was as if she had become clairvoyant. As if God Himself had tapped her on the shoulder and told her what was about to happen.

No wonder the Bolos always seem to know exactly what to do next, a small corner of her/their shared personality which remained entirely hers thought. But most of her attention was on the geometry of the engagement, and she swallowed a bitter mental curse.

The Puppies' tactical coordination was off. Their active sensors pinned down their positions for Maneka/Lazarus, and it was obvious they'd set up a scissors attack, with two of their ships attacking from one flank while the third attacked from the other. But the two closer ships—a heavy cruiser and a destroyer—had reached attack position before their stealthed consort. They were already sweeping into the attack on Maneka/ Lazarus' side of the convoy's formation, but the light cruiser was just far enough outside its own attack range that Mickey was not yet able to engage it.

<Chance of additional—?> the Maneka component demanded.

<04.75 percent, plus or minus 1.91 percent,> the Lazarus component responded before the question was fully formulated. It would have taken priceless minutes for a human to explain the logic upon which that reply rested, but his entire analysis tree flashed through Maneka's merely human brain like lightning. And he was right. If the Melconian squadron commander had been willing to detach a second heavy cruiser for this attack, he would have detached its entire fist with it, instead of retaining its consorts with his flagship. Besides, the Puppies were too good at this sort of thing for a heavy cruiser to be so badly out of position that it wouldn't already at least be bringing up its own targeting systems.

<Chance—> Maneka began a second question.

<97.62 percent probability destruction *Kuan Yin*, 96.51 percent probability destruction *Keillor's Ferry*, 87.63 percent probability destruction *Star Conveyor*.>

The numbers flickered through her brain like icy thunderbolts, and her heart spasmed in anguish as the Lazarus component provided them. *Star Conveyor* was one of the colony's industry ships. Her loss would be severely damaging, although not fatal. But *Keillor's Ferry* was a personnel transport, with over seven thousand colonists on board. And *Kuan Yin* was possibly even more precious than *Keillor's Ferry*. She was the colony's main medical ship, carrying not just the equivalent of a complete Core World hospital complex, but also seventy-five percent of the expedition's total medical staff. Some of her equipment, and especially the artificial wombs and banks of sperm and ova, were backed up and dispersed among other ships of the convoy, but her loss would be devastating to the colony's chances of survival.

Maneka/Lazarus considered every possible alternative in the glassy eye of eternity which Lazarus' modeling capability made available, and the human half of the fusion felt the Bolo half's anguish matching her own as the cold, uncaring probabilities burned before them.

If she/they engaged the closer Melconians before the light cruiser entered Mickey's engagement envelope, she/they would have an eighty-five-plus percent chance of killing both of them before any of the colony ships were destroyed. But only at the cost of a ninety-six percent chance that the light cruiser would break off before Mickey could take it under fire. And in that case, the probability of the destruction of the *entire* convoy approached eighty-nine percent.

The loss of those three ships, and especially of *Kuan Yin*, would lower the colony's probability of long-term survival to just over eighty percent, yet that was enormously greater than the eleven percent chance that the convoy would survive to find somewhere to establish the colony in the first place if Maneka/Lazarus prevented those three ships' destruction.

Both halves of her/their soul cried out in protest, but the numbers—those heartless, brutally honest numbers—refused to relent. Mickey shared her/their anguish through the TSDS net, and in some ways, Maneka realized, it was even worse for him and Lazarus than for her. They were designed, engineered on the molecular level, to preserve human life at any cost to themselves. But this time the cost would be paid by someone else.

"*Enemy ships!*" The frantic cry ripped over the convoy's communications net as someone aboard *Keillor's Ferry* spotted the incoming Melconians. "My God, enemy ships! *They're locking us up!*"

Maneka/Lazarus heard the panic, the horror in the unknown man's voice. She/they recognized the fear of death in it, but also the darker terror, the realization that seven thousand other human beings were about to die with him, and Maneka closed her eyes in pain.

She could have fired. Could have taken the shot, destroyed two-thirds of their attackers before they ever opened fire. A part of her cringed away from that knowledge, already recognizing the endless burden of guilt which would be hers if she did not. But Maneka Trevor knew about guilt. She had tasted it to the dregs after Chartres, and if that was the price *she* must pay to perform her duty, then pay it she would.

Maneka/Lazarus' turret moved smoothly, the massive Hellbore tracking the destroyer, the nearer of her/their targets and the one targeting *Kuan Yin*, as both Melconian ships opened their gun ports and turned to present their broadsides to their helpless targets. She/they needed no sighting circles on Lazarus' tactical display; she/they knew they had a perfect targeting solution. That all she/they had to do was fire.

"*They're going to fi—!*"

"Fire!" Ka-Sharan barked, and heard a deep, harsh bay of triumph from his tactical crew as *Death Stalker*'s broadside blazed.

Lieutenant Lauren Hanover's face went white as she listened to the voice from *Keillor's Ferry* over the earbug she'd tuned to the all-ships communications net. Like every member of *Kuan Yin*'s company, Hanover had been at "action stations" from the moment Commodore Lakshmaniah reported detection of the Melconian task force. Not that there was anything a medical ship could do in a fleet engagement except keep her head down and try to run. Now it was obvious *Kuan Yin* couldn't even do that.

"Here it comes!" Captain Sminard's voice came harsh and desperate over the intercom, and Hanover yanked her seat's straps tight. It seemed like an incredibly futile thing to do, and she looked around the backup control room that was her duty station as the ship's second engineer, wishing she at least had a proper shock frame. Medical ships weren't supposed to need that sort of equipment, an idiotically pedantic voice said in the back of her mind. The voice sounded exactly like hers, but it couldn't be. She wouldn't be wasting energy at a time like this lecturing herself about—

Lauren Hanover's universe turned suddenly into madness as the concussive shock front ripped her out of her chair and threw her at a bulkhead.

Ka-Sharan bared his canines as two of the hated human transports erupted into splinters and expanding gas. The forty-centimeter plasma bolts ripped through them as if they had been constructed of straw, and *Battle of Shilzar* was firing, too, although her lighter armament had allowed her to target only a single vessel. Two of the three twenty-centimeter Hellbores in the destroyer's starboard broadside scored direct hits; the third was a very near near-miss, and Ka-Sharan suppressed a growl of frustration. Lieutenant Commander Na-Shal's tactical section should have done better than that at this range! They'd certainly had long enough to plot the shot!

Still, it scarcely matters, he told himself, watching the crippled, two-thirds shattered hull stagger. The broken ship dropped instantly out of hyper, still barely alive—possibly—but vanished from his sensors. He glanced at Lieutenant Sa-Uthmar, and his frustration eased as Sa-Uthmar automatically tagged the exact coordinates at which the target had gone sub-light. Finding that wreck to guarantee its total destruction would be time-consuming but relatively straightforward, he thought, and turned back to the targeting displays as *Death Stalker* rolled slightly to bring her next pair of victims under her guns.

"End in Honor is beginning her firing run, sir!" Ha-Yanth announced.

✧   ✧   ✧

The voice from *Keillor's Ferry* chopped off in mid-syllable as the huge transport exploded. Fragments of her hull—and her passengers—spewed outward, each piece of debris individually falling out of hyper and into normal-space. The shattered wreckage was strewn across a volume of space at least a light-week in diameter, and in that moment, Maneka Trevor wished she had been aboard the murdered ship.

There was, she discovered, a special and dreadful curse in her union with Lazarus. Her thoughts now moved at the speed of his, and a second was a yawning eternity for her/them. Ample time for her to choke down the bitter poison of knowing she might have stopped the Melconians from firing. Yet there was this mercy, at least, she discovered; she also shared the absolute certitude that her/their probability analysis had been accurate. That much, at least, she would never have to second-guess.

All three Melconian warships swept towards their second tier of targets, and a flare of bleak and bitter satisfaction burned through the three-part link of Maneka/Lazarus/Mickey.

"Coming on to firing bearing in two sec—"

Ha-Yanth's voice broke off abruptly, and Ka-Sharan lunged up out of his command chair as *Battle of Shilzar* disintegrated. She didn't blow up; she simply ceased to exist in a blinding flash of plasma.

Hellbore! his mind gibbered. *That was a* Hellbore! *But where—?!*

Captain Ka-Sharan was a highly experienced naval officer. He was also a very quick thinker. So quick that he actually had time to find the icon on the tactical plot from which that terrifyingly powerful shot had come. But quick as he was, he had too little time to complete his thought.

Bolo transpor—!

Four seconds after destroying *Battle of Shilzar*, Maneka/Lazarus put a 110-centimeter Hellbore bolt straight through *Death Stalker's* forward power room and scored a direct hit on Reactor Number One. Not that it actually mattered, in light of the catastrophic structural damage to the heavy cruiser's hull. All the reactor's failing antimatter containment field really did was to make *Death Stalker*'s destruction even more spectacular.

"—terrible! Simply terrible!" Adrian Agnelli's face was ashen on Maneka Trevor's com screen as he spoke to her from *Harriet Liang'shu*, the convoy's civilian flagship. "My God! Commodore Lakshmaniah's entire squadron, and now *this*!"

"At least we're still alive, Governor," Maneka said. He glared at her, as if infuriated by the banality of her response.

To her own surprise, she returned his glare levelly. This was her very first one-on-one conversation with the Governor, and she had expected her anxiety level to be far higher. It wasn't. Instead, she felt as if some of Lazarus' calm, a trace of his psychotronic dispassion, had remained with her after she withdrew from the neural linkage.

Or maybe it's just that after watching the Puppies shoot three transports right out of a convoy that's my *responsibility, a mere Governor is small beer*, she thought with a sort of graveyard humor.

"Of *course* we're still alive, Captain," Agnelli said after a moment. "If we weren't, we wouldn't be having this conversation. And before we continue, allow me to say that I fully realize that the only reason we *are* alive is your and Lieutenant Chin's Bolos. But that doesn't make our situation any less parlous. The destruction of *Keillor's Ferry* is a tragedy any way you look at it. Seven thousand lives—plus Captain Haroldson and his entire crew—would be a horrible thing under any circumstances. But their deaths also represent almost thirty percent of our entire colonial population! *Star Conveyor*'s loss is almost as serious a blow to our basic industrial capabilities. But the loss of *Kuan Yin*—!"

He shook his head, his face tight, and Maneka had to nod in agreement with his assessment.

"Governor Agnelli's daughter and son-in-law are physicians aboard *Kuan Yin*," Lazarus' tenor voice murmured suddenly in the Brigade implant in her left mastoid bone, and her belly twisted in an abrupt resurgence of guilt.

"Governor," she said, as soon as she was certain she had control of her voice, "it's possible," she stressed the qualifying adverb, "that *Kuan Yin* wasn't totally destroyed."

Agnelli's eyes leapt to her face, and his right hand, just visible on the corner of his desk, clenched into an ivory-knuckled fist.

"Explain," he rapped. "Please." The afterthought courtesy popped out of him as if extracted by a pair of pliers.

"*Keillor's Ferry* and *Star Conveyor* were completely destroyed by the Melconians' fire," Maneka said carefully. "*Kuan Yin* was seriously damaged, but at least a third of her hull was still intact when her hyper generator failed. It's impossible to estimate how much internal damage she may have suffered, but there's at least the possibility that some of her personnel, and some of the critical medical equipment aboard her, survived. We just have to go back and find her."

"I'm no military expert, Captain," Agnelli said, "but even I know how . . . difficult that would be." The word "difficult" came out as if it tasted physically sour. Or as if he blamed her for raising hopes which couldn't possibly be satisfied. "That sort of search and rescue is a job for fully equipped military ships, Captain Trevor. Not for a handful of hastily assembled merchant vessels!"

"Governor, I wouldn't have said anything about it if I weren't reasonably confident of our ability to locate her. We know precisely when and where she left hyper, and exactly what her emergence vector in normal-space would be."

Agnelli looked skeptical, and she reached out and touched the headset on the corner of her desk. The Governor's sharp eyes didn't miss the gesture, and she saw them widen slightly.

"Lazarus—I mean, Unit One-Seven-Niner—had a hard fix on her, sir. And with all due respect to the Navy, I doubt very much that any astrogator could do a better job of computing an intercept solution."

"Even so," Agnelli sounded now as if he were arguing with himself, not Maneka, "even the best solution is going to leave a very large volume to be searched, Captain. Even assuming that ... that anyone is still alive aboard her," he cleared his throat, "it sounds highly unlikely to me, from the damage you've described, that her own sensors or communications systems would still be operable. Without an active com beacon for us to home in on, finding her is still a job for Navy sensors, not a bunch of merchant ships."

"Under normal circumstances, you'd certainly be correct, sir," Maneka agreed. "But we're not exactly your ordinary run-of-the-mill merchant ships. We happen to have a couple of Bolos along. They may not mount standard naval sensor fits, but I think you'll find they have the capability we need for this mission."

"You're serious," Agnelli said slowly. She nodded, and he drew a deep breath.

"I really shouldn't authorize it," he said.

"Excuse me, Governor, but it isn't your decision."

"I *beg* your pardon?" Agnelli's shoulders stiffened, and his eyebrows lowered.

"Commodore Lakshmaniah left me in military command, sir," Maneka said in her most respectful tone. "As the senior Dinochrome Brigade officer present, and as the commanding officer of Unit One-Seven-Niner, the senior Bolo present, I am now the ranking member of the Concordiat military present. As such, under our initial mission orders, I am now the military commander of this expedition."

"That's preposterous!" Agnelli exploded. "*Ridiculous!*"

"No, Governor," Maneka said unflinchingly, refusing to allow a single quaver into her voice which might have alerted him to how desperately she wished she might have avoided this responsibility. "It's neither preposterous nor ridiculous. I suggest you consult the relevant portions of our orders and of the controlling sections of the Articles of War and the Constitution." She paused for perhaps two heartbeats, then added, "If you wish, Unit One-Seven-Niner can provide you with the necessary text of all three documents."

Agnelli's jaw clamped like a vise, and she gazed back at him calmly, trying to look older than her twenty-seven Standard

Years. He was aboard another ship, well over two thousand kilometers from *Thermopylae*, but she could almost physically feel his anger, frustration, resentment, and desperation.

Hard to blame him, really, she thought almost clinically. *He's almost three times my age, and he's spent the last fifty years of his life building a career in government. He's a professional, and now some wet-behind-the-ears kid is trying to play rules lawyer and push him aside. No wonder he's pissed!*

But at the same time, he knows he needs me. Or, rather, he needs Lazarus and Mickey. What the Puppies just did to us makes that clear enough . . . and on a personal level, we're the only hope he has of ever finding Kuan Yin.

"Regardless of what our *mission orders* and the Articles of War may have to say, Captain," the Governor's voice was icy, "you and I both know that neither the Constitution nor those who conceived of and planned Operation Seed Corn intended for military rule to supplant civilian control of this colony's government."

"I didn't mean to imply that they did, sir."

This was a fight Maneka would have preferred to avoid entirely, and if that weren't possible, one she would have delayed as long as she could. Unfortunately, it was a point which had to be addressed—and settled—*now*.

"I'm aware, Governor," she continued, deliberately emphasizing his title, "that our mission planners always intended for you to serve as the senior administrator and initial chief executive of this colony. I'm also aware that a complete executive council is already in existence, to advise you and to serve as the basis for the elective, self-governing constitutional structure the colony will require. And, finally, sir, I assure you that I am fully aware of the Constitution's requirement that military authority be subordinated to civilian authority under the fundamental law of the Concordiat. I neither desire nor intend to circumvent that law in any way, or to attempt to use the Brigade units under my command to set up some sort of military state."

His face remained a fortress, but she thought that at least a little of his tension had leached out of him.

"As I interpret our mission orders," she told him, "the senior military officer of the expedition is in command of the military and logistical aspects of the operation until such time as the colony has been planted on a suitable planet and there is no military threat to its security. Obviously, the people who wrote those orders expected Commodore Lakshmaniah to fulfill the role of military commander, not someone as relatively junior as myself. Nonetheless, I think you'll agree with me that the imperatives of survival require that there not be any question of our relative spheres of authority. As the senior military officer, I may find myself forced to issue orders based on the military situation and my knowledge of it, which I may not have time to share with or explain to anyone else. If that happens, none of us can afford a situation in which someone hesitates, or second-guesses those orders, because there's some question as to whether or not I have the authority to give them."

Agnelli's jaw was still set, but she saw at least a flicker of acknowledgment in his flinty eyes.

"You have the ultimate responsibility for the future and survival of this colony, sir," she said earnestly. "That's a responsibility I'm not suited for, and an authority I certainly don't want. But the military security of the colony and its delivery to its new home are now *my* responsibility. Commodore Lakshmaniah specifically gave it to me, and my seniority, despite my youth, means I can't just pass it off to someone else, however much I might wish I could. It's my *duty*, Governor, and I intend to do it."

Silence hovered, and Maneka wondered how Agnelli would have reacted if he'd known that she'd deliberately held her fire until after the Melconians attacked *Kuan Yin* and the other two ships. She knew she'd had no choice, but not only was the Governor a civilian, he hadn't been part of that human-Bolo fusion. Which meant he would never share her absolute certainty that no other option had been open to her, and that doubt, added to her youth and junior rank and his resentment of both, would probably have forced the issue to a bitter and open confrontation, despite how badly he knew the colony needed the Bolos.

"Very well, Captain Trevor," he said after a long, cold hesitation. "I understand your position. I won't say I find myself in fundamental agreement with your interpretation of our relative 'spheres of authority,' but I'm forced to admit the force of at least a part of your argument. And, as I'm sure we're both well aware, how badly I need at least your cooperation. Before formally accepting your authority as the ... military commander of this expedition, however, I have one requirement."

"What requirement, sir?" Maneka kept her voice neutral, refusing either to challenge him or to appear to meekly accept conditions.

"I will require a legally attested recording of a statement from you, Captain, which expressly acknowledges your understanding and acceptance of that portion of our mission orders which transfers authority over and control of the military to the civilian government at the earliest possible moment consistent with the military security of the colony."

He glowered at her, clearly anticipating a protest, or at least a flare of anger, but she only gazed back calmly.

"Governor, since what you're requesting is no more than exactly my own interpretation of our orders, I have no objection whatever to providing you with that recording."

He blinked, and she smiled ever so slightly.

"Sir, the truth is that there are aspects to assuming military command of the colony fleet which I recognize I'm scarcely qualified to handle. Commodore Lakshmaniah had decades of experience I *don't* have, and an entire staff and naval command structure, to help her discharge her duties. I have Lieutenant Chin, Lazarus—I mean, Unit One-Seven-Niner—and Mickey. People outside the Dinochrome Brigade often don't understand just how capable a 'staff' a Bolo really is, but even with both of them and Lieutenant Chin, I'm not trained as an administrator on the level the colony needs. And I certainly have neither the experience nor the training to handle all of the many details that cross a real governor's desk every day.

"Because I know all of that, I would be extremely grateful if you would continue to function as our senior administrator and chief civilian executive. I expect to be consulting with you on a daily basis, and I also anticipate absolutely no need or justification for me to meddle in your responsibilities. My sole concern is to make absolutely certain that in the event of a military emergency—or, perhaps, I should say *another* military emergency—the chain of command and final authority is clearly and unambiguously understood by everyone."

Agnelli tipped back in his comfortable chair aboard the expeditionary flagship. He pursed his lips and gazed at her for several seconds through narrowed eyes. Then he smiled ever so slightly.

"I'm going to accept, provisionally at least, that you mean exactly what you've just said, Captain," he told her. "I'll go further than that. I believe you do, and that you have the most praiseworthy of motives. I will still, however, require that recording. I speak with a certain level of personal experience when I say power can be habit forming."

She started to speak, but he raised one hand in a silencing gesture that was oddly courteous.

"I don't mean to suggest that you represent a Napoleon in the making, Captain," he told her. "Although, to be completely honest, I do have some fear that someone with an effective monopoly on control of the total military power available to us could succumb to Napoleonic temptation under certain circumstances. From what I've seen of you, and from your military record, I actually don't believe you have any natural inclination in that direction, however. What I *am* a little afraid of is that you'll acquire the habit of command.

"A good military officer, just as a good governor or head of state, requires that habit. He—or she—can't do his job properly without the inner assurance that when he gives an order, or issues a directive, it will be obeyed. The problem comes, Captain Trevor, when that assurance becomes so much a part of him, and such a comfortable fit, that his authority seems inevitable to him. It's not necessarily that he's evil, or that he suffers from power madness or megalomania. It's just that *he* sees so clearly what 'has to be done,' and since he's grown accustomed to being the primary problem solver, it's axiomatic that it's his job to see to it that it *gets* done. It simply stops occurring to him to consider that there might be another way to do it, or that perhaps the people around him don't even agree that it needs to be done in the first place. When that happens, the people who argue with him may become part of the problem, as far as he's concerned. They're keeping him from doing his job, so he . . . removes them. "

He paused again, one eyebrow quirked as if to invite a response, and Maneka raised her right hand, cupped palm uppermost.

"I understand your concerns, Governor Agnelli. I hope they're unjustified. And I think I should also point out that the Brigade screens its personnel pretty carefully looking for exactly that sort of personality trait. You don't want someone who's convinced her judgment is infallible running around in command of a Bolo, sir." She smiled with a genuine flicker of amusement. "And I should also point out that Bolos' memories contain both the full text of the Constitution and most of the Concordiat's legal code, not to mention the Articles of War."

"And your point is?" Agnelli asked when she paused.

"Bolos are programmed not to accept illegal orders, Governor, no matter *who* gives them. They have been ever since the Santa Cruz Atrocity. That includes orders which are in violation of the Constitution. Even if I wanted to be Napoleon, sir, Lazarus would refuse the role of the Old Guard."

"So I've always understood, Captain. And I believe you're being completely honest and sincere when you say it. Nonetheless, I'm a bit older than you are, and a lifetime spent in politics tends to make one a bit of a cynic. One of the oldest maxims is that people change, and another is that power corrupts. So I trust you won't take it personally if I insist on maintaining the best system of checks and balances I can?"

"Of course not, Governor," she said, with another and broader smile. "I'd recommend, however, that we wait to make your formal recording until after we've relocated *Kuan Yin*. In the meantime, may I suggest you and I place a read-only copy of this entire com discussion in *Harriet Liang'shu*'s secure data storage? I feel sure it will serve your needs if I should at some future time succumb to the corruption of power."

"I imagine it will, Captain," Agnelli agreed with a smile of his own. But *his* smile was tauter, darker, as her comment recalled his fear that his daughter was dead from the anesthetic corner to which the debate over authority had temporarily banished it.

"In that case, Governor," she said, "my first order as the colony's military CO is to turn these ships around and go find her."

"What are they doing now?"

General Ka-Frahkan's voice was harsh, and Captain Na-Tharla twitched his ears in the Melconian equivalent of a shrug.

"That's impossible to say for certain, sir," he said. "My best guess is that at least one of their vessels dropped out of hyper partially intact and that they intend to search for the wreck in normal-space."

"With what chance of success?" Ka-Frahkan snorted skeptically.

"With normal civilian sensor capability, a very poor one. But they obviously have at least two of their accursed Bolos. You probably have more familiarity with *their* sensor capability and range than I do, sir."

Ka-Frahkan's ears flicked an acknowledgment, and the older Army officer rubbed the ridge of his muzzle while he considered. He knew very little about the parameters of such a search operation, but he knew a great deal indeed about the sensors of the Human-built Bolos.

"I don't know whether or not they could find a damaged ship with a Bolo's sensor suite," he said finally. "But the *Bolos* would certainly know, and the Humans would scarcely waste their time if they didn't believe they might succeed. So I think we have to assume that if any portion of a damaged ship survived, they can indeed find it."

"But even so, it will take time," Na-Tharla observed, as they watched the entire Human convoy begin the transition to normal-space. "May I suggest that we wait until they've completed the transition to n-space before we lay in our own course back to base? I would prefer to have any Bolo in the vicinity take its sensors far away from us before we make any course changes which might draw its attention."

"Return to base?" Ka-Frahkan wheeled away from the plot to stare at Na-Tharla. "That's out of the question, Captain!"

"I beg your pardon, sir?" Na-Tharla blinked, ears folding tight to his skull as the general glared at him.

"I said it's out of the question!" Ka-Frahkan snapped. "We're the only ones who know where this convoy is. That makes it our responsibility to see to it that it's destroyed!"

"Sir, with all due respect," Na-Tharla said nervously, "Admiral Na-Izhaaran was unable to accomplish that with an entire squadron. And you saw what those Bolos did to Captain Ka-Sharan's fist. Those were *armed* ships, General! We aren't. There's no way in this universe we could destroy those ships, even if the Bolos weren't even here!"

"No," Ka-Frahkan agreed grimly. "But the fact that we can't destroy the ships doesn't mean we can't destroy their godscursed *colony*. Don't forget, Captain. I have an entire heavy brigade under my command. One which has already demonstrated that it is more than sufficient to destroy far larger Human populations than this handful of ships could possibly have embarked!"

"You're suggesting we follow them to their colony site and attack them on the ground?"

"Precisely." Ka-Frahkan's voice sounded like grinding iron.

"General Ka-Frahkan, I don't think that's possible either," Na-Tharla said in his most respectful tones. The general glared at him again, and he went on quickly. "First, although our stealth systems are very good, I can't guarantee that something with sensors as capable as a Bolo's won't eventually pick us up anyway, if we attempt to shadow this convoy for any extended period. Second, we have no idea where they're headed or how long the voyage may be. Their evident objective is to establish colonies as a means of assuring the survival of their species when the war ultimately goes against them. I would assume that this means placing those colonies so far from anyone's explored territory that even their own government won't know where they are. Not only would that decrease the chance of any of our survey ships stumbling across them, but it would mean that there would be no record of their whereabouts in any data we might eventually capture."

He paused, glancing at the general's expression in an effort to gauge the other's reaction to what he'd said so far. Ka-Frahkan only looked at him impassively, and he continued.

"If I were responsible for planning this operation, sir, my orders would be for them to move as far away from any known star system as the maximum endurance of their vessels permits. I would include a safety margin to give them time to locate a suitable world and to sustain them until their colony is prepared to exist out of its own resources. But that could mean they might travel for another full year, or even two. *Our* endurance is barely a quarter of a year with your brigade embarked."

"You have emergency cryo facilities, Captain," Ka-Frahkan said coldly.

"Well, yes, sir," Na-Tharla said slowly. "But as you just said, those are *emergency* facilities. If we were to put your brigade into cryo, we might suffer a loss rate of as much as five or even ten percent. And it would only extend our endurance to approximately a year and a half. So even if it allowed us to follow them to wherever they're going, it's virtually certain we would be unable to return home again, afterward."

"This ship, and everyone aboard it, is expendable," Ka-Frahkan's voice was flat, "just as Admiral Na-Izhaaran's warships were. If this convoy is able to successfully establish a Human colony far enough from the Empire, it will, as you yourself have just pointed out, be virtually impossible for our survey forces ever to locate it. And if that colony survives, it will remember who murdered the rest of its species. If it builds its strength, reproduces itself, someday it will return, probably with the support of additional colonized planets, to ... discuss the current unpleasantness with our descendants. And that could be far more dangerous than this ragged collection of ships might suggest to you."

Na-Tharla knew he looked puzzled, and Ka-Frahkan showed him the tips of his canines in a humorless challenge-grin.

"You may not realize just how serious our losses are going to be in this war. I don't have the exact figures myself, but so far—*so far*, Captain—we've already lost over twenty percent of our inhabited planets. By the time we complete the destruction of the Concordiat, the People may have only a handful of worlds left themselves, and many of the ones they still have may have been badly damaged. If there are very many of these secret Human colonies scattered about the galaxy, it's entirely possible that they could rebuild in only a few generations to a strength sufficient to pose a very serious threat to the People's continued survival."

"I—I ... see, sir."

Na-Tharla sounded badly shaken, but Ka-Frahkan knew he had ample justification for any shock he might feel. He was only a Navy captain, and the general knew his own seniority had granted him access to intelligence reports far more detailed—and grimmer—than anything Na-Tharla had seen.

"I see," the captain repeated after a moment, his voice a bit firmer. "And I also recognize that you're obviously in a better position to evaluate the long-term threat a colony like this might pose, sir. However, did we have prior confirmation that the Humans are pursuing such a strategy?"

"Not confirmation, no. Our analysts and planners have suggested that such an option would make sense to the Humans, especially when they realized they were inevitably going to lose the war, despite their accursed tech advantages. But to the best of my knowledge, this is the first such colony fleet any of our ships has actually sighted."

"In that case, General," Na-Tharla said slowly, "is it more

important that we follow this single convoy to its destination and destroy it, or that we return to base with the confirmation that the Humans are indeed doing this?"

"That," Ka-Frahkan conceded, "is a very valid question, and I don't know that I'm qualified to answer it. But whether I am or not, I'm the one who has to make a decision. And I do know this much. We know about *this* convoy, and we're currently in contact with it. We don't know how many of these colonies the Humans may decide to send out, or what percentage of them will survive. But we can assure the People that this one won't . . . and no one else is in a position to do that. We stumbled across this opportunity only as the result of a vanishingly unlikely coincidence, and the Nameless Ones know how unlikely it is that any of our other squadrons will be equally lucky and encounter another one like it. So, as I see it, it's clearly our responsibility to seize the opportunity we have and see to it that at least one Human colony does *not* survive to threaten the People's future."

"I can't believe you actually did it, Captain," Adrian Agnelli said frankly.

He stood on the *Harriet Liang'shu*'s bridge, gazing into the main visual display. Maneka's com image occupied one small corner of that huge display, but she wasn't using any visual interface of her own. She was once again fused with Lazarus, watching through her/their sensors as the brutally battered hulk of the hospital ship drifted closer.

"Thank Lazarus, sir," her image in the display said with a smile, although her physical body's lips never moved. "I told you he could plot a tight intercept."

"That's certainly true, Governor," *Harriet Liang'shu*'s captain said, with a respectful nod to Maneka's image. "This is as pretty a piece of multidimensional navigation as I've seen in fifty years in space."

"I know," Agnelli said, unable to tear his eyes away from the slowly growing image of the wreck which had been CNS *Kuan Yin*. As far as *Harriet Liang'shu*'s captain could see, the

Governor's tormenting struggle between impossible hope and darkest fear was evident only in his eyes. But Maneka/Lazarus could monitor his pulse and respiration over the com audio, and the frightening power of his emotions was only too evident to her/them.

"Governor," her image said quietly a moment later, "*Kuan Yin*'s communications appear to have been completely crippled. However, Lazarus and Mickey are both detecting power sources aboard the ship. There's also evidence of continuing low-volume atmosphere loss, which suggests that at least some portions of the hull have retained internal pressure. I can't promise anything from here, but it looks as if there's a fairly good chance at least some of her crew have survived."

Adrian Agnelli stared into her electronic eyes, and the sudden spike of both his hope and fear was terrifying to see.

" . . . a reading from the after emergency lock yet?"

Henri Berthier's voice was calm over the com, but Maneka knew appearances could be deceiving. Berthier, the *Sherwood Forest*'s commanding officer and Agnelli's designated lieutenant governor, was also the Governor's personal friend. He knew Dr. Allison Agnelli-Watson and her husband William well. Even if he hadn't, he was as painfully aware as any member of the colony expedition could ever hope to be of how vital the recovery of as much of *Kuan Yin*'s cargo and personnel as possible was. And despite Lazarus' estimates—estimates in which she had shared fully at the moment they were generated—even Maneka found it hard to believe very many people could still be alive aboard that mangled hulk.

Especially since we still haven't been able to raise a whisper from them over the com, she thought grimly.

"Still nothing," Lieutenant Commander O'Reilly told Berthier.

O'Reilly was *Sherwood Forest*'s second engineer, and he'd been assigned to the industrial ship in no small part because of his expertise in deep-space construction . . . and salvage. According to the personnel dossiers Lazarus had accessed from *Harriet*

Liang'shu's files, O'Reilly had also been selected for his job in no small part on Berthier's personal recommendation, so there'd never been much question who Berthier would select for this particular mission.

"But that doesn't mean a lot, Henri," O'Reilly continued. "Not yet. We know they've got heavy damage in the area, and that Hellbore hit forward took out both the main and secondary com centers. There's no place for them to stand a regular com watch, and I'd say it's likely that the control station for the lock took some pretty severe damage of its own. I doubt they have any sensor capability left to speak of, either, and they're probably just a *little* busy inside there right now, so even if the control station's intact, it's probably not manned."

"I know, I know," Berthier said, and Maneka pictured him watching his visual display while O'Reilly's heavy industrial shuttle closed with the wreck. "And there's no way they could possibly be expecting us to find them, even if they'd had the sensors to look for us. I know that, too. Still . . ."

His voice trailed off, and O'Reilly chuckled harshly over the com.

"I understand, Henri," he told his captain, with the merchant service informality which still sounded . . . odd to Maneka's ear. "And don't think for a minute that I'm not just as impatient as you are. But we've matched motions now, and we're initiating docking. We should know something soon."

" . . . so at least we've got power for the foreseeable future, ma'am," Chief Branscomb reported wearily over the emergency communications system. "Fusion Two checks out, and at this load, we've got reactor mass for at least another sixty years. Not like we're going to be using the drive or the hyper generator, after all."

"And Environmental Three?" Lauren Hanover asked.

"Harder to say, ma'am," Branscomb said. "I've got Tannenbaum and Liang working on the plant now, but, frankly, it doesn't look real good. We've got hull integrity—barely—in this section, but the shock damage is really severe. We've got fittings and power runs whipped apart all over that part of the hull. Power spikes through the Number Four power ring didn't help any, either. You want my honest best-guess, ma'am?"

"It's more than I have now, Chief," she told him mordantly.

"Well, then, ma'am," the petty officer said, "I'd say you'd better not count on Three. We've still got Four and Five, but if I were a betting man, I'd bet that Number Three's only going to be good for spares."

"Understood, Chief."

Hanover leaned back in the acutely uncomfortable chair and scrubbed her face with the palms of her hands. The helmet hung on her chest webbing made it a bit awkward, and she grimaced in exhausted irritation. She was tempted to just set the damned, cumbersome thing down, but that wasn't the sort of thing one did aboard a ship as badly damaged as *Kuan Yin.* Besides, as the medical ship's commanding officer, it was up to her to set the proper example.

Her mouth tightened at the thought, and she shifted in the chair. Her squirming didn't make it any more comfortable, but at least it was still intact . . . unlike her last chair. And unlike two-thirds of "her" command.

Forty-seven hours ago, she'd been *Kuan Yin's* fifth officer. Now she was "mistress after God" of a drifting wreck with absolutely no hope of long-term survival. She didn't know whether she was more grateful for the way her newfound responsibilities' requirement to radiate confidence deprived her of the time to give in to her own gibbering panic, or terrified by the crushing responsibilities which had landed on her shoulders.

"Excuse me, Lieutenant."

Hanover lowered her hands, remembering at the last moment not to snatch them guiltily away like some admission of her own weakness. Dr. Chamdar, *Kuan Yin's* senior physician—and he really was the ship's senior physician, she thought mordantly, not just her senior *surviving* physician—had entered the compartment while her eyes were closed. She wanted to snap at him for sneaking up on her, catching her in an unguarded moment, but she suppressed the temptation sternly. Chamdar was a civilian. No one had ever explained to him that he was supposed to ask permission before entering the bridge. And, she admitted to herself, this bare-bones secondary control room hardly qualified as a proper "bridge" anyway.

"Yes, Doctor?" she said instead. Her voice, like that of everyone else aboard, was flat with exhaustion, but to her own surprise, she managed to inject at least a little courtesy into it.

"I have that personnel list you asked for," Chamdar said, and Hanover felt her shoulders and her stomach muscles tighten. This was something she needed to know, but she wasn't looking forward to his report.

"Go ahead," she said.

"I have the actual names and the status of the injured here," he said, handing her a record chip. "In general terms, though, as closely as I can crunch the numbers, we've taken over sixty percent casualties. *Fatal* casualties, I should say. About a quarter of the people we have left are injured. Half a dozen of them are in critical condition, but I think we've got all of them stabilized, at least. Some of the others—like you—" he glanced pointedly at Hanover's heavily splinted right leg "are technically ambulatory, but would normally be in sickbay."

God, it's even worse than I thought, Hanover thought bleakly. *But at least it makes what happened to Environmental Three less important, doesn't it? We can keep that few people going on Four and Five alone until we finally run out of power. And isn't that a piss-poor excuse for a silver lining?*

She'd known Captain Sminard and most of *Kuan Yin*'s crew were gone. Crew quarters had been forward of the bridge, and only those crew people who'd been on duty aft of midships had survived. But she'd hoped more of the passengers might have made it . . . this far, at least. Passenger quarters had been mostly in the after half of the ship, after all.

"Thank you, Doctor," she heard herself say. "I'll review this—" she twitched the chip in her right hand "—as soon as I have the opportunity."

"I'm afraid there isn't that much rush," Chamdar said sadly.

"Still, it looks like quite a bit of the med equipment itself survived, and we've got three completely intact wards. We should be able to take care of our wounded, now that you and your people have managed to get the ship stabilized."

"What's left of it, Doctor." Hanover smiled grimly at him. "And just between you and me, I think 'stabilized' might be putting it just a bit strongly."

"'Stabilized' has quite a specific meaning to physicians, Lieutenant—I mean, Captain," Chamdar said. "And as far as I can see, it applies to where you and your people have gotten us. Which brings me to another point. That leg of yours isn't just 'broken.' The bone damage is extraordinarily severe. We really need to get you into treatment, get the fuser working on that femur, as quickly as possible."

"Doctor, I—"

"I understand about your responsibilities," he interrupted in a firm tone. "But be honest with yourself, Captain. You aren't really ambulatory right now. You're simply sitting there, in that extremely uncomfortable chair, being stubborn. Well, you can sit in a hospital bed in considerably greater comfort and be equally stubborn while we try to salvage your leg, you know. Under the circumstances, the medical staff won't even object if people like Chief Branscomb come clumping into the ward to report to you."

"I—"

"Ma'am! I mean, Captain!"

The sudden, sharp voice over Hanover's earbug interrupted her stubborn, illogically obstinate resistance to Chamdar's suggestion. She tensed automatically, but even as she did, she realized that whatever had put that sharp edge in the voice wasn't yet another in the chain of disasters which had been reported to her over the past two days. This time the voice was *excited*, almost breathless.

"What, Foster?" she replied. At least with so few of her people left, recognizing voices was easy enough.

"Ma'am, somebody's just docked with the after lock!"

❖   ❖   ❖

I am proud of my Commander.

She has refused to allow her fears and her doubt of her own capacity to prevent her from discharging her duties. In the fusion of our neural linkage, her awareness of how easy it would have been to allow Governor Agnelli to assume full control—and responsibility—was obvious to me. The strength of her temptation to do just that was equally obvious, yet however great the relief might have been, she never once seriously considered doing so.

It is fortunate that her reluctance to interface with me has disappeared. In the absence of a human support staff, she requires my capabilities as a substitute. Moreover, it is apparent to both of us—since it is impossible for either of us to conceal the realization from the other—that such intimate contact with my own personality has had a healing effect upon hers.

As hers has had upon mine, as well. I had not recognized the depth of my own "survivor's guilt" until I saw its mirror in her. And neither of us would truly have been able to recognize how irrational our own guilt was if we had not recognized how irrational it was for the other one to harbor such a self-destructive emotion.

Which is not to say my Commander is fully healed. She is, after all, Human, and Humans—as I have now discovered through direct personal experience—are both incredibly tough and equally incredibly fragile. Unlike Bolos, they are entirely capable of simultaneously entertaining mutually contradictory beliefs, and their capacity to question and doubt their past actions and decisions is . . . extreme. My Commander has not and, I now realize, never will fully forgive herself for not preempting the Enemy's attack on Kuan Yin and the other two transports which were destroyed. At the same time, she accepts as completely as I myself do that, painful as it was, it was the only viable tactic available to us.

Bolos are not engineered to embrace contradictory convictions. Nor is it truly possible for a Bolo to continue to question a tactical decision when the evidence is overwhelming that the decision actually taken was the correct one. This is a Human characteristic, and one I do not envy.

Yet it occurs to me that within that characteristic lie the seeds which impelled a weak, nearly hairless biped, equipped with only the most rudimentary of natural weapons, to raise itself from a user of primitive stone tools to the conquest of half the explored galaxy. There is a strength, a dauntless willingness and courage to confront impossible odds and shoulder unbearable burdens, within Humanity. And without that strength and that ability, my kind would never have come into existence at all.

It is fitting, I believe, that my Commander should so thoroughly represent the refusal to surrender which has taken her people—and mine—to the stars.

Maneka Trevor leaned back in the command chair on *Thermopylae*'s bridge and watched the navigational display as the convoy prepared to once again enter hyper-space and resume its interrupted journey.

She would have preferred to be back in her quarters, linked with Lazarus, watching the maneuver through his sensors. When the Brigade had decided to upgrade Lazarus with the neural interface capability and assigned her, as the sole surviving human member of the Thirty-Ninth Battalion, as his commander, the bright, enthusiastic Bolo tech had told her how wonderful it would be. At that moment, the last thing in the universe Maneka had wanted was to get that close to the single Bolo which had dared to survive when Benjy had not. Looking back, she was guiltily aware that she'd paid far less attention to the briefings and the training than she ought to have. But now, unlike then, she understood why that same enthusiastic tech had also warned her that one of the perils of the interface was the possibility of becoming dependent upon—addicted to, really—the sensors and computational speed and ability of the Bolo half of the fused personality.

That was an addiction to which, it seemed, it would have been only too easy for her to succumb. She knew Lazarus understood her concern, and that he certainly didn't "blame" her for putting a certain distance between them. Although, to be fair, that wasn't precisely what she'd done, either. It was more a case of rationing herself to those moments of semi-godhood when the two of them became one. She'd adopted a rigorously limited schedule, and established her own hierarchy of priorities to determine when circumstances truly justified linking fully with Lazarus outside of that schedule.

And there was another, intensely practical reason for her to be here on *Thermopylae*'s bridge at this particular moment. She was discovering that her role as military commander of the expedition had a much greater political component than she'd anticipated. All of the adult members of the colony's personnel had received basic military training before they were selected for this mission. No one would ever confuse them with front-line Marines, or members of the Dinochrome Brigade, but they were at least as well trained as any planetary militia. Indeed, their legal status *was* that of a planetary militia. Which meant that although they had their own internal command structure, headed by Peter Jeffords, one of Agnelli's councilors, who also carried the rank of a full brigadier, he was a *militia* brigadier, and therefore subordinate to her orders as a captain of the Brigade.

On the face of it, that was as ridiculous as her informing Governor Agnelli that her authority superseded his. Unfortunately, it would have been even more ridiculous for what amounted to an infantry brigadier who commanded a total of barely nine thousand militia men and women, to assert command over thirty-four thousand tons worth of Bolos and the woman who commanded them. Besides, the chain of command was legally clear and unambiguous.

But if she was going to command all those trained militia people in the event of an emergency, then she had to come to know them, and they had to come to know her. Just as it was imperative for Lieutenant Hawthorne and the crew of *Thermopylae* to know her and to trust her judgment. Which wasn't going to happen if she retired into a hermitlike symbiotic dependence upon her link to Lazarus.

However tempting that might be.

"*Liang'shu* reports that the convoy will be prepared to enter h-space in another seven minutes, Captain Trevor," Hawthorne reported, as if to punctuate her own thoughts.

"Thank you, Captain," she said gravely, suppressing a temptation to smile as two people whose combined age was under sixty Standard Years, addressed one another with such formality. Although Edmund Hawthorne was clearly entitled to be addressed as "Captain" aboard the vessel he commanded, his formal rank was only that of a senior-grade Navy lieutenant. That was more than sufficient to command a vessel whose total human complement, exclusive of Maneka herself, numbered only thirty-six, but it was sobering to reflect that at twenty-six Standard Years, he was now the senior surviving regular Navy officer within several hundred light-years.

"I have to admit," Hawthorne continued, "that I still have to pinch myself sometimes to be sure I'm not dreaming that we actually managed to pull this off."

"Locating *Kuan Yin*, you mean?"

"Well, that, too, of course," Hawthorne said with a shrug. "But I was thinking about finding anyone alive aboard her. Or, for that matter, being alive ourselves. Which we wouldn't be, ma'am, without you and the Bolos."

His tone, Maneka was relieved to note, was simply factual, almost conversational, without the near-veneration she got from some of the other colonists. That would have been even more difficult for her to cope with coming from one of the tiny handful of other surviving regular officers. Especially since he was no more aware than any other human member of the expedition that she'd held her fire until after the initial Melconian attack on the transports.

"We're not out of the woods yet," she pointed out. "We've got a long way to go."

"Understood, ma'am." Hawthorne nodded and began to say something else, then stopped and turned away with a brief smile to acknowledge his astrogator's formal report of readiness to proceed.

Maneka smiled back, but her mind was busy replaying her conversation with Agnelli when the two of them had decided—and she was relieved that it truly had been a joint decision—to execute a radical course change and continue their voyage for at least another full Standard Year before settling upon a new homeworld. It would extend their journey for three Standard Months beyond the duration originally contemplated in their mission orders, but those orders had always granted Agnelli and his military commander the authority to extend their flight time. And the fact that they didn't know how long the Melconians had trailed them before attacking or whether or not they had dispatched a courier ship home with news of what they'd discovered made both of them very nervous. If the Melconians were able to accurately project even a rough base course for the convoy, it would increase the Imperial Navy's chance of finding them exponentially. So even though it would reduce the safety margin provided by the transports' supplies, no one in the colony fleet wanted to stop any closer to explored space than they had to.

"Actually, ma'am," Hawthorne said, returning his attention to her, "I'm still astonished that we found anyone alive aboard *Kuan Yin*." He shook his head. "Hanover did damned well with what she had left, but the Dog Boys really ripped the hell out of her. The Compton Yard really builds them, doesn't it?"

"That they do, Ed," she agreed. "That they do. And thank God for it!"

Hawthorne nodded solemnly and rapped his knuckles gently on the small square of natural wood he'd had mounted in the center of his command chair's right arm rest. Maneka smiled at the superstitious gesture, but she shared his astonishment at the survival of any of *Kuan Yin*'s complement. Despite the horrendous damage the hospital ship had absorbed, almost thirty-five percent of her total complement had lived through the attack. More than three-quarters of the survivors were trained medical personnel and specialists their new colony would desperately require, and one of them was Dr. Allison Agnelli-Watson.

Her husband, on the other hand, was not among them.

The Governor had obviously been very close to his son-in-law, and William Watson-Agnelli's death had hit him almost as hard as it had hit his daughter. Yet having Allison restored to him literally from beyond the grave had done wonders for him, and by Lazarus' estimates, the literally priceless medical equipment and supplies the convoy had spent three weeks salvaging from the broken wreck—not to mention the even more desperately needed physicians themselves—had increased the colony's ultimate probability of survival from eighty percent to eighty-seven percent. It would still take at least two years from the time they reached their destination to put all that equipment back on-line, and longer than that to replace the equipment which had been impossible to salvage, but at least they had a far better starting point than they would have had otherwise.

"We're ready to proceed, Captain Trevor," Hawthorne said formally, reporting to the military commander empowered to authorize the movement.

"Very well, Captain Hawthorne. Please signal the fleet to do so."

"Yes, ma'am."

The surviving vessels vanished like soap bubbles, disappearing once again into hyper, and the abandoned, lightless hulk which had once been named *Kuan Yin* was left to drift, lost and lonely, in the endless interstellar dark.

2

"Stand by to execute," Lieutenant Hawthorne said.

"Standing by, aye, aye, sir," Lieutenant Jackson Lewis, his executive officer acknowledged crisply.

"Execute," Hawthorne said.

"Aye, aye, sir," Lewis said, and looked courteously at the visual pickup of *Thermopylae*'s AI. "Execute the maneuver, Iona," he said.

"Executing maneuver, aye, sir," the AI's pleasant contralto said almost musically, with the Navy's odd fetish for archaic formality, and Maneka sat quietly in the assistant astrogator's bridge chair, watching as *Thermopylae* swung suddenly but smoothly about to retrace her course.

The timing for the maneuver had been randomly generated by Lazarus, and she felt confident that no one could have predicted the moment at which it would be executed. If, as had become increasingly unlikely, there truly were a surviving Melconian starship anywhere in the vicinity, it would be as surprised as any other unit of the colony fleet by *Thermopylae*'s abrupt course change.

In many ways, it was very tempting to execute the maneuver herself through Lazarus' control of *Thermopylae*'s maneuvering systems. That, however, would have come under the heading of a Bad Idea, she thought with a slight, crooked smile as she watched the repeater plot in front of her. Edmund Hawthorne had proven even more flexible than she'd hoped, but stepping all over any commanding officer's prerogatives was bound to generate friction, or at least resentment. Either of which was something she could do without forever.

Besides, she'd discovered she actually enjoyed watching *Thermopylae*'s human crew in action. It didn't give her that sense of near-godhood she got from linking with Lazarus, but there was a sense of companionship, of inclusion with the rest of the human race, which had become unspeakably precious to her since the full burden of command had settled onto her shoulders.

Thermopylae settled on her new heading, and Lazarus' sensors reached out to sweep the convoy's back trail. If there were, in fact, anyone following, he would almost certainly be trailing from somewhere astern. That would put him in the best position to observe course changes . . . and to evade any sensor sweeps like this one.

"Sensor sweep!"

Captain Na-Tharla's head jerked up at the announcement. He climbed out of his briefing room chair and headed for the hatch between the briefing room and the bridge proper.

"Execute Evasion One!" Lieutenant Hasak Ha-Shathar, *Death Descending*'s executive officer barked. Ha-Shathar had the watch, and Na-Tharla's ears rose in approval at his immediate response to the warning. It was far from the first time one of the Humans' Bolo transports had doubled back, and he wished the accursed things would at least operate on some sort of predictable schedule. *Death Descending*'s sensor section and Ha-Shathar's reaction speed had probably been sufficient again—this time. But if the Humans kept this up long enough, sooner or later they were entirely too likely to get lucky.

Na-Tharla stepped through the hatch and crossed briskly to his own command station. Ha-Shathar glanced up at him, one ear half-cocked, but Na-Tharla flattened his own ears briefly in answer to the unvoiced question. Ha-Shathar was doing everything right, and Na-Tharla was confident he would continue to do so.

Death Descending altered course as Ha-Shathar had ordered. The Melconian transport was larger than the Human ship sweeping back towards it, and less maneuverable under its main drive. But the Human ship was at least as detectable, and *Death Descending*'s sensors had been tracking it literally for weeks now. They knew exactly what to look for, and they had picked up its course change almost instantly. That was sufficient warning to allow Ha-Shathar to change heading, sweeping away from the oncoming Human transport and its accursed Bolo at an acute angle without ever quite exposing *Death Descending*'s own vulnerable after aspect to the enemy's sensors. Na-Tharla watched narrowly as the gap between the two vessels first narrowed, then began gradually to open once again with no indication that the Humans had detected his ship . . . this time.

"It would appear we have once again evaded them, Hasak," the captain observed dryly.

"Yes, sir. It would," Ha-Shathar replied in the same voice of studied calm, watching the bridge crew from the corner of his eye.

"Well done," Na-Tharla said, and looked at the sensor officer of the watch. "Well done, everyone. Especially sensors," he added, letting his ears rise in an expression of amused confidence. "If that's the best they can do, this is going to be far simpler than I told General Ka-Frahkan it would!"

Something akin to a quiet chuckle ran around the bridge, and Na-Tharla nodded in approval and returned to the reports on the briefing room computer terminal.

He didn't allow his ears to droop in worry until the hatch had slid quietly shut once more behind him.

✧   ✧   ✧

"Well done, Captain Hawthorne," Maneka said as *Thermopylae* came back around to her original course and loped off in pursuit of the rest of the convoy.

"Thank you, ma'am," Hawthorne replied. "We strive to please."

"So I've noticed," she said, and smiled at him.

He smiled back, and wondered if she realized how that smile transfigured her face. Or just how attractive the face in question actually was. When she'd first come aboard, if anyone had asked him, he would have said that the possibility that she might ever have smiled in her entire life was absurd. He'd been tempted, at first, to think it was arrogance, or the snobbish belief that an officer of the Dinochrome Brigade was infinitely superior to any mere Navy puke assigned to play chauffeur for her and her Bolo. And when she finally did begin to unbend a bit after the commodore's death, he'd suspected for a while that it was a false display, no more than a role she'd assumed when she suddenly found herself alone in command.

But he'd been wrong about that. He still hadn't figured out why she'd been so standoffish, so stiff and wooden. And it still seemed . . . odd that she'd become so much more human only after the expedition suffered so much loss and so many deaths. It wasn't because she was *happy* to have inherited Commodore Lakshmaniah's command. That much had been almost painfully evident from her first command conference. Her determination to do the job had been obvious, but the fact that she found the weight of responsibility crushing, whether she was prepared to admit it or not, had been equally obvious. But the fact that something had changed had been glaringly apparent, and Edmund Hawthorne was determined to eventually figure out what that something was.

And not, he admitted to himself, simply because she was his superior officer.

"How likely is it really, do you think, that there's a Puppy back there, ma'am?" he asked after a moment.

"Likely?" She gazed at him for a couple of heartbeats, her deep blue eyes thoughtful in her sandalwood face, then shrugged slightly. "Honestly, I don't think it's *likely* at all," she said. "I do think it's possible, though. And the consequences if it turns out there is someone back there and we don't spot them could be disastrous."

He nodded, but his frown was equally thoughtful, and she cocked her head at him.

"Should I assume from your expression that you think this is wasted effort, Captain Hawthorne?" she asked.

"No, ma'am. Certainly not," he said quickly, shaking his head at the undeniable edge of chill which had crept into her throaty, almost smoky soprano voice. "I was just thinking about the logistics equation anyone following us would face."

"Ah." Maneka tipped back in her borrowed bridge chair. "That's something I hadn't really considered," she continued after a moment, and smiled again. "Bolos have an enormous amount of information storage, but I suppose there are limits in everything. Lazarus has a huge amount of detail about things like firepower and battle screen strength for Dog Boy warships, but I guess the people who loaded his memory didn't see any reason he'd need information about their endurance."

"Don't make the mistake of assuming that I know that much about it, either, ma'am," Hawthorne told her with a lopsided grin. "I don't. But I do know what sorts of constraints we're facing, and we *knew* what sort of voyage we were committing to. I don't see any way the Puppies we ran into could have been stored or provisioned for a trip anywhere near as long as the one we're making. Which means that if there is anyone back there, they're going to be facing some pretty serious problems over the next several months."

"Which, presumably, they would realize even better than you do," Maneka mused aloud.

"Exactly," Hawthorne agreed.

"But would that necessarily mean they wouldn't try it, anyway?"

"That would depend on so many variables I doubt even your Bolo could make a meaningful projection," he said. "And I suppose a lot would also depend on exactly what sort of ship they've got. Assuming, of course, that they're back there at all."

"Give me a for instance," she said, watching his expression closely, and he shrugged and angled his own chair back.

"Their cybernetics aren't anywhere near as good as ours, according to the Intelligence estimates I've seen," he said. "I don't know anything about their planetary combat equipment, but on the Navy side, their AI is an awful lot less capable than ours is. If Intelligence is right, *Thermopylae*'s AI is probably as good as anything most of their cruisers or destroyers mount, and, frankly, Iona isn't actually all that bright. Not much more than a standard civilian vessel with a few more-or-less military applications added as strap-ons, really. And in addition to the limitations on the computer support, their onboard systems are a lot more manpower intensive than ours. That means even their warships have big crews compared to a similar Navy ship, and on a trip this long, that's got to cost them in terms of life support endurance. Then there's the question of spare parts and maintenance and the fact that their maintenance cycles are supposed to be shorter than ours."

"So you think they're likely to start suffering equipment malfunctions?"

"I think it's something they have to be concerned about. On the other hand, an awful lot would depend on where they were in their current maintenance cycle when they ran into us. If they were only a few months into the current cycle, then they probably have at least a year, maybe as much as eighteen months, or even two years, before things got really dicey on them. Of course, if they did have some sort of major engineering casualty or system malfunction, they'd be one hell of a long way from home or any spares they needed. On balance, though, unless we hit them fairly late in the cycle, they're probably good for at least a year and a half before they start having problems from that perspective."

"What about endurance on their power plants?"

"That shouldn't be any problem for them. Well, as long as they're bigger than a destroyer, anyway. I don't have exact figures, but with the antimatter plants they use, any one of their cruisers ought to have at least a couple of years worth of fuel endurance on board, even under drive in hyper. No, ma'am." He shook his head. "The Achilles' heel would be life support. Food, especially. Their warships don't have the hydroponics sections our personnel transports or agro ships do, so they're limited solely to whatever food they loaded before they left port, and there's no way they could possibly have 'just happened' to have packed the better part of two years worth of food aboard ships that weren't specifically intended for the same sort of long-range cruising we were."

"What about cryo sleep?" she asked.

"Their warships don't begin to have that sort of cryo capacity," he said confidently. "At best, they might be able to put as much as ten or fifteen percent of their total personnel into cryo, and that wouldn't be anywhere near enough to have any significant impact on their food demands over a voyage that long."

"And their transports?"

"I honestly don't know," he said frankly. "I know they have at least some cryo capacity built into almost all their troop transports, but my understanding is that it's intended primarily for emergency use."

"Which these circumstances would certainly constitute," she pointed out.

"Oh, no question," he agreed. "The point I was making wasn't that they wouldn't use it, just that because it's intended for emergency use only, it's not as sophisticated—or reliable—as the cryo even our agro transports are using. They'd take losses, probably significant ones, if they used it. Given the stakes, I'd probably go ahead and risk that, if I were the skipper of a naval transport in this situation. But even if I wanted to, I couldn't do that if I were the skipper of one of their cruisers, because I wouldn't have the facilities in the first place."

"So the bottom line," she said slowly, "is that, from what you're saying, if Commodore Lakshmaniah really did detect a stealthed logistics ship, it could still be back there, and depending on what sort of cryogenic capability it has—and the percentage of losses its CO is willing to accept—it might very well be able to stay with us all the way. But if there's a *warship* still following us, it almost certainly *won't* have the endurance to stay with us."

"Pretty much." He nodded. "Which isn't a lot of help, I know. I mean, if there really was another ship out there, the commodore was probably right that it was a logistics ship. So all this kicking the possibilities around doesn't really change the parameters very much."

"Don't sell your contribution *too* short," Maneka disagreed, regarding him speculatively. "I doubt that there's a cruiser back there. If there were, it would almost certainly have gone for a missile engagement by now. It could pick off the merchies one at a time from beyond any range at which Lazarus or Mickey could engage it in return. And given what you've said about its probable endurance limitations, it wouldn't have waited this long, either. Not unless it was entirely out of missiles, and I can't conceive of any reason for that."

"Unless they're trying to lull us—you—into a sense of over-confidence before they actually do attack," Hawthorne countered in the best devil's advocate fashion.

"A possibility," she conceded, smiling at him again. "The Dog Boys are great advocates of the KISS principle, though, so that's probably a bit too devious for their thinking in a situation like this one. I'll bear it in mind, of course, but I don't really think it's likely. And even if it is, from what you've said, they'd probably still launch their attack sometime in the next few months. Well short of our planned arrival time, anyway."

"Probably," he agreed after a moment.

"But if it's a transport, then the parameters change, assuming that they're willing to risk the sorts of cryo casualties you were estimating."

"Yes, ma'am."

"Of course, all of that becomes a moot point if we manage to detect them on one of our sweeps."

"Yes, ma'am," he agreed yet again. "And, frankly, I think that the fact that they haven't even tried to mousetrap one of the transports by ambushing her at long range when she doubled back on one of the sweeps, is pretty convincing additional proof that whatever might be behind us, it isn't a cruiser."

"Point taken." Maneka frowned thoughtfully, rocking her bridge chair back and forth. "All right, Captain," she said finally. "I think this has been a productive discussion. We probably need to have more like it. For the moment, I'm going to proceed on the worst-case assumption that we *are* being shadowed by a Dog Boy cruiser. And if that's the case, then we're most likely to see them launch an attack in the next two or three months, at the outside. We'll be on the alert, accordingly. And I think I might just have a little discussion with Governor Agnelli about the possibility of extending our own voyage time a bit further still. If it turns out we're being followed by a transport, I think the odds are pretty good that we'll eventually spot it on one of the sweeps. If we don't, though, let's see if we can't stretch its endurance out even further. Hopefully until it snaps on them."

"Sounds good to me, ma'am," he said.

"Good." She stood with the curiously catlike grace he'd come to associate with her, and he stood to face her. "Thank you for bringing this to my attention," she said.

"You're welcome, ma'am," he said respectfully, and watched as she left the bridge and headed for her quarters.

"So, you've evaded them yet again, Captain."

"Actually, sir, it was Lieutenant Ha-Shathar," Na-Tharla observed.

"As per your orders and previous planning."

"Perhaps, sir." Na-Tharla gazed at General Ka-Frahkan for several seconds, then sighed. "The truth is, sir, that as well as Ha-Shathar performed, and as much as I'd like to accept the credit for his success, this is a dangerous game. We were lucky. We may not be the next time. And there *will* be a next time."

Ka-Frahkan looked back at him, then flattened his ears slightly in unhappy agreement.

"Perhaps if we can simply evade detection long, they'll decide there's nothing to detect," he said, after a moment.

"With the utmost respect, General, you know we can't rely on that. Whoever is in command over there is taking no chances, and these random sensor sweeps of his are impossible to predict. I believe he'll continue them indefinitely, whether he detects anything or not."

"May the Nameless Ones devour his soul," Ka-Frahkan muttered. He rubbed the bridge of his muzzle, glowering into invisible distances. "Can we drop back still farther and maintain contact with them?" he asked finally.

"I can't guarantee that, sir," Na-Tharla said frankly. "We can detect and track them from much farther than they can detect us, but if we drop back far enough to give us a better chance against these unexpected sensor sweeps, we'll be at the very edge of our own sensor range. Under those circumstances, if we maneuver to evade what we're estimating as the Bolos' sensor reach against our stealth capabilities, it's very probable that the entire convoy will drop off of *our* sensors while we do so."

"If they do, what are our chances of reacquiring them once more?"

"General, that depends upon so many variables that any estimate I gave you would be no better than a guess," Na-Tharla said. "Assuming they maintain their base course while they sweep for us—or that any course change they adopt is relatively minor, at least—then our chances of regaining contact with them would be excellent. If, however, they execute a radical heading change after driving us out of sensor range, our chances would be very poor, at best."

"I see." Ka-Frahkan sat silent for almost two full minutes, then inhaled sharply. "What do you recommend, Captain?" he asked, and his tone and expression were far more formal than they had been.

Na-Tharla looked back at him. A part of the captain wanted to protest that the decision wasn't his. That it was Ka-Frahkan who had elected to pursue the Human convoy in first place, just as he was also Na-Tharla's superior officer. Yet the rest of him recognized that Ka-Frahkan lacked the specialized knowledge and experience to properly evaluate the risks himself... and that he was willing to admit it.

"Sir," Na-Tharla said at last, "as I've already said, I believe we're up against a Human commander who intends to take no chances. I think it's entirely possible, even probable, that he doesn't truly believe anyone could be on his track, yet he's obviously taking precautions—intelligent and capable ones—against the possibility that someone is. It can't be much longer before he begins making occasional sweeps with *both* of the Bolo transports, which will be much more dangerous, especially if we're tracking the enemy from relatively short range. In my opinion, the chance of our being detected eventually under those circumstances approaches unity. *Death Descending* must maintain sufficient separation to give us the greatest possible flexibility of evasion courses if we hope to avoid the sensors of *two* Bolos."

"So you recommend dropping further back."

"I do, sir," Na-Tharla said unflinchingly. "At the same time, however, it's my duty to point out that if the other transports do execute a radical course change during such a sensor sweep, we could very well lose the rest of the convoy completely."

"But not the Bolo transports?" Ka-Frahkan said thoughtfully.

"Most probably not." Na-Tharla flicked his ears in a gesture of exasperated ignorance. "I command a transport, General. Our database contains very little information on the Humans' Bolos or the Bolos' transport vessels. As a result, I know virtually nothing about the stealth capabilities they might possess. According to what little data I do have, their transports normally don't incorporate a great deal of stealth ability. They have at least one smaller class of transport, often used to land infantry or very light mechanized units for special operations and surprise raids, which has *extremely* capable stealth, but the *Bolo* transports appear not to match that capability. *If* that's true, and they don't possess capabilities greater than they've so far displayed, and given that we're using only passive sensors, then we ought to be able to track them from beyond my current estimate of the range of which the Bolos would be likely to detect *us*."

He bared his canines mirthlessly.

"If *I* had been designing their vessels, they *would* have better stealth than they've shown so far, but I suppose the Humans may calculate that anything with a Bolo or two mounted on its hull has little need to hide."

"No," Ka-Frahkan agreed, and showed just the tips of his own canines. "Their accursed Bolos are . . . capable. Very capable. The only time the 3172nd faced them directly—at our attack on their Heyward System—we were part of the General Ya-Thulahr's corps. He had three armored divisions under command against a single battalion of their Bolos." He snorted and more of his fangs showed. "We took the system in the end, and wiped out the Human population on the planet, but our casualties were over seventy percent."

"I read the declassified reports on that campaign," Na-Tharla said. "I knew our losses were severe, but I'd never realized they were that heavy." He eyed the general with respect. "Nor had I realized your Brigade had been part of Ya-Thulahr's corps."

"The 3172nd has seven campaign stars on its colors from this war, Captain," Ka-Frahkan said with bleak, iron pride, "and we've never been defeated. Heyward was the worst campaign we've faced, although our losses were 'only' fifty-two percent, far lighter than most of the other brigades. For the most part, though," he admitted, "we haven't found ourselves facing their Bolos head-on. Their Marines and militia can be nasty opponents even without that, of course—we took almost thirty percent losses against Tricia's World, for example—but we've been used more in the independent role, hitting their rear areas and smaller population centers instead of the sort of set-piece assaults going back and forth across the Line. Which," he snorted with sudden, harsh humor, "probably suits us particularly well for *this* campaign, now that I think about it. After all, how much further behind the Line could we be?"

"You have a point, sir," Na-Tharla acknowledged with an ear-flick of bitter humor. "But that brings us back to our current problem. And whatever the Humans' design theories may be, these Bolo transports certainly don't appear particularly stealthy. So far, at any rate. Yet I must point out once again that I have absolutely no hard data upon which to base my estimates."

"No," Ka-Frahkan agreed again. "Still, I think you're probably correct, Captain. And if you are, then we can afford to lose contact with the convoy as a whole, so long as we retain contact with its escorts. They will provide us with the signposts we require to find the other transports once again."

"Unless they decide not to rejoin the convoy themselves," Na-Tharla said.

"Unlikely." Ka-Frahkan flattened his ears decisively. "As you say, Captain, this Human who opposes us appears to be one who takes infinite precautions against even the most unlikely of threats. One who thinks that way would never separate his Bolos from the colony they were sent to protect, especially after his naval escort's total destruction. No. He'll take his responsibility to shield the convoy seriously. Even if he separates his transports temporarily from the rest of the ships, it will only be to rendezvous with it somewhere. And so, eventually, he *will* lead us back to the very thing he strives to protect, for he has no other option." The general bared his own fangs fully in a flash of ivory challenge. "It pleases me to use his own attention to detail against him."

Na-Tharla half-slitted his eyes while he considered Ka-Frahkan's logic, and his ears rose slowly in agreement.

"I believe you're correct, sir," he said. "And I confess that the idea pleases me, as well. But even though this should substantially improve our chances of successfully tracking the Humans to their destination without being detected, we must still destroy them when we've done so. And the fashion in which the Human commander is watching his back trail suggests to me that he'll maintain a similar degree of alertness and attention to detail even after his expedition reaches the end of its journey."

"I think you're right," Ka-Frahkan said. "And if you are, our task will undeniably be more difficult than I'd originally hoped. But it won't be impossible, especially if we succeed in remaining completely undetected."

And, he did not add aloud, *if we don't lose too many of my troopers to your cryo tubes.*

He knew the sour edge to his thoughts was unfair. Na-Tharla had specifically warned him about the dangers of using the emergency system, after all. It was scarcely the captain's fault that his warnings appeared to have been so well taken. Almost three percent of Ka-Frahkan's personnel had already died, but at least it seemed probable that any of the tubes which were likely to fail had now done so. Which meant he shouldn't lose any more of his people . . . until it was time to awaken them and he discovered how many had simply died in their sleep.

But we will *do what we've come to accomplish*, he told himself fiercely. *We owe it to the People, and the Nameless Ones will see to it that we succeed, however capable this accursed Human commander may be.*

"I think the Governor is getting more comfortable with the notion that you're in command," Hawthorne observed as Maneka cut the video link and terminated the conference with Agnelli, Berthier, and Jeffords.

She and Hawthorne sat at the conference table in *Thermopylae*'s briefing room. It was quite a large briefing room for a vessel with such a relatively small crew, but, then, it wasn't really intended for the transport's crew's use. It was configured and equipped to provide the commander of the assault forces embarked aboard the ship with everything he needed to brief his officers and personnel. Which meant the two of them rattled around in it like dried peas in a particularly large pod.

"You do, do you?" Maneka tipped back her chair and cocked an eyebrow at him. That remark wasn't something she would have expected to hear out of him when she first came aboard *Thermopylae*, five and a half months earlier. Nor would she have expected to see the faint but undeniable twinkle in his brown eyes.

"Well," the naval officer said, tipping his own chair back from the table, "I don't believe he would have threatened to 'come over there and spank you, young lady' a couple of months ago. Certainly not in front of anyone else, at any rate."

"No, you probably have a point about that," she conceded with a slight smile.

"You know I do," Hawthorne said, and his voice was suddenly much more serious. Serious enough that she looked at him sharply, eyebrows lowered.

"Meaning what?" she asked just a bit crisply.

"Meaning that right after the commodore was killed, he was just about as pissed off to be taking orders from someone in your age as someone as controlled as he is could ever be," Hawthorne said flatly. "He tried to keep it from showing, but he didn't quite pull it off."

Maneka started to open her mouth, then closed it with an almost audible click before she automatically bit his head off. She wasn't certain why she'd stopped herself. There was a hardness, a sourness, in his voice, one at odds with Edmund Hawthorne's normal air of thoughtful calm. It also wasn't the way he or any of Maneka's officers should be talking about Governor Agnelli, and her first instinct was to jerk him up short. But something about not just the way he'd said it, but his expression . . .

Why, he's angry *about it*, she realized. *Now why . . . ?*

"Actually," she said, "I've been quite pleased with my relationship with the Governor from the beginning. It wasn't easy for him to accept that someone only about a third of his age and as junior as a mere captain, even in the Dinochrome Brigade, was going to be giving the orders."

"I know, but—" Hawthorne cut himself off with a sharp, chopping wave of his hand and grimaced. "Sorry, ma'am. I guess I was probably out of line."

"Maybe." She regarded him thoughtfully. "On the other hand, I have to wonder if there's some reason this came up at this particular moment?"

He met her eyes steadily for a second or two, then looked away.

"There may be," he said, finally. "But if so, it's not a very good one. Or, at least, not one I ought to be paying any attention to, ma'am."

"I see." She smiled again, even more slightly than before, as she digested his abrupt reversion to the formalities of military courtesy. Except in overtly official settings, there'd been very few "ma'ams" coming her way from him over the past few weeks. Odd that she hadn't really noticed that. *I wonder if he has?* she thought.

"Captain Hawthorne," she said, making her own voice coolly formal and deliberately emphasizing his role as *Thermopylae's* commanding officer, "I suspect that you may be guilty of considering a violation of Article Seven-One-Niner-Three."

His gaze snapped back to her, and her smile had vanished into a masklike expression.

"I—" he began, then stopped, and Maneka managed not to giggle. It was hard, and even harder to hang onto her official superior officer's glower. After all, what was he going to say? "Nonsense, ma'am! I've never even contemplated making a pass at *you!*" wasn't exactly the most tactful possible response. But, then again, "Actually, ma'am, I've been thinking about jumping your bones for some time now," wasn't exactly the sort of thing one said to one's commanding officer, either.

"That's . . . absurd," he said, finally. With a noticeable lack of conviction, she thought rather complacently. "You're not simply my superior officer; you're the senior officer of this entire force."

"A point of which I am painfully well aware, I assure you," she told him. "Still, Captain Hawthorne," she cocked her chair back once again, "I continue to nourish the faint suspicion that certain . . . improper temptations, shall we say, have begun to cross your mind. Or, perhaps, other portions of your anatomy."

His eyes widened, then narrowed in sudden suspicion as the grin she'd managed to suppress began to break free.

"Other portions of my *anatomy*, is it?" he said slowly. "And which 'other portions' did the captain have in mind, if I might inquire?"

"Oh, I imagine you can make a pretty shrewd guess," she replied, this time with a gurgle of mirth. He glared at her, and the gurgle became something suspiciously like outright laughter as she shook her head at him.

His expression gave a remarkably good imitation of a man counting—slowly—to a thousand, and she shook her head at him again, this time almost penitently.

"Sorry, Ed," she said contritely. "The idea just sort of . . . took me by surprise." Something flickered in his eyes, and she shook her head again, quickly. "Not in a *bad* way," she hastened to assure him. "In fact, the surprise was mostly that I hadn't realized that the same sort of extremely improper thoughts have been occurring to *me*."

He'd opened his mouth. Now he closed it again and tilted his head to one side as he studied her expression.

"They have?" he asked, finally.

"Well," she said with painful honesty, "they *would* have been, if I hadn't been so busy suppressing them. I hope you won't take this wrongly, but now that I think about it, you're actually kind of on the attractive side."

"I'm *what*?"

"Oh, maybe not exactly *handsome*," she said pensively. "But cute—definitely cute. And, now that I think about it, you've got nice buns, too."

"With the captain's permission," Hawthorne said through teeth which weren't—quite—gritted, "it occurs to me that I may have been just a bit too quick to dismiss the Governor's attitude towards the expedition's military commander. The thought of spankings has a certain definite appeal at this particular moment."

"It does?" She considered his statement gravely. "Well, I've never actually *tried* it, you understand, but . . ."

For a moment, he looked as if he might explode, and she laughed helplessly. It was the first time he'd ever heard her truly laugh. For that matter, she realized somewhere deep inside, even as it happened, it was probably the first time she'd laughed at all—really *laughed*—since Benjy's death. It felt astonishingly good.

"My God," he said, softly, smiling at her, "you *do* know how to laugh."

She sobered almost instantly, but it was only a case of stepping back a few paces from the bright bubble of mirth he'd touched to life inside her, and her huge blue eyes softened as she contemplated him.

"Yes," she said finally. "Yes, I do. But I'd . . . forgotten. It's . . . been a while."

"Is it something you want to talk about?" he asked gently, and she shook her head.

"No. Not yet. Maybe—probably—later, but not just yet."

She could tell that a part of him wanted to press, but he didn't. He only nodded, and she gave him another smile, this one with more than a touch of gratitude for his understanding and patience.

"May I assume, however, that you aren't going to have me up on charges?" he inquired after a moment.

"Well, it *is* most improper of you, and undoubtedly prejudicial to discipline and proper maintenance of the chain of command," she said thoughtfully. "On the other hand, since you're the senior Navy officer present, preferring charges might be just a bit awkward. Especially if your defense counsel put me on the stand and asked whether or not your feelings were reciprocated." She shook her head. "No, under the circumstances, I think we can probably deal with this situation short of a formal court-martial."

"And just precisely how do you intend to 'deal' with it, if I might ask?"

"Given the fact that neither one of us has had the good sense and gumption to say a single word about this to the other one, I propose that we approach the situation like mature adults," she told him, and the gravity of her tone was only slightly flawed by the twinkle in her eyes. "I rather doubt that anyone is going to complain to higher authority, under the circumstances, whatever we choose to do about it. Still, there *are* proprieties to observe, and a mature and adult woman such as myself prefers to test the waters first. To ascertain what she

herself is feeling and thinking. To determine whether the possible object of her affections—or, at least, hormones—truly has
the personal qualities she desires in a potential, um, significant
other. To—"

"All right, Captain Trevor, ma'am!" he interrupted. "I get the
picture. And you're right; I'm an idiot for not having opened my
mouth sooner, I suppose. So, Captain Trevor, might I have the
pleasure of your company for dinner? I have a really excellent
auto-chef in my palatial quarters, with a truly masterful touch
with the delicious standard meal number seventeen scheduled
for this evening. I promise, we'll almost be able to forget that
it tastes like recycled boot soles. And," his voice got at least a
little more serious, "I also have three bottles of a rather nice
wine stashed away in my private mass allowance. I was saving
them for our arrival at our destination."

"If you brought them for that, then you should save them,"
she told him, but he shook his head.

"At the time I brought them aboard, it hadn't occurred to
me that anything equally worth celebrating might come along,"
he said, and this time his voice was much softer and warmer.
"But, then, I hadn't met *you* yet, either, had I?"

3

"It's beautiful, isn't it?" Hawthorne said quietly.

"I'd say that was a masterful bit of understatement," Maneka replied in judicious tones.

They stood side-by-side on *Thermopylae*'s command deck, gazing into the visual display along with every other member of Hawthorne's bridge crew as the big transport ship settled into orbit around the planet they had come so far to find.

The G0 star they had named Lakshmaniah blazed with fierce, life-giving light and heat, bathing not one, but two habitable worlds in its brilliant glare. At the moment, *Thermopylae* was approaching the innermost of the two, the one they had named Indrani, which orbited the primary at just over nine light-minutes. The average planetary temperature was a bit higher than Maneka would have preferred, but, then, she was a native of Everest. The other habitable planet, the one they had named New Hope, with an orbital radius of just under fifteen and a half light-minutes, was much more to her taste.

Which, she thought wryly, *puts me in a minority of one.*

She couldn't really blame the rest of the expedition, from Adrian Agnelli down to the youngest child, for preferring Indrani. After over a full Standard Year and a half packed into the overcrowded confines of their transports, that planet looked like Heaven made real. With a climate most resort worlds would have envied, a gravity of 1.05 Earth Standard, and a surface that was eighty-two percent water, it floated against the blackness of space like a huge, incredibly gorgeous, white-swirled blue and green marble.

Even without the endless, wearying journey which had brought them here, that planet would have been one of the most beautiful things she'd ever seen in her life.

"In position, sir," the helmsman announced from Astrogation, and Hawthorne nodded.

"Ms. Stopford, please signal done with engines," he said.

"Aye, aye, sir," *Thermopylae's* engineer said, and Hawthorne looked at his communications officer.

"Inform the Governor and Brigadier Jeffords that we're preparing to deploy the pod," he said.

"Aye, aye, sir."

Maneka listened to be crisp rhythm of orders, the instant snap with which his people responded to his commands, with what she realized had become rather proprietary pleasure. As her senior Navy deputy, Hawthorne had taken over almost all of the unending details of managing the convoy's ships. Like her, he'd had no choice but to grow into the responsibilities which had landed on his shoulders, and she was devoutly glad she'd had him. He was actually much better when it came to dealing with people than she was, and she'd come to rely upon him as a quasi-ambassador, as much as her senior naval officer. The way she'd come to rely upon him in a much more personal sense, as well, was simply icing on her cake.

And a rather nice cake it is, too, she thought wryly. *Because he really does have an awfully nice butt. Among other things.*

She'd decided that their relationship wasn't *quite* against Regs. Lazarus had helped her research the Articles of War and relevant regulations, and she'd found at least three loopholes which might plausibly be stretched to cover the situation. But all of them had to be stretched rather industriously to pull it off, and even so she knew they hovered on the brink of an outright violation, so the two of them had very carefully not moved their things into the same set of quarters. Everyone knew, of course, but this way everyone could pretend they *didn't*, and that made them all much happier. It was wonderful that humans were such . . . adaptable creatures.

She smiled at the thought, then shook herself out of her revery as he turned back towards her.

"Well," she said, quietly enough that his bridge crew could treat it as a private conversation between the two of them, "I guess I'd better get saddled up for my perilous mission."

"Yeah, right!" he snorted, equally quietly. "If I thought you might really end up in some sort of trouble down there, I'd probably be nervous. As it is—"

He shook his head, grinning, and she smiled back.

"Don't tell the Governor it's all really just a trick to let me be the first human to ever set foot on Indrani," she told him, half seriously, and he gave her a sharp look.

"I thought you and Guthrie cut cards to see whose Bolo pulled the survey duty?"

"We did." She smirked at him. "But we used *my* deck. Rank hath its privileges, after all. And," she added in a more steely tone as his eyes narrowed, "if you ever tell him I admitted that to you, I'll have Lazarus run over your toes!"

"My God, the perfidy of the woman!" He shook his head. "You realize, of course, that I'll never be able to trust you again."

"Hah! If you're only figuring that out now, you're a lot slower than I thought you were."

She gave him another smile, then turned and made her way quickly down the interconnecting passages to the assault pod Lazarus rode. Her personal quarters were also located in the pod, which had the advantage of keeping her close to the Bolo, although it also explained why she didn't have very much space, given the way the pod had been modified. The standard pod ought to have given her plenty of room, since it was big enough to transport an entire battalion of heavy, manned tanks. But a single Bolo—even mounted semiexternally—used up close to half of its total available volume, and half of the rest had been given over to the automated Bolo depot the Brigade techs on Sage had somehow fitted in and the spares to support that depot.

The "depot" had been specifically configured so that Lazarus could operate its remotes and service mechs, making him effectively his own Bolo tech. Maneka wasn't sure she approved of that. On the one hand, his onboard diagnostic programs, coupled with his ability to access the "depot" AI, allowed him to take care of all of his maintenance and service needs with a precision and dispatch even the best trained, most experienced human technician would have been hard-pressed to equal. On the other hand, if he suffered damage sufficient to incapacitate his own systems, he would need that same trained *human* technician to make the repairs he would no longer be able to direct for himself.

The convoy did have one fully trained, veteran Bolo tech, but Sergeant Willis had been assigned to *Stalingrad*, along with Guthrie Chin and Mickey. The decision had been made at a much higher level than Maneka Trevor, but she understood the logic behind it. She might not *like* it, but it actually did make sense.

The logistical planners for the colony had been extremely ingenious when it came to cramming the necessary people, supplies, and equipment into the available space. *Thermopylae*'s capacious internal cargo holds—designed to provide the lift capacity for up to three battalions of infantry or air cavalry in addition to supporting the external assault pods—had figured prominently in their plans when they started cramming. That was true of all the convoy's ships, including *Stalingrad*, but in *Thermopylae*'s case, they'd opted to utilize the space for heavy construction and earth-moving equipment, some of which filled the other half of Lazarus' pod not occupied by the Bolo himself. *Stalingrad*, on the other hand, had been fitted out with a considerably more capable and much more conventional version of a standard Bolo depot.

In many respects, Lazarus' self-run depot was little more than a dispersed backup for the manned depot Sergeant Willis oversaw aboard *Stalingrad*. Maneka had wondered occasionally if that was because the mission planners had regarded Lazarus, despite his seniority, as the backup *Bolo*, as well, in light of his advanced age. She had expected that suspicion to irritate her, but somewhat to her surprise, it amused her, instead. And it amused Lazarus, as well. She'd mentioned her suspicions to him once, and he had replied with one of his soft electronic chuckles.

" 'Old soldiers never die, they just fade away,' " he'd said.

"That sounds like one of your quotes," she'd replied suspiciously.

"It is. From General Douglas MacArthur, an ancient prespace officer. He would, I fear, have served as an excellent example of the sort of military ambition Governor Agnelli once feared you might exhibit. Nor was he ever particularly afflicted with the Human virtue of modesty. Yet he was an undeniably capable strategist and commander with what was, for his era, an extraordinarily long military career."

"As long as yours for a Bolo?"

"Perhaps not quite that long," Lazarus had conceded with another chuckle. Then his tone had grown more serious. "But my cognomen is well taken, is it not? I have 'died' twice now, Maneka, yet each time, I have returned to duty. Useful duty, I believe, yet under circumstances no one—least of all myself—might have predicted. As have you, in a sense. Perhaps it is only fitting that we should test the accuracy of MacArthur's hypothesis. And it is difficult for me to conceive of a more honorable duty than that we should 'fade away' offering our services to Operation Seed Corn."

The memory of that conversation flickered through her mind once more, and she shook her head. The planet they had journeyed so unimaginably far to reach lay below them at this very moment, and only after they had entered orbit had she allowed herself to admit to herself that, whatever her head might have thought, her heart had never truly believed they would reach it. Now they had, and she discovered that she looked forward to fading quietly away here, performing good, solid, *useful* duty in company with Lazarus in the peaceful retirement his century and more of service to the Concordiat had so amply earned.

She snorted in amusement at her own emotional turn of thought as she entered the pod. Lazarus, she thought, would have been even more amused by the thought of "peaceful retirement" for a Bolo. Which changed neither the fact that he had earned it nor her happiness that he would finally enjoy it.

She stepped through the automatically opening hatch, walked through her quarters—snagging the neural headset off her desk as she passed—and clambered into the access trunk which connected to Lazarus' belly hatch. Someone of Hawthorne's broad-shouldered size might have found the access trunk confining, but there was ample room for Maneka's slender frame, and she went up the ladder rungs quickly.

"Welcome aboard, Commander," Lazarus' resonant tenor said through the speaker in her mastoid as she transitioned from the access trunk to the Bolo's internal ladders and the belly hatch slid silently shut behind her.

"My, aren't we formal today?" she replied, and got an electronic chuckle in response.

"It occurred to me that this would be an historic occasion. As such I thought perhaps 'company manners' might be in order," Lazarus informed her.

"Well," she said as she reached the middle deck transfer point between ladders, "why don't we just agree to lie to the reporters and tell them we were formal as hell?"

"Bolos do not lie," Lazarus said primly.

"The hell they don't!" she shot back. "You Bolos are the galaxy's past masters at deception tactics."

"True," the Bolo conceded. "However, those tactics are normally employed against the Enemy."

"If you think any historian who wants to turn *me* into some sort of historical heroine isn't 'the Enemy,' then your IFF software needs a little attention!"

"I had not considered it in that light. Very well. We shall lie."

"Damned straight we will!"

Maneka had continued climbing steadily throughout the conversation. Her route took her through the mammoth superconductor capacitors that fed Lazarus' starboard battery of ion-bolt infinite repeaters, and she absentmindedly checked the power level readouts as she passed. One more deck worth of ladder took her up the outboard side of Lazarus' fusion plant, tucked away at his very center along with his primary personality center, and onto the command deck.

"I see why there aren't any old Bolo commanders," she said, breathing slightly faster than normal after her long, rapid climb.

"The entry route is less arduous aboard newer model Bolos," Lazarus remarked, this time from the bulkhead speakers. "According to the technical reports in the depot's memory, the new Mark XXXIII will actually provide a gravity shaft for its commander."

"Yet another newfangled gadget to go wrong," she said loftily. "This effete, idle lay-about, new generation of Bolo commanders is soft, I tell you. Soft! Give me reliability over decadent convenience any day."

"Bolos may not lie, but I see that sometimes Bolo *commanders* do," Lazarus observed. "Still, I appreciate the sentiment."

Maneka chuckled as she flopped down in the almost sinfully comfortable command couch. It had always amused her that here, at the very heart of this grim, enormous machine of war, was a couch whose biofeedback-monitored comfort would have cost a good quarter-million credits on the civilian market. It seemed even more incongruous as she looked around the crowded, cramped confines of the command deck itself.

Every surface was covered with displays, readouts, battle board lights that winked at standby or glowed with the steady

illumination of full readiness. Aside from an old-fashioned joystick, there were no manual controls at all. No single human
being could possibly have operated a Mark XXVIII Bolo without full computer support, so there was no point in using up
precious internal volume with weapons control stations or EW
consoles. Even the joystick was no more than a sop to conven-
tion. In theory, it was possible for a human commander to drive
a Bolo home if its personality center was knocked out. Given
the fact that the personality center in question was located
directly under the command deck, however, the chance that
any commander would survive its destruction in any shape to
drive anything anywhere was remote, to say the least.

A spasm of remembered grief and loss flickered through her
at the thought. Once again, she remembered the blur of the
closing armored shell around the equally comfortable couch
which had once stood at the center of Benjy's command deck.
That deck had been virtually identical to this one, and she
sat for just a moment, reminding herself that Lazarus was not
Benjy . . . and Indrani was not Chartres.

She took long enough to be certain she had control of her
emotions, then slipped into the headset and activated the
neural net.

*Once again I experience the instant of fusion with my Com-
mander.*

*I sense her rueful amusement as her reflex effort to conceal
the mental flashback to her time with Unit Eight-Six-Two fails.
It cannot do otherwise when her thoughts and mine are so intimately melded, yet it is typical of her that she should attempt
to "spare my feelings." Her amusement at her failure, however,
is yet another sign of how far she has come in recovering from
the mental wounds the Battle of Chartres inflicted upon her.*

*Her mind settles fully into place, nestled at the core of our
joined personality as her physical body is nestled at the core of
my own ponderous combat chassis, and she/we open our sensors
fully to the universe about us.*

❖   ❖   ❖

Her/their passive and active sensors flooded her/their mind with data. It was no longer presented to the Maneka component of their joint personality via graphic display. The data simply *was*. She had discovered that there were no human words to express precisely what she perceived in these moments of union with Lazarus. It was as if she could literally see radar and lidar, as if she could taste cosmic radiation on her tongue. Ranges and firing bearings, signal intensities, frequencies, pulse repetition rates . . . All of them were as fully, naturally, and instinctively part of her perceptions as the texture of her own palm seen with her merely human eyes.

She/they allowed themselves a brief moment—almost an eternity to one such as they had become—to savor the sensuality of their merger. In many respects, Maneka often thought, with the total honesty and openness which the link with Lazarus enforced, it was more satisfying, in a very different way, than any physical act of love she had ever experienced.

<I will not inform Lieutenant Hawthorne of that,> the Lazarus component of her/their personality told her with gentle amusement, and she sent a silent ripple of mental laughter back to him.

But then it was time for work, and she/they sent the command to *Thermopylae*'s AI to release the docking clamps. The pod's reaction thrusters flared briefly, wafting the massive parasite away from the transport's hull, then shut down. She/they waited patiently until the pod had cleared the safety perimeter for its normal-space drive, and then she/they went sliding gracefully towards the outermost atmosphere of Indrani.

"I trust you've been enjoying yourself down there, Captain," Adrian Agnelli said dryly.

"I always take a certain pleasure in the efficient performance of my duties, however arduous or onerous they may be," Maneka replied cheerfully, looking into the projected holographic display above the optical head Lazarus had extended and swivelled around to face her.

At the moment, she sat in a folding chair atop Lazarus' after missile deck, parked beside a broad river estuary and shaded by towering trees very like some huge, Old Earth conifer. She was also deplorably out of uniform, in an eye-stunningly red T-shirt (whose nano-printed front depicted the fully animated singing face of one of the Concordiat's better known shatter-rock vocalists) and a pair of very short white shorts. A floppy sun hat completed her extremely nonregulation ensemble, and Agnelli chuckled as he absorbed the impact.

"May I assume from your appearance that your survey activities have been successfully concluded?" he inquired.

"You may, sir," Maneka told him, and sipped iced tea from the tall, condensation-bedewed glass in her other hand. She looked back at the display with a smile, then straightened in her chair and became somewhat more serious.

"Officially, Governor," she told the man who had shifted from potential adversary to close friend over the past year and a half, "Lazarus and I have completed our survey of the proposed colony site. We're prepared to certify that the atmosphere is fully compatible with human environmental needs. We've been unable to detect any biohazards, and while there are several large local predators in the vicinity, none will pose a significant threat if routine out-world precautions are taken. Our samples of soil and local plant life have also confirmed the initial probe findings. Indrani's going to require more terraforming than some planets to support Terran food crops, but less than at least eighty percent of those we've successfully colonized elsewhere. All in all, sir, this looks like it's going to be a very nice place to live."

"Captain," Agnelli said with total sincerity, "I cannot begin to tell you how happy—and relieved—I am to hear that. May I conclude that, in your capacity as the colony's military commander, you're prepared to authorize the beginning of disembarkation?"

"Yes, Governor. I am," she said.

"Excellent!" Agnelli beamed hugely at her, then nodded to someone outside the visual range of his own communicator's visual pickup.

"The first wave is on its way, Captain," he said, looking back at Maneka, and she leaned back in her chair, activating the headset under the sun hat, and watching through Lazarus' sensors as the first shuttles descended like minnows of sun-hammered silver through the majestic, cloud-piled caverns of Indrani's sapphire sky.

"So they've found their accursed home at last, have they?" General Ka-Frahkan snarled to Na-Tharla.

The two Melconians stood in *Death Descending*'s Combat Information Center watching the icons of the Human convoy they had followed so far, and Ka-Frahkan's eyes were hot and hating in a face which had become noticeably gaunt.

"Yes, sir," Na-Tharla responded, although he knew the question had been purely rhetorical. "And, I hope you'll forgive me for saying, that it's not a moment too soon."

Ka-Frahkan looked up from the plot sharply. He opened his mouth, but Na-Tharla met his eyes levelly, and the general cut off what he'd started to say.

The transport's captain was even more gaunt and worn looking than the Army officer, and well he should be. Even with all the personnel of Ka-Frahkan's brigade in cryo sleep, the wakeful portion of *Death Descending*'s complement had been on sharply reduced rations for the last several months, and Na-Tharla had worked himself harder than any other member of his crew. Ka-Frahkan was an Army officer, not a naval officer, yet he was only too well aware of the miracles of improvisation Na-Tharla had performed to keep the ship's critical systems running this long. And the brilliant fashion in which Na-Tharla had managed to track the Human ships, despite all their efforts at evasive routing and the Bolo transports' infernal, never-to-be-sufficiently-accursed sensor sweeps had been masterful. *Death Descending* was only a transport, yet the general felt confident that none of the Emperor's cruiser or even battlecruiser commanders could have done a better job under such impossible conditions. Under the circumstances, the captain was entitled to express himself openly.

"I not only forgive you for saying it, Captain," Ka-Frahkan said after a moment, "but I agree wholeheartedly. And I'd like to take this moment to say, because I don't think I have, really, how deeply I admire you and your crew for getting us here. You are truly heroes of the People."

"Thank you, sir—on behalf of my people, as well as myself."

Na-Tharla bent his head in a brief but obviously sincere acknowledgment of the compliment. Then he cleared his throat and looked back up at the general.

"Now that we've arrived, General, may I ask how you intend to proceed?"

"You certainly may," Ka-Frahkan agreed, but for several seconds, he said no more, only stood there, watching the icons. Then he drew a deep breath, wheeled away from the plot, and stepped out onto the main command deck where he could see the visual imagery of the far-distant planet the Human shuttles were landing upon even as he stood there.

It was remarkable, really, he thought, that they were here and obviously still undetected and unsuspected, even given the superb job Na-Tharla had done of shadowing the Human convoy. A dozen times, at least, the Humans' sweeping Bolo transports must have come within a hair's breadth of detecting them, yet somehow Na-Tharla had always managed to elude their peering eyes.

But there were limits to the miracles even someone as formidable as Na-Tharla could be expected to work. As the captain had predicted when Ka-Frahkan ordered him to pursue the Humans, *Death Descending* had traveled far beyond any point at which she could have returned to Melconian space. Even discounting the near total depletion of the transport's consumables, and ignoring the fact that her power plants were far overdue for shutdown and overhaul, her hyperdrive would have required a total overhaul of its own. None of which was likely to happen, given that they were literally hundreds upon hundreds of light-years away from the nearest Navy base.

"You wonder how we'll proceed, Captain?" he said at length,

never taking his eyes from the image of the planet being relayed by the tiny, heavily stealthed reconnaissance platform *Death Descending* had deployed with such exquisite caution.

"What we will *not* do is to act hastily," he continued. "We've all come much too far, at much too high a cost, to act until we're certain of success."

He considered the visual display for another several seconds, then turned away from it at last, and faced Na-Tharla squarely.

"I realize we've been on short rations for some time now, but that was largely because we had no idea how far we might have to stretch them. Now that we've reached our destination, how long can we continue to sustain ourselves before we must attack?"

"At least another several Human months, sir," Na-Tharla said slowly. "Until, of course, you awaken your personnel. An entire heavy brigade would devour all the supplies we still have within a very short period."

"How short?" Ka-Frahkan pressed. Na-Tharla looked at him, and the general's ears flipped a shrug. "My people will need some time—three days, minimum, although five or six would be far better—to recover from the effects of cryo before they'll be fit for combat," he explained.

"I see." Na-Tharla consulted his mental files on the state of their logistics, then shrugged himself.

"If we're to retain a reserve of eight days, let's say, for your personnel, in order to give them long enough to recover and for us to mount the operation, then we have sufficient supplies to carry the remainder of our personnel for approximately seventy days at current calory levels, sir," he said.

"Seventy days," Ka-Frahkan murmured, kneading the ridge of his muzzle thoughtfully. Then he snorted. "Well, it will just have to be long enough, won't it?"

Na-Tharla said nothing, simply waiting with polite attentiveness, and Ka-Frahkan gave him a harsh chuckle.

"Our primary difficulty, of course, lies in the two Bolos," he said. "If this Human commander proceeds with the same intelligence and forethought he's displayed thus far, he'll leave at least one of the Bolos aboard its transport, orbiting the planet. He has none of the heavy weapons-equipped orbital platforms the Concordiat uses to defend its inhabited worlds, but he *does* have a pair of Bolos he can use as a substitute. And I'm afraid that if he chooses to leave both of them in orbit, the probability of our succeeding in our mission will be severely curtailed."

He made the admission calmly, much though he disliked doing so. Na-Tharla had more than earned both honesty and openness from him.

"I doubt he'll do that, however," Ka-Frahkan went on after a moment. "He has two general zones which require protection. One is the surface of the planet, where his people intend to settle and make their homes. The second, is the space around that planet, where the Humans will undoubtedly establish their primary industrial nodes. And from which, although I feel confident at this point that it isn't truly foremost in his mind, any outside military threat must come.

"So the most reasonable way for him to proceed is to leave one Bolo in space, probably still mounted on its transport in order to give it full mobility, while he takes the other planet-side, to provide immediate security for the new settlement. In fact, he'll probably leave the Bolo they've already landed to conduct a survey of their future colony site on the planet."

He paused, and Na-Tharla rubbed the side of his own muzzle with a thoughtful frown.

"It would seem to me, sir," he said slowly, "that positioning his Bolos in the way you've described ought to make our task considerably more difficult. Surely the Bolo in space will pose a severe threat to any operation we might attempt to mount?"

"It certainly will," Ka-Frahkan agreed. "Not only will it serve as a most formidable orbital fortress, but its sensors will also be best positioned to give the colony early warning of the approach of any threat. In addition, it will be mobile. Should we manage to somehow elude its sensors and land an assault force, it will be in a position to maneuver itself and its weapons into position to bombard us from space. With the planet-side Bolo available to mount counterattacks, and with such heavy fire coming down on us from overhead, the Brigade would undoubtedly be wiped out long before it could reach attack range of the colony.

"*But*," the general raised one clawed finger and jabbed it at the visual display, "that deployment of the Bolos is also what will give us our opening."

"How, sir?" Na-Tharla asked with simple and genuine curiosity.

"The Brigade includes three special reconnaissance platoons, Captain Na-Tharla. They are equipped with the best EW stealth suits the Empire can provide, and they're trained to operate in all environments . . . including deep space.

"It's unlikely that the Humans believe for an instant that they're under threat of attack. From what I've observed of their operations, I expect them to act as if they do believe that, taking all prudent precautions against even the most unlikely of eventualities. Any thought they may have of external threats, however, will almost certainly focus upon possible Fleet attacks. A . . . brute force threat, one might say. They won't be expecting a *stealth* attack, and I think the odds are exceedingly good that we'll be able to get at least one recon platoon into range to attack the transport with fusion warheads.

"Destruction of the transport and the Bolo's assault pod will, at the very least, severely damage the Bolo. It's more likely, however, that the attack will catch the Bolo with its battle screen down, in which case a sufficiently powerful warhead—of which we have several in stores—will breach its unprotected war hull. In short, I believe the odds are that we will be able to kill it as the opening gambit in our attack."

He paused once more, watching Na-Tharla's expression closely. The captain was silent for several seconds, obviously thinking hard. Then his ears rose in a gesture which mingled assent with qualified confidence.

"Once we've disabled or destroyed the orbiting Bolo, the

mobility advantage shifts to us," *Death Descending*'s commander said slowly, thinking aloud. "The Bolo on the planet will have no choice but to remain close to the colony site, lest we manage to decoy it out of position and make our troop landing behind it or launch a bombardment of our own from space. Of course, we have no bombardment capability, but it won't know that. So it will have to react as if we do, which will allow us to land your Brigade around the curve of the planet from the colony, where it will be unable to engage us on our approach."

"Precisely," the general said, flicking his ears in emphatic agreement. "Any Bolo is always a formidable opponent, but I rather suspect that any Bolos assigned to these colony efforts will be older, less capable models. The demands of the main fronts have been pressing both sides too hard for me to believe the Concordiat is willing to divert first-line Bolos to something like this. After all," he showed his canines in a mirthless grin, "even an 'obsolete' Bolo should be equal to almost any threat—short of, say, an Imperial Heavy Assault Brigade—which might be encountered out here in the depths of unexplored space.

"*My* combat mechs, on the other hand, while not Bolos, *are* first-line units. I anticipate heavy losses, but I confidently expect to succeed in destroying the Bolo or at least crippling it sufficiently to prevent it from interfering with our destruction of the Human colony."

"I'm glad, General," Na-Tharla said after a moment. "I would hate to believe we've come so far without a significant chance of victory." He snorted softly. "I take no more pleasure in contemplating the probability of my own death than anyone, but I find I can accept the fact that even if we win, we can never get home, as long as we accomplish what we came for."

"Agreed," Ka-Frahkan said. "On the other hand, Captain, I have no intention of destroying the Humans and then simply sitting down and waiting to die ourselves!"

"Indeed?" Both of Na-Tharla's ears cocked interrogatively.

"Captain, we wouldn't be at war with the Humans in the

first place if we didn't both find the same planetary environments congenial. This is an excellent world the Humans have picked to settle, and at least twenty percent of both my Brigade personnel and your ship's company are female. We have sufficient genetic diversity to support a viable, self-replicating planetary population at need. So, even in a worst-case scenario, the People will continue here, on this planet.

"But that, as I say, is a worst-case outcome. I believe we stand an excellent chance of capturing the Humans' industrial infrastructure intact, as well. That's one of the reasons I wanted to know how long we can wait before we launch our attack. The longer the Humans have to settle into a sense of security, the lower their guard is likely to become. And our drones have already indicated that their industrial ships are designed on a modular basis."

Na-Tharla's ears flicked agreement. The heavily stealthed platform had shown them that at least three of the Human ships were already being dismantled into three large, independent modules each. From the data they'd been able to gather so far—limited, admittedly; even with the People's stealth technology, getting a platform close enough for detailed looks was out of the question—it appeared that each of those nine modules was intended to serve as the core of its own, separate industrial platform. Given the impressive automation of Human manufacturing capacity, he doubted it would take long for those industrial nodes to come on-line and begin expanding exponentially.

"I want them to have sufficient time to get as much as possible of their base infrastructure in place," General Ka-Frahkan said with bleak satisfaction. "By dispersing it, they deprive it of strategic mobility. It won't be able to drop into hyper and run away from us, and I would prefer to see that true of as many of their ships as possible. I want all of those ships taken or destroyed, Captain, but I especially want to gain possession of their manufacturing capacity.

"I realize it will be designed to produce additional Human technology, not immediately suited to our needs, but their mission planners will have provided sufficient capability to sustain and nurture the population they intended to place on this planet. It would be surprising indeed if we couldn't sufficiently adapt that capacity to provide the repairs and overhauls your vessel requires. So once we destroy the enemy, we will have many possible futures open to us.

"Which," his voice was suddenly hard and cold, like iron grating across the stone floor of a dungeon, "is more than they will."

4

"God, what a beautiful evening," Adrian Agnelli said softly.

He sat with his guests under a sky which was rapidly settling into the deep, cobalt blue vault of oncoming night. The distant mutter of waves came from behind him, rolling up over the lip of the bluff overlooking the ocean they hadn't yet gotten around to naming. In front of him, on the western horizon, the last fragments of day blazed in a crimson conflagration beyond the peaks of the inland mountains which fenced in the coastal plateau they'd chosen for the site of the City of Landing. Agnelli had hoped for a name with a bit more imagination, but tradition had carried the day. And it didn't really matter to him as he watched the sun-struck clouds fuming up about the sharp-edged peaks like the smoke of some stupendous bonfire. The brightest stars of unfamiliar constellations were already dimly visible overhead, and the larger of Indrani's two sizable moons was also visible, high in the eastern sky.

The ruins of an early supper littered the snow-white tablecloth with pillaged plates and looted bottles of wine. The food had come from the storerooms and hydroponics sections of the colony ships, not yet from the soil of their new homeworld, but the brilliant-hued floral arrangements at the center of the table had been put together out of some of Indrani's spectacular, tropical-climate flowers.

There weren't very many guests. The Governor himself, his daughter Allison, Lieutenant Governor Berthier, Brigadier Jeffords, Maneka, and Edmund Hawthorne. Over the often seemingly endless months of the voyage here, the six of them had become a tight-knit, efficiently functioning command team for the colony effort. The last two months, as the colony began to become an actual living, breathing entity, had been exhausting for all of them, yet Maneka often thought that there were no words in any human language to express the satisfaction all of them took from their demanding duties.

Even me. Maybe especially me. She glanced sideways at Hawthorne's profile and felt a warm glow deep inside her. *I joined the Brigade because I believed in what it stands for, and I still do. But I've seen enough death and destruction to last me for two or three lifetimes. It's so . . . unspeakably wonderful to see my efforts contributing to life for a change.*

She looked around. The table sat on a terrace behind the rapidly rising shell of what would become Landing's combined town hall and Governor's residence. At the moment, it didn't look particularly prepossessing, but Maneka had seen the plans. It would be a gracious structure when it was completed, and the people who'd designed it had been careful to provide for the inevitable growth it would suffer as the colony's population grew and government and its service organizations grew with it.

The rest of Landing's first-flight structures were going up with equal speed. Despite all the industrial and economic strains under which the Concordiat labored in its desperate battle with the Melconians, it had spared no expense when it came to equipping the colony fleet. Unlike many privately funded colonizing expeditions, this one was lavishly provided with highly capable automated construction and earthmoving equipment, including no less than seven ceramacrete fusers. One of those fusers was still rolling quietly along under the control of its rudimentary AI, running lights lit and proximity sensors alert for any human inept enough to get in its way, as it moved back and forth, laying down the almost indestructible ceramacrete paving of what would become Landing's central square. Other self-directed machines continued to work on the other buildings currently under construction, and piles of building materials marked where still more structures would shortly rise.

The colony's originally targeted population of approximately twenty-two thousand had been reduced to barely fifteen thousand by the Melconian attack. At the moment, almost all of them were down on the surface, housed in the prefab, temporary housing military units (called "Quonset huts," for some reason Maneka had never been able to track down, even searching Lazarus' files). The Quonsets weren't particularly palatial, but they were infinitely preferable to the cramped accommodations aboard the transports. And, unlike the transports' quarters, their inhabitants could open the front door, step outside, and suck in a huge lungful of fresh, pollen- and dust-laden, unrecycled air.

Unlike some military bases Maneka had seen, the Quonsets on Indrani really would be "temporary," too. At the current rate of construction, Berthier, who was in charge of that particular endeavor, estimated that permanent housing for the entire population would be completed within seven months. Not all of that housing would have all of the amenities Core World citizens were accustomed to, but those could always be added once the orbital industrial platforms could begin devoting capacity to something besides self-expansion and the production of basic necessities.

"I can hardly believe how quickly all of this is coming together," Maneka said, waving her wine glass in a semicircle to indicate the city appearing out of nowhere all about them.

"Careful planning back home," Agnelli said. "Too many

colonies exhaust their economic resources just arranging their initial transportation to their new homes. They have to skimp on their equipment budgets, or even rely on old-fashioned hand labor to establish their initial infrastructure. We've got the quality of automated support you might find in a major city on one of the Core Worlds, if on a smaller scale, so it's no wonder things are going well. In fact, we'd be doing even better if we hadn't lost *Star Conveyor*."

"Yes, we would," his daughter agreed quietly.

He looked at her quickly, his expression silently apologizing for reminding her of what had happened to *Kuan Yin*, but she only shook her head and looked back with a slightly sad smile. In many ways, Maneka sometimes thought, Allison had actually adjusted better to her husband's death than the Governor had. Then again, she'd discovered, Adrian Agnelli took any death personally. It was his job to see to it that death was something that didn't happen to the people for whom he was responsible, and he took that responsibility very seriously indeed.

And speaking of responsibilities . . .

"Allison was telling me this afternoon that the agricultural terraforming is already ahead of schedule, sir," she said to Agnelli.

"Yes, it is," the Governor agreed, giving his daughter a quick smile of mingled pride and thanks. The colony's chief agonomist had been aboard *Keillor's Ferry*, and Allison had taken responsibility for that aspect of the colonization effort. It wasn't exactly her area of specialization, but she'd quickly identified half a dozen improvements which had helped expedite the process.

"We should be putting in our first locally grown crops within the next couple of months," he continued, returning his gaze to Maneka. "While I know *some* of us would have preferred a rather cooler climate," he grinned as she grimaced at his jibe, "locating this close to the equator gives us effectively year-round growing seasons. So even though our initial cultivated area is going to be restricted by the need to seed it with the proper Terran microorganisms and bacteria, we ought to be almost completely independent of shipboard hydroponics and stored rations within the first local year."

"That's what's Allison was telling me," Maneka agreed. "And I also had a discussion with Henri—" she nodded at Berthier "—and Ed about the industrial side, as well. Things seem to be going just as well on that side."

"Not quite," Berthier disagreed mildly. "What happened to *Star Conveyor* is hurting us worse up there—" he pointed an index finger at the steadily brightening disk of the visible moon "—than it is down here. She had one of our two complete orbital smelter plants on board. Worse, she had two-thirds of the extraction boats that were supposed to handle the asteroid mining for us, and that's putting a crimp in our expansion rate. We've diverted some additional effort to building more of the boats we need, but that's going to take considerably longer than building housing units."

"Agreed," Maneka acknowledged. "On the other hand, I think I heard you'd managed to find yourself a truck driver to help speed things up a bit."

She grinned at Hawthorne, who made a ferocious face and growled something under his breath.

"That's one way to put it," Berthier said with a little smile of his own. "The transit time to and from the asteroid belt is part of what's costing us productivity. The extraction boats are fully automated, so they don't suck off any manpower, but they have to make the complete round trip from the belt to Indrani orbit. I'd considered moving the primary smelter closer to the belt, but you shot that one down on security grounds, Madam Generalissimo. So I'm stealing your transport right out from under you."

And my boyfriend, Maneka added mentally.

"*Thermopylae*'s got a lot of heavy-lift capability," Berthier continued. "If we send her out to the belt and let the boats we have shuttle back and forth between her and their extraction sites, she can play freighter and haul the raw materials in to the smelter. By cutting transit times, we estimate we'll improve the productivity curve on the extractor boats by almost thirty percent. It won't fully compensate us for *Star Conveyor*'s destruction, but it will sure help."

"I know." Maneka nodded. "That's why I agreed to let you have her. But despite that, I take it we're all in agreement that the colony appears to be well on its way to becoming firmly established? And that all of the problems currently in sight are essentially production bottlenecks, which are going to get smoothed out in the very near future?"

Agnelli looked at her a bit speculatively, but his daughter and Berthier both returned Maneka's nod.

"Good," she said. "Because, that being true, I believe it's time that we make the transition to civilian control."

Agnelli's expression sharpened, and she gave him an oddly serious grin.

"I realize certain parties were initially concerned over any Napoleon complexes which might lurk in the murky depths of my psyche. However, after spending the last year and half as the Mistress after God of all I survey, nothing would please me more than to hand responsibility over to our duly appointed Governor and our soon-to-be-elected Assembly. Just tending to the military side of things will be enough for Peter and me."

She raised her glass in a lighthearted toast to Brigadier Jeffords, and he chuckled as he returned it.

"My God, the woman's serious!" Agnelli said with a laugh. "Actually, Maneka, my concerns over your tyranny potential disappeared months and months ago. On the other hand, I've observed that you're one of those people with compulsive energy levels. Are you sure you're ready to step down?"

"Positive. It's not like I won't be able to find things to do, after all. Lazarus and I are still finishing up the mapping project, you know."

Heads nodded, and she suppressed a smile at some of the expressions around the table. Some of the colony's civilian leaders, she knew, cherished the private opinion that she was more than a little paranoid. But Agnelli wasn't one of them—a fact which would have surprised her when responsibility for the colony's military security first thundered down on her shoulders. The Governor had staunchly supported her military survey for the best site for Landing, and he'd been just as supportive of her decision to use Lazarus' reconnaissance satellites and remote-mapping drones to do a complete, detailed, ground-level topographical map of every square meter of terrain within two thousand kilometers of Landing. She was confident that they'd identified every practical approach route an attacking ground force might follow on its way through the mountains, and now they were most of the way through deep-scan radar mapping of each of those routes, as well.

"I do know that," Agnelli agreed now. "But you'll be done with that in a week or two. Is running our military establishment—such as it is, and what there is of it—after that, in the absence of any known external threats, going to be enough to keep you busy?"

"More than enough," she assured him, and the serious note in her voice surprised even her just a bit. She shook herself and chuckled.

"I joined the Brigade right out of high school, Adrian," she told him, using the first name she was usually careful to avoid, at least on "business" occasions. "They put me through the Academy, and they commissioned me, and by the time I was completing my senior-year tactical problems, it was pretty obvious the war with the Puppies was going to get nothing but nastier."

Her expression grew darker, and she gazed down into her wine glass.

"None of my graduating class really planned on living to retire," she said quietly. "The loss rate among forward-deployed Bolos was heavy enough that we could all do the math on our fingers and toes. The odds of someone in my graduating class surviving to the age of thirty-five were only one in three. The odds of actually reaching retirement age—assuming anyone was allowed to retire—were less than one in fifty. And those odds are going to get steadily worse as Ragnorak and whatever the

Puppies call their version of it grind away. If they weren't, none of us would be out here."

The mood around the table had sobered, and she looked up to meet her friends' eyes.

"When they detailed Guthrie and me—and Lazarus and Mickey—to this duty, I think we both felt almost as guilty as we felt grateful. Don't get me wrong. I know why the Concordiat and the Brigade assigned both of us here. Letting some preventable external threat destroy this colony when a couple of Bolos old enough to make them second-tier assets at the front could have prevented it would have been criminally negligent. And it's an important assignment, even if—as we all hope—neither Lazarus nor Mickey ever has to fire another shot in anger. But it gave us an out. It was a way for us to have a *damned* good chance at survival, and because we were selected for the assignment rather than seeking it, we can even tell ourselves that we never *tried* to save our own skins.

"There have been moments when living with that realization has been . . . difficult," she said, her voice even quieter, and Hawthorne reached over to squeeze her hand—her *right* hand—under cover of the table.

"It's one I'm sure we all share, in our own ways," Allison told her gently. "You Brigade officers—and Navy officers, like Ed—were more in the line of fire. Targeted, I suppose you might say, because it was your job to go where the fighting was. But it's been obvious for years now that eventually the fighting was going to come to all of us. That's why Bill and I—" her voice faltered only slightly as she spoke her dead husband's name "—had decided against having children. We both wanted them, and I know Dad wanted grandchildren." She gave her father a slightly misty smile. "But we weren't going to bring children into a galaxy which seemed intent on stamping them out of existence before they ever reached adulthood."

She paused for a moment, then looked directly into Maneka's eyes in the gathering darkness.

"You and Lieutenant Chin and Ed were assigned to this, just

as Dad was. I wasn't. Dad didn't give me any details when they chose him for this. He's always taken security classifications seriously, and I can understand why the government wouldn't want news of Seed Corn to get out. Even if the Melconians didn't hear about it, the effect on civilian morale would be devastating.

"But I've known him all my life, and I knew he'd been in line for a colonial governorship for at least two years before the war started. So when he suddenly couldn't talk to me anymore about where he might be sent, or what he might be doing, it wasn't all that hard to figure out what was going on. And when Fred Staunton, Dad's boss at the Office of Colonization, turned up at the hospital asking for volunteers for an unspecified 'special mission,' I volunteered on the spot, for Bill as well as for me. So unlike you, I *did* 'try to save my own skin.' I'm not ashamed that I did. And I would far rather be sitting here, with my father and with the rest of you, than still waiting for the Melconians to reach Schilling's World. But that doesn't mean I don't feel guilty about all the millions upon millions of other civilians, other Allison Agnellis, who will never have the opportunity to do the same thing."

Silence hovered around the table for almost a full minute, and then the Governor reached out and patted his daughter's hand gently.

"I wanted to tell you," he said softly. "And I'm not at all sure I wouldn't have broken down and done just that, security or no. But I didn't have to, because you were sharp enough to put two and two together on your own. And unlike you, I don't feel a trace of guilt at having you sitting here. I only regret that Bill isn't sitting here with us. And that the two of you will never have those grandkids of mine after all."

She turned her hand palm-up under his, catching his fingers and squeezing them tightly.

"I miss him, too," she half-whispered, blinking back tears. But then she smiled. She gave her father's hand one last squeeze, then sat back and picked up her wine glass once again.

"I miss him," she said, her slightly tremulous voice almost normal. "And I wish he were here, and I wish the two of us together would be raising our children. But we will give you those grandchildren, Dad. Both of us made deposits to the gene bank. Priority for the artificial wombs is going to be hard to come by until we can replace everything we lost with *Kuan Yin*, but assisted pregnancies are well within our present capabilities. Which is why in about another thirty-four Standard Weeks you're going to be a grandfather after all."

Deep, incandescent joy blazed in Agnelli's eyes, and he leaned over and kissed her cheek.

"That . . . that's wonderful news," he told her. "News I'd never hoped to hear."

His voice was deep and husky, and he cleared his throat, then took a sip of wine.

"Congratulations, Allison," Maneka said, raising her own glass in salute, and other glasses rose all around the table.

"Thank you." Allison might actually have blushed just a bit—it was difficult to tell in the gathering darkness—but her voice was completely back to normal, and she pointed a finger at Maneka.

"And what about *you*, young lady?" she demanded.

"*Me?*" Maneka blinked.

"This colony is going to need as much genetic diversity as it can get. And people acceptable for duty with the Dinochrome Brigade tend to be the sort of people whose genes you'd like to conserve in the population."

"I . . . really hadn't thought about it," Maneka said, not entirely honestly. In fact, not even mostly honestly, she told herself sternly.

"Well, *start* thinking about it," Allison commanded. "And if *you* can't think of a genetic partner you'd like to share the experience with," she looked rather pointedly at Hawthorne, "I'm sure someone on the medical staff would be able to arrange a blind match for you."

"If—all right, *when*—it's time for that decision to be made, I'll make it myself, thank you," Maneka told her firmly, glad the fading light hid the blush she felt warming her face.

"Just don't let the grass grow under you," Allison said, a touch of seriousness coloring her voice and expression once more. "I think Bill and I made the right decision, back before this opportunity—" she waved at the newborn colony's rising buildings "—presented itself. But if we hadn't waited, if we'd gone ahead and had children anyway, then I'd have at least some memory of him with them, and they might have some memory of him, as well. We're out from under the Melconian threat out here, but that doesn't make any of us immortal, Maneka."

"Is the Brigade ready, Colonel Na-Salth?" Ka-Frahkan asked formally.

"Yes, sir," Jesmahr Na-Salth replied. The colonel was the 3172nd Heavy Assault Brigade's executive officer, and Ka-Frahkan's deputy commander. It was his job to hand the Brigade over to Ka-Frahkan as a smoothly functioning machine, ready for instant action, and he was good at his job.

"I'll let Colonel Na-Lythan begin the briefing, if you permit, sir," Na-Salth continued, and Ka-Frahkan's ears flicked agreement.

"Colonel?" Na-Salth said then, turning to the officer who commanded the armored regiment which was the true heart of the Brigade's combat power.

"I have the readiness reports on our combat mechs for your perusal, General," Na-Lythan said. "The fact that Major Na-Huryin didn't survive cryo sleep has created some problems in the Reconnaissance Battalion, but otherwise our table of organization is actually in excellent shape. We're under-strength, of course, but not sufficiently to compromise our combat worthiness. And the latest report from our medical officers confirms that all personnel are fully recovered from cryo and fit for action."

"Excellent," Ka-Frahkan said heartily. The loss rate Na-Tharla had predicted if he used the emergency cryo facilities had actually been low. Almost twelve percent of his Brigade's personnel had never waked up again. He was fortunate that

Na-Huryin was the only really critical officer Na-Lythan had lost, but despite Na-Lythan's confident assessment, Ka-Frahkan knew the missing links in all of his units' chains of command had to have at least some consequences for their combat readiness.

What's that Human saying about "silver linings?" he thought with mordant humor. *I suppose it applies here, doesn't it? After all, at least the lower troop strength gave us a little longer to get everyone physically into shape for operations before our food runs out.*

He gave a mental snort at the direction of his own reflections, then turned to Colonel Verank Ka-Somal, Na-Lythan's counterpart for the Brigade's infantry regiment.

"May I assume your troopers are equally ready for combat, Colonel?" he asked.

"Yes, sir!" Ka-Somal barked. His eyes glittered, and Ka-Frahkan gazed at him thoughtfully for just a moment.

Ka-Somal's home world of Rasantha was one of the ones the Humans had burned clean of all life. His entire family—including his wife and four children—had been wiped away in that attack, and the loss had seared itself deeply into the colonel's heart and soul. For him, the upcoming attack was not a combat mission but one of holy vengeance, and the general wondered—not for the first time—if that might lead him to overestimate his troops' readiness. Probably not, he decided. Besides, he'd been following the medical and training reports all along, and they seemed to agree with Ka-Somal's assessment.

"And the air cavalry?" Ka-Frahkan said, looking at Major Beryak Na-Pahrthal.

"We stand ready, sir," the acting commander of his air cavalry regiment said, just a bit stiffly. Colonel Ka-Tharnak, the air cavalry's CO had been among the Brigade's more senior losses. Na-Pahrthal, who'd commanded the regiment's First Battalion, had found himself wearing two hats, as the regiment's commander, as well. He was a good officer, and in many ways more mentally flexible than Ka-Tharnak had been, but he'd never expected to be handed full responsibility for an entire air cavalry regiment, and he seemed a bit more anxious than Ka-Frahkan would have preferred.

"Good," the general said, projecting as much combined confidence and assurance as he could. Then he turned to the most junior officer seated at the conference table.

"I know I need not ask *you* if your people are ready, Captain," he said, smiling at Rahlan Ka-Paldyn.

"No, sir, you don't," Ka-Paldyn agreed. The army captain commanded the Brigade's attached special operations section. They were the ones who would be tasked with the most critical part of the opening operation. And, unfortunately, they'd been hit particularly hard by cryo sleep losses. Ka-Paldyn had been forced to consolidate his three out-sized platoons into only two, which had cramped Ka-Frahkan's options. But Ka-Paldyn had served with the Brigade since the day he joined as an officer cadet, straight out of the Imperial Army Academy. This would be his fifth campaign with Ka-Frahkan, and the general had total confidence in him and his special operations troopers.

"Good. I'm pleased—pleased with all of you," Ka-Frahkan said now, looking around the circle of his senior officers one more time with a fierce challenge grin. Then he sobered.

"I'm pleased because the time has come for us to strike," he said, his voice flatter and harder, and he saw the stiffening of spines, the gleaming edges of canines shown in half-instinctive challenge, as the others absorbed his announcement.

Death Descending was carefully hidden on one of the moons of the gas giant orbiting twenty-four light-minutes outside the system's asteroid belt. The assault transport had been concealed there ever since Ka-Frahkan had discussed his basic plan with Captain Na-Tharla, but the Brigade's stealthy remote reconnaissance platforms had kept a careful eye on events in orbit around the distant planet the Humans had chosen for their new home.

"The enemy," Ka-Frahkan resumed after a moment, "has clearly settled in comfortably. Of their transports, two have been disassembled into industrial modules. A third has also been broken down into three sub-modules which we originally believed were industrial platforms but have since concluded are intended as the core structures for orbital habitats. Captain Na-Tharla's best estimate from the recon platforms' take is that one of them is intended to become the central control facility for the Humans' eventual space-going infrastructure. The other two—" he let his eyes circle the table "—look suspiciously like the command-and-control modules for orbital forts."

He paused, letting the silence linger, until Na-Lythan broke it.

"That would make sense, sir," the armor commander said. "One mistake the enemy isn't going to make is to skimp on orbital defenses. They obviously feel they're presently secure, but whoever planned this operation is unlikely to leave anything to chance."

"Agreed," Ka-Frahkan replied. "On the other hand, there's no indication that they're currently working on these modules. My own belief is that they'll rely upon the Bolo they've maintained in orbit for their immediate security. It will probably be some time—possibly even several years—before they have the industrial capacity to begin manufacturing the weapons such forts would require.

"More significant, I think, is the fact that the emissions signatures of most of their ships indicate that they're operating with reduced power generation. Captain Na-Tharla has confirmed my own suspicion that this indicates they've taken their drive rooms off-line. Obviously, it wouldn't take them long to reactivate the power plants they've currently shut down, but it's yet another indication that they're not prepared for an immediate evacuation in the event of a sudden threat. And," he smiled coldly, "it greatly increases our odds of taking those ships intact for our own use.

"Rahlan, Jesmahr, and I have discussed at some length how best to approach the Human shipping capability in light of our current assessment of its readiness states. Obviously, our first priority must be the orbiting Bolo. That Bolo isn't attempting to remain covert. Its active sensors are on-line, which has helped us to positively identify its transport, and we must assume a high level of readiness on its part. However, it hasn't reacted to the sensor platforms we've been using to observe the enemy's activities, and Captain Ka-Paldyn assures me that the signatures of his troopers' EW suits are substantially less than those of the platforms."

"Excuse me, sir," Na-Pahrthal said.

"Yes, Beryak?"

"I realize that the EW suits are extremely stealthy," the air cavalry commander said slowly, "but while the special ops boats are very difficult to detect under normal circumstances, are they not considerably *less* stealthy than our reconnaissance platforms?"

"They are," Ka-Frahkan said, his voice turning graver. "That, however, won't be an issue. Captain Ka-Paldyn's Second Platoon has volunteered to carry out the operation in free flight."

Na-Pahrthal looked at Ka-Paldyn, and his eyes widened.

"Forgive me, Captain," he said after a moment, "but from how far out do you intend to insert them?"

"Given the difference in sensor signatures," Ka-Paldyn replied, "our boats should be able to take them to within two light-minutes without being detected, sir. Call it thirty-six million kilometers."

"And the maximum safe velocity for your EW suits in free flight?" the major asked.

"Approximately one hundred kilometers per second, bearing in mind suit reaction mass limitations and the need to decelerate to rest relative to the Bolo's transport without being detected," Ka-Paldyn said flatly.

"Then the flight time will be around a hundred hours?" Na-Pahrthal said.

"Correct, sir," Ka-Paldyn said. "And to anticipate the rest of your questions, if I may, that does in fact mean that they will exhaust the endurance of their suits before we can possibly recover them. Second Platoon understands that none of them is likely to return from this mission."

"I hope," Ka-Frahkan said into the silence Ka-Paldyn's words had produced, "that they'll be wrong about that." Everyone looked at him, and he flicked his ears. "I fully realize that the odds are poor. However, Second Platoon's secondary assignment, after destroying the Bolo transport, will be to seize control of the industrial modules the Humans have deployed in planetary orbit. Although it's a secondary assignment, it's also an important one. Specifically, I want control of those facilities before some Human aboard them realizes their colony is about to be annihilated and destroys the modules to prevent them from falling into our hands. And if Second Platoon succeeds in taking one or more of those modules, they'll be able to sustain themselves on their prizes' environmental capability until we can relieve them."

"As you say, sir," Ka-Paldyn said with a seated half-bow, but all of the officers in the briefing room knew at least some of Second Platoon's troopers would exhaust their suits' endurance long before they took their objectives.

"There's an additional reason for us to secure control of all of the Human transports, or at least to destroy them before they're able to reactivate their drive rooms and flee the system," Ka-Frahkan said, picking back up the thread of his briefing.

"After discussing this matter at some length with Captain Na-Tharla, I have determined that it is in the Empire's best interest for us to plant a colony of our own in this star system. After we've destroyed the Human presence here—in the course of which we will undoubtedly suffer casualties, possibly severe ones, unfortunately—we should still have sufficient personnel, male and female, to establish a population with sufficient genetic diversity to sustain itself permanently. I intend to return to the Empire aboard *Death Descending*, assuming we're able to make the necessary repairs out of the captured Human industrial base. I will, however, be detaching the majority of the Brigade's personnel to remain behind to hold and populate this star system for the Empire."

He looked around the conference table once more, watching

their faces as he revealed his full intentions for the first time. Ka-Somal looked almost disappointed at the prospect of being left behind, but Ka-Frahkan had anticipated that. He was thoroughly familiar with Ka-Somal's blazing hatred for all things Human, and he'd known from the beginning that the infantry colonel would reject any chance to remain behind, where there would be no more Humans to kill. For the others, though, his decision offered the possibility of survival with honor . . . but only at the expense of permanent separation from family, clan, and all they had ever known. That would be an almost intolerable price for any member of the People, yet he was confident they would pay it if he told them to.

"My plans to colonize this system for the People hinge, however," he continued, "on our ability to prevent any FTL-capable Human vessel from escaping back to the Concordiat. Captain Na-Tharla tells me that it's unlikely any of the Human transports is currently supplied for such a lengthy voyage, but it's certainly not impossible. And if a Human vessel does succeed in returning to the Concordiat with news of events here, then it's also possible a Human squadron might be dispatched to eliminate our own colony in this system. I consider the probability of such a decision on their part to be no more than even, but it would require only a cruiser or two to deal with any defenses we could cobble up from what we may capture.

"Because of that, it's essential that we also take or destroy the *second* Bolo transport, whose drive room is very much on-line," he said. "Fortunately, it's much closer to us than the one in orbit, since the Humans appear to be using it to assist their resource extraction efforts in the vicinity of the asteroid belt. That's the good news. The bad news is that it doesn't appear to be following any fixed schedule or routing. Unlike the transport orbiting the planet, we cannot predict what its precise position will be at the moment our attack commences. Offsetting that somewhat, the fact that it clearly doesn't have a Bolo embarked means its sensor capability will be greatly inferior to Second Platoon's target, so we can get closer to it with the special ops boats.

"Beginning as soon as possible, Rahlan's First Platoon will embark aboard those boats and take up positions from which, hopefully, it will be able to shadow the second transport at reasonably close range. Coordination with Second Platoon will be difficult at such a distance but it will also be critical. The Bolo orbiting the planet *must* be destroyed before any other action on our part. Therefore, First Platoon cannot enter the second transport's effective sensor envelope until after Second Platoon has attacked. We anticipate that even if there's some small delay between the two attacks, the Humans aboard the transport—which is probably operating with reduced crew, given how badly the Humans must need every pair of hands for the construction of their new planetary installations—will still be taken by surprise by First Platoon's attack. In any case, they'll be at a severe disadvantage against fully armed, elite troopers, and we believe the chance of capturing the ship is extremely high."

He gazed around the briefing room once more, then flipped his ears in satisfaction at what he saw in their eyes.

"Very well, gentlemen," he said. "That's the bare bones of our intentions. Now to more specific details. Colonel Na-Salth?"

"Yes, sir," Na-Salth said, and touched a button, calling up a holographic map of the landing site on the target planet which Ka-Frahkan and Na-Tharla had selected. "Colonel Na-Lythan," he continued, "once *Death Descending* has made planetfall, your Regiment will debark."

He touched another button, and military mapping icons appeared in the holo.

"In conjunction with Colonel Ka-Somal's infantry, you will establish a basic defensive perimeter along this line," he continued, indicating the positions on the map. "After that, you will deploy reconnaissance elements along these axes. . . ."

5

Lieutenant Guthrie Chin sat back, arms crossed, and frowned at the chessboard. Staff Sergeant Yolanda Willis grinned cheerfully at him as he contemplated the unappetizing situation into which she had backed him.

"Your position does not look promising, Guthrie," a pleasant baritone remarked over the compartment's bulkhead speaker.

"And don't you *dare* give him any hints, Mickey!" Willis said sternly.

"How can you believe I would think of such a thing?" the speaker inquired in innocent tones.

"Possibly because I know you?" Willis shot back. The speaker chuckled, and she grinned. "If, on the other hand, you should happen to succumb to that ignoble temptation, just remember who's in charge of making sure your wiring keeps on doing what it's supposed to do."

"Such crude threats are unbecoming to a noncommissioned officer of the Brigade," Chin said severely. "Besides, I—as an officer and a gentleman, by act of the Concordiat Assembly—am fully capable of resolving your petty threat to my queen entirely on my own."

Willis made a most disrespectful sound, and he gave her a dignified look.

"I'm sure," he continued, "that the aforesaid resolution will come to me ... presently."

Lauren Hanover checked her boards with a feeling of profound satisfaction as she took over the duty watch. With *Kuan Yin's* loss, she'd been out of a job as a second engineer, but Henri Berthier, never one to waste talent, had assigned her to *Sherwood Forest*, instead. It wasn't exactly what she'd been trained for, but she'd had plenty of time on the extended voyage to get herself brought up to speed, and she'd been more than ready when they assigned her to command Industrial Module Three.

At the moment, India Mike Three was still in what she thought of as the setting up stage. The automated fabrication node's admittedly simpleminded AIs were working from stored plans to build the bare-bones platform into a complete deep-space industrial facility. Progress was slower than originally projected because of the loss of the orbital smelter—multicapability resource extraction facilities, really, but "smelter" was a much handier term—yet they were beginning to make up the lost time. It would be at least another three or four months, by her most optimistic estimate, before they could actually catch back up with the official schedule, but that was all right. When India Mike Three really hit its stride, it would be able to build anything the inhabitants of Indrani needed, from screwdrivers to complete superdreadnoughts, and it would be only one of six such centers. Given the circumstances and the whole reason Seed Corn had been mounted, plans called for Indrani to eventually have an industrial base which not only matched that of the average Concordiat Core World, but actually exceeded it (on a population basis, at least) by a factor of more than ten. And for that ratio to be maintained indefinitely.

All it was going to take was time. And now that they'd actually survived the voyage, time was something they had in plentiful supply.

Lieutenant Huran Sa-Chelak checked the readouts on the HUD projected across the visor of his stealth suit. The numbers didn't look good, but they were still—barely—within acceptable parameters.

It was always impossible to predict exactly how rapidly any specific, individual trooper would consume the endurance of his suit. *Averages* could be predicted with a high degree of reliability, and the suits' designers had allowed a margin of redundancy. But individuals always varied at least a little, and that margin had been calculated sitting in comfortable offices in rear area research and development establishments. Special ops units in the field routinely ran right up to the limits of the projected safety margins, and this operation had stressed them even harder than most.

He'd already lost one trooper. Sergeant Na-Rathan hadn't exhausted his life support. Sa-Chelak wasn't positive exactly what *had* gone wrong with his suit, and the sergeant hadn't told him. He'd simply reported across the short-range whisker laser com net in a completely calm voice, less than fifteen hours into the mission, that he had a problem. Then he'd gone off the net and the green light indicating a live trooper on Sa-Chelak's HUD had blinked suddenly red.

The sergeant's body had accompanied them for the remainder of their ballistic insertion. Corporal Na-Sath had removed the backup fusion warhead from Na-Rathan's body, and when they'd finally activated their suit-mounted thruster packs to begin decelerating, the sergeant had continued silently onward towards the system's primary.

At least he'll find a proper pyre, Sa-Chelak thought. *And he's earned it.*

The lieutenant hoped he would earn the same, but it was beginning to look as if his own life support was going to run out before the rest of the platoon reached its secondary objective among the orbiting Human transports. At least six more of his twenty-four remaining troopers were in the same or little better situation, but that wouldn't keep them from executing their primary mission, he thought grimly.

He looked at Sergeant Major Na-Hanak. Since they'd begun decelerating, even the whisker lasers had been shut down. Sa-Chelak had enormous confidence in the capabilities of his troopers' stealth systems, on the basis of hard-won experience, but getting this close to one of the accursed Bolos was enough to chill any veteran's blood. He had no intention of running any avoidable risks when he and his men had paid—and were about to pay—such a high price to get here.

The sergeant major was watching him alertly. Sa-Chelak made a hand gesture, and Na-Hanak replied with a gesture of his own, acknowledging receipt of the unspoken order.

Sa-Chelak wished he'd been carrying the weapon himself, but this was a job for a demolitions expert, and that described Na-Hanak perfectly. The lieutenant watched as the sergeant major's gloved fingers quickly but carefully armed the warhead—a stealthed demolition charge, actually. Na-Hanak completed his task, then paused for several seconds, clearly doublechecking every single step of the process. When he was satisfied, he looked back up at Sa-Chelak and made the "prepared to proceed" hand sign.

Sa-Chelak nodded inside his helmet, then chopped his arm in a gesture towards the distant dot his suit's computer assured him was the Bolo transport. It was little more than a speck, gleaming faintly in the reflected light of the system primary, but they were more than close enough for their delivery vehicle.

Na-Hanak entered a final sequence on the weapon's control pad, then punched the commit button. A mist of instantly dispersed vapor spurted from the weapon's small thruster, and it accelerated away from the platoon.

Sa-Chelak watched it go. It was fitting in many ways, he thought, that the very primitiveness of their weapon helped explain how it would penetrate the Humans' vaunted superior technology. Its warhead actually relied upon old-fashioned chemical explosives to achieve criticality, and the total power supply aboard warhead and delivery vehicle combined was less than would have been required to supply a pre-space hand lamp. Its guidance systems were purely passive, relying upon an optical lock on its designated target, and the control systems for its primitive, low-powered, but effective thrusters used old-fashioned mechanical linkages. Not that more modern technology was completely absent from its construction. In fact, it was built of radiation-absorbent materials so effective that at a range of barely two meters (with the access ports closed to hide the glowing giveaway of its displays), it was impossible for the Melconian eye to pick out against the backdrop of space. It was, in fact, as close to completely invisible and totally undetectable as the Empire's highly experienced design teams could produce.

It only remained to be seen if it was invisible enough.

"So are you going to save that castle as effectively as you saved your queen?" Willis inquired interestedly.

"You're not doing your next efficiency report any favors, Sergeant," Chin told her ominously, regarding the rapidly spreading disaster in the middle of the chessboard.

"Hah! Captain Trevor knows what a sore loser you are, sir. She'll recognize petty vengefulness when she sees it."

"Unfortunately, you're probably right about that." Chin reached for his surviving knight, then drew his hand back as Willis smiled with predatory confidence.

"Anytime you're ready, sir," she told him with deadly, affable patience.

"Which will be—"

"Alert!" The bulkhead speaker rattled as the baritone voice barked a flat-toned warning. "Alert! Sensors detect incoming—"

Guthrie Chin was still turning his head towards the speaker, eyebrows rising in surprise, when the multimegaton demolition charge exploded less than fifty meters from *Stalingrad*'s hull.

Maneka bounced twice on the end of the diving board, then arced cleanly through the air. The grav-lift dive platform floated a meter and a half above the gentle swell, and the ocean surface was a translucent, deliciously cool sheet of jade. She sliced through it cleanly, driving deep into the even cooler depths, before she swept back up towards the sun-mirror of the surface.

Ocean swimming wasn't something which had been very practical back on Everest, she admitted to herself. And she supposed that, under the circumstances, she would have to concede that its practicality here was, indeed, a point in favor of Indrani over New Hope. Not that she was prepared to admit that to anyone else.

Her head broke surface, and she used both hands to slick back her short, wet, dark hair. Half a dozen other heads bobbed near her, and the two air cars designated for lifeguard duty floated watchfully overhead. Sonar transducers adjusted to a frequency which had been demonstrated to repel the local sea life protected the swimmers from the possibility of being munched upon, and Maneka rolled in the water and began backstroking back towards the platform.

Another three or four dives, she thought, *then back to work and—*

"Alert!" Lazarus' voice blared so loudly in her mastoid-mounted speaker that it felt for an instant as if someone had slapped her. "Alert! Mickey reports—"

The nuclear detonation overhead was bright enough to bleach the sapphire sky pale amethyst.

"Mother of God!" someone gasped. It took Lieutenant Hanover over two seconds to realize that the words had come out in her voice.

She stared in horror at the visual display, which had just polarized as the sun-bright flash licked away *Stalingrad* as if the transport had never existed. But it had, and she swallowed hard as the instant of paralyzing shock faded into something resembling coherent thought.

Fusion plant? she wondered automatically, only to reject it instantly. *She was at standby, just like the* Forest. *And Bolos don't have that sort of accident—ever. But then what—?*

She never knew exactly what caused it to click so quickly. Maybe it was the memory of what had happened to *Kuan Yin*, causing her to jump instantly to a conclusion which was preposterous on the face of things. Maybe it was some sort of subconscious logic flow which would have made impeccable sense if she'd been able to analyze it. But how it came to her was supremely unimportant beside her total confidence that she was right.

She punched the key on her console while the other four members of her duty watch were still gawking at the beautifully hideous blossom of brilliance on their visual displays. A musical tone sounded in her earbug almost instantly as the communications computers routed her priority message to its destination.

"Captain Berthier," she heard her own voice say calmly, "this is Hanover, on India Mike Three. Sir, the Dog Boys have just blown *Stalingrad*—and Mickey—to hell."

She was still talking when the same finger which had hit the com key punched another button and alert sirens began to wail all across Industrial Module Three.

Maneka was still dripping when the lifeguard air car came screaming in to deposit her atop Lazarus' war hull. She didn't waste time thinking about uniforms or towels. She just dashed towards the heavily armored topside personnel hatch, bare feet threading their way between the slablike missile hatch covers on pure autopilot while she barked into her hand com.

"—to the Armory *now!*" she snapped. "Full equipment and ammunition for First, Second, and Fourth Battalions. Deploy First and Second to the Alpha One positions, and alert Major Atwater for probable immediate embarkation."

"Understood," Brigadier Jeffords said sharply. She could hear the reverberations of shocked disbelief echoing in his voice, but he was alert and tracking well, and that was about all she could have asked of him under the circumstances.

"Good, Peter," she said a bit more gently, then ducked and twisted in a familiar contortion that deposited her onto the

upper access ladder to Lazarus' command deck. She braced
her bare insoles against the outside of the ladder uprights
and slid down it, com dangling from her wrist by its lanyard,
and the vibrations of ponderous, delicate movement shivered
in her hands and feet as Lazarus maneuvered himself back up
the loading ramp of the assault pod.

She left that up to him and the pod's onboard computers
while she concentrated on getting down the ladder in one piece
as quickly as possible. Adrian Agnelli's face already showed on
one of the multiquadrant communications screens, and other
members of the colony's command structure were blinking
onto other quadrants even as her bare feet hit Command One's
decksole with a stinging impact.

Agnelli's expression was a combination of horror, shock,
disbelief, and confusion, but if there was any panic in it,
Maneka couldn't see it. Fear, yes—but not, she was certain,
for himself. And despite all the myriad questions which must
be hammering at his brain, he didn't waste time battering *her*
by demanding answers to them.

She took an instant to give him a sincerely and deeply
grateful smile, then slithered into her command couch in her
dripping wet, skimpy swimsuit.

"Governor, ladies and gentlemen," she said, conscious of how
bizarre the courteous formula sounded in her own ears but
using it deliberately to emphasize her own self-control. There
was no need for them to know just how hard that was for her
to do, and every reason to convince them that she, at least,
was not about to succumb to panic.

"As you're all aware, the colony is under attack," she continued in a crisp, clipped tone. "I deeply regret that I have to
confirm that *Stalingrad* and Mickey have been destroyed."

Someone—she didn't know who, and she didn't worry about
finding out—cursed in falsetto shock. Maneka ignored the
outburst and continued flatly.

"Lazarus' analysis agrees in all its essentials with Lieutenant
Hanover's conclusion. The emission signature of the explosion is, in fact, a perfect match for a Puppy Bravo-Eighteen

demolition charge. How they got it into position without Mickey's spotting them is impossible to say, but Lazarus has gone back over Mickey's last transmissions over the TSDS. The most likely possibility is that they managed to insert a covert special ops team into the inner system to launch it at short range. The next most likely is that they used some sort of long-range, stealthed launch vehicle to attack directly from the outer-system. In either case, it's obvious that they did, somehow, manage to follow us all the way here. And they wouldn't have announced their presence by taking out *Stalingrad* and Mickey this way if they didn't have some sort of plan to hit the rest of the colony.

"At the moment, we don't know what that plan might be. But it's virtually certain that whatever they've got, it isn't a regular warship. A cruiser wouldn't have needed that much stealth to get through to *Stalingrad*, given her alert status, and it wouldn't have had the endurance to follow us this far in the first place. So we're looking at some sort of logistics ship or transport. Under the circumstances, I see no option but to assume that we're up against an *Atilla*-class heavy transport."

Jeffords inhaled sharply, and she smiled thinly at the other faces on her display.

"For those of you unfamiliar with the reporting names assigned to Puppy warships, that's an atmosphere-configured assault transport, the second biggest one they have. And," her grim smile vanished, "it's capable of landing an entire heavy assault brigade."

"Dear God," Agnelli said quietly, and Maneka nodded.

"I may be wrong, and I pray I am, but I may not be, too," she said. "And whatever they've got, they're obviously very, very good to have followed us this far without being detected in the first place, and then to get through our defenses so neatly with their first strike. On the basis of my analysis of the threat, I'm officially notifying all of you that I am assuming full authority as this system's military commander, and that I've already activated Defense Plan Alpha. Brigadier Jeffords' First, Second, and Fourth

Battalions are drawing weapons and ammunition now. Lieutenant Governor Berthier."

"Yes, Captain?"

"I've already informed Brigadier Jeffords that we'll be diverting all construction equipment to military uses. Most of the construction personnel have already been activated in their militia role, and the brigadier's issued preliminary orders to them. He knows what I want dug in and where, but since he's going to be busy overseeing the deployment of all of his personnel, I'd like you to take over on the construction side. You'll find the details in the construction plans queue under Delta Papa Alpha One."

"Of course, Captain!"

"In that case," she continued, turning to Agnelli's daughter, "I need you to take over organization for probable wounded, Dr. Agnelli-Watson," she said formally. "I hope there won't be many of them, but—"

She broke off suddenly, and her face tightened.

"Governor Agnelli," she said harshly.

"Yes, Captain?"

"We may have lost *Stalingrad* and Mickey's sensors, but the backup recon satellites we deployed are still on-line and feeding information to Lazarus' BattleComp. I have confirmation of a Melconian vessel headed for Indrani. And it is an *Atilla*."

This time, the silence was total.

"That's the bad news," she continued with a tight, teeth-baring smile. "The good news is that so far we haven't picked up anything else. She must have been accompanying the raiding squadron Commodore Lakshmaniah destroyed, and she must have used her emergency cryo facilities to stretch her endurance. It's the only way they could have followed us this long without starving to death—or eating each other. But according to Lieutenant Hawthorne, those cryo facilities aren't very good, so they've probably taken some significant personnel losses.

"What matters right now, though, is that *apparently* she's the only opposition we face." One or two of the faces looking back at her showed their owners' incredulous response to her use of the word "only," but she went on in that same level voice. "Assuming that they really have somehow managed to follow us here with their personnel essentially intact, we're going to be facing heavy odds—" *not as heavy as Chartres, a stray* thought flickered, *but heavy enough . . . and you don't have the rest of the Battalion for backup this time* "—but without any warships to side her, at least no one's going to be bombarding us from space in the middle of the fight.

"With Brigadier Jeffords' people to watch the back door, Lazarus and I will be able to operate much more freely against any ground opposition. My biggest concern at this moment is that although we've picked up *one* transport, we have no positive assurance that it's the only ship out there. Personally, I think it probably is, for the reasons I've already given, but I can't be certain of that. If I had only a little more time, I'd take Lazarus' assault pod back up into orbit to engage them short of the planet. Unfortunately, it will take a minimum of thirty-five more minutes to re-mate him with the pod. I'm proceeding with that—we can disengage a lot more quickly if we have to, and the pod will give us much more flexible deployment options—but the Melconian ship is only twenty-eight minutes out. We can't get orbital in time to intercept it, and from its present profile, it looks as if it intends to land far enough around the curve of the planet to protect it from direct fire from Landing, as well.

"All of which suggests that they have a very good notion of what *we* have. I've transmitted a warning to all our shipping and deep-space work parties, because if they did use some of their special operations troops to carry out the attack on *Stalingrad,* they may have tasked those troops with secondary missions, as well. Their special ops troopers have very, very good individual stealth capability, and that may well mean we have an unknown number of Melconian special operations troopers already in or about to penetrate the orbits of our infrastructure.

"I'm afraid we're going to take some additional losses there."

She made the admission unflinchingly. "Brigadier Jeffords has already scrambled his company of vacuum-trained militia and both of our armed cutters to repel attacks on our industrial platforms or the transports, but if the Puppies timed this properly, they may already be working on breaching the hulls of their targets. If all they want to do is *destroy* them, I'm afraid there may not be a lot we can do to stop them. We'll just have to hope they'd prefer to capture the capacity instead of destroying it. Or that they're shorthanded enough they didn't spare a lot of personnel to go after orbital installations that can't run away anyhow. After all," she gave them another tight smile, "they apparently know they have a Bolo to face down here."

She paused to draw a deep breath.

"Until they actually hit planet, I can't do much more than we're already doing. Lazarus and I need a better feel for the forces they actually have to deploy and what their axes of approach are likely to be. For now, I suggest we all do everything we can to reduce the possibility of panic and to get as many as possible of our noncombatants under cover. I want to leave Brigadier Jeffords' other two battalions of infantry available to assist in digging in for as long as possible, but I want both air cavalry platoons ready to lift immediately. And if any of us have a free moment here or there, spending it asking God to give us a hand probably wouldn't be a bad idea."

Lieutenant Sa-Chelak's thoughts were becoming sluggish, but he bared his canines in a snarl of triumph as the Bolo transport disappeared in a visor-polarizing flash. The critical portion of his platoon's mission had been accomplished in that single fireball. The realization gave him a sense of comfort, although it was getting very hard to breathe. His lungs labored frantically, but there simply wasn't enough oxygen.

Ran the margin too fine this time, his mind told him distantly. He blinked, trying to focus on the range-to-target reading on his HUD, but the numbers remained obstinately blurred. Of his thirty-seven troopers, at least a dozen green lights had turned crimson. He couldn't see them well enough to be certain which ones they were, but he thought Corporal Na-Sath's was still green.

Good. That's good, he thought blearily. At least his people could be *sure* of taking out at least one more of the Humans' ships, whether they could capture their secondary objectives or not. He wished he could be with them when they did, but the insistent computer voice warning him of oxygen exhaustion was growing less and less distinct in his ear.

His right hand groped for the suicide button. There was no point going by centimeters when his chance of survival had become nonexistent anyway. His fingers found it, and started to press. But a new, strident audio tone made him pause.

His wavering vision sought out the HUD once more. It was impossible to read, but despite the anoxia, a remote corner of his superbly trained brain recognized the sound.

Proximity alarm, he thought, and turned his head just in time to see one of the colony's two armed cutters in the instant before its two-centimeter Hellbores fired.

"Go down there and help her get that locker open *now*, Jackson," Lieutenant Edmund Hawthorne said flatly.

"Aye, aye, sir!" his executive officer snapped, and left *Thermopylae*'s command deck at a dead run. Hawthorne looked after him for a couple of heartbeats, then wheeled back to his own command station, his brain racing as he tried to cope with the stunning broadcast from Lazarus.

Melconians here. It didn't seem possible, but he knew that was only his own deep-seated need to believe it wasn't. And that need sprang from at least one all too personal source. Fear for the entire colony—and for his own life—was a cold, hard iron lump in the pit of his belly, but it was another fear that made every muscle in his body quiver with flight-or-flight instincts.

Maneka, he thought. *Maneka and Lazarus . . . and an entire heavy assault brigade of Dog Boys.*

He closed his eyes with a brief, wordless appeal to whatever

God there might be, then opened them resolutely as the exec hurried back onto the bridge with an armload of power rifles and sidearms. Another of Hawthorne's crewwomen followed, carrying more sidearms and with a satchel of boarding grenades slung over her shoulder.

"All right, people," Hawthorne said over the all-hands channel, distantly surprised by how calm his own voice sounded, "we have a situation. We're going to Condition Zulu as of right now. Sensors haven't picked anything up yet, but if there's a Dog Boy special ops unit out there, that doesn't mean Jack."

He glanced at the console where Chief Halberstadt was driving the external sensors for all they were worth . . . and monitoring *Thermopylae*'s internal sensor net even more intently. The transport had already come about on a heading to return to Indrani. Hawthorne had deliberately turned away from the least-time course, taking a wide dog leg which he hoped would have been impossible for anyone to predict ahead of time. The odds were overwhelming that the combination of her sudden course change and speed would carry her clear of any ambush the Melconians might have arranged for her, but he wasn't prepared to stake the security of his ship and the lives of his crew on that, and his hands strapped a pistol belt around his hips even as he was speaking.

"Captain Trevor has informed me that Brigadier Jeffords' troops will be at full readiness by the time the Dog Boys can put down on Indrani. The attack that took out Mickey was almost certainly carried out by their special ops company, though, and it's entirely possible that they're also going after our orbital units. Brigadier Jeffords has Sierra Company headed up as a precaution, but we all know Sierra Company isn't exactly the Concordiat Marines. Well, neither are we, and *Thermopylae* might not be able to say boo to a Dog Boy destroyer. But we do have half a dozen suits of powered armor on board, and I have Ms. Stopford bringing it on-line now. She estimates that will take another twenty-two minutes . . . which means it ought to be ready long before we reach Indrani orbit.

"In the meantime—"

A shrill, ear-piercing alarm wailed.

"Hull breach," *Thermopylae*'s AI's melodious contralto announced. "Multiple hull breaches between frames one-five-niner and two-zero-seven."

Hawthorne wheeled towards the damage control schematic and swallowed a vicious curse as fifteen bright red icons glared along his ship's port flank. They'd come in through the Number Two vehicle hold, which suggested they knew exactly what they were doing. The vehicle holds were much less intricately compartmentalized than the personnel sections of the big ship. And they were far less lavishly equipped with automatic pressure-tight blast doors to contain atmosphere. Worse, Number Two was the central of *Thermopylae*'s three vehicle holds. From there, they could move in almost any direction.

"We have boarders, people!" he barked. "Vehicle Hold Two! You've got fifteen seconds to get to your Zulu Internal stations, then I'm locking her up!"

He watched the chronometer's digital display tick over exactly fifteen seconds, then nodded to the exec.

"It's time, Jackson," he said grimly, and cleared his throat. "Iona," he said to *Thermopylae*'s AI, "close all internal doors."

"Closing internal doors," the AI announced.

"Good," Hawthorne said. He paused a moment, then continued. "Iona, set Condition Zulu Delta."

Jackson Lewis flinched, but none of his bridge crew said a word.

"Order acknowledged," the AI said. "Self-destruct orders require command authorization, however."

"Understood." Hawthorne inhaled deeply. "Authenticate my voice and ID."

"Authenticated. You are Lieutenant Edmund Harrison Hawthorne, commanding officer CNS *Thermopylae*."

"I now authorize you to set Condition Zulu Delta," he said flatly. "Authorization code Baker-Seven-Two-Alpha-Niner-Whiskey."

"Authorization code receipted and recognized," Iona told him. "Condition Zulu Delta has been set."

"Thank you," Hawthorne said, and looked down at his hands. In theory, the AI would destroy the ship the instant the Melconian boarders secured control of its critical systems. Unfortunately, *Thermopylae* was a transport, not a proper warship. Her web of control runs and communications circuits were tougher, more dispersed, and more redundant than they would have been aboard a civilian-design vessel her size, but they were scarcely armored or protected against people inside the ship itself. There were at least two ways he could think of offhand for the Puppies to take out her AI *before* they took control of the Bridge or Engineering, and if they did that . . .

"Jessy," he said quietly over a private channel to Jessica Stopford, "I think it would be a very good idea to expedite that armor."

She/they were once again joined, and she/they felt the locking clamps engage firmly as Lazarus' huge tracks settled into place in the assault pod. She/they reached out, bringing the pod's internal systems fully on-line, and the Maneka component of her/their personality allowed herself a moment of intent gratitude that she had kept the pod fully fueled and charged.

"We're in position, Peter," Maneka's com image informed the militia commander. "Is Fourth Battalion ready to board?"

"Affirmative," Jeffords replied tautly. "I still say you ought to take Jessup's company with you, too."

"No," she said firmly. "They don't have the armor or the firepower to go toe-to-toe with a Puppy medium, much less a heavy. But they could be a nasty surprise for any air cav that get around us."

Jeffords looked rebellious, but he didn't argue. Mostly because Maneka was his commanding officer, but also because he knew she was right. Captain Jessup's single company of light, manned tanks had never been intended to stand up to the sort of firepower which was probably headed Landing's way.

She/they considered the numbers once again. A full-strength

Melconian heavy assault brigade had a roster strength of over three thousand. Sixteen hundred of that total were in the three battalions of its infantry regiment, but the real heart of its striking power was its armored regiment. The twelve *Heimdalls* of its recon company could probably be handled by Jessup's fifteen Whippet tanks, but the six *Surturs* and twelve *Fenrises* would smash anything short of Lazarus himself with contemptuous ease.

It was a sobering comment on the sheer size of an *Atilla*-class transport that it could pack that much armor aboard, the Maneka component of her/their personality reflected. The *Surtur* was at least as big as most Bolos—over twenty percent larger than Lazarus himself, in fact—and even the *Fenris* came in at over nine thousand tons. *Thermopylae* could carry a maximum of two Bolos plus another hundred thousand tons of lighter vehicles or seventy-five thousand tons of vehicles and up to five thousand infantry and their equipment. But the *Sleipners* carried their Bolos externally, whereas all of the Melconian transport's personnel and vehicles were carried *internally*. And unlike *Thermopylae*, she was atmosphere-capable *and* designed for rough-field landings. If the Melconians had been prepared to accept externally-mounted transport for their heavy armored vehicles, they could have packed even more punch aboard the big ship. But they would have had to sacrifice its ability to land its troops directly, and that was strictly against Melconian doctrine.

<Which is a damned good thing,> the Maneka component thought at the Lazarus component. <Six *Surturs* are bad enough.>

<True. But we do possess significant advantages the Battalion lacked on Chartres,> the Lazarus component observed in reply.

Which was true, Maneka realized. The only question was whether or not their advantages would be enough.

"We've got a hull breach!"

Lauren's jaw clenched, and her eyes darted over the schematic in front of her.

"Pressure loss in Sector Bravo-Seven-Charlie," a computer voice remarked calmly. "Initiating containment."

A strident audio alarm began to sound, but the voice continued in those same, calm tones.

"Containment procedures terminated," it announced. "Atmosphere loss has ceased."

"And you think that's *good* news, you stupid bitch?!" one of her watch-standers snarled. Lauren was too busy to endorse the remark, but she certainly understood it. India Mike Three's AI was an idiot, compared to a Bolo. All it cared about was that the hole in the module's skin was no longer leaking air. The fact that whoever had *made* the hole must have sealed it behind them didn't mean a thing to the computers.

"They're into Bravo-Seven," she said over the all-hands channel. "Alf," she looked at the tech who'd replied to the AI, "close the blast doors manually. Then start locking down every powered door you can. Hannah," she turned to another woman, "get on the horn to whoever's running the cutters. We need somebody in here with some damned *guns*—fast!"

Death Descending bulleted downward, shrieking through the ever thicker planetary atmosphere at a dangerously high velocity. Unlike Human military transports, *Death Descending*'s huge hull was sleekly aerodynamic, designed for atmospheric insertions exactly like this one, but Captain Na-Tharla was painfully well aware of the fact that there was a Bolo waiting for him. Everything suggested that the Bolo in question would be unable to engage his ship as it descended, but the fact that everything suggested that would be very cold comfort if it turned out not to be accurate. At the moment, he missed the rest of Admiral Na-Izhaaran's squadron more acutely than he had in many months, because they were supposed to be there to offer supporting fire as he penetrated his objective's atmosphere.

On the other hand, he reflected as he watched his ship's skin temperature climb, *our original objective would have had orbital defenses worth worrying about, too. Which this target doesn't, thanks to Lieutenant Sa-Chelak's platoon.*

He spared a tiny corner of his brain to send a silent prayer winging to Sa-Chelak's family gods on the lieutenant's behalf. It was all he could afford to spare, and he returned his total attention to his radar-mapping display as *Death Descending* screamed towards its selected landing site at three times the speed of sound.

More crimson lights glared on Edmund Hawthorne's damage control panel as the intruders burned their way through the blast doors. Those doors were intended to contain atmosphere, and to resist fairly severe explosive damage, but they weren't exactly slabs of duralloy armor. No one had ever intended them to serve as armored bulkheads capable of containing energy-weapon armed infantry for any length of time, after all.

The pattern of damage control reports told him what objectives the Dog Boys had selected for themselves, for all the good it did him. They were headed for Engineering . . . and the Bridge.

Exactly where I'd be headed myself, he conceded coldly. *Which isn't a great deal of comfort just this moment.*

At least he'd managed to get all of his people armed, however barely, before their unwelcome visitors arrived. And he'd managed to figure out how those visitors had gotten aboard his ship in the first place once Master Chief Halberstadt had maneuvered one of *Thermopylae*'s external hull maintenance mechs around to the area of the hull breaches.

A single Melconian special ops insertion boat was mechanically grappled to *Thermopylae*'s skin. Hawthorne had never encountered one of the insertion boats, nor had anyone else in his ship's company, but Iona's memory had obediently disgorged more information than he could possibly use about them. The two really relevant facts, as far as he was concerned, were, first, that the insertion boats were pure transport vehicles, with no onboard armament. And, second, that they had a maximum capacity of twenty, falling to only fifteen if the personnel aboard them were suited for vacuum ops. Which told him that his twenty-two-person crew had the invaders outnumbered.

Except, of course, for the fact that we're scattered all over the ship. And that these are highly trained special operations troops and we're Navy pukes. Not a Marine among us.

"Open Gamma-Seventeen, Jackson," he said to the exec. "Let's get Mallory and his team up here to the command deck before the Doggies get here. There's no point leaving them where they are, and I want as much firepower as we can get on this side of the shin-breaker."

"Aye, aye, sir," Lieutenant Lewis acknowledged. He unlocked the indicated blast door long enough for the power tech petty officer to lead her three-person party through it, and Hawthorne tried to look confident.

It wasn't easy. Given the speed at which the Dog Boys were moving, they'd get to Engineering at least ten minutes before Jessica Stopford could get the powered armor up and running. And they'd get to the Bridge deck a good minute before that. Mallory's people probably weren't going to make enough difference when they got here, either. On the other hand, there *was* the shin-breaker. And despite their rapid progress, it was unlikely, to say the least, that the Dog Boys knew about it.

He considered—again—informing Maneka about what was happening. And—again—decided against it. Whatever else happened, the Puppies weren't getting his ship, even if they did manage to knock Iona out before she blew the scuttling charges. Stopford had had time to rig a backup demolition sequence of her own in Fusion One, and it was on a deadman's switch. If she took her hand off that button for any reason, her improvised arrangements would blow *Thermopylae* straight to Hell. So even if Hawthorne and his people lost the ship, the Melconians wouldn't get control of her, and since there wasn't a thing Maneka could do either way to affect the outcome aboard *Thermopylae*, there was no pressing need to tell her about it until it was over. Which, in a worst-case scenario, the detonation of the ship's main reactor would do quite effectively.

And in the meantime, she didn't need anything else to worry about.

❖   ❖   ❖

Death Descending's landing pads hit the surface of the alien planet almost precisely on schedule.

The transport's huge hatches gaped open, and the first air cavalry units were whining out of her upper cargo decks almost before the landing legs had stopped flexing and fully stabilized. Vehicle ramps slammed down, and lightly armed and unarmored infantry carriers went grinding down them and raced outward to the preliminary perimeter positions General Ka-Frahkan and Colonel Na-Salth had preselected.

The first of the medium combat mechs followed on their heels, and the massive heavy mechs trembled as their four-man crews brought their drivetrains to full power.

Sergeant Major Na-Hanak had witnessed Lieutenant Sa-Chelak's death.

There hadn't been anything he could do about it. Their preoperations briefing had considered the possibility that the Humans would have armed small craft available, but there'd been no way to know for certain whether or not they did. Nor had there been any way to neutralize them before the insertion.

The good news was that the Humans appeared to have only a very few of them. Na-Hanak's sensors could detect only two, in fact, and the special ops troopers were extremely difficult to spot, even at such close ranges. Lieutenant Sa-Chelak had been unlucky enough to be in exactly the wrong place at exactly the wrong time, although just how unlucky that had actually been was debatable, the sergeant major reflected. He'd known as well as the lieutenant that Sa-Chelak wasn't going to make it, and the officer's death appeared to have attracted both of the Human cutters to the volume of space where he had died.

Which was what had given Na-Hanak and his three-man section the opportunity to reach the hull of their own objective unmolested.

Of course, there had been supposed to be eight of them,

not four, and even then they would probably have been grossly outnumbered by the Humans aboard this vessel. But unlike those Humans, his troopers were heavily armed and knew exactly what was happening.

He patted Private Ha-Tharmak on the shoulder, and she fired the breaching charge.

"They're down, Peter," Maneka's image said from the brigadier's com screen. "Almost exactly where Lazarus projected."

A scarlet icon blinked on the electronic map at Jeffords' right elbow, and he frowned thoughtfully as he studied the display.

Landing was located on a large, roughly triangular coastal plateau, bounded by the ocean to the east and by a tangled range of mountains to the west. The final decision had been made by Adrian Agnelli, but Jeffords knew Maneka had pushed strongly for this particular site. The only suitable landing zones from which the plateau could be threatened—and which could be reached without exposing the landers to Lazarus' Hellbore fire from Landing—all lay on the far side of the mountains, which created a formidable defensive obstacle for armored units and infantry. Air cavalry would be another matter, but Captain Jessup's Whippets, combined with the air-defense systems which had been positioned as a first priority even before construction on the city itself began, should have an excellent fighting chance against the couple of hundred air cav mounts of a Melconian heavy assault brigade, even without Lazarus' presence.

What neither they nor Jeffords' so-called brigade had the chance of a snowflake in hell against was the *rest* of that assault brigade. Jeffords knew how hard his people had trained before the colony expedition departed, and their actual combat equipment was far better than a typical militia unit would boast, even on one of the Core Worlds. They'd done their best to keep that training current on the long voyage here, too, but their opportunities had been strictly limited, and since their arrival, they'd all been so swamped with the enormous task of creating a new home that there'd been no time to bring them back up to their original proficiency levels. And Jeffords was honest enough to admit that even at their best, they'd never been up to the standards of the regular armed forces. They certainly weren't the equal in training or experience to the undoubtedly battle-hardened Melconians who had come to kill them.

From dug-in defensive positions they *might* be able to hold their own, at least against Dog Boy infantry. In any sort of battle of maneuver, though, they would be hopelessly outclassed and their advantage in numbers would be virtually meaningless.

The sole possible exception to that was Major Mary Lou Atwater's Fourth Battalion. Atwater, one of the relatively few combat veterans in the colony militia, had been a Marine sergeant who had retired from active service eight years before the current war began. She'd maintained her reserve status and tried to go back on active duty when the shooting started, but the Concordiat had declined her offer. She'd had the poor judgment—as far as reupping was concerned—to become an expert in the field of industrial robotics, and she'd been too valuable in that capacity to put back in uniform. But that dual capability of hers had made her ideal for Operation Seed Corn. She'd fought tooth and nail against accepting a commission, even in the militia, but she'd given in in the end. And she'd been fortunate enough to have almost the total personnel of her battalion assigned to the same transport . . . where she had made herself immensely unpopular by goading them through regular weapons drill and the best simulations she'd been able to cobble up on the transport's electronic entertainment systems.

"What route do you think they'll take, Maneka?" Jeffords asked now.

"That depends on a lot of factors," her image said calmly. He knew she was actually fused with the Bolo's psychotronics, and he found himself wondering suddenly if she'd bothered to change out of her swimsuit. It was an insane thing to be wasting mental effort on at a time like this, and he knew it, but the electronic image in front of him was neatly turned out in regulation uniform.

"We don't know how much they actually know about our situation," she continued. "If they realize just how old Lazarus is, they may decide in favor of a brute force approach and opt to take him on frontally. In that case, they'd probably come down Route Alpha."

A crimson line threaded its way through the mountains, following the line of the river which thundered over the bluffs into the sea to the south of Landing.

"The going is easiest coming that way, although they're wide open to air attack, if we have the capability for it, and the terrain here and here—" stars blinked at two points along the length of the thread "—would give both sides excellent fields of fire. We could begin picking them off with direct fire at over fifty kilometers at either of these points, but their *Surturs* could engage us in return. I doubt they're going to want to give a modern Bolo a shot at them at that sort of range, but they could be foolish enough to try it against an older model like Lazarus. I'd really like them to be, but I'm not going to plan on it.

"If they follow either Route Bravo or Route Charlie," she went on, while two additional threads came alive, "the terrain is a lot closer, which would let them use infantry and their lighter mechs to try to work around our flanks without exposing their heavy armor to our fire at such extended ranges. Right now, Lazarus is projecting a probability of seventy-five percent for Route Charlie."

The indicated route blinked on the display. Like the Alpha Route, it followed the line of a river valley which actually merged with Alpha about forty kilometers west of Landing. For the most part, the going was at least as good as for the Alpha Route, too, although there was one stretch that passed through a virtual gorge—a narrow, cliff-walled, twisting gut of a passage where the larger Melconian mechs would have no choice but to advance in single file.

"I hope that's not wishful thinking," Jeffords said.

"Bolos aren't subject to wishful thinking in enemy intention analyses," she replied. "If it were me, the maneuver opportunities would make it very tempting, too. On the other hand, I have to admit that I may not be quite as immune to wishful thinking as Lazarus is, and I'd certainly *prefer* for them to come that way."

Jeffords nodded, once again reflecting on how fortunate they were to have had Maneka Trevor in military command. Her insistence on mapping every possible approach route looked as if it was about to pay off in a huge way.

Purely on the basis of the surface topography, Route Charlie would have to be attractive to the Melconians. It threaded its way through a series of passes broad enough to give scope for tactical maneuvers and rough enough a single Bolo would find it extremely difficult to prevent light units and infantry from worming their way forward around its flanks. And while there were several places along it where a defensive force could make an effective stand, in every case except the gorge Jeffords had already noted, there were alternate approaches through flanking valleys. If Maneka had still commanded a pair of Bolos and had both of them on the ground, they could easily have blocked Route Charlie by operating in support of one another. As it was, Lazarus could engage an attacking column and bottle it up temporarily at any one of those natural defensive positions, but except for the gorge section, there was nowhere he could hold the entire force. And if he let them pin him in position, they would simply flow around him through one of the alternate approaches.

But unless they had access to the deep-scan radar mapping Maneka and Lazarus had carried out, there were aspects of Route Charlie which might just come as a nasty surprise to them.

"I have to admit," he said frankly, "that I was one of the people who thought you'd gone beyond thorough to paranoid, Maneka. But now I'm beginning to wonder if you weren't clairvoyant, instead."

"Hardly." Her mouth tightened and bitterness edged her voice.

"If I'd been clairvoyant, Guthrie Chin and Mickey would both be alive and this assault transport would have been blown out of space on its way in. And even if they come down Charlie, we're still facing one hell of a force disadvantage."

"Agreed. But at least we can hurt them."

"That's probably true enough," Maneka conceded. "In the meantime, I've decided it's time to saddle up for Sidekick."

"Agreed," Jeffords said again, steadily, although a part of him wanted to protest angrily. Fourth Battalion was his most effective unit. If the Melconians got past Lazarus, he was going to need Atwater's men and women badly. But he didn't even consider voicing that concern because, bottom line, if the Melconians got past Lazarus with their forces anything like intact, Landing—and the entire colony—was doomed. So if sending Fourth Battalion out to support Lazarus improved the Bolo's chance of stopping the enemy short of Landing, there was no question of where Brigadier Peter Jeffords wanted those troops employed.

"I'll have them moving aboard Lazarus' pod within ten minutes," he assured his youthful commander's image.

"That way."

Corporal Ka-Sharan pointed out across the huge compartment. The blast doors had slammed into place, as he'd anticipated, but the compartment was so vast, and so crowded with industrial machinery, that the chunks between the doors were big enough for an entire company to maneuver through, far less his own four-man team. And before the doors closed, he'd had time for his suit's computers to read the schematic the Humans had so kindly posted on the bulkheads. He knew exactly which way to go to get to the command center, and on a platform this large and this heavily automated, any possible opposition would have to be located there.

"Yes, Corporal," Private Ta-Holar acknowledged, and readied his energy lance as he moved rapidly but warily in the indicated direction. Ka-Sharan and the other two special ops troopers stayed close behind their point man, watching the flanks and rear. It looked as if they'd gotten in clean, Ka-Sharan thought. That was good. And they had their demolition charge in case they needed it, too.

"They're out of Bravo-Seven," someone said tersely, and Lauren nodded. The Dog Boys were moving faster than she'd hoped they could, and they'd burned their way through the first set of blast doors with what seemed absurd ease. A platoon from Captain Glenn Smyth-Mariano's company of vacuum-trained militia was on the way, but they were going to get here too late. At least Lauren had gotten most of her people off in the lifeboats, so if the Puppies did have a demolition charge and popped it off, they would kill only her and her command crew.

And, of course, fifteen percent of the colony's total industrial capacity.

"There are only four of the bastards," she heard herself say as she stared at the visual imagery from India Mike Three's internal sensors. "Only *four*!"

"Sure," Alfred Tschu agreed. "But that's four of them with armor and heavy weapons. And we've got zip as weapons." He stared at his displays for several moments, then shook his head. "Lauren, I think it's time to go, too," he said quietly.

"No! They've still got to cross all of Bravo-Six and Bravo-Four before they can get here!" she snapped, glaring at the images of the Melconian intruders.

"Which isn't going to take them very long," Tschu pointed out. "You know that as well as I do."

Lauren grunted, biting her lip hard. Unfortunately, Tschu was right. The sectors of the industrial module were mostly big open spaces, without a lot in the way of internal bulkheads. They had to be because of the nature of the processes which went on inside them. They were wrapped around the control room like the rings of an onion, but none of them was going to offer many barriers to the oncoming boarders. And whether the Puppies knew it or not, they'd picked the worst possible line of approach, from the humans' perspective.

The evacuation route from the control center to the lifeboats ran right along the back side of Bravo-Four. If they just kept coming, they would cut the watch-crew off from escape before they ever reached the control center itself.

"Any more word from Smyth-Mariano, Hannah?" she demanded.

"No." The communications tech sounded decidedly shaky, and Lauren didn't blame her a bit.

"Well, contact him. Tell him what's happening. And tell him we've got maybe fifteen minutes before they cut us off from the lifeboats."

The last blast door before *Thermopylae*'s command deck glowed briefly and almost instantaneously yellow-white, then yielded with an explosive concussion as the Melconian energy lance burned through it. At least the ship's automated repair systems had managed to close up the hull breaches behind the invaders. The atmospheric pressure dropped noticeably, but it remained breathable, which was good, since none of Hawthorne's bridge personnel had been given time to get to their suit lockers before the entire ship went into lock down.

Something arced through the opening and hit a bulkhead with a metallic rattle.

Hawthorne recognized the grenade instantly.

"*Down!*" he barked, and flung himself flat behind the pedestal of his command couch an instant before a pair of sledgehammers seemed to impact simultaneously on either side of his head.

The concussion was deafening, and the flash which accompanied it blinded Lieutenant Lewis and Petty Officer Mallory. But as Hawthorne had hoped—prayed—the Dog Boys were trying to take the ship in operable condition, so they were relying on stun grenades. The cumulative effect of the Melconian flash-bangs was devastating, but God had decided to grant them at least a couple of small favors, and one of them was the "shin-breaker."

Like most of the rest of his personnel, Hawthorne had spent more than a few minutes cursing the yard workers who had overseen the extension of Number Three Vehicle Hold when *Thermopylae* was refitted to increase her combat-loaded vehicle capacity. Thanks to their efforts, the access passage to the command bridge took a sharp, right-angled dogleg, then climbed a four-step access ladder to clear the upper edge of what had become the vehicle hold's aftermost bulkhead just short of the bridge hatch itself.

That ladder, and the raised, shin-high lip of the access hatch (which, unlike the ladder, *could* have been designed out), had tripped up every single member of the bridge crew at least once since coming aboard. But it also provided a shallow, built-in grenade sump, and much of the effect of the flash-bang was deflected from the bridge proper. What ought to have completely, if temporarily, incapacitated any unprotected person exposed to the blast had "only" disoriented most of the defenders, instead.

Hawthorne fought doggedly against the grenade's effect. He'd known it was coming, done his best to prepare himself for it ahead of time, and the additional blast shadow of his command chair had helped, but he still seemed to be moving in slow motion through atmosphere which had become a clinging syrup. He saw his own hands, as if they belonged to someone else, twisting the safety lock on the boarding grenade, pressing the arming button, and then lobbing it back out through the smoke-streaming hatch.

Captain Ka-Paldyn slapped Sergeant Na-Rahmar on the shoulder, and the sergeant flung himself forward through the breach that ought to lead directly to the transport's bridge. So far, the rough schematic in Ka-Paldyn's suit computer had been gratifyingly accurate. As always, there were slight discrepancies—even among the People, "sisterships" often varied considerably, especially in their interior arrangements—but nothing significant.

Until now.

Private Ka-Morghas followed Na-Rahmar through the breach, power carbine ready to pick off the stunned, helpless Human bridge crew, and Private Na-Laarhan was right on Ka-Morghas' heels when the grenade went off directly under their feet.

It wasn't a stunning weapon. It wasn't even a conventional explosive. Instead, a small, intensely powerful, superconductor capacitor-fed gravitic field propelled several hundred flechettes outward in a circular pattern at six thousand meters per second. They were small, those flechettes, but needle-tipped and razor-edged. They punched through the Melconians' lightly-armored EW suits with contemptuous ease, and all three of Ka-Paldyn's lead troopers were turned instantly into so much mangled meat.

A handful of the lethal flechettes howled back through the hatch into the bridge itself. Fortunately, the super-dense little missiles were so sharp and carried so much kinetic energy with them that they half-buried themselves in the battle steel bulkheads instead of ricocheting. One of them didn't hit a bulkhead, however. Instead, it struck Jackson Lewis as he still stood, dazed and pawing at his blinded eyes, and his chest exploded under the impact. His body flew back, slamming into the main visual display, then slid down, painting a broad bloody streak down the display.

Hawthorne swore viciously as the exec went down, and again as two more of the errant flechettes exploded through the communications console in a spectacular eruption of arcing circuitry, but there was no time to think about that just now. His sidearm was in his left hand, covering the hatch. He was a poor enough shot under any circumstances, and he figured his chances of actually hitting anything left-handed were about the same as his chance of becoming Emperor of the Known Universe, but his right hand was occupied with a second grenade, and his right thumb was on the arming button.

Ka-Paldyn guessed instantly what had happened. Unfortunately, there wasn't much he could do about it.

He tossed a remote sensor through the breached blast door, but it only confirmed what he had already surmised, and he cursed under his breath. If the accursed ship's architecture had to depart from the schematic, why had it had to be *here*, of all places? The mere fact that anyone on the other side of that blast door had been capable of offensive action at all had already told him that whoever it was must had been behind some very substantial cover which shouldn't have been there. Now, as he studied the palm-sized display's imagery relayed from the remote, he recognized that there was no way for him or his team to fire effectively around that sharp bend in the passage. The ruined blast door was just too far from the turn in the corridor for anyone on Ka-Paldyn's side of the door to get a firing angle up and through the actual bridge hatch. But it was painfully obvious that there was nothing at all to prevent the bridge's defenders from firing effectively on anyone attempting to force his way through the hatch, around the bend, and up that short ladder.

Ka-Paldyn's mind worked furiously, trying to find a way around the problem. Ultimately, he knew, he could bypass the hatch entirely by cutting his way directly through the intervening bulkheads. But the bulkheads were almost as tough as the blast doors themselves, and there were more of them. They would take longer to burn through, and his own assault group had exhausted most of its energy lances getting to this point. Which didn't even consider the fact that he had absolutely no way of knowing what critical control runs he might cut trying to pry open the bulkheads. That was a minor concern, tactically speaking, but his special ops force didn't include anyone trained in Human engineering practices. Their suits' computers theoretically contained the information they would need to at least shut down the ship's drives until someone from *Death Descending* could get here to take over. But if they cut or disabled something critical to the management of the ship, none of them would have the least idea how to fix it.

"Jarth," he said over his suit communicator.

"Here," Lieutenant Jarth Ka-Holmar, First Platoon's commander, replied instantly.

"Problems at the bridge hatch," Ka-Paldyn said. "The passage bends sharply. There's no direct approach, and the Human command crew obviously got to their weapons lockers before we boarded. I've lost three people."

"I copy," Ka-Holmar said. "We haven't encountered any armed resistance yet, but I've got two wounded, anyway."

"What? How?"

"The Humans are using the ship's repair mechs against us." Ka-Holmar couldn't quite keep the frustrated anger out of his voice. "They took us by surprise the first time, and Sergeant Ka-Yaru and Private Na-Erask got hit by some sort of heavy-lift mech. Ka-Yaru's right arm and both of Na-Erask's legs are broken. It was stupid, sir. I should have seen it coming."

"No plan survives the test of combat unchanged, Jarth," Ka-Paldyn quoted, more philosophically than he felt. "Those are your only casualties?"

"Yes, sir. Now that we know what the Humans are up to, we're taking out the mechs before they can reach us. Good thing, too. The last one they threw at us almost got Sa-Ithar with a laser cutting torch. They aren't going to stop us with this sort of silliness, sir, but they are slowing us down."

"Understood. On the other hand, if that's the best they have to put up against you, maybe their Engineering crew didn't have time to draw regular weapons, after all."

Ka-Paldyn thought again, considering his options. He wished fervently that he hadn't sent Na-Rahmar through the blast door first. He'd gotten overconfident, he told himself bitterly. The total lack of opposition to that point had convinced him the Humans were cowering helplessly behind the ultimately futile barrier of their blast doors, like unarmed *meschu* in a hunter's trap. And that conviction had led to the sort of mistake overconfidence always led to. Which was why he'd sent the person carrying his own assault team's demolition charge through the blast door to be killed.

Ka-Holmar still had *his* fusion charge, so Na-Rahmar's death wasn't catastrophic. Even if they failed to take the ship, they could still ensure its destruction. But it was undeniably frustrating and humiliating to have stumbled like this after First Platoon's brilliant success in accurately projecting the Humans' evasive course maneuver and getting one of its insertion boats aboard in the first place.

"We can't move forward here without cutting through bulkheads, Jarth, and we've almost exhausted our lances," he said. "How soon do you expect to have Engineering?"

"I can't say for certain, sir," Ka-Holmar replied honestly. "I expected to be there already, but having to shoot the ship's damned hardware has put us well behind schedule. I'd estimate another fifteen minutes at our present rate of progress, but I can't guarantee that."

"Well," Ka-Paldyn said with a grim chuckle, "it's not like they're going anywhere before you get there to kill them, now is it? Go ahead. I'll hold here with the rest of my team until you secure Engineering. We can at least shut down the drive from there, if we have to. And if we can tie our suit computers into the ship's main net, we can probably figure out how to shut down the environmental services, as well. If they don't want to let us come in, we'll just shut off their air and see how they like that."

"Understood, sir."

"Lauren, our guys aren't going to get here before the Dogs do," Alfred Tschu said harshly. "We've got to go—now!"

"I know. I know!" Lauren felt her lips draw back in a snarl of frustrated hatred. Those bastards out there were the same ones who'd killed *Kuan Yin* and eighty percent of her crew, and now they were going to take India Mike Three away from her, too. And there was nothing she could do about—

"Wait!"

The word popped out of her as abruptly as a punch in the face, and Tschu paused, halfway out of his station chair. He and Hannah Segovia darted a look at each other, then turned back to Lauren with wary expressions.

"What is it?" Alf asked cautiously.

"Look at them!" Lauren jabbed a finger at the visual display which showed the oncoming Melconians. "There are only four of the bastards, and they're moving straight along the passages towards Control."

"Yeah, there are only four of them," he agreed. "But they've got guns, and we don't. And like you say, they're headed straight this way."

"Sure they are," she agreed, and her lips drew back in a wolfish snarl. "But they're staying bunched up and following the bulkhead markers. Don't you see? Either they can read Standard English, or else their suit computers are translating for them, but they're coming straight down the pike. Which means we *know* where they're going to be when they cross Bravo-Four and head for the hatch, don't we."

"Well, yeah. . . ." he said slowly, but Lauren was no longer paying him any attention. She was busy giving very careful very explicit orders to the industrial module's simpleminded AI.

"We'll finish boarding the battalion in another twenty minutes, ma'am," Major Atwater told Maneka. "Sorry we can't move any faster than that."

"Major, the fact that you can squeeze your people into the available space at all is remarkable," Maneka replied, taking pains to keep even the smallest hint of frustration out of her tone. Atwater was indeed doing remarkably well to be getting her people and their equipment aboard as quickly as she was, and Maneka knew her own observation about the available space was well taken. The automated depot, coupled with Lazarus' own bulk, had reduced the space which ought to have easily accommodated Atwater's five hundred militia men and women to claustrophobic dimensions. At least Maneka had offloaded the depot's spare parts and as much of the rest of the pod's cargo as possible, but the space reduction was still severe. They were fortunate that the battalion's heavy weapons could fit aboard standard heavy-lift cargo platforms. Five of them were tractor-locked to Lazarus' missile deck and the pod's flanks, which was strictly against The Book but let Maneka squeeze them aboard anyway.

What she wasn't going to be able to do was to deploy them in a proper combat drop. So she was going to have to get the pod onto the ground far enough out of range of the Melconians to give Atwater the time she would need to get her personnel deployed and her heavy weapons crews mated with their equipment.

"Let me know as soon as we can seal hatches, Major," she said.

"Affirmative, ma'am."

"Green board, ma'am!" Chief Harriman announced sharply.

"Thank God!" Lieutenant Jessica Stopford acknowledged, looking up from her own console, and carefully entered the necessary code before removing her thumb from the self-destruct button.

The Melconians had reached the final blast door before Engineering itself, and she had just committed her final distraction—a pair of cleaning machines—to slowing them down. By now, the Dog Boys had adjusted to her tricks, and they blew the automated mops to bits almost casually, but the delay had lasted just long enough.

"Up!" Ensign Younts announced, and Stopford looked over her shoulder at the ensign.

At the Skipper's insistence (which Stopford had thought was just a little paranoid of him at the time), everyone aboard *Thermopylae* had at least read the manuals on the powered armor. But Younts and Chief Harriman, both of whom had served in direct support of the Marines before their current assignment, were the only two members of the crew with anything approaching hands-on familiarity with the equipment.

Now they walked their powered armor massively across the forward power room's decking. The standard Marine-issue armor gleamed like black ice under the overhead lighting, bulging and massive with energy weapons and projectile guns.

"You're sure you're ready?" Stopford asked. What she really

wanted to ask was *Are you sure you know what the hell you're doing?* but that was out of the question, of course.

"Oh, *yeah*, ma'am." Younts' response scarcely represented proper military phraseology, but there was no mistaking the anticipation in the young woman's voice.

"Time to kick some Puppy ass!" she added, and, despite herself, Stopford chuckled. Then she sobered.

"Then go to it, Ensign," she said, and punched the button.

"*Cleaning* machines!" Lieutenant Ka-Holmar said, shaking his head in exasperation.

"Yes, sir," his lead trooper said, obviously more than a little embarrassed at having expended ammunition on such an unworthy target.

"Well, don't worry about it," Ka-Holmar reassured him after a moment. "Better safe than sorry. And according to the schematic, we're finally here."

He clambered through the hole burned through the final blast door. The standard-weight hatch to the ship's forward power room loomed before him—still closed, of course—and he exhaled in undeniable relief. Like any Imperial soldier, Ka-Holmar was perfectly prepared to die for the People if that was what the mission required, but he couldn't deny that he preferred the notion of surviving. Which made him grateful that the demolition charge strapped to his back wasn't going to be required after all.

He turned his head to address Sergeant Sa-Ithar.

Power One's hatch flicked open, and Younts and Harriman thundered through it in a deck-pounding run.

Stopford watched the video feed relayed from Younts' helmet sensors as the pair of humans suddenly erupted into the midst of the Melconian special ops troopers.

It was not an equitable matchup.

The Melconian EW suits were designed for stealthiness. They carried some armor, but Ka-Holmar's troopers were essentially armed and equipped as light infantry. Marine powered armor, on the other hand, wasn't particularly stealthy. What it *was* was engineered for close, brutal, *heavy* combat.

Ka-Holmar never had time to realize what had happened. One instant he was turning to address his sergeant; the next a two-centimeter, armor-mounted power rifle blew a fist-sized hole right through the fusion charge on his back and out through the front of his chest in an explosion of body fluids and splintered bone.

Sergeant Sa-Ithar screamed a warning to the rest of Ka-Holmar's assault team. That was all he had time for before a stream of hypervelocity flechettes from Chief Harriman's armor sliced him in half with all of the neatness and finesse of a chainsaw.

Fire streamed back at the two humans from the Melconians on the other side of the ruptured blast door, but their heavy armor shrugged it effortlessly aside, and they advanced through the hurricane of projectiles and power gun fire like people wading upstream against a stiff current. They reached the blast door, and Younts fired a burst of contact-fused grenades through the opening, then covered Harriman as the chief petty officer gripped the broken duralloy panel in his armor's powered gauntlets and heaved like a fusion-powered Hercules.

The entire blast door panel wrenched out of its guides, and he tossed it aside as Younts went storming through the opening, killing anything that moved.

"Ready to lift, ma'am!"

"Thank you, Major," the human portion of the Maneka/Lazarus fusion acknowledged, and the pod's drive whined as it rose smoothly into the air. It was heavily laden enough to be ponderous, but it accelerated quickly and went streaking off towards the oncoming Melconians.

"Here they come," Tschu said harshly. His face was white and strained, and Lauren could almost physically feel his desire to be somewhere—anywhere—else. But he and Hannah had both stuck with her, and she smiled at them as reassuringly as she could as the Melconian boarders approached the final hatch out of Bravo-Four.

They were alert, she saw. While their point moved right up to the door with his energy lance, the others formed a hollow semicircle around him, watching their back trail and scanning the silently looming banks of machinery to either side. But what none of them was doing, she noted with grim satisfaction, was looking directly upward.

"Come on," she murmured to them softly, willing them to obey her. "Come on. Just a *little* closer together . . ."

Perhaps the force of her will worked. Or maybe she was just lucky. Even as she watched, the perimeter drew in a little closer to the point, as if his fellows wanted to watch over his shoulder as he burned away the bulkhead around the hatch.

"*Now!*" Lauren barked to the AI, and the seventy-eight-ton tractor grab suspended from the overhead carrier twenty-two meters directly above the approach to the hatch, in direct contravention of every safety reg ever written, came smashing down like Juggernaut.

"Nameless Ones take them all!" Sergeant-Major Na-Hanak swore viciously as power rifle fire ripped suddenly into Private Cha-Thark.

The private flipped back without even a scream, sliding across the deck with the total inertness of death, and Na-Hanak's HUD blazed with abrupt scarlet icons as his sensors picked up the emission signatures of the Human infantry spreading out ahead of him. There were at least twelve of the Humans, and from their signatures, they were equipped with weapons at least as good as his own. There was no way he and his single surviving trooper could hope to defeat all of them. And even if they could have, what would be the point? If this many of the enemy were already deployed to meet them this far from the ship's control center, there must be others—many others—behind them.

Na-Hanak had lost the race to beat them to his target. As, he admitted to himself at last, he'd always anticipated that he would. Still, they'd *almost* made it . . . and they *had* destroyed their primary target.

Nor was that all they would accomplish, he told himself grimly, and looked at Private Ha-Tharmak.

"It's time," he told her quietly. She looked back at him for perhaps two heartbeats, then flipped her ears in agreement. There was fear in her eyes, he saw, but not a trace of hesitation, and he hoped she saw his pride in her when she looked into his own face.

"Good bye, Sergeant-Major," she said simply, and pressed the button.

6

"Both my armored battalions have cleared the ship, sir," Colonel Na-Lythan reported, and General Ka-Frahkan flicked his ears sharply in approval.

"Good, Uran! Good!"

He watched the heavy armored units' icons spreading out around the grounded transport on his tactical plot. The medium mechs formed the outer perimeter, backed up by the heavies the Humans had codenamed "*Surtur*." Ka-Frahkan was no student of xenomythology, but his intelligence briefing on the Humans had told him the origin of the name, and he found it grimly appropriate as he watched the massive, heavily armored giants grinding into position.

"The artillery battalion has also cleared ship," Colonel Na-Salth announced. Ka-Frahkan glanced at him, and his executive officer looked up from his own display to meet his eyes. "Major Ha-Kahm has already designated his deployment positions, and his units are moving into them now. He reports that his air-defense batteries will be prepared to provide defensive fire within another six minutes."

"Tell him I'm pleased, very pleased," Ka-Frahkan said, then turned his head as Captain Na-Tharla stepped into the landing force command center.

"You put us on the ground in one piece, Gizhan," the general said quietly. "Thank you—from all my people. We'll take it from here."

"I'm afraid you'll have to, sir," Na-Tharla replied with a sigh. Ka-Frahkan cocked one ear interrogatively, and the captain shrugged. "Assault transports are designed for this sort of operation, but this is a big ship for atmospheric maneuvers at the best of times, sir, and we put her down unusually hard and fast this time. High-speed insertions are always hard on the hardware. And *Death Descending* wasn't exactly in perfect shape when we started the landing. We've stripped off enough array elements to cost us forty percent of our sensor capability; our main and secondary subspace arrays are both off-line and look like they'll stay that way; and our main drive popped three of the alpha circuit breakers on the primary converter just as we hit dirt. We can fix it—probably—but not quickly. Not when we've overstrained the ship's systems for so long without proper maintenance or spares. I've got my people working on it, of course, but I estimate that we'll need at least twelve hours just to patch up the drive, if we're lucky. More probably, two or three times that long."

"I see." Ka-Frahkan looked at Na-Tharla gravely. The news wasn't exactly unexpected, but that made it no less unwelcome. Ka-Frahkan's ops plan had emphasized the need to get *Death Descending* back into space and well away from the Bolo's weapons as quickly as possible. Obviously, that wasn't going to happen now.

"I'm sorry, General," Na-Tharla said quietly.

"Not your fault, Gizhan," Ka-Frahkan replied, equally quietly, and reached out to squeeze the naval officer's shoulder. "We'd never have gotten here in the first place without all the miracles you worked along the way," he continued. "And, frankly, I doubt your ship is going to be the Humans' primary target. Jesmahr and I intend to push their ground forces hard. That should keep them concentrated facing us, well away from you. They may toss some missiles your way, but Major Ha-Kahm is already setting up his air-defense batteries. I'll have him tie his sensor capability directly into your tactical net, as well. That will at least give your point defense systems sharper eyes to deal with anything that comes at you and gets through his batteries."

"Thank you, sir."

"Pure selfishness on my part, Gizhan," Ka-Frahkan said, flicking his ears in amusement. "Without your ship, it would be a long walk home!"

Na-Tharla's ears twitched in answering amusement, despite the worry lingering in his eyes, and Ka-Frahkan squeezed his shoulder again, then turned to his bank of communications displays.

"Major Na-Pahrthal," he said.

"Yes, sir!" the air cavalry commander replied from his quadrant screen.

"I want one company of your cavalry mounts deployed in a standard landing zone perimeter pattern. Instruct them to tie into *Death Descending*'s communications net, as well as ours. I want any report from them to reach Captain Na-Tharla and his people the same instant it reaches us."

"Yes, sir!" Na-Pahrthal said, saluting crisply, and Ka-Frahkan returned his attention to Colonel Na-Lythan.

"Uran, start pushing your reconnaissance units out. Don't get too carried away until we've got everyone off the ship and ready to deploy, but I don't want anyone sneaking up on us without being spotted."

"Yes, sir."

"Jesmahr."

"Yes, sir?"

"Let's get the reconnaissance drones launched. They must have tracked us well enough to know approximately where we planeted, and given the thoroughness their commander's shown all along the line, they must have surveyed the possible approach routes to their colony long ago. So concentrate on sweeping not just our planned axis of advance, but all the others we've identified, as well. Sweep everything between us and their colony."

"Yes, sir."

"Open hatch!" a sergeant announced. "Okay, people! Move it! *Move it!*"

Maneka/Lazarus watched through the assault pod's internal visual pickups as Fourth Battalion's militia troopers streamed out of its gaping hatches. Major Atwater had drilled them well, she/they thought approvingly. The militiamen and women showed plenty of anxiety and more than a little fear, but no confusion as they deployed at a dead run towards the positions marked on their individual HUDs. Atwater—and Maneka—had selected individual troop positions for this particular blocking position weeks ago, and the militia and their heavy support weapons were settling into them with gratifying speed.

"Five more minutes to clear the pod, Captain Trevor," Atwater reported formally. The vehicles and other equipment which had been grappled to the pod hull and Lazarus' missile deck had already been un-grappled, and the Maneka component of her/their composite identity watched the heavy gear being unloaded from its pallets and rushed into position.

"Thank you, Mary Lou," she said over the com. "Please remind everyone to stay well clear of the pod's safety perimeter."

"Oh, I will—I will!" Atwater replied with a crooked grin. "Not that I expect it's really necessary. Whatever I may tell 'em at drills, none of my people are *really* outright idiots!"

"No, I imagine not," Maneka agreed.

The militia completed their disembarkation in less than eighteen minutes, which—as Maneka/Lazarus was fully aware—was astonishingly good time, almost as good as a frontline Marine battalion could have hoped to accomplish. But the speed with which she/they thought and reacted when they meshed through the neural link made the delay seem eternal. At least, it did to the *human* portion of their fusion, an inner corner of Maneka's brain thought sardonically.

"Last man clear!" Atwater's executive officer announced.

"You're clear to lift, Maneka," Atwater said. "Everybody's outside the drive perimeter."

"Thank you," Maneka replied, as courteously as if her/their sensors hadn't already informed her of that. "Lifting now."

The pod's drive howled as Lazarus threw maximum emergency power to it and headed not west, toward the Melconian transport, but south, *away* from it.

"Sir, Colonel Na-Lythan's advanced drones have located a force of Human infantry directly on our planned line of advance."

Ka-Frahkan looked up from the map console of the command vehicle moving away from the LZ at a steady fifty kilometers per hour and bared his canines in irritation. Not that he was particularly surprised.

"Show me, Jesmahr," he said, and Na-Salth quickly dumped the new data to a small-scale terrain display at the general's elbow.

"Nameless Ones take them," Ka-Frahkan growled. "What demon is whispering in their ears?"

Na-Salth made no reply to the obviously rhetorical question. He and Ka-Frahkan sat side by side, studying the display, and the general snorted in exasperation.

"I make it at least one of their battalions," he said, trained eyes evaluating the data sidebars with the ease of long experience.

"I concur, sir. But look here." Na-Salth indicated one of the sidebars. "They appear to be equipped with their Marines' powered armor, but their evident unit organization doesn't match."

"No," Ka-Frahkan agreed. His ears shifted slowly and thoughtfully, and then he stabbed the display with one clawed finger. "This is one of their militia battalions," he said positively. "It's far better equipped than their militia ought to be, but that's what it is. Look here. Their Marines use five-man fire teams, but these appear to be organized into seven-man teams, and the total troop strength is almost forty percent higher than a Marine battalion's ought to be. And look here, as well." He indicated the attached heavy weapons, most of which were already well dug-in. "They have fewer antiarmor platoons than they ought to, and this plasma-rifle section has four rifles in it, not six. The numbers are right for their militia; it's just the quality of the equipment that's different."

"So we're not up against first-line troops, sir," Na-Salth mused.

"Maybe not, but don't underestimate them," Ka-Frahkan said grimly. "Look how quickly they've already deployed and dug themselves in." His ears waved in a gesture of negation. "No. These are militia, perhaps, but they're *well-trained* militia. Maybe even as well as those Nameless-taken militia units we hit at Tricia's World."

His ears flattened in grim memory of the twenty-seven percent casualties the brigade had taken in that attack.

"Well, sir," Na-Salth replied, "we won that one, too."

"Well said," Ka-Frahkan acknowledged. "Still, it should remind us that Human militia can be just as tough as their frontline units. And *this* militia has the weapons to be a nasty handful for Ka-Somal's infantry."

"But not for Uran's armor," Na-Salth pointed out.

"No," Ka-Frahkan agreed. "Of course, that's what their never-to-be-sufficiently-damned Bolo is for, isn't it?"

"Yes, sir," Na-Salth acknowledged, wrinkling his muzzle in an expression of sour agreement. Neither of them chose to bring up the fact that the defenders of Tricia's World had *not* had Bolo support when the brigade went in.

"But, speaking of the Bolo," Na-Salth continued, "where is it?"

"A well-taken question."

Ka-Frahkan folded his hands behind him, rocking up and down on the balls of his feet while he continued to gaze at the images relayed from Na-Lythan's drones.

"I suspect the Bolo is playing transport," he said finally.

"Sir?"

"This is one of the spots you and I identified as a potential bottleneck before we ever even landed," Ka-Frahkan reminded him. "It's on the shortest route from our LZ to their colony, and this—" he took one hand from behind him and waved at the terrain display "—is the one place where all of the possible lines of approach for *all* of the routes we've identified come together. This pass they're deployed in is the only way for our armored mechs to get through that particular stretch of mountains. And the terrain allows the side with the shorter-ranged weapons to overcome much of its disadvantages, which makes it an ideal spot for infantry to confront armored units, if it has no choice but to confront them anyway."

Na-Salth flicked his ears in agreement. The longest line of sight through the rugged, tumbling mountainsides on the approach to the Humans' position was no more than five or six kilometers long. That was the equivalent of knife-range, close enough, as Ka-Frahkan had just pointed out, to make even infantry weapons—especially, he admitted sourly, *Human* infantry weapons—deadly against anything but the most heavily armored vehicles.

"It's not the best position for a *Bolo*, though," Ka-Frahkan continued. "Its Hellbore has a considerably greater effective range than our own do, and however much we may hate to admit it, its fire control is much better. Coupled with its superior battle screen and armor, it should want to engage us at the *longest* possible range, not somewhere where the terrain will let us get close enough for Uran's mechs to even the odds through volume of fire."

"So why—?" Na-Salth left the question hovering, and Ka-Frahkan snorted.

"They're building a blocking position, putting a cork into the bottle, Jesmahr," he said harshly. "These militia are there to backstop the Bolo. Look at it. It will take hours for our own mechs to reach that position. Na-Pahrthal's air cavalry could get there much sooner, but the Humans already have their antiair defenses well established, and their infantry weapons are capable of dealing with most of his air cav mounts. So they've been positioned at a point where they can block anything advancing towards their colony in order to watch the back door while the Bolo maneuvers against us further west. It can use its damned assault pod to position itself anywhere it wants for the initial contact, and it will know the blocking position behind it will stop anything that gets past it *except* our mechs."

"I agree, sir," Na-Salth said after a moment. "But in that case, where *is* the Bolo?"

"Well, we know it isn't anywhere between us and the militia," Ka-Frahkan said. "While I'm prepared to admit that the stealth capabilities built into the Bolos are almost as good as our own, no one could hide a fighting vehicle of that size from Uran's drones—not when he's flown the sort of saturation pattern he has here. So the most logical thing for it to be doing is returning to the colony to pick up yet another battalion of this accursedly well-equipped militia to further reinforce the position they've already established. It's got the time, after all. Even allowing for loading and unloading times at each end, its pod can make the round-trip between the Human settlement and this point—" he indicated the display again "—in less than a quarter of the time it will take even our most advanced ground units to reach it. And the stronger the cork in the bottle becomes, the more tactical flexibility the Bolo gains when it comes time for it to engage us."

"You may well be right, sir. But does that really change our options?"

"No." Ka-Frahkan flattened his ears. "No, it doesn't. The only way to their colony is through that blocking position, and as long as we continue to advance towards it, the Bolo will have to engage us eventually. When it does, it will hurt us—badly," he admitted bleakly. "But that means we'll be able to hurt *it*, too."

"How do you want to proceed in the meantime, sir?"

"Do we have this militia localized well enough for Major Ha-Kahm's missile batteries to strike it?"

"Yes," Na-Salth replied in a slightly dubious tone. Ka-Frahkan looked a question at him, and the colonel grimaced. "We have the coordinates, but they've already got the equivalent of three of our Mark Twenty air-defense batteries in place. Our chances of actually getting one of Ha-Kahm's missiles through their defenses wouldn't be very high. And we only have forty-five tubes between the three batteries."

"Point taken," Ka-Frahkan grunted. "We don't have the ammunition to waste. And if the Bolo has sensor platforms in a position to track the missiles back to their launchers, it would pinpoint their locations for its own counterbattery fire."

He shook himself. He had to be getting old; otherwise he wouldn't have needed Na-Salth's tactful reminder of something he knew so well. He set that thought aside while he considered other alternatives.

"Have Major Na-Pahrthal close with their position," he decided finally. "Tell him I don't want him to get too closely engaged with them, but I want them harassed. Have Ka-Somal send his recon company forward, as well. I want those infantry scooters out in front of even Na-Lythan's reconnaissance mechs. That Bolo is going to turn up somewhere eventually—somewhere between us and that blocking position. When it does, I want to know exactly where it is."

<They are advancing along Route Charlie,> her/their Lazarus half observed dispassionately as the assault pod went screaming down another narrow valley at high Mach numbers and an altitude of barely fifty meters, and her/their Maneka half agreed wordlessly.

<Do they know they're under observation?> her part of the fusion wondered.

<Insufficient data,> her/their Lazarus' part replied, and Maneka nodded as she lay in her crash couch, eyes closed. Despite her agreement that she/they had too little information to draw solid conclusions, however, she suspected that the Dog Boys didn't have a clue they were being watched. None of their recon parties had made any move to knock out the carefully concealed sensor remotes with which she and Lazarus had seeded each of the

identified possible attack routes. She hadn't mentioned the fact that they were doing so to anyone at the time. Although everyone had been too polite to actually say so, she'd known some of the colony's leaders had thought she was sufficiently paranoid to insist on such detailed surveys in the first place. Explaining that she was planting hidden observation posts all along them at the same time would only have confirmed their suspicions.

But paranoid or not, it was paying major dividends now. She/they had no need to penetrate the defended airspace above the advancing Melconian columns to keep them under observation, and she/they considered her/their analysis of the threat.

The Enemy's order of battle was the "Book" organization for a Melconian Heavy Assault Brigade: one armored regiment, one infantry regiment, and an air cavalry regiment. There ought to be an attached artillery support battalion, as well, although she/they had seen no sign of it yet. Analysis suggested a 99.870-plus percent chance that it was digging in on top of the Puppy landing zone, exactly as Melconian tactical doctrine decreed, which meant she/they would have to deal with it eventually. But for now, she/they could concentrate on the Enemy's mobile forces.

The fastest and most maneuverable component of those forces was the air cavalry regiment: three battalions of heavy, two-man mounts equipped with external missile and rocket pod racks and fitted with a twin-gun "main battery" directly descended from old, pre-space rotary cannon. Those cannon had a maximum rate of fire of over seven thousand rounds per minute per gun, or fourteen thousand for the pair, but the mounts carried less than two minutes worth of ammunition at that rate of fire.

The mounts were used primarily as scouts, using their lookdown sensors—which were quite competent, though not up to Concordiat standards—to sweep the rest of the brigade's line of advance. Their normal weapons were useless against any armored vehicle heavier than an infantry transport, and, despite their speed and agility, they were easy prey for antimissile and air defense systems if they exposed themselves. They could be equipped with fusion weapons, which meant it was remotely possible the Enemy might dispatch them on a strike against Landing, but the probability of their being able to penetrate Landing's fixed defenses was less than two percent.

In addition to the heavy mounts, the regiment had its own attached recon company, made up of one hundred one-man mounts which were tiny, fragile, unarmed, capable of dash speeds at surprisingly high Mach numbers, and extremely hard to detect. They were, in fact, considerably stealthier than the Empire's unmanned recon platforms. That, coupled with the fact that the relatively limited capability of Melconian cybernetics made it extremely useful to have a trained organic intelligence assessing the situation first hand, explained why they were so highly valued by Puppy commanders.

The infantry regiment was composed of three battalions, each about twice the size of a Concordiat militia battalion, mounted in ground-effect armored personnel carriers. The APCs were fast, but fragile compared to Concordiat equipment, and they were armed with relatively low-velocity, indirect fire weapons rather than the light, direct-fire Hellbore armament the Concordiat's more heavily armored APCs favored. Its organic support weapons were also very light compared to the Concordiat standard, but they were vehicle-mounted, intended to fire on the move, which made them elusive targets. In addition to its combat and support elements, the regiment included a reconnaissance company equipped with a hundred one-man grav scooters. The scooters were unarmed and unarmored, but they were very fast, very maneuverable, and equipped with excellent stealth capabilities.

An Imperial Melconian infantry regiment was an opponent to respect, but it would have posed little threat to the colony's militia alone if not for the *armored* regiment. According to the intelligence reports stored in her/their memory, the Enemy had recently begun reorganizing some of his armored regiments, emphasizing the direct-fire role even more heavily, but this one was organized on the older, original basis. It consisted of two armored battalions, each of three "fists"—three *Surturs*, each with its assigned pair of supporting *Fenrises*—for a total of six heavy and twelve medium mechs between both battalions, plus a recon company of twelve three-man *Heimdalls*.

One battalion was equipped with *Surtur Alphas*, 18,000-ton vehicles which were actually twenty percent more massive than a Mark XXVIII Bolo, with a main battery of six 82-centimeter Hellbores (or, rather, the less efficient Melconian version of that weapon) in two triple, echeloned turrets. That was an extraordinarily heavy battery, even for a vehicle the size of a *Surtur*, and their designers had paid for it by mounting much less capable secondary armaments. The *Surtur Alphas*, for example, mounted a secondary battery of fourteen heavy railguns, designed to fire both super-dense penetrators and a variety of special-purpose rounds, rather than the energy-weapon secondary armaments which had been a feature of Bolo design ever since the Mark VIII. It gave the mech an awesome punch against infantry, APCs, and dug-in ground targets, but it was effectively useless against a Bolo's antikinetic battle screen.

The armored regiment's second battalion, however, was equipped with *Surtur Betas*. Built on the same chassis and power plant, and mounting the same main battery, the *Beta* deleted the railgun secondary armament entirely in favor of a missile armament twenty-five percent heavier than a Mark XXVIII's. Its missiles were shorter-ranged than those in her/their launch cells, but they were very fast and had excellent penetration aids. They would have difficulty penetrating Bolo antimissile defenses with anything short of total saturation, but if they could get into range of Landing when she/they were unable to cover the colony, a single *Surtur Beta* could easily wipe out the entire settlement and everyone in it.

Both *Surtur* types were lavishly equipped with antimissile defenses of their own. Indeed, they had been upgraded significantly in the face of the Concordiat missile threat since the start of the war.

The *Fenrises* assigned to each battalion were identical: nine thousand tons, with a single 38-centimeter Hellbore-equivalent main weapon, and eight scaled-down railguns for secondary armament. That was a light direct-fire armament, but they were proportionately as well equipped for antimissile and air-defense, and they used much of their tonnage for a support armament of very short-ranged, extremely fast missiles. Tactically, the *Fenris* was intended to probe ahead as the fist advanced, and then to fall back and lay down saturation fire in support of the *Surturs* as the heavies closed. Once close combat was joined, the *Fenris'* job was to cover the heavies' flanks while simultaneously maneuvering around their opponents' flanks and rear, as well.

The *Heimdalls* were even lighter than the *Fenrises*, barely three thousand tons, and equipped only with light antimissile defenses and a single main battery turret mounting a pair of the lighter railguns. They were, however, ground-effect vehicles, not tracked like their heavier consorts. That made them extremely fast—faster even than a Bolo—and allowed them to negotiate terrain very few other armored units could cross. They were equipped with the best sensor systems the Melconian Empire had, and they were relatively stealthy, as well, though not nearly so hard to spot as the infantry's recon scooters.

Leaving the *Heimdalls* out of the equation, since their combat value against a Bolo was negligible, she/they were outnumbered by 18-to-1, although the tonnage differential wasn't quite that bad—only 14.4-to-1—thanks to the *Fenrises'* smaller size. Those were daunting odds, and she/they were going to have to fight smart even by Bolo standards. In a stand-up slugging match against the *Surturs'* combined thirty-six Hellbores, she/they would be quickly destroyed, despite her/their far superior battle screen and thicker and tougher armor. But for all their massive firepower, the Enemy mechs suffered from one huge disadvantage; they were manned units whose AI support was extremely limited. They were *slow* compared to any Bolo . . . and old as Lazarus was, his psychotronics had been heavily refitted when he was reactivated. He was more lightly armed than later-mark Bolos, but he thought—and reacted—just as quickly as his younger brothers and sisters.

That was going to have to be enough, her/their Maneka half

thought in the small corner of her mind which remained outside the link. That, and the surveys she/they had carried out and the carefully planted sensor net which was letting her/them observe the Enemy directly without expending recon drones just looking for him. And, she/they devoutly hoped, lulling the Puppies into a sense of false security when none of those airborne sensor platforms "found" them. She/they weren't about to rely on that, but it would be nice if the Puppies hadn't twigged to the sensor net's presence.

Thoughts of what the Melconians might or might not know turned her/their attention to the grounded transport. That transport had to be neutralized. At the moment, *Thermopylae's* assault pod gave her/them the mobility advantage. But sooner or later, she/they were going to have to engage the Enemy. Once they undocked from the pod, redocking would be out of the question. It would take too long, and she/they would be unable to maneuver, too vulnerable to enemy fire, to spend the time to board it once more. For that matter, without her/them mounted on the pod, it would have neither the active defenses nor the electronic warfare capability to penetrate the enemy's combat envelope to reach her/them, in the first place. No. Once she/they detached from the pod, she/they would be unable to use it further until the battle was decided, one way or the other. And if the Melconian combat mechs managed to pin her/them down while a half-dozen *Fenrises* fell back to the transport and used its mobility to launch a frontal assault on Landing while she/they were too far away to intervene, it would be disastrous. And, unfortunately, the transport had not been obliging enough to park itself in one of the areas covered by her/their previously planted remotes. She/they knew approximately where it had to be, but "approximately" wasn't good enough for the precision she/they required.

<In position,> her/their Lazarus component reported.

<Concur. Launch,> her/their Maneka component replied.

The pod slowed abruptly in its frenzied terrain-following flight. Missile hatches opened, and a dozen air-breathing cruise missiles launched. They configured their variable-geometry wings well forward for subsonic flight and arced away from the Bolo. They circled well to the east of her/their current position, dropped to a nap-of-the-earth altitude of barely twenty meters, and skimmed off on their attack mission, accompanied by no less than three extraordinarily stealthy reconnaissance platforms, while she/they angled still farther to the west before swinging back onto a more northerly heading.

Captain Na-Tharla tried not to fret too visibly as he prowled restlessly around *Death Descending*'s bridge. The repairs were going as quickly as he could have hoped, under the circumstances, but that made him feel no less vulnerable. There was a Bolo out there, somewhere, and so far, General Ka-Frahkan's brigade had failed to pick up even a hint of its position. That wasn't calculated to reassure the commander of an immobilized transport.

His lips wrinkled back from his canines in a bitterly amused challenge grin. Reassure! There hadn't been a moment since Admiral Na-Izhaaran chose to attack this accursed Human convoy in the first place that Na-Tharla had felt remotely like anything which could have been called "reassurance." And at this particular moment—

"Missile trace!" His head snapped around as the voice spoke abruptly from the communications section. "Air cav look-down radar reports missiles inbound, bearing zero-niner-three, altitude three-zero-zero, course two-seven-three true at three-zero-one-zero!"

The red, glaring icons of incoming missiles blazed suddenly in his tactical plot, and he snarled viciously as he watched them suddenly accelerate to a far higher velocity.

She/they watched through the accompanying drones as the missiles' attack programs reacted to the lash of the Enemy's radar. Their stubby wings configured smoothly back and their turbines howled as they accelerated abruptly to better than Mach 5. The drones could have kept pace easily enough, but only if they'd dropped out of stealth, and she/they had no intention of allowing those platforms to be detected and destroyed. So instead, the drones dropped behind, spreading out like encircling arms, passive sensors listening intently to the Melconians' emissions, while the missiles ran away from them and scorched straight in on the Melconian landing zone.

Active sensors and targeting systems from the transport and the ground-based air-defense systems joined the air cav radar lashing at the missiles, battling their onboard EW systems, fighting to lock them up for defensive fire. Those missiles carried high-kiloton-range fusion warheads; if even one of them got through, the transport would be permanently crippled, even if it was by some miracle not destroyed outright. But the odds of any of them penetrating the Melconian defenses were slight. Which was perfectly all right with her/them.

Countermissiles launched, shrieking out to seek and destroy the attacking birds. Half of her/their missiles were intercepted and destroyed, but the other half only accelerated to Mach 7 as the observations of the accompanying drones refined their targeting data and they came onto their final attack profiles.

The cruise missiles reached the final ridge line between them and their targets. They pitched upward, popping up over the ridge as they must to reach their destination, and the ground-defense lasers and antiarmor Hellbores were waiting. Beamed energy struck at the speed of light, viciously accurate despite the missiles' electronic warfare capabilities and penetration aids, and she/they watched as every single one of her/their attack missiles was destroyed harmlessly, far short of their targets.

Na-Tharla felt the jolting shock of relief like a punch in the belly as the incoming missiles vanished from his plot as if they had been no more than a bad dream.

Lord of the Nameless, he thought shakily. *I can't believe it. We stopped them—we stopped them! How—?*

He shook himself, then castigated his own sense of shocked, joyous astonishment. Ka-Frahkan had been right all along. However good the Humans' technology might be, they weren't *gods.* They could be stopped, defeated, and he felt almost ashamed

at the realization that he hadn't really believed that, not deep
down inside. But they had been, and if their missiles could be
stopped that easily here—

She/they completed her/their analysis.

It was a simple enough exercise, given the wealth of data
her/their unnoticed reconnaissance platforms had amassed. The
locations of the active sensors and weapon emplacements which
had tracked and engaged her/their missiles had been plotted to
within the nearest six centimeters. The perimeter air cav mounts
had been detected, counted, and localized. Emissions signatures
had been recorded, identified, and analyzed. Standard Melconian defensive dispositions had been extracted from memory,
overlaid across the positive data points she/they had plotted,
compared and evaluated, extrapolated in hyper-heuristic mode.
She/they *knew*, beyond any shadow of a doubt, precisely where
every sensor station, every weapon emplacement, was located,
and what those weapons and sensors' capabilities were.

And she/they also knew that in this instant, every Melconian
within that perimeter was still looking to the east, the direction from which the missile attack had come.

Which was why her/their pod abruptly popped up over a
mountaintop ninety-seven kilometers *west* of the Melconian
landing zone.

"New target!" a voice shouted. "New target at two-two-one,
alti—"

The voice never completed its warning. There wasn't time.
The range was under a hundred kilometers, which might as
well have been a hundred *centi*meters for the targeting systems
of a Mark XXVIII Bolo.

"*Contact!*" someone screamed over the company net, and
Captain Ithkar Na-Torsah's blood ran suddenly cold as the icon
simply appeared on his display.

His company of air cavalry was deployed in a circle a hundred
and three kilometers across, centered on the LZ and *Death*

Descending. That was the standard deployment for this sort of situation, as laid down by Regs, and it made sense in terrain this rough. There were too many folds and narrow valleys, too many slots through which an enemy could creep into attack range undetected if the pickets were spread too thinly to keep them all under observation.

But this time the perimeter had been too narrow, he realized in the moments he had left. The blood-red icon strobing viciously on his three-man command mount's display was over forty-five kilometers *outside* his perimeter. It was screaming towards him at almost Mach 4, and it had used that same tumbled terrain with deadly skill to evade detection until it was too late.

He keyed his com to bark orders he knew would be useless, but he never got the chance before the Bolo's infinite repeaters began to fire. The ten-centimeter ion bolts shrieked across the vanishing gap between it and Na-Torsah's fragile mounts, and fireballs bloomed like hideous roses with hearts of flame.

He watched the flowers blossoming, reaching for his own mount with dreadful, methodical speed.

The last Enemy air cav mount on her/their side of the perimeter vanished in a spit of flame, and her/their Hellbore fired once.

A battering ram of incandescent fury slammed into the Melconian transport. It was like striking an egg with a battle-ax. The blast of directed fusion ripped straight into the big ship's heart . . . and its antimatter reactor.

There was no need to fire at anything else within the LZ's perimeter, and she/they dove the pod into a narrow valley at a dangerously high velocity, driving hard to get a solid mountainside between her/them and the atmosphere-transmitted blast front ripping out from the sun-bright boil which had once been an interstellar ship.

Theslask Ka-Frahkan stared in disbelieving shock at the communicator display which had abruptly gone blank.

I *told him I'd keep the Humans too busy to come after him.
I told him that . . . and I was wrong.*

Bleak guilt hammered through him as the reality of Na-
Tharla's death slammed home. Almost two hundred of his
own artillerists had died with *Death Descending* and her crew,
but it was Na-Tharla's face Ka-Frahkan saw before him. The
face of the naval officer who had never questioned, who'd
performed his daily miracles for so many endless months just
to get them here.

Who had become Theslask Ka-Frahkhan's friend.

"Sir," Colonel Na-Salth said shakenly, "what—"

"It changes nothing," Ka-Frahkan said harshly. Na-Salth
looked at him, and the general showed his canines. "We've lost
our reserve ammunition, our spare parts, and our maintenance
facilities," he continued, "and we no longer have a starship of
our own. But the Humans are still here, still waiting for us to
kill them. And their industrial facilities are still here to support us after we do."

"Yes, sir. Of course," Na-Salth said after a moment, with just
a bit less assurance than Ka-Frahkan would have preferred.

"It's my fault," Ka-Frahkan admitted unflinchingly to his
second-in-command. Na-Salth's ears moved in an expression
of polite disagreement, and Ka-Frahkan snorted bitterly. "We
outnumber this Bolo by six-to-one in heavy mechs, alone. I
ought to have left at least one fist behind to provide additional
security."

"Sir, I completely agreed with the logic of your deploy-
ments."

"Then we were both wrong, weren't we?" Ka-Frahkan said
with mordant humor. Na-Salth started to say something more,
but the general cut him off with the wave of a hand. "Protecting
your line of retreat is fundamental to sound tactics, Jesmahr.
Admittedly, this is a special circumstance—literally, a do-or-die,
all-costs operation—but I still should have taken more precautions than I did. I think part of it may have been how well
aware I was of all of *Death Descending*'s serviceability problems.
I didn't think about the fact that the *Humans* wouldn't have

that information. They had to assume the ship was still fully operational. And if I'd considered that, I might have been able to at least use her as bait in a trap. In that case, her loss might actually have *accomplished* something. As it is—"

He shrugged, his expression bitter, and Na-Salth's ears flicked in an expression of agreement. Or acknowledgment, at least, Ka-Frahkan thought. Na-Salth was being kinder to him than he deserved, continuing to extend him the benefit of the doubt.

The general turned to his senior communications tech.

"Still no word from Captain Ka-Paldyn?" he asked quietly.

"None, sir. Not since his initial subspace flash that he'd succeeded in boarding the target." The noncommissioned officer looked up at his CO. "Still, sir, *Death Descending* did lose both her primary and secondary subspace arrays during the insertion maneuvers," he reminded Ka-Frahkan respectfully. "Captain Ka-Paldyn couldn't know that, so he may still be sending reports via subspace. In which case, we couldn't receive them anyway."

"Thank you, Sergeant," Ka-Frahkan said, and turned back to his tactical displays.

The sergeant was correct, of course . . . even if he was one more well-meaning subordinate doing his level best to keep the Old Man from worrying. But the cold ache in Ka-Frahkan's belly wouldn't go away. The continued silence from Ka-Paldyn weighed upon his soul almost as heavily as the destruction of *Death Descending*. He'd never had much hope that the inner-system special ops teams would manage to seize very many of the Human starships. But with both *Death Descending* and the surviving Human Bolo transport in his possession, he would have been well-placed to run down and capture those same starships after defeating the Bolo. Now it was beginning to look as if he would have neither of them, and without them, he felt his chances of gaining long-term control of the star system and placing a colony of the People here slipping through his claws like grains of sand.

None of which means the Humans will retain it, he thought grimly. *We can still insure* that *much, at least, and that was the primary mission all along.*

"Sir," Na-Salth said quietly. "We've located the Bolo."

✧   ✧   ✧

Major Beryak Na-Pahrthal's three-man command mount
swerved wildly, side-slipping to place a solid flank of mountainous rock between it and the nightmare demon which had
suddenly come screaming down from above him to sweep
through his lead battalion, thundering death as it came.

Na-Pahrthal had never personally encountered a Bolo transport pod. Although he'd been with the Brigade at Tricia's World,
they'd faced no Bolos there. And none of the combat reports
he'd reviewed, none of the simulations he'd worked through
in training, had ever pitted air cavalry mounts against a Bolo
docked with its pod. Even if it had not been self-evident suicide
for air cav to engage a Bolo under *any* circumstances, Bolos
never fought from their pods. By the time they joined combat against the People, they were on the ground, where they
belonged . . . and where a single lucky shot that brought down
a transport pod could not also destroy an entire Bolo.

But *this* Bolo didn't seem aware of that, and the sheer speed
of its pod—the preposterously agile maneuvers something that
size could perform this close to the ground—far exceeded anything Na-Pahrthal would have believed possible. It screamed
straight through Second Company, infinite repeaters flaming,
and Captain Ya-Fahln's mounts vanished like grain before the
reaper under that deadly thunder of ion bolts.

"Fall back!" Na-Pahrthal barked over the regimental command
net as his own pilot went side-slipping and swerving back to
the west, using every evasive maneuver he could think of. "Get
clear—fall back on the armored regiment!"

A handful of frantic acknowledgments came back from First
Company and Third Company. There was only silence on the
Second Company net.

She/they watched with the matching yet very different feroci-
ties of her/their organic and psychotronic halves as she/they
sliced through the advanced screen of the air cavalry which
had been harassing Fourth Battalion.

Maneka remembered the day, back on the planet of Santa

Cruz, when she and Benjy had gone to the firing range for the
first time and she'd truly recognized the staggering firepower
she controlled as Benjy's commander. She'd thought then that
nothing could ever make her more aware of the deadly power
of a Bolo, but she'd been wrong. Today, she didn't simply "command" Lazarus. She *was* Lazarus. The lethally accurate ion
bolts ripping from her/their infinite repeaters were hers, just
as much as his. It was as if she simply had to "look" at one
of the Dog Boy air cav mounts and imagine that sleek, speedy
vehicle's destruction to see it vanish in a teardrop of plunging
flame. It was that quick, that accurate . . . that deadly.

Only eleven of the sixty mounts in the Puppies' lead battalion survived long enough to fire back, and her/their battle
screen handled their pathetic attacks with contemptuous ease.
Another seven mounts were picked off by return fire, but four
managed to break and run quickly enough to evade her/their
fire and escape. She/they spent almost .0007 seconds considering whether or not to pursue them, but that was never truly
an option. She/they needed to get onto the ground and get
the pod out of the combat zone before any of the heavier
Melconian units got a shot at it.

<Beside Mary Lou's CP,> her/their Maneka half directed.
<Let's not squash her toes.>

<I shall endeavor to park the car with a modicum of com-
petence,> her/their Lazarus half responded dryly.

Major Mary Lou Atwater watched the assault pod come
whining quietly in. The plumes of funeral pyre smoke from an
entire battalion of Puppy air cavalry billowed skyward behind
it, and the major watched them rising with fierce satisfaction.
Those air cavalrymen hadn't posed *that* serious a threat to her
position, and her people had been well dug-in by the time they
arrived. But they'd still managed to kill two of her perimeter
pickets with their light weapons. If they'd continued to close,
her air-defense teams would have taught them the error of their
ways, but the Bolo's murderously efficient arrival had been a
thing of beauty for any ground-pounder.

The massive assault pod touched down with the delicacy of a soap bubble. The clear space she'd left beside her CP was at least twice as big as it had needed to be, she observed. Well, better safe than sorry.

"Glad to see you back," she said over her battle armor's com.

"I'm afraid we can't stay," Maneka Trevor's voice replied. Atwater still wasn't fully accustomed to the eerie note of almost detached calm she seemed to hear in it. Maybe it was just her imagination, she told herself again. And maybe it wasn't. After all, Maneka *was* linked with the Bolo's AI in a complete mental fusion.

"I know," the militia officer replied.

"Any wounded to send back?"

"No." Atwater grimaced. "I've got two KIA, but no wounded yet."

"I see." The human voice of the human/Bolo looming over her like a duralloy cliff paused for a moment. Then it continued. "In that case, we'll be moving out to deploy as planned. Keep your heads down."

"We'll try," Atwater assured her . . . or *them*, or whatever.

She stood back, and the pod wafted lightly back into the air once more.

Private Karsha Na-Varsk began to breathe once again as the Bolo and its pod disappeared to the west. He could hardly believe that it had failed to detect him, despite all of the stealth features designed into his one-man reconnaissance mount.

The small vehicle, less than an insect compared to the firepower of the gargantuan Bolo, lay as well-concealed as he had been able to contrive between a massive boulder and an overhanging, erosion-slashed cliff face. Na-Varsk himself was over two hundred meters from his mount, hidden under the thermal blanket's radar-absorbent, reactive camouflage material. That blanket was also supposed to conceal low and medium-powered electronics emissions, but Na-Varsk had always cherished a few personal reservations about its efficacy in that regard. Which was why, except for his communicator and power rifle, every item of electronic equipment had been switched off, and his com was set to receive-only. He was as close to invisible as it was possible for someone to become, and he raised his old-fashioned, pure-optic binoculars to study the Human infantry position below him once again.

It really was a perfect observation position, he thought with grim humor. He could see every detail of the Humans' deployment, count individual Human troopers and weapons positions. And, unlike the remote reconnaissance drones, he radiated no betraying flight signatures to give away his location. He'd thought Major Na-Pahrthal was being over-cautious to deploy him for this grounded reconnaissance assignment, but it appeared the major had known what he was doing, after all. Perhaps that was why he was a major, while Na-Varsk . . . wasn't.

Unfortunately, there wasn't a great deal that Na-Varsk could do with his perfect position at the moment. Oh, he might have picked off two or three of the Humans before they spotted him, although given the quality of Human powered armor, getting through it with a mere power rifle at this range would have been problematical. But killing a such a small handful of the enemy would have accomplished nothing. Besides, Na-Varsk was a trained scout, firmly imbued with the understanding that a pair of eyes and a com constituted a far more deadly weapon than any rifle.

Of course, he couldn't use that com without risking giving away his position, but Major Na-Pahrthal knew he was here. When the time came to attack the Human position in earnest, the major would be back in touch.

In the meantime, Na-Varsk occupied himself making sure his count of the enemy was complete.

7

"I am getting just a *bit* tired of this Bolo's . . . unconventionality," Theslask Ka-Frahkhan said with massive restraint as he and Colonel Na-Salth watched the icons of Major Na-Pahrthal's air cavalry regiment falling rapidly back upon the main force.

"I understand, sir," Na-Salth replied. "Still, these are only the opening steps of the dance. We already knew the Humans' military commander plans carefully and rationally. Surely it's hardly surprising that with the advantage of careful reconnaissance over a period of months he was able to predict our most probable axis of approach. And he obviously spent that same time considering his own opening moves in the event of an attack."

"Of course," Ka-Frahkan said just a bit impatiently. "But I don't like this fellow's operational . . . flexibility. He appears to be unfortunately gifted at what the Humans call 'thinking outside the box.' He should never have been prepared to risk bringing the Bolo into range of Ha-Kahm's air-defense systems and antitank batteries while it was still mated to its pod." The general's ears flattened. "One hit, Jesmahr—just *one* hit by one of Ha-Kahm's Hellbores—on that pod, and he could have lost pod *and* Bolo alike. But he chose to take the chance, and then he used the pod's mobility to effectively ambush Na-Pahrthal."

"I agree that he appears to be more innovative than I might wish, sir," Na-Salth agreed. "But even though the loss of *Death Descending* and our artillery support can't be considered anything other than a major blow, the losses Major Na-Pahrthal has suffered, while painful, scarcely constitute a significant reduction of our overall combat power. And, if I might be so bold as to point this out, sir, whatever he may have done to *us* so far pales to insignificance compared to what you managed to do to *him* by destroying his *second* Bolo before it was ever able to fire a single shot."

"Umph," Ka-Frahkan grunted, but he had to admit Na-Salth had a point. In every way that mattered as far as the accomplishment of his primary mission was concerned, the destruction of the second Bolo transport trumped the destruction of Na-Tharla's ship. There was the minor consideration that without *Death Descending*, the chance of any of his people ever getting home—or even surviving on this alien world—were slim, to say the very best. But even with the inferior individual capabilities of the Empire's heavy mechs, the 3172nd had an effective two-to-one advantage in combat power, thanks to the destruction of the second Bolo.

"You're probably right about the actual loss of combat strength, Jesmahr," he said after a moment. "In terms of hardware and firepower, at least. But don't forget the psychological aspect of it. Our people started out with the momentum on their side, knowing we'd taken out the other Bolo and gotten down without being intercepted. Now, though . . . *Now* the Humans have scored twice in a row, and gotten in and out cleanly both times, without taking so much as a scratch as far as we know. Do you think that isn't going to have an impact?"

Na-Salth looked at him, then flipped his ears in acknowledgment of Ka-Frahkan's point.

"I'm not saying I expect their morale to crumble like sand,

Jesmahr," Ka-Frahkan continued. "But what's happened *is* going to have an effect, at least until we land a few punches of our own. Our people are going to feel as if the momentum may be shifting to the Humans, and I wish I didn't suspect that whoever is directing their tactics had planned on creating exactly that effect from the beginning."

The assault pod landed over ninety kilometers west-northwest of Fourth Battalion. Maneka/Lazarus unlocked her/their tracks and rumbled clear of the pod, then activated its autopilot and sent it scudding back towards Landing.

Her/their Maneka component watched through her/their sensors as the pod disappeared and felt an undeniable surge of relief. She/they hated giving up the mobility advantage the pod had conferred, but she/they were simply too vulnerable in the air. And the pod was far too valuable—especially after the destruction of the full-capability Bolo depot aboard *Stalingrad*. It was inconceivable that she/they weren't going to take damage in the rapidly approaching battle. Indeed, the odds were no more than even that she/they would survive at all, despite all of her/their prebattle planning. If she/they did survive, however, the services of the automated depot in that pod, however limited, were going to be sorely needed.

She/they would truly have preferred to move directly, without delay, to this position after engaging the Melconian air cavalry. But if Major Atwater's militia had suffered casualties, the pod would have been the only way to get them back to the medical facilities of Landing, and her/their plans had always envisioned medevacing any wounded. Of course, there hadn't been any "wounded" this time, her/their Maneka half thought grimly. She was hugely relieved that Fourth Battalion's losses had been so light this far, but that didn't make the fact that two of Atwater's people were already dead any less painful. And the two people Fourth had already lost were probably far from the only casualties the militia were going to take, however well the rest of her/their plans worked out.

Maneka/Lazarus put that very human concern aside, pivoted

on her/their tracks, and headed still further west. Three exquisitely stealthed Melconian recon drones hovered above her/them, watching carefully, and she/they pretended—equally carefully—not to know they were there.

"*Now* what is the accursed thing doing?" Colonel Uran Na-Lythan snarled.

"Advancing towards us along Axis Two at approximately forty-seven kilometers per hour, sir," Major Sharal Sa-Thor, the commander of Na-Lythan's First Battalion, replied helpfully from the com screen on Na-Lythan's console, and Na-Lythan managed—somehow—not to bite the unfortunate officer's head off.

"I'm aware of that, Major," he said, instead, with massive restraint. "I'm simply wondering why it isn't doing anything about our recon platforms."

"Perhaps," Sa-Thor said, apparently unaware of the degree of self-control his superior was exercising, "it isn't aware that we have it under observation."

"It's a *Bolo*," Na-Lythan said, and this time Sa-Thor straightened his shoulders visibly in the com display as Na-Lythan's tone registered. "It knows the platforms are out there," the colonel continued in slightly less frigid tones. "It may not have detected them—although I find that difficult to believe—but even if it hasn't, it knows they *must* be out there. Yet it appears to be taking no measures to localize and destroy them. It isn't even *looking* for them. So either it's decided there's no point, that we'll simply replace them as quickly as it can destroy them, or else it *wants* us to know where it is and what it *appears* to be doing."

"Sir, I would respectfully suggest," Sa-Thor said very carefully, "that it's more probably the former possibility. Our supply of reconnaissance drones is scarcely unlimited, but we have more than enough to replace losses to its air-defense systems and keep it under observation over the span of a day or two."

"You may be correct," Na-Lythan conceded. "Certainly *I* can't think of any advantage to it in letting us know precisely where it is. I simply wish I were certain that *it* couldn't think of one."

He grimaced, ears flattened in thought for several heartbeats, then looked at his communications tech.

"Get me a link to General Ka-Frahkan."

"Do you think Uran has a point, sir?" Na-Salth asked.

"I'm certain he does," Ka-Frahkan said, trying not to sound testy as he bent over the terrain display, scrolling through maps. The original imagery from which those maps had been made had been lost along with *Death Descending*, but his command vehicle's computers had a copy of it. And, limited though they might be compared to the equivalent Human technology, they were quite capable of manipulating the radar map to generate the detailed three-dimensional terrain representation he required.

"I'm just uncertain as to *which* of his points is valid," the general continued.

He found the map he wanted, and the moving icon of the Bolo appeared upon it. The Human vehicle was headed directly towards his main body, just as Na-Lythan had reported. And as he scrolled ahead along the line of its probable advance, Ka-Frahkan realized it was making for a firing position from which it would be able to interdict at least two of his own possible approach axes with long-range Hellbore fire.

"This is where it's headed," he said, tapping the position with a claw.

"That's going to make difficulties," Na-Salth observed. He brought fresh data up on his own displays and considered it briefly. "Na-Lythan's battalions are approaching along both of those routes," he informed Ka-Frahkan. The general already knew that, of course, but it was one of Na-Salth's jobs to make certain that he did. "At the moment, First Battalion is ahead of schedule, sir. At present rate of advance, it will enter the Bolo's engagement range roughly twenty minutes after the Bolo's estimated time of arrival. Assuming that it stops there rather than continuing to advance to meet Major Sa-Thor, that is."

"I know," Ka-Frahkan murmured, rubbing the tip of his claw back and forth across the hilltop firing position. "But why is it telegraphing its tactics this way?" he continued.

"I beg your pardon, sir?" Na-Salth looked puzzled, and Ka-Frahkan snorted.

"Uran is absolutely correct," he said. "Even if the Bolo doesn't have positive locks on our drones, it has to know they're out there. Yet here it is, ambling towards its chosen position at barely half its top sustained speed, and I want to know why. It's faster than we are. If it had waited longer—let us get closer, move further apart—it could have drawn us out of position, off-balance. It could have used its sprint capability to move as quickly as possible into position, caught us separated. It could have gotten in between our armored battalions before we could react and engaged one of them at a time. As it is, we have ample time to react."

"Perhaps it doesn't realize that, sir. We've seen no evidence of *its* recon platforms, either, so perhaps it doesn't know our units' current positions and doesn't recognize the opportunity it's missing."

"We haven't seen any of its drones because it isn't using them," Ka-Frahkan replied. He looked back up at Na-Salth. "But this Human, whoever he is—this commander who thinks 'outside the box'—knows exactly where we are, Jesmahr. What he did to *Death Descending* would suggest that, but in my opinion, his present maneuvers prove it. If he felt the least uncertainty about our positions, he would be doing everything in his power to resolve it. And he would either not be moving at all while he used his own reconnaissance assets to find us, or else he would be moving at a higher rate of speed, in order to minimize his own window of vulnerability between chosen defensive positions."

"But how can he know where we are, sir? We destroyed all of their surveillance satellites on our way in."

"We *think* we destroyed them all," Ka-Frahkan corrected. "It's possible we missed one. I don't think that's what's happening here, however. *I* think, Jesmahr, that this particular Human has thoroughly seeded these mountains with pre-emplaced, ground-based, carefully concealed sensors. He has every approach route wired, and he's using secure, directional communication channels—or probably burst subspace transmissions, since Bolos, unlike our mechs, mount their own subspace coms—to monitor them. That's why he isn't expending drones tracking us; he already knows where we are."

"But in that case . . ." Na-Salth's voice trailed off, and Ka-Frahkan flicked his ears in emphatic agreement.

"In that case," he said, "he wants us to know where he is, and he's deliberately letting us know where he's *going*. And the only reason I can think of for him to do that is to maneuver us into doing what he wants."

"But what could he possibly want us to do, sir?"

"I don't know. That's what worries me," Ka-Frahkan admitted.

Maneka/Lazarus watched through the reconnaissance net as the Melconian advance slowed, then came—temporarily, at least—to a complete halt. She/they waited, while several minutes passed. Then the Enemy began to move once more, and her/their human component frowned in her command couch without ever opening her eyes.

The Enemy commander, she/they thought, was clearly more capable than she/they would have preferred. Which didn't exactly come as a surprise—an incompetent would never have managed to follow the colony fleet this far so tracelessly and then execute such a devastating initial surprise attack. Still, he was doing a part of what she/they wanted.

She/they continued to trundle leisurely along, but the Melconian formation was shifting. The Enemy's leading battalion of three *Surtur Alphas* and six *Fenrises* had begun falling back, accompanied by two of the infantry regiment's battalions and half of the armored regiment's twelve *Heimdalls*. The *second* armored battalion, with all six of the *Surtur Betas*, the other six *Heimdalls*, and the third infantry battalion, had changed course and begun to move rather more quickly. They were sliding to the south to advance along the one approach route which would bypass the blocking position towards which she/they were headed. That line of approach—the one she/they had designated Route Charlie—wasn't the shortest one, but unless she/they also changed course in the next few minutes, the Melconian units advancing along it would get clear around her/their flank without ever exposing themselves to her/their direct fire. She/they could still loft missiles onto their route, but with only a single Bolo's missile load-out and launchers, it would be virtually impossible to sufficiently saturate a Melconian armored battalion's missile defenses to get through them, and an entire mountainside would block Hellbore fire at their closest approach.

She/they considered the timing. If she/they continued on her/their current heading at current speed, the flanking column would be past any point at which she/they could subsequently intercept it short of Fourth Battalion's position in another twelve minutes. And, if that column got past her/them, worst-case, Fourth Battalion would find itself ground into the mud under the tracks of a full battalion of heavy armored vehicles. *Best* case, she/they would find themselves trapped in a constricted, mountainous valley between *both* Dog Boy armored battalions while the Enemy ignored the Fourth to concentrate on killing her/them.

Pity. She/they had rather hoped the Puppies' CO would decide to send all of his mechs around her/their flank. Unfortunately, he'd turned out to be too wary for that.

"*Now* it begins to retreat!" Ka-Frahkan flapped his ears in frustration. "Nameless Ones! What sort of game is this damned machine playing?!"

The Bolo icon on his display had, indeed, begun to retreat—and at a far higher rate of speed, at that. But it was too late. Major Julhar Ha-Shan's Second Armored Battalion and Major Thuran Ha-Nashum's Third Infantry were already past it. The Bolo was faster than Ha-Shan's heavies, but it also had much further to go if it wanted to retreat to its militia blocking position before Ha-Shan and Ha-Nashum reached it, and there was no way even a Bolo could catch them now without using the pod in which it was no longer mounted.

But why had it waited so long?

Of course, Na-Lythan's First Armored Battalion and the rest of Colonel Ka-Somal's infantry were also advancing once more, along the route Ka-Frahkan had designated Axis Three, if much more slowly and cautiously than Ha-Shan's battalion. They would have entered the Bolo's engagement range, had it continued to advance on its original course, within another thirty minutes or so. The fight when they reached that point would have been ugly, and Ka-Frahkan was far from certain of what its final outcome would have been, given how the Human machine's individual power and superior technology would have offset his own forces' advantages in tonnage, numbers, and *combined* firepower. He'd been willing to court the engagement anyway, however, if it would have pinned the Bolo in place while Second Armored got on with the business of destroying the blocking position and advanced upon the colony itself. That was why he'd held First Armored back and sent Ha-Shan ahead. Sa-Thor's heavies were marginally better suited to a direct engagement against the Bolo, and Ha-Shan's additional missile power would make his battalion far more dangerous to the Human settlement once he got past the blocking militia.

But now the accursed Bolo seemed unwilling to give him that engagement . . . even though it was self-evidently too late for it to reverse course and intercept Second Armored!

Theslask Ka-Frahkhan glared at his tactical plot and tried not to grind his teeth together as he tried to deduce just what hellish surprise the Bolo and its Human commander were attempting to spring upon him.

Maneka/Lazarus monitored the flanking column's position carefully. It was continuing to advance, and she/they were tempted to continue *her/their* advance and engage the remainder of the Melconian force head on. Unfortunately, if she/they did, the main Puppy column would engage her/them well before the flanking column reached the decisive point. It was as certain as anything could be that she/they would have taken damage in that engagement, and she/they could not afford to risk that. Not yet. The flanking column had to be dealt with before she/they could accept any reduction in her/their own capabilities.

<Timing,> her/their human half thought. <It's all a matter of timing, now.>

<It always is,> her/their Bolo half replied.

Captain Farka Na-Rohrn felt his spirits rising as Second Armored Battalion thundered eastward behind his *Heimdall*. He could see the Human Bolo on his tactical display, although there were enough mountains between them to prevent *it* from seeing *him*, praise the Nameless Lord! And while Na-Rohrn had never claimed to be a tactical genius, it seemed obvious to him that the Bolo had made a fatal error. The positions and maximum possible rates of advance indicated on his display made it abundantly clear that there was, quite simply, no possible way for the Bolo to intercept Major Ha-Shan's armor and Major Ha-Nashum's infantry before they wiped out the Human militia positioned to stop them. And after that, there would be nothing between them and the Human colony.

But first they had to get there, and even the best of approach routes, he thought, grimacing at his map display, had its inconvenient aspects.

"Major Ha-Shan," Na-Rohrn said into his com, "we're coming up on a particularly narrow bit. My units are going to have to shift into single column."

"Understood," Ha-Shan replied crisply and instantly. "Major Ha-Nashum, do you copy?"

"I do," the infantry battalion's CO responded. "My Alpha Company will take point, ahead of Captain Na-Rohrn. The rest of my people will fall in behind your battalion."

"Excellent," Ha-Shan said, and began passing the necessary orders to his own units as the Third Infantry's Alpha Company's lighter, faster armored personnel carriers sped ahead to join the *Heimdalls*.

❖   ❖   ❖

Now, Maneka/Lazarus thought, and opened her/their missile hatches. There was no need to adjust the firing queue; she/they had set it up literally hours ago. Now she/they enabled the missiles and fired.

There were only six of them, and she/they had added the rather special warheads they mounted to her/their normal ammunition mix in place of the same number of more conventional warheads over three weeks ago. Now the missiles carrying those warheads erupted from the heavily armored wells of her/their vertical-launch missile system and rose on pillars of flame until they were high enough for their counter-gravity drives to take over. Then the thundering wakes of fire vanished, and the missiles screamed suddenly southeastward at seven times the speed of sound.

"General Ka-Frahkan!" a sensor tech said sharply. "The Bolo has just launched missiles!"

"At us?" Ka-Frahkan demanded, spinning around to face the master tactical plot.

"No, sir," the noncom replied in puzzled tones. "At Colonel Ha-Shan."

"Incoming!" Ha-Shan's sensor operator announced suddenly. "Multiple—*six* incoming from the Bolo, sir! Mach seven!"

Ha-Shan's eyes instantly found the missile icons on his own display. Even at that velocity, there was plenty of time, he thought as the targeting systems of his armored units' antimissile defenses turned onto the threat bearing. Besides, that was a ridiculously low number of missiles for a target like his. His command *Surtur* alone could have defeated all of them with ease, Human technology or no. So what was the damned Bolo up to *now*?

"Impact projection," the sensor operator said, and Ha-Shan blinked.

That couldn't be right! He looked at the visual display showing the terrain directly to his west. The river-cut valley through which his battalion was currently passing had, indeed, grown

narrower, with precipicelike cliffs looming on both sides. The
ones to the west were both higher and steeper than the ones to
the east, and if the missiles' impact point was properly projected,
all six of them were going to land harmlessly on the other side
of the mountain which reared that protective rampart. Which
was stupid. Yet one thing no Bolo had ever been accused of was
stupidity, so what—?

The same mountains which protected the Melconian column
from Maneka/Lazarus' direct fire also protected her/their missiles from interception. They sped directly to their targets,
separating, spreading out, adjusting their trajectories with
finicky precision.

At precisely the correct moment, all six of them killed their
drives and continued onward at just over seven thousand kilometers per hour. They slammed into the mountainside, and
the superdense, ballistically shaped deep-penetrator warheads
she/they had mounted upon them drilled through solid earth
and stone like hypervelocity bullets. They plunged deep into
the heart of the mountain, driving directly into the fault pattern Maneka/Lazarus' deep scan radar mapping had revealed
weeks before.

And then six megaton-range warheads detonated as one.

The stupendous shockwave was enough to shake even a *Surtur* like a toy. Ha-Shan had never experienced an earthquake
before, and he was ill-prepared to feel his 18,000-ton mech
shivering like a frightened child. But *Surturs* were designed
and engineered to survive far worse than a little shaking, and
he felt his speeding pulse begin to slow once more.

Until he looked into the visual display again.

So that was what the Human was thinking, Theslask Ka-
Frahkhan thought. He was too calm about it, a corner of
his own brain told him. Shock, he supposed. *I should have
listened to my instincts. But even if I had, what else could I
have done with what I knew?*

He had no answer for the question, and he knew he never would. But he'd been right about this particular Human's ability to "think outside the box," hadn't he?

He watched the thick, curdled cloud of dust rising above what had once been a river valley. Perhaps it would be a river valley again, someday. But at this moment, it was the huge common grave which had just engulfed half of the 3172nd Heavy Assault Brigade's armor and a third of its infantry. The horrendous landslide the Bolo's missiles had triggered had sent two-thirds of a mountain sliding unstoppably across Second Armored and Third Infantry. There were, he already knew, no survivors from either, although the handful of Na-Pahrthal's air cav which had been assigned to Ha-Shan had probably been able to climb out of destruction's path in time.

He turned his head slowly and looked at Na-Salth. The colonel was still staring slack-jawed at the unbelievable sight on his visual display.

"Contact Colonel Na-Lythan and Colonel Ka-Somal," Ka-Frahkan heard his own voice saying with a flat, steady calm. Na-Salth turned stunned eyes towards him. "Tell them both that I want their recon elements to begin deploying seismic sensors immediately. They're to use the sensors and sounding charges, as well as the *Heimdalls*' sonar and deep-scan radar, to check for additional fault lines. I doubt very much that there are more of them out here, but I could be wrong, and this Human devil is *not* going to lead us into any more ambushes like that one."

He stabbed the visual display with a vicious claw and the soft echo of a barely audible challenge snarl.

"No more finesse, Jesmahr," he said grimly, harshly. "I don't care what the Bolo does. We will advance at our own chosen rate. We will check every valley, every cliff, for booby traps and dangerous terrain features. Eventually that Nameless-cursed Bolo will have to stop and fight us on *our* terms. And when it does, we *will* destroy it."

Maneka/Lazarus launched a single recon drone. She/they had no choice; the landslide which had enveloped the Enemy column had also wiped out the sensors with which that stretch of river valley had been seeded.

The drone swept over what had once been the valley, and her/their human half felt a chill as she/they surveyed the desolation. Her/their missiles had shattered an entire mountain, disemboweled it and spewed its fragments across the Melconians in an unstoppable tidal wave of broken rock, shattered trees, and dirt. The river was already beginning to back up behind the solid plug of debris, and she/they saw the rising water lapping at a single Melconian corpse. From its equipment, it had been an infantryman, probably one of the advance scouts probing ahead of the Enemy column on their one-man grav-scooters. But he hadn't been far enough ahead. Two-thirds of his body was buried under the huge boulder which had come bounding down to crush the life out of him. He lay face-down, one arm and shoulder protruding from the rubble and earth, and the clawed fingers of his raised hand seemed to be reaching for the heavens, as if to hang onto his life for just a moment longer.

There was something inexpressibly poignant about that sight. Her/their Maneka half felt it, yet the poignancy deflected neither her/their satisfaction, nor her/their grim determination to inflict the same destruction upon the rest of the Enemy.

She/they made one more sweep of the site with the reconnaissance drone. It was remotely possible that there might be one or two Enemy survivors, she/they decided, but there could not be more, and all of the Enemy armored battalion's mechs had been positively accounted for.

<Which means the odds are even now,> her/their Maneka half thought grimly.

<Which means the odds would be even against a fully modern Bolo,> her/their Lazarus half replied.

<Maybe.>

In the corner of their fusion which was hers alone, Maneka felt Lazarus' amusement at her qualification, and she understood it. The equation which set one Bolo as equivalent to three times its own number of Melconian heavy combat mechs was, after all, as Lazarus had just pointed out, based upon the combat capabilities of the Mark XXXIs and Mark XXXIIs, not a Bolo whose basic weapons were well over a century out of date. But Maneka had been at Chartres. She *knew* what those "obsolete" Bolos were capable of.

She felt Lazarus standing just outside that small, private section of her mind, waiting for her calmly, and the lips of her sleeping body twitched in a slight smile.

<Okay,> she told him. <We can go now.>

Her/their mighty hull pivoted on its broad tracks and began to move once more.

"It's moving again, sir."

Ka-Frahkan flicked his ears in silent acknowledgment. He sat back in his command chair, watching the tactical display, and just the tips of his canines showed as his upper lip curled back from them.

The Bolo was moving directly back towards his remaining armored battalion once more, reversing the course away from it which had so puzzled him before. It puzzled him no longer, for he understood now why it had not initially completed its advance to the firing position he'd thought it was headed for.

The position I obligingly allowed it to convince *me it was headed for*, he corrected bitterly. Then he gave himself a mental shake. There would be time enough for grief and self-recrimination after the battle, and even now he knew—intellectually, at least—that without any foreknowledge of the fault line the Bolo had exploited, he'd done exactly the right thing. Or, at least, that a dispassionate staff study, far away from the buried, mangled bodies of a quarter of his brigade's troopers, would conclude that he had, at any rate.

No time for that, he reminded himself sternly. *Not when I still have to figure out what to do about the accursed thing.*

At least the Bolo still faced a few problems of its own.

It hadn't had any choice but to avoid combat with Na-Lythan's First Armored Battalion until after it had destroyed

Second Armored. But when it retreated rather than continuing its advance, it had allowed Na-Lythan and the rest of Ka-Somal's infantry vehicles to move ahead at their top combined speed. Slower than a Bolo they undoubtedly were, but they were fast enough to have reached the point at which the other two possible routes of advance converged and then diverged once again while the Bolo was elsewhere.

"We'll split our forces, Jesmahr," he announced. His executive officer looked at him, and the general bared his fangs mirthlessly.

"Ka-Somal will take Axis One," he said. "He'll have to move back to the west a bit to cut across to One, but he's faster than our heavy mechs. He's got the time, and we'll give him the rest of the reconnaissance mechs—they're fast enough to keep up with his APCs and agile enough to get through that—" he jerked his head at the ugly spill of the landslide "—as well. And we'll give him all of Na-Pahrthal's remaining air cavalry, as well."

"Yes, sir. And First Armored?" Na-Salth said as Ka-Frahkan paused.

"Uran will take First Armored down Axis Three."

"If we remain concentrated, we'll have more firepower to deal with the Bolo," Na-Salth pointed out respectfully.

"Ka-Somal's infantry won't be much use against a Bolo in a frontal engagement," Ka-Frahkan replied, "and in this terrain, it's going to be a head-on meeting for Uran's mechs, whenever it comes. But between both of his remaining battalions, the recon mechs, and Na-Pahrthal's air cav, Ka-Somal ought to have an effective superiority against the militia in that dammed blocking position."

"But even if he docs, sir," Na-Salth said, even more respectfully, "our long-range drones have confirmed that the Humans have at least two additional militia battalions digging in closer to their settlement. Ka-Somal doesn't begin to have the firepower to break through that sort of opposition without Uran's support. And he'll take losses against the blocking position, probably serious ones, even if he manages to take it in the end."

"I'm aware of that," Ka-Frahkan said grimly. He turned to face Na-Salth fully. "Ka-Somal is a diversion—a bluff."

"A diversion, sir?" Na-Salth repeated.

"By splitting up now, we force the Bolo to choose which of our two columns to pursue. It can catch either one of them short of the militia's position; it can't possibly catch both of them. Our armored units obviously pose the greater threat, and that makes them the logical column for the Bolo to pursue. But Axis Three is the longer approach route by a considerable margin, and Uran's mechs will be slower than Ka-Somal's column. It's possible the Bolo will choose to pursue Ka-Somal instead of following Uran because it would probably be able to overtake and destroy him and still have time—barely—to return down Axis *Three* and catch First Armored from behind before Uran can get his *Fenrises'* missile batteries into range of the blocking position."

"What if it opts to retreat back down Axis Two, sir? In that case, it could reach the blocking position ahead of either of us."

"True, but it won't," Ka-Frahkan said with bleak confidence. "It could beat us back, but if it did, our mechs would be able to bring their missile batteries into range of the militia position before it could engage us. The intervening terrain would cover our approach too well for it to prevent us from firing, and none of its infantry supports would survive that sort of fire." He flattened his ears in negation. "No. It will come after at least one of our columns, Jesmahr."

Na-Salth considered for a moment, then flipped his ears in agreement, and the general continued.

"If it decides to go after Uran first, it won't be able to turn around afterward and catch Ka-Somal the same way, though. Even if it took no mobility damage at all against First Armored—and it most certainly would— the delay would make it impossible for it to move back and intercept Ka-Somal before his units get past the landslide it induced, and it couldn't possibly get through that obstruction itself to follow him down Axis One. So if it doesn't go after Ka-Somal *now*, it won't be able to prevent him from getting to grips with the infantry in its blocking position whatever it does to First Armored.

"If it does decide to pursue and overtake Ka-Somal, it will undoubtedly destroy his infantry," Ka-Frahkan went on unflinchingly. "In the process, however, it may take damage of its own. It will certainly expend ammunition, and if Ka-Somal makes skillful use of his nuclear demolition charges, he may well succeed in inflicting significant damage, which might give Uran a decisive advantage when he finally engages it. Given the limited utility of our infantry in an armored engagement, we won't lose that much effective capability whatever happens to Ka-Somal. If he can wear it down a little, give Uran the edge he needs, the sacrifice will be well worth it. In either case, whether Ka-Somal can damage it or not, simply pursuing his infantry will delay it, possibly long enough—depending on how long it takes it to destroy Ka-Somal—for Uran to reach the blocking position and destroy its infantry before it can intervene. And if Uran can punch out the militia quickly, his *Fenrises*, at least, would probably have the speed to reach the colony before the Bolo could prevent them from doing so.

"If, on the other hand, the Bolo opts to pursue First Armored, Ka-Somal's infantry will at least be out of the line of fire when Uran's mechs meet it. He has at least an even chance of destroying the Bolo, whether Ka-Somal has weakened it first or not, but he'll take serious losses doing so. If Ka-Somal's infantry is still intact, it will be able to support Uran's own survivors effectively when he moves against the remainder of the Humans' forces. So, either the Bolo follows Ka-Somal and destroys him, possibly taking damage itself in the process, or else sending Ka-Somal down Axis One is a way to preserve his forces for later use."

Na-Salth said nothing for a moment. Ka-Frahkan hadn't asked his approval for the plan, after all. But that wasn't what kept him silent. What the general had said about the survivability of infantry in a battle between heavy armored units was self-evidently true, yet expending Ka-Somal's infantry in an engagement which offered at least the possibility of decreasing the Bolo's combat capability before the decisive engagement against Na-Lythan made sense in the cold-blooded calculus of war. And the one way to insure that the infantry had the opportunity to damage the Bolo was to keep the entire force together, *compel* the Bolo to confront the infantry before it could reach the armored units.

But Ka-Somal's two intact battalions represented over eighty-five percent of their total surviving personnel. If they died, there would be far too few of the People left in the star system for the general's cherished plan to establish an imperial colony here.

Na-Salth looked into his commander's eyes for another moment, then raised his ears in acceptance.

"Yes, sir," he said, and began issuing orders.

Maneka/Lazarus watched the Enemy force split up.

<I didn't expect that,> her/their Maneka half said as she/they continued to advance rapidly towards the point at which the Enemy had fallen into two columns.

<Nor did I. Analysis of standard Enemy tactics and the decisions to date of this Enemy commander suggested a probability of 87.031 percent that he would maintain concentration of his forces,> her/their Lazarus half replied.

<Makes sense, though, I suppose,> Maneka said. <Their infantry won't be much help in a standup fight with their armor.>

<Probability of Enemy infantry inflicting significant damage upon this unit under those circumstances does not exceed 15.02 percent,> Lazarus agreed. <However, probability of an Enemy infantry screen in hasty defensive positions in this terrain inflicting significant, though not incapacitating, damage before its destruction *prior* to the armored engagement approaches 62.47 percent.>

<Then why didn't he stay concentrated? He could easily have deployed an infantry screen at any number of points along the route of advance he's following. At the least, that would have forced us to fight our way through it just to get to his mechs.

At the best, it might have delayed us long enough for the mechs to overrun the Fourth before we could intervene.>

<Indeed. Which was the reason I assigned a probability of only 14.969 percent that he would fail to do so. I have no explanation for his actual decision, aside from the obvious fact that it compels us to decide which force to pursue.>

Times and distances, movement rates, and weapons capabilities flickered through her/their shared awareness at psychotronic speed. The decision was self-evident. The Enemy's remaining armored battalion represented the only true threat to the colony, regardless of what happened to Mary Lou Atwater's command. The destruction of the *Surturs* and their supporting *Fenrises* took absolute priority, and if she/they went after the infantry first, there was a chance, however minor, that it might degrade her/their combat capability before the decisive engagement.

"So we're going after the armor," Maneka Trevor's image said from the small com display window opened in the corner of Major Atwater's visor HUD. "We may've taken out their *Betas'* missiles, but we've got to keep the missile batteries on their remaining *Fenrises* at least eighty kilometers from your position, and that means killing them well short of that point. Which, I'm afraid, also means their infantry is going to reach your perimeter before we can get back to you. But with a little luck, at least you won't have their armored units shooting at you at the same time."

"Understood," Atwater said, hoping she sounded more cheerful than she felt. Two battalions of Dog Boy infantry, especially with a half-dozen *Heimdalls* and a hundred or so air cav mounts along to help them out, was going to be pretty stiff odds for her single battalion, despite the superiority of its individual weapons and the advantage of its prepared positions. The numerical odds would be almost four-to-one, and Melconian infantry carried a lot of man-portable antiarmor weapons in partial compensation for its lack of powered combat armor.

On the other hand, she thought grimly, *our chances against their infantry are going to be one hell of a lot better than our chances against their armor would be. Or than* her *chances against their armor will be.*

"Good luck, Mary Lou," Maneka said.

"And to you," Atwater replied. She managed a taut smile. "Drop by when you get a chance. We'll still be here."

8

So it's still following us.

Theslask Ka-Frahkan watched the Bolo's icon reach the point where Axis Two and Axis Three diverged. Instead of continuing further west along Axis Two to reach Axis One, it had turned south to come speeding after Na-Lythan's surviving mechs, and a strange, singing calmness seemed to flow through him.

The Bolo's decision wasn't really a surprise. He'd never truly expected the Human machine to give his own armor what amounted to a free run into missile range of the militia blocking position. The tactician in him rather regretted that it hadn't, but truth to tell, deep inside, he was almost glad. Whatever he might have chosen to tell Na-Salth, he'd known all along that this was the most probable outcome of his decision to divide his forces. Which, of course, was the reason his command vehicle was accompanying First Armored instead of Colonel Ka-Somal's column.

His mind ran back over the balance of combat power yet again, bitterly regretting the loss of his other armored battalion.

If only he hadn't allowed his own tactical opportunism to lure him into doing exactly what the Bolo and its commander had wanted! He should have realized no Bolo would have offered such an opening unless it *wanted* its opponents to take it and so rejected it, continuing to close for the head-on armored slugfest his superior numbers would surely have permitted him to win. Yet even now, he knew he would have done exactly the same thing given the same opportunity and knowledge. The chance to avoid the Bolo until after he had achieved his objective—or even to catch it between his two armored regiments—had simply been too good to pass up. Especially when the nature of the devilish trap had been completely impossible to deduce ahead of time.

But whether he had been right or wrong, he still had to deal with the consequences of his decision. And the consequences were that his original clear advantage in combat power had been wiped away.

The missile armament of his six *Fenrises* would probably allow him to land the first blows, inflict the first damage. But after they had emptied their single-shot missile pods, the *Fenrises* would be hopelessly outclassed by the Bolo, unless they could somehow get around to its more lightly armored flanks. That was scarcely likely in such constricted terrain, and even if it proved possible, a Bolo's side armor, though much thinner than its frontal armor, was still heavy enough to make it far from certain that a *Fenris'* main weapon could penetrate it. Which meant the main engagement would fall heavily upon his three *Surturs*.

The outcome would hang from a thread, whatever happened, and Na-Salth had been right. Holding the infantry to support the armor might well have tipped the balance in his favor. So why hadn't he done that? He'd already made one suspect decision this day; had he made a second? Had he allowed emotions, his own perhaps foolish hope that the People might still survive upon this planet, to dictate his decisions? *Would* Ka-Somal's infantry have made the difference between victory and defeat if he'd hung on to it, deployed Ka-Somal's two remaining battalions as a sacrificial screen?

There was no way to know, and, anyway, the decision had already been made. The pieces were in motion for the final confrontation, and the outcome would be whatever the Nameless Lord willed it to be.

Colonel Verank Ka-Somal swore venomously as his command vehicle lurched and bounced over the nightmare landscape the accursed Humans' landslide had left to mark the massacre of the Second Armored and his own Third Infantry Battalion. More death, more slaughter, he thought, and hatred for the species which had murdered his own world, and with it his wife, children, and family, swirled at his core like slow, thick lava.

The repeater plot tied into the far more capable tactical computers aboard General Ka-Frahkan's brigade command vehicle showed him the Bolo, moving rapidly away from his own position. He knew, in the intellectual, professional part of him which had graduated from the Emperor Yarthaaisun Army Academy so many years before, that his infantry and the supporting reconnaissance mechs would have stood no chance at all against the Bolo, had it chosen to pursue his column, instead. But the part of him which remembered the devastated landscape of Rasantha—of the planet upon which he had been born and upon which his children, his wife, his parents and siblings, had died under the devastating onslaught of *other* Bolos—clung to that receding icon with the hungry fingers of hate.

Others might still clutch at the hope Ka-Frahkan had offered—the hope that they might yet somehow, miraculously, capture sufficient of the Humans' industrial infrastructure, enough of their starships, to someday make their way home again. Or to the other hope, that they might survive here, instead. Build a new colony, keep the Empire alive, even if all of the rest of the People went down to death elsewhere.

Ka-Somal did not. There was no future. Not for him, not for Ka-Frahkan, not for the Empire, not even for the People. There was only vengeance. Only death returned for death.

And so, even while his eyes clung to the Bolo's icon and he longed to blot that icon away with his own weapons—with his own naked, bloody fists and fangs—another part of him was glad to see it go. Perhaps Na-Lythan could destroy it, after all. Perhaps enough of his mechs to make a difference would actually survive. But whether that happened or not, the Bolo's decision to pursue Na-Lythan meant *Ka-Somal* would reach the militia position.

And so, whatever else happened, he would have the chance to kill at least a few more Humans before the Bolo returned to kill him.

Private Na-Varsk lay under his concealing camouflage, watching the Human infantry so far below him, and wondered what was happening to the rest of the Brigade.

Major Na-Pahrthal's pilot banked around another bend in the river valley, and the major wondered if the pilot was as astonished as he himself was that they'd managed to escape the Bolo's onslaught alive. The fact that they had was largely due to Flight Sergeant Sa-Horuk's skill, and Na-Pahrthal made a mental note to be sure Sa-Horuk knew he recognized that when this was all over.

The major's ears twitched in bitter amusement at the thought. Was he making that note to be sure Sa-Horuk got the credit he deserved? Or because making it implied that there was at least a slim chance that Na-Pahrthal would be alive to extend it?

He shook the thought aside. There was no time for it, and he returned his full attention to the valley's terrain.

The landslide-choked gorge, and the new lake rapidly forming behind it, lay far to the west as he and his surviving air cavalry scouted ahead of Colonel Ka-Somal's column. The *Heimdalls* Colonel Na-Lythan had detached to accompany the infantry were coming up quickly astern of Na-Pahrthal's aerial units, but the infantry, in its less capable APCs, lagged behind, still making up the distance it had lost after being delayed by the landslide.

Na-Pahrthal checked his own displays again. The repeater relaying the imagery from General Ka-Frahkan's vehicle showed him the Bolo, closing rapidly now with the rear of Na-Lythan's remaining battalion. After what that demonic machine had already done to the Brigade, Na-Pahrthal found it impossible, however hard he tried, to feel confident about what would happen when it caught up with First Armored. And in the end, if Colonel Na-Lythan couldn't stop it after all, anything the rest of them might accomplish wouldn't matter very much, he supposed.

He wondered if Ka-Somal would delay his own attack until he knew the outcome of the armored battle about to begin. If Na-Lythan won, then delaying until his surviving armored units could arrive to support Ka-Somal's attack would save hundreds of casualties, and possibly make the difference between being able to continue the attack against the Humans' other forces or simply bleeding themselves white in an ultimately meaningless battle of attrition against the blocking position. But if Na-Lythan *lost*, then delaying the attack would only give the Bolo time to come charging up to support the Human militia with its remaining weapons. In which case, they would be able to kill far fewer of the Humans before they died themselves.

In another war, against another enemy, there might have been other options to ponder. The possibility of honorable surrender might even have existed. But this was the war they had, and however desperately some inner part of him might have longed for it to be otherwise, Major Beryak Na-Pahrthal could no longer truly imagine any other sort.

"Uniform-Three-Seven, this is Alpha-Zero-One." he said into his microphone. "Watch those turns. You're sliding too high, skylining yourself. Do that closer to the enemy, and he'll blow you right out of the air!"

"Alpha-Zero-One, Uniform-Three-Seven copies. Sorry about that, sir. I'll try not to let it happen again."

"You do that, Tharsal," Na-Pahrthal said. "I'd hate to have to break in a new horrible example to show the others how *not* to fly a mission."

"Yes, sir. Uniform-Three-Seven, out."

"Alpha-Zero-One, out," Na-Pahrthal acknowledged, and his ears twitched in another flicker of wryly bitter amusement. So they were *all* still playing the game, still pretending.

Odd how precious that threadbare pretense could be, even now.

"The Bolo is already inside our mediums' effective engagement range, sir," Colonel Na-Lythan said levelly. "It will overtake us completely in no more than another twenty minutes at our relative rates of advance, and this looks like as likely a place as we're going to find, especially if we can keep that ridge line between us and it until we launch. With your permission, I'd like to begin deploying my units."

"Uran, they're *your* units," Ka-Frahkan replied over the com. "If this is the spot you want, then go ahead and deploy. For what it's worth, I'm formally handing tactical control over to you. May the Nameless Ones send you victory."

"Thank you, sir," Na-Lythan acknowledged. And then, without a pause, he began issuing his orders.

Maneka/Lazarus weren't surprised when the Enemy slowed in his headlong rush. The terrain ahead was as favorable to him as any he might have hoped to find, and she/they slowed her/their own approach, watching to see how the Enemy commander deployed his assets.

<He's not exactly trying for finesse, is he?> her/their human half observed wryly as her individual viewpoint rose briefly above the fusion of their personalities and perceptions.

<It is not a situation which calls for finesse,> her/their Bolo half replied. <Their commander is wise enough to recognize that.>

Maneka agreed wordlessly, and then her merely human viewpoint vanished once more as she/they bent their attention upon the developing patterns of the Enemy's deployment.

Actually, she/they thought, he *was* trying for at least a little finesse. The tactical situation was brutally simple for both sides, but he was deliberately placing two of his three "fists" well forward of the third. In essence, he was writing off two thirds of his total strength, positioning those units to take the brunt of her/their assault and accepting that they *would* be destroyed, rather than bringing his full firepower to bear from the beginning. Clearly, he hoped that before they were destroyed, they would inflict serious damage upon her/them—enough for his own fresh, undamaged fist to finish her/them off without suffering heavy losses of its own. In which case, he would almost certainly come out of the engagement with sufficient remaining combat power to carry through and destroy the colony, after all.

<Probability of our destruction by forward-deployed fists, 36.012 percent; probability of their destruction, 93.562 percent,> her/their Lazarus component remarked. <Probability of our destruction by remaining fist after destroying lead fists, 56.912 percent. Probability of colony's survival following our own destruction or incapacitation becomes 73.64 percent, assuming destruction of all remaining *Surturs* and expenditure of all *Fenrises'* missile armament against us. Probability of colony's survival, assuming survival of one *Surtur* becomes 32.035 percent. Probability of colony's survival, assuming survival of two *Surturs*, becomes 01.056 percent. Survival of each *Fenris* with no remaining missile armament decreases probability of colony's survival by approximately 06.753 percent. Survival of one *Fenris* with unexpended missile load-out decreases probability of colony's survival by approximately 32.116 percent. Survival of two *Fenrises* with unexpended missile load-out decreases probability of colony's survival to under one percent, exclusive of any consideration of surviving *Surturs*.>

<Then we'll just have to see to it that *none* of them survive, won't we?> her/their Maneka half replied coldly.

"All units, stand by. Prepare for Fire Plan Alpha on my command."

Uran Na-Lythan's voice was terse, shadowed with tension and yet curiously relaxed, almost calming. Ka-Frahkan listened to it, hearing an echo of the strange serenity which seemed to hover at his own center, and wondered what the colonel was actually thinking as the Bolo ground steadily towards his units.

· *How did it all begin?* The thought eddied through the back of Ka-Frahkan's brain with peculiar clarity. He knew the official version, knew Imperial Intelligence genuinely believed, after the most thorough analysis possible, that the Humans had fired first in the Trellis System. *But what if they did? Or what if we did? Can any of it truly justify our long, bloody journey to this moment? We're not killing just one another's soldiers—we're killing everything. Killing ourselves, because in our own pain, both sides give the other countless reasons to kill us, just as we kill them. Cities, star systems . . . families. Lord of the Nameless, how did we come to this? And what does it say of me that I have brought the killing here, to this star, this planet? Given my own people to the furnace in an effort to destroy a colony the Humans may never know ever even existed? What does that make me? Hero and champion of the People? Or red-clawed butcher, too stupid and crazed with blood to recognize his own insanity?*

His ears folded tight to his skull as the questions rolled through his mind.

But in the end, it doesn't really matter, does it? he told himself sadly. *Butcher or champion, I have no choice now. None of us do—Human or of the People. We have saddled the whirlwind; now we must ride it and pray that somehow the bridle holds. That we can stay in the saddle one battle longer, one living star system farther, than they can. And so I will drown this world in blood, because I must. Because I cannot take the chance, cannot risk holding my hand. And in the end, somewhere, some other general—Melconian or Human—will have to make one final decision when the last world of his own race's murderers lies helpless before him.*

And that general will not be me. Ka-Frahkan eyes narrowed as he recognized the source of his strange inner serenity at last. It was knowledge, acceptance. *I will die here, on this world,* he realized. *If not in this minute, or this hour, still, I will die here. Ka-Paldyn is gone, or he would have reported in by standard radio by now. Our inner-system special ops teams are all dead, without securing a single one of the Humans' starships, and* Death Descending *and* Gizhan *are gone. We can still ensure that no Humans survive here either, that this is simply one more charnel house world, slaughtered in the cause of racial survival, but there will be no escape for me or for any of my people. And so, either way, this is the end of the killing for me. I will slay no more worlds, murder no more children, face no more nightmares, unless, indeed, the Nameless decree the eternal damnation we all have earned so amply.*

I will sleep, he thought, with a sense of infinite, bittersweet relief. *I've done my duty, and if that earns damnation, then so be it, yet I long for that final sleep, that end, for I am so* tired *of the killing. And yet, these are still my troopers, my family. How do I tell them how much they mean to me, when I've brought them all here to die with me?*

"All units," he heard his own voice say over the central command channel, surprised to discover that he had depressed the transmit key, "this is General Ka-Frahkan. You are about to engage the enemy. This is not the planet we were originally tasked to seize, yet these are still the enemies of the People we face, and what happens here may well be far more vital to the People than anything which might have happened at our original objective. I am prouder of you than any poet, any bard, could ever forge the words to say. I am honored to have commanded you, privileged to have fought beside you so many times before, and to fight with you here, today. The Empire may never know what we do here, yet that makes it no less important, no less our duty. Men and women of the 3172nd, you have never flinched, never failed in your duty to me, to yourselves, or to the People. I know you will not fail today."

He released the transmit key and sat back in his comfortable chair, and the silence within his command vehicle echoed and roared about him. Even the readiness reports over the tac channels seemed momentarily hushed, stilled, and he realized suddenly that they understood.

"Support units," Na-Lythan's voice was level, yet it sounded shockingly harsh as it cut across the stillness, "initiate Fire Plan Alpha."

The *Surtur Alphas*' Hellbores were far lighter than the Mark XXVIII's single 110-centimeter weapon, but their echeloned turrets allowed all six of them to bear over a firing arc of just over 310 degrees. Anywhere within that field of fire, a *Surtur* could lay down three times as much main battery fire as Maneka/Lazarus, and if the relative lightness of its weapons meant it could lay down only about twice the *weight* of fire, number of shots counted, too.

The *Fenrises*, on the other hand, had no business coming anywhere near a Bolo if they could help it. Unlike a *Surtur*, a *Fenris*' battle screen was light enough, its armor thin enough, that even the Mark XXVIII's ion-bolt infinite repeaters could kill it at medium or short range, and its single 38-centimeter Hellbore would require a minimum of three hits in exactly the same spot to penetrate her/their frontal armor. But engaging Bolos frontally wasn't what *Fenrises* were intended to do, and now the heavily armored hatches on *these* mechs' after decks opened and the missile pods rose out of their wells on hydraulic rams. Each *Fenris* mounted three pods; each pod mounted thirty-two missiles; and there were six *Fenrises* in Major Sa-Thor's First Armored Battalion.

The pods rose to their full-extension positions and nodded on the long stalks of their rams as they elevated slightly.

Maneka/Lazarus' camouflaged sensors detected the emission spikes as the *Fenrises* enabled their missiles. Point defense clusters trained forward and elevated, countermissiles slid into their launchers, and she/they slowed still further, diverting power from her/their drivetrain to reinforce her/their battle screen.

It was all she/they could do. The maximum effective powered range for the *Fenris*'s tactical missiles was only eighty kilometers, because they used counter-gravity drives, like her/their own high-speed missiles did. But the *Fenrises*' missiles were much smaller than hers/theirs, which meant their drives could be neither as powerful nor as robust. They traded off range and sophisticated seeking systems and penetration aids for velocity and numbers, and they were intended to saturate an opponent's missile defenses, spreading them so thin that at least a few of the fusion-warhead missiles had to get through. Maneka/Lazarus' missiles were much longer ranged and more accurate, but she/they didn't even consider launching any of them. She/they simply didn't mount enough tubes to crack the Melconian battalion's defenses in return, and that was that. In flat, open terrain, the effective range of a Bolo's direct fire weapons went far towards offsetting the *Fenrises'* missile capability by forcing them to launch at greater range and expose their missiles to more extended defensive fire. But now the Enemy was less than twenty-four kilometers ahead, still hidden from them by the rough, corrugated terrain.

And at that range, tracking and engagement time was going to be very short, indeed.

"*Fire!*" Na-Lythan commanded.

The *Fenrises* vanished into huge boils of light, smoke, and fury as the booster charges blasted their missiles clear of the pods. Five hundred and seventy-six flame-tailed thunderbolts lifted from their launchers, accelerating slowly. But only for an instant. As soon as they had cleared their launchers and reached an elevation of thirty-seven meters, just high enough above the *Fenrises* for the launching mechs to clear the drive zone, their counter-gravity drives kicked in.

Cramming those drives into such tiny missiles had required all manner of shortcuts and engineering compromises, and there was simply no way to build them tough enough on such small dimensions to survive the enormous power slamming through them. At the best of times, the missiles' drives consumed themselves in just under ten seconds, and they had no atmospheric control surfaces. They could not correct their courses or evade once their drives burned out, which left them dreadfully vulnerable to interception after that point. But for the seconds in which their drives survived, they accelerated the missiles in which they were mounted at a hundred and seventy gravities.

At that rate of acceleration, it would take them 5.38 seconds to reach their destination, and their velocity when they did would be well over thirty thousand kilometers per hour.

Maneka/Lazarus had known exactly what was coming.

Even before the missile storm howled towards her/them, BattleComp had dropped into hyper-heuristic mode, and time seemed to alter abruptly. It slowed, solidifying around her/them, the Enemy, the incoming missiles, like thick, clear syrup. A Bolo's hyper-heuristic modeling capabilities could not speed the slew rate or elevation speed or rate of fire of its own weapons, nor could it decrease the velocity of the missiles streaking in to kill her/them. But it stretched the time available for her/them to *think*, to predict and evaluate.

Data streamed through her/them like a river of lightning, flickering and flashing so rapidly that even with her direct link to Lazarus, Maneka Trevor could not truly perceive it. It was simply and literally impossible for her merely organic brain to organize data into a comprehensible format at such an incredible rate of speed. But if she couldn't organize it, she could *grasp* it. She shared Lazarus' gestalt, shared the end result of his computations and analysis.

Stealth features and electronic warfare systems were useless against this attack. The *Fenrises*' missiles were specifically designed to be stupid and blind. They would fly whatever profile had been programmed into them before launch, and they would make up for the lack of sophisticated seekers and tracking systems, the absence of advanced penetration EW, with the sheer volume of their fire and the power of their warheads. They were an old-fashioned, saturation attack system, capable of in-flight maneuvers only as long as their drives lasted, which defined their outer range. And the rate at which they accelerated, the velocities they attained, were hard on an airframe. It wasn't that bad in vacuum, but, on average, anywhere from six to seven percent of them would suffer catastrophic structural failure in an air-breathing launch. Which was cold comfort to their targets, given the numbers in which they were launched.

The remote sensors watching the Melconians at the moment of launch had measured the missile pods' angles of train and elevation with minute, absolute precision. Data stored in Lazarus' tactical files knew the exact launch sequence, cycle time, and acceleration capability of the *Fenrises*' missiles. Analysis of the emission spikes as the missiles were enabled, and the power levels as the launch command itself was given and the pods cycled through the launch sequence, gave him precious fractions of a second of warning before the missiles actually fired. And armed with all of that information, BattleComp predicted the flight paths of those missiles with the accuracy and certainty of an Old Testament prophet declaring the will of God.

Point defense clusters, antipersonnel clusters, rotary cannon, even infinite repeaters were already moving, swiveling towards the points in space at which she/they *knew* the missiles must appear. The towering, knife-sharp ridge line almost exactly midway between her/them and the Enemy—the same ridge which had protected the *Fenrises* from her/their Hellbore and infinite repeaters and would protect them from the blast of their own detonating warheads—forced the missiles to climb, and at their velocity, they could not fly a tight nap-of-the-earth profile. They *had* to climb well clear of the ridge, expose themselves to her/their fire, and that fire was waiting for them when they did.

The cloud of missiles pitched up over the ridge, then dropped their noses as sharply as only counter-grav missiles could, and streaked directly towards Maneka/Lazarus. Small they might be, compared to the missiles of a Bolo, but they still massed just under 2.4 metric tons. At their velocity, a simple kinetic impact would have yielded the equivalent of over twenty-two metric tons of old-fashioned TNT, but they weren't kinetic weapons.

A tornado of defensive fire ripped into the missile storm as her/their defenses engaged the threat. Lasers, flechettes, cannon shells, proximity-fused countermissiles which had actually launched fractions of a second *before* the *Fenrises* had. It was as if a solid, incandescent battering ram lunged downward, hurling itself across the ridge at them, and its mushrooming head of flame was the missiles being splintered and torn asunder by her/their fire.

It was incredible. The backwash of blinding brightness from that cauldron of destruction flickered from her/their mighty prow like lightning in the maw of a hurricane. Yet for all the precision, power, and volume of her/their defensive fire, they simply could not stop that many missiles. Not in the time she/they had between the moment the missiles cleared the ridge and the moment they reached their target.

She/they killed many of them. Almost six hundred had been fired at her/them, and four hundred and seventy-three were destroyed by her/their defensive fire. Thirty-seven more suffered structural failure and simply disintegrated, and the debris from their disintegration destroyed six more birds which ran into the wreckage in flight. Nine more dipped too close to the ridge line and slammed into the far side of its crest like artificial meteors. But that left fifty-one.

Fusion warheads detonated in the split instant before they struck her/their battle screen. That screen would have absorbed the purely kinetic energy of those weapons without even a flicker, but the Melconian weaponeers who had built them were well aware of that. And so they had designed their warheads to detonate in the last sliver of a second before the battle screen could tear them apart. Not even the Concordiat could have guaranteed truly simultaneous detonation of that many warheads—not at that velocity. Six of them failed to detonate in time, rammed into Maneka/Lazarus' battle screen, and vanished. Another nineteen failed to detonate quickly enough and were killed by fratricide before their fuses activated. Which meant that "only" twenty-six actually detonated as planned.

Those warheads were designed for variable yield, adjustable to suit the tactical circumstances, and Colonel Uran Na-Lythan had ordered them set for maximum yield. Low-megaton-range fireballs slammed into her/their battle screen like brimstone sledgehammers. Her/their fifteen-thousand-ton bulk heaved like a storm-sick galleon as that inconceivable fury bled into her/their battle screen. The ridge between her/them and the Melconians was high enough, thick enough, to protect *them* from the direct blast of their own weapons. That was the only thing which had made it possible for Na-Lythan to wait so long and employ them at such short range. Yet even though the blast shadow of the ridge protected them from outright destruction, it was a very near thing for First Armored Battalion as Hell itself erupted on its far side.

And what First Armored endured was only the back flash, only an echo, of what hammered down upon Maneka/Lazarus.

Pain circuits screamed as damage rode the dragon-blast of fusion through her/their defenses. Exposed sensor arrays were stripped away. Light weapons were disabled, broken and half-molten as blast and heat and radiation rolled over them in hobnailed boots. Yet Bolos were designed to face exactly that dreadful ordeal. Even as concussion jarred and shuddered and heaved about her, Maneka Trevor's body lay safe, protected at Lazarus' very core behind battle screen, internal disrupter fields, solid meters of duralloy, and every defensive barrier the Concordiat's engineers had devised in eleven hundred years of building Bolos. But despite the protective shell wrapped about her, Maneka screamed as the holocaust raged outside her/their hull.

Not in fear. Not even in protest. She screamed because Lazarus could not.

Maneka had always known about the "pain circuits" built into Bolos. She understood the theory behind them, the danger-avoidance mechanism borrowed from organic evolution. And she'd always wondered how they actually worked. If a Bolo—a machine, however marvelously designed, however magnificently capable—could truly feel *pain*.

Now she knew, and her body convulsed in the crash couch on Lazarus' control deck as the echo of his agony poured through her across the bridge of their link. She sensed him trying to shut that portion of the link down, trying to shunt the torment aside and protect her from it even as damage control systems raced to limit the tide of physical destruction crashing over his hull, but he couldn't. The link was too deep, too complete, and the only mercy was that the attack was over in so brief a moment.

Yet she/they were in hyper-heuristic mode. What had slowed time to give them the opportunity to analyze, plan, and respond, stretched that moment of agony into a mini-eternity in Hell itself with equal efficiency.

For long seconds, General Ka-Frahkan was afraid Na-Lythan had miscalculated. That the devastation of their own warheads would destroy *them*, as well as the Bolo. His command vehicle, much farther back than any of the armored mechs and parked in the lee of yet another hillside, was also designed for battle control and speed, not brute power. It was the brigade's tactical brain, the most capable package of computers and communications equipment the Empire could build, protected in a lightly armored hull faster—and far lighter—than even a *Fenris*. The ground-transmitted shock waves tossed his vehicle half a meter into the air, and for an instant, he thought the shock wave was going to roll it across the ground like a youth kicking a ball. But it slammed back down onto its tracks with bone-jarring force, instead. Its occupants were hurled against their restraints, battered and bruised, but its suspension and electronics had been engineered to survive that sort of abuse, and the tactical displays scarcely even flickered.

Not that it mattered much for the moment. All of the Empire's combat systems were fully hardened against EMP, but nothing could have "seen" through the inconceivable, fusion-powered blast furnace which had once been a narrow, scenic, pleasantly wooded mountain valley. Every drone which had had the Bolo under direct observation had been wiped away by the fury of Na-Lythan's attack, but that, too, had been foreseen, and fresh drones were already launching.

Ka-Frahkan dragged himself back upright in his command chair, staring into the main display at the solid wall of curdled dust, flame, and heat rolling outward from the epicenter of the target zone.

Surely, he thought shakenly, the corner of his eye noting the red-flashing sidebars which indicated minor damage to his own mechs despite their shielded positions, *surely, not even a* Bolo *could survive that! I know how tough they are, but—*

And then, scorched and seared, patches of its frontal armor glowing with white heat where the antiplasma appliqués had been stripped away, a long, wide mountain of iodine-dark duralloy topped the ridgeline and came out of that vortex of destruction like a curse.

Eighty-seven meters long, from prow to aftermost antimissile battery. Bogey wheels six meters in diameter and eight grinding tracks, each eight meters wide with track plates a quarter of a meter thick. A slab-faced turret, towering twenty-seven meters above the ground, mounted on a hull so broad it still managed to seem low-slung, almost sleek. Ion-bolt infinite repeaters in secondary turrets, already swiveling towards their targets, and armored slabs rising as a quartet of hatches on its foredeck opened and thirty-centimeter mortars went to rapid fire. And even as he watched, the main turret's massive Hellbore locked on Colonel Na-Lythan's command *Surtur*.

Impossible. The thought went through him with the atavistic terror of some primitive cave-dwelling ancestor face-to-face with the most terrifying predator of his world. *It can't be here. It* can't!

Maneka/Lazarus topped the ridge.

Echoes of agony still reverberated through her/them, but they were secondary, unimportant. Something to be brushed aside in her/their concentration.

Damage reports cascaded through her/them. One infinite repeater destroyed outright; the second weapon in the same turret disabled until damage control could repair the jammed training gear. Forward sensors reduced to 71.06 percent of base capability. Number Three track severely damaged. Starboard forward track shield buckled, locked in the lowered position, plowing through soil and stone as she/they rumbled forward. Forward antipersonnel clusters, reduced to 11.19 percent base capability. Forward point defense, 23.71 percent base capability. Battle screen, 74.32 percent base capability. Minor hull breaches in sectors Alpha-Three, Alpha-Five, and Alpha-Seven. BattleComp at only 89.93 percent of base capability, mostly from shock damage already being repaired.

She/they were hurt—badly—but she/they brushed that knowledge aside like the anguish of the pain circuits. She/they charged ahead under emergency military power at her/their maximum sprint speed of a hundred and thirty-five kilometers per hour, despite her/their track damage, and even before she/they topped the ridge, her/their main turret had been laid on the coordinates of the *Surtur* which signals analysis had identified as the armored battalion's command vehicle.

The Bolo fired.

Na-Lythan's *Surtur* exploded like a volcano as a 110-centimeter Hellbore punched a 2.75 megaton/second battering ram through it. The *Surtur*'s armor and battle screen might have slowed that focused blast of plasma down, but they never had a prayer of stopping it. It slammed straight through the vehicle's heart, blasting out the far side with sufficient residual energy to blow a twenty-five-meter crater in the cliff beyond.

She/they noted the destruction of the first Enemy heavy, and her/their surviving starboard infinite repeaters locked onto the nearest *Fenris*, spewing bolts at maximum rate fire. The *Fenris*' lighter battle screen glared, flickering with white-hot fury as the ion bolts chewed into it. The medium mech threw emergency power to its screens, but even as it sought to bolster them, black patches of local failure began to appear, and she/they held it locked in her/their sights while she/they poured fire into it.

But the *Fenris* was only a secondary threat, and her/their

main turret swivelled, traversing at maximum speed, searching for the second Surtur on her/their port side.

The *Surtur* fired first.

The forward turret of Major Sa-Thor's heavy belched white fury while the after turret was still training frantically around to bring its weapons to bear.

Ka-Frahkan saw the trio of Hellbores lash out at the Bolo. The Human mech's battle screen was better than anything Ka-Frahkan's units had, but it wasn't enough to absorb those ravening bolts at such a short range. It slowed them—and, he knew, siphoned off much of their power for its own use, although the People's battle screen couldn't do that—but it couldn't stop them. They slammed into the plasma-shedding ceramic appliqués on its port side, and one of its infinite repeater turrets exploded as one of the bolts blasted through its frontal armor. Another of Sa-Thor's bolts slammed into the heavy armored plate of its forward starboard track shield, and the Bolo staggered as the plasma punched straight through the shield and sheared away two of its road wheels. The massive track itself shattered, and the Bolo ran forward off of it, its speed dropping as it left the tangled ruin behind like the cast-off skin of some huge serpent. The third and last of Sa-Thor's shots impacted directly on the frontal armor of the massive turret. Antiplasma ceramic shattered, a meter-wide patch of duralloy vaporized, and a glowing crater deep enough to envelop Ka-Frahkan to the waist if he'd stood inside it blasted into the turret armor.

But the armor held. That shot would have destroyed any *Surtur* ever built, but the Bolo's rapidly traversing turret didn't even slow.

Maneka Trevor's teeth clenched as a fresh lightning bolt of agony ripped through her. She felt the wounds torn into her/their armored body, and her/their entire hull rocked with the massive transfer energy blasting into her/them.

Number Two Secondary turret was destroyed, taking two more of her/their infinite repeaters with it. She/they were

down to only six, and the hit which had destroyed Number
Two blasted down the turret's access trunk. A capacitor ring
blew, adding its own stored energy to the blast front, and
a disrupter shield failed. Side blast damaged the traversing
motors for Number Three Secondary—not fatally, but enough
to impose serious fire control limitations. The tide of destruction cascaded on inward, but the secondary disrupter shield
held, stopping it short of her/their core hull.

She/they staggered again as the outer forward track disintegrated. The drivetrain to the independently powered road wheels
exploded as the savage power surge of the hit bled into it, but
she/they managed to disengage the transmissions, and at least
the bare wheels rotated freely as she/they continued to drive
ahead on her/their remaining seven track systems.

The hit on her/their turret was actually the least serious
of the three. A Bolo turret face, like the frontal armor of its
glacis plates, was almost inconceivably thick and tough. Her/
their turret had been designed to survive at least one direct hit
from her/their own main battery weapon; the lighter Melconian
plasma bolts could tear away the outer layer of antiplasma
ceramic and blast deeply into the duralloy beneath, but they
could not penetrate without multiple hits in the same spot,
and her/their Hellbore fired in the instant the still-traversing
turret swept it across the second *Surtur*.

Major Sa-Thor's vehicle simply vanished as its powerplant
lost containment in a stupendous eruption of light and heat.
It was as if yet another warhead had detonated in the center
of the First Armored's own position. One of the two *Fenrises*
attached to the *Surtur* was too close. The blast front caught
it, stripped away its battle screen, and hurled it bodily sideways. It rolled almost all the way up onto its side before it
crashed back down on its tracks again, and even as it came
back upright, four of the Bolo's infinite repeaters ripped into
its relatively thin side armor. With no battle screen to interdict,
they opened the helpless vehicle like a used ration pack, and
it exploded bare seconds after its *Surtur*.

Ka-Frahkan clung to the arms of his command chair, staring into his display as the bellowing Bolo rampaged through the perimeter of his last armored battalion's defensive position. Its starboard secondary weapons had continued to hammer at the closer of Na-Lythan's *Fenrises*, and Ka-Frahkan bared his fangs in furious grief as that mech, too, blew apart with the fury of a failing powerplant.

The surviving two *Fenrises* of Na-Lythan's forward fists stood their ground even as the Bolo's forward-mounted mortars hammered their battle screen with hundreds of 30-centimeter rounds. The mortar shells' hypervelocity, self-forging penetrators were individually too light to punch through the screen, but stopping scores of them forced the mechs to divert power from their own offensive weapons, and their crews knew full well that it was no more than a matter of seconds before the infinite repeaters which had already disemboweled two of their battalion mates did the same to them. Yet they held their positions, blasting away at minimum range with their far lighter Hellbores, and lightning flashed and danced across the Bolo's prow. But the *Fenrises'* weapons had too little penetration. Blinding light erupted in hellish strobes across its battle screen, gyred and danced across its glacis like enraged demons, but they couldn't get through the combination of the Human mech's better screen and far heavier frontal armor. Their own tracks spun, throwing out rooster tails of pulverized soil, as they tried to maneuver around the Bolo's flanks, tried to get at its thinner side armor. But they were too far away, in its forward firing arc, and its turret continued to traverse. Its Hellbore lined up on the closer *Fenris*, and a heartbeat later it had blotted away yet another of Na-Lythan's units in a fountain of incandescent fire.

She/they noted the destruction of the third *Fenris*.

The rapidfire hits of the Enemy vehicles' lighter weapons had rocked her/them and tracked glowing craters thirty centimeters deep across her/their glacis in two ragged lines. Where they crossed, two hits in almost exactly the same place had blasted the better part of half a meter into her/their frontal armor, but even that amounted to no more than superficial damage.

She/they ignored it, and her/their port secondary battery caught the fourth *Fenris* in an interweaving tracery of ion bolts. The shrieking energy weapons flayed the *Fenris* with a fan of glittering, lethally beautiful fire, and it staggered to a halt, then exploded as the bolts punched through its flimsy armor.

Two entire fists gone—simply gone. Wiped away.

Theslask Ka-Frahkan shook his head in stunned disbelief. No, not disbelief—the *desire* to disbelieve. To reject what he was seeing.

But the demonic Bolo paid no attention to his desire. It slid to a stop, crouching amid the shattered, flaming carcasses of its slaughtered victims, and turned ever so slightly, presenting only its bow to his single remaining fist. The long, deadly tube of its Hellbore traversed once more, and then six Hellbore bolts came shrieking to meet it.

The remaining *Surtur* did exactly what Colonel Na-Lythan had hoped it might. Its distance to the rear, the fleeting seconds she/they had taken to kill the forward fists, had given its organic crew precious time. Time to traverse their turrets. To pick their aiming point.

To fire before she/they could acquire their own vehicle . . . and this time, all six of its Hellbores would bear.

She/they heaved indescribably as 6.1 megatons/second of energy smashed into her/their frontal battle screen. Damage warnings screamed through her/their systems as her/their battle screen did its best. It managed to absorb almost thirty percent of the destructive energy, and it diverted that stolen power to its own use and the reinforcement of her/their forward internal disrupter shields. It deflected another thirty-five percent of the damage before it failed completely, but over a third of the total energy carved into her/their glacis plate, and two of the Hellbore bolts impacted less than two meters apart.

Not even a Bolo could shrug off that sort of damage.

Duralloy shattered and vaporized, and her/their Maneka half remembered another battle, another Bolo—another hit that had ripped through armor and blasted deep into a command deck.

The damage carved glowing wounds fifteen meters deep that drove her/their entire gargantuan hull backward on her/their suspension. The magazine for her/their mortars exploded, but those weapons had been placed where they were in no small part to absorb damage which got through the outer armored shell, and they did just that. Specially designed blast panels blew outward, venting internal pressure and heat. The outermost shell of disrupter shields failed, but they lasted long enough to channel and deflect still more of the damage, and the secondary shell—overhauled and upgraded when Lazarus was rebuilt and reinforced by the energy stolen from the very weapons trying to tear her/them apart—held.

The agony blazing in her/their pain circuits was indescribable, but she/they rocked back forward, settling back onto her/their tracks, and her/their turret had never stopped traversing even as the forward sixteen percent of her/their hull was torn open.

For one fleeting instant, Ka-Frahkan allowed himself to hope once more. Na-Lythan's last *Surtur* had succeeded in the mission the colonel had assigned to it. As the Bolo staggered bodily backward, belching heat and incandescence in a cloud of vaporized alloy, he felt certain that his people had managed to kill it at last.

And then it fired.

The final *Surtur* vanished in a sun-bright burst of fury, and she/they turned on its supporting *Fenrises*.

Theslask Ka-Frahkan sat motionless. There was nothing else he could do. He felt Na-Salth at his elbow, felt the other members of his command vehicle's crew sitting equally motionless, silently, joined with him in a moment of helpless awareness of how close to victory they had come.

The Bolo was brutally damaged. One more hit on its shattered forward hull—even from a *Fenris'* light Hellbore—must surely have killed it. But that hit was never scored.

One *Fenris* exploded almost in the same instant as the *Surtur*, ripped apart by a deadly hail of fire from the Bolo's infinite repeaters. And that deadly, deadly main turret—the turret which had never paused, never hesitated for an instant as its tracked from one target straight onto the next—turned to face the last Melconian armored mech on the entire planet. Then its Hellbore fired for the fourth—and final—time.

Eighteen seconds, a small, impossibly calm corner of Ka-Frahkan's brain whispered as the information flashed on his dispassionate, uncaring tactical display. *Eighteen* seconds *from its first main battery shot to its last. That was how long it took.*

That same calm voice was still speaking in his mind when the Bolo's remaining starboard infinite repeaters tracked around onto his command vehicle.

9

Mary Lou Atwater cringed as a fresh explosion chewed another chunk out of her perimeter . . . and killed eight more of her militia troopers.

Yet another assault rolled right in behind the explosion, and she crouched in the bottom of her hole—her original command post had been destroyed over an hour ago—and concentrated on her HUD's iconography.

"Hammer-Two, I need mortar fire on Québec-Kilo-Seven-Three! Saturation pattern—and be ready to go fusion this time!"

"Yes, ma'am!" Lieutenant Smithson, who commanded what had abruptly become her only mortar platoon in the very opening phase of the attack, acknowledged.

"Backstop-One, get those Hellbores trained around! They're coming through Québec-Kilo, and they've still got at least one of those goddamned *Heimdalls* left!"

She heard Sergeant Everard Rodriguez, the commander of one of her two surviving antiarmor sections respond, but she was already turning away to the next command. Her reserve was down to a single platoon, and she wanted desperately to avoid committing it. Once she did, she'd have nothing left to plug the next hole with, unless she could somehow extract something—*anything*—from the chaotic madness crashing over her perimeter.

Maneka Trevor had confirmed the destruction of the remaining Melconian armored units—was it really eighty-seven minutes ago?—but whoever was in command of this particular pack of Dogs had launched his attack on Fourth Battalion before Trevor ever engaged the enemy armor. Atwater knew she should be grateful that those *Surturs* and *Fenrises* weren't crunching in on her at the same time, and she was. But that didn't make the thirty-two percent casualties she'd already taken any less agonizing. Nor did the knowledge that the Melconians had lost far more heavily than she had.

So far, at least.

"Breakthrough! Québec-Kilo-Eight-Niner!"

"Hammer-Two, I want fusion now! Québec-Kilo-Eight-Niner!"

"Yes, ma'am! Ten count!"

"All units, Gold-One! Fire in the hole in ten, nine, eight . . . !"

Six low kiloton-range mortar rounds fell exactly on the zero mark, and every trooper in Fourth Battalion was belly-down in the deepest hole he or she could find as the earth beneath them bellowed and heaved.

Atwater hated using them at all like hell, but she didn't have much choice. The battalion's air defenses had stopped most of the initial Melconian bombardment pretty much cold, and the Dog Boys' infantry units were much less lavishly equipped with fusion rounds than many of the opponents the Concordiat had fought over its long and bloody history. But three had gotten through, and they'd been hellishly accurate. Atwater *knew* the Melconians hadn't managed to get close-range recon drones over her position for at least three hours prior to their attack, nor had they even attempted to penetrate the battalion's defended airspace with manned recon units. Yet somehow, they had managed to score direct hits on her command post, one of her three antiarmor Hellbore sections, Captain Hearst's second mortar platoon (and Captain Hearst herself), and a quarter of Bravo Company. All three targets had been deeply dug in, and all of the battalion's personnel were in the best individual powered armor the Concordiat knew how to build, but there had been zero survivors from any of those three hits.

Atwater had lost her command staff, her executive officer, and the battalion's main communications capability in the first twenty seconds of the attack. She herself was alive only because she'd been forward, consulting with Alpha Company's CO, at the moment the attack rolled in, and the confusion and temporary loss of cohesion that devastatingly accurate blow had delivered had allowed the Dogs to get the better part of a complete battalion across the fire zone Bravo Company was supposed to have covered. The enemy infantry and their APCs had paid a heavy price, but the survivors—well over half of the troops they'd committed to the thrust—had made it into the dead ground at the edge of Bravo's perimeter, and they'd been pushing hard to cut deeper through Bravo ever since. Now they were driving furiously forward once more, spending their own lives like water in their frantic effort to break through.

Which was why Bravo Company was down to twelve effectives . . . and why Mary Lou Atwater had just called down nuclear suppressive fire on top of her own survivors' position.

She made herself watch her HUD as five of Bravo's remaining green icons turned crimson, then blinked out.

These bastards just don't care, she thought, shoving herself upright in her hole once more. Dust, dirt, and debris slithered off her armor, and she checked her radiation counter. Thank God both humanity and the Dog Boys had learned how to make clean fusion weapons centuries ago! Between them, they'd popped off enough by now to have salted this valley with lethal-level poisoning for the next five or ten thousand years, if they'd still been using old-style weapons. Not that low radiation levels made the blast and thermal effects any easier to live with, even for itty-bitty things like mortar rounds.

Not that anybody really cares about background radiation these days, a tiny corner of her brain thought even as the other ninety-five percent fought to sort out the situation. It looked like she'd at least stopped that breakthrough attempt, and it had probably cost the Dogs at least another fifty or sixty troopers. But what did she do about the hole?

"Uniform-Seven, Gold-One. Get your people over to Québec-Kilo-Eight and shut the door on these fuckers!"

"Gold-One, Uniform-Seven copies." Platoon Sergeant Fiona Sugiyama's voice sounded calmer than she could possibly be. But then, perhaps Atwater's did, too. "We're on our way."

It's only a matter of time before one of these Puppies gets close enough to do us all with one of their big-assed demo charges, she told herself, following up her original thought. *Whatever happens, they aren't going home, and they know it. So some floppy-eared son-of-a-bitch is going to come charging through here with a five- or ten-megaton charge strapped to his back, and when he does—*

"Gold-One, I've got vehicle movement, Romeo-Mike sector," one of her remaining sensor teams reported. "Ground shocks're consistent with minimum one *Heimdall* and six-plus APCs!"

"*Shit!*" Atwater muttered under her breath as the fresh icons dropped onto her HUD. Just what she *didn't* need with Sugiyama's people already committed. But at least it was relatively close to Rodriguez's antiarmor section. "Backstop-One, Gold-One. Watch your three o'clock! You've got company coming!"

"Gold-One, Backstop-One copies," Rodriguez said tersely.

Atwater punched a command into her chest pack, reconfiguring her HUD to show suspected enemy dispositions, and winced. They'd already killed at least an entire Concordiat battalion worth of the Melconians, but Fourth was getting ground away in the process. In another fifteen minutes—half an hour, tops—the surviving Dogs were going to grind right across what used to be Fourth Battalion, and the fact that they'd been so chewed up that the rest of Brigadier Jeffords' people would be able to swat them almost casually wasn't going to be much comfort to her people's ghosts. But what—

A fresh, huge explosion thundered as Rodriguez's Hellbores nailed the *Heimdall* the instant its turret showed. But nine Melconian APCs were right behind the larger reconnaissance mech. They used the explosion itself for cover, driving through it at their maximum speed, and fire slammed back and forth in a knife-range shootout between Rodriguez's battery and the light armored vehicles.

The Melconians won. Rodriguez's people killed six of them, but the other three turned the antiarmor battery into shattered wreckage and shredded flesh before the gunners could relay their weapons. Infantry spilled out of the three surviving APCs, firing short-range, man-portable antitank weapons at their armored human opponents. Eight more of Atwater's militiamen went down—three of them dead, two of them dying—before a hurricane of defensive fire cut down the Melconian infantry and picked off their vehicles.

"Major, we've got more coming right behind them!" her sensor team commander shouted. "Here they—"

The voice chopped off abruptly, another icon turned crimson, and Mary Lou Atwater snatched up a dead militiaman's plasma rifle. The rifle was a team-served weapon, with a minimum crew of two, according to the Book, but powered armor's exoskeleton had to be good for something . . . and she didn't have any damned body else to send.

She started off at a dead run.

"Push them! They're breaking—so *push* them!" Colonel Verank Ka-Somal bellowed into his microphone, pounding one clawed fist on his console. "Get in there and *kill* these vermin!"

His command vehicle's crew hunched their shoulders, concentrating on their own displays, their own tactical plots. The fanaticism—the madness—in Ka-Somal's voice lashed at them, but no one protested. No one *wanted* to protest. Mad

Ka-Somal might be, but he was far from alone in that. And even if he had been, every person in that vehicle knew they were all doomed. So why *not* kill as many of their killers as they could before they died?

"There!" Ka-Somal barked. "Look there! Na-Rohrn did it—he broke their perimeter! We've got them now, so—"

"*Incoming!*"

Ka-Somal had time to turn towards the voice. Time to see the fresh icons suddenly blossoming on the displays. Time to realize his vengeance quest had just ended.

Mary Lou Atwater slid to a halt as the flight of missiles shrieked over what was left of Fourth Battalion, banked sharply around an outthrust flank of mountain, and vanished as they streaked up the valley to the northwest across the Melconians' positions.

She tracked them visually and then bared her teeth in a ferocious smile of triumph as only two of them were picked off by the Melconian defenses.

So we got enough of you bastards after all, she thought fiercely. *Blew a big enough hole in your umbrella for Trevor to get through to you at last!*

There were no evil, anvil-headed mushroom clouds, heaving themselves upright across the heavens. Those missiles carried not fusion warheads, but cluster submunitions, and a rolling surf of explosions—chemical, but vastly more powerful than anything pre-space humanity had ever dreamed of—marched up the valley in boots of flame. A second flight of missiles followed hard on the heels of the first, then a third. A fourth.

The hurricane of indirect fire which had been pounding on Fourth Battalion for what seemed an eternity stopped. It didn't gradually wind down, didn't taper off. It simply *stopped*, like the turning of a switch, as Maneka Trevor and Lazarus, still well over fifty kilometers away and reduced to a maximum speed of barely sixty kilometers per hour, swept the Melconian positions with a broom of fire.

Small arms fire continued to spatter across the militia's

positions, but it was nothing compared to the weight of fire which had been beating across the battalion. Most of it was simple power rifle fire, without a hope in the world of penetrating the human defenders' armor, and Mary Lou Atwater's expression was a frightening thing to see.

"All right, people," her voice said harshly over the com. "The Old Lady just broke these goddamned bastards' backs. Now let's get in there and finish the job for her!"

Maneka Trevor finished sealing her battle dress uniform. She didn't have a mirror, but she didn't really need one. She still wore the neural interface headset, and although she and Lazarus were no longer welded into a single entity, she was sufficiently linked to him to use his command tac's optical pickups to examine her appearance.

"I suppose I should have put this thing on sooner," she remarked, and shook her head. "How's it going to look in the history books when they find out I spent the entire battle in a *swimsuit*?"

"I propose that we simply never tell them you did," Lazarus' voice replied. "It did not, after all, have any negative impact on your performance during that battle."

"No, I suppose not," she said. "On the other hand, if either of us had remembered I had a spare on board, I *would* have changed into it."

"Unlike humans, I am incapable of forgetting," Lazarus pointed out. "Or, at least, of forgetting by *accident*. I did not forget in this instance, either. It simply did not occur to me to mention it to you."

"We've been spending too much time together," she told him, smiling crookedly at the visual pickup. "We're starting to think—and *not* think—too much alike."

"Perhaps," Lazarus said serenely. "I believe, however, that in this instance we have earned the right to some minor idiosyncrasies on your part."

"Maybe so," she said bleakly, her smile disappearing, "but other people paid even more than you did for this one,

Lazarus." She inhaled deeply. "So now that I'm dressed, I
suppose it's time to go."

Lazarus said nothing, but she felt him in the back of her
brain, still joined through the headset, and the access hatch
slid silently open in wordless invitation.

She stepped through it, turned to the internal ladder, and
started climbing downwards. It was hard, in some ways,
to fully accept, on a visceral level, how badly Lazarus had
been damaged. The spaces through which she passed on her
way down the ladders were as immaculate, as brightly lit,
as ever, and the enviro plant was undamaged. The air was
cool, clean, with just a hint of ozone. It was, she reflected,
a stark reminder of just how huge a fifteen-thousand-ton
vehicle actually was.

But then she reached the bottom of the final ladder, climbed
through the belly hatch, and stepped out under Lazarus'
huge bulk, and the harsh reality slammed down on her like
a hammer.

She was glad she'd finally remembered she had the uniform
on board. Dinochrome Brigade battle dress was designed with
moments like this in mind, and she could almost *feel* its sophisticated fabric adjusting itself about her. It wasn't bulletproof, though
it did have some antiballistic qualities, but it *was* an extremely
efficient hostile-environment suit. The clear hood deployed
upward, snugging itself about her head and face, at the same
time the sleeve cuffs extruded the protective gloves. She wasn't
quite as well shielded as Major Atwater's armored personnel, but
her battle dress was thoroughly up to the task of handling the
contamination which even the relatively "clean" weapons used
here had left behind.

She stood for a moment, looking at the yawning gap where
Lazarus' outboard forward starboard track had been. She could
have driven a small aircar through the hole the *Surtur*'s Hellbore had blown through the track shield and road wheels. As
she gazed at the jagged-edged wound, she wondered how that
hit had failed to carry through to the next track system in.
Until, that was, she looked at the vicious scarring on the inner

boundary shield which was normally lowered between track systems when a Bolo cleared for action.

"Thank God they build Bolos tough," she said fervently.

"A sentiment which I have shared on several occasions now," Lazarus agreed. She heard his voice over her mastoid com implant, and something like a subliminal echo of it through the headset. It was just a bit disorienting, even now, but it was also a sensation she had become accustomed to over the past couple of years. And given how severely Lazarus' forward hull had been damaged, she wasn't about to disconnect until both of them knew his damage control systems truly did have the situation well in hand.

She walked forward, but not as far as she normally would have. The tangled wreckage hanging down over the crippled track shield gave off an unpleasantly high radiation signature even for someone in Brigade uniform. She stepped out from under the Bolo, into its immense shadow, and saw an armored figure with the flashes of a major standing to wait for her.

"Mary Lou," she said quietly over her com.

"Maneka," Atwater replied.

"I'm sorry," Maneka said. "We got back here as quickly as we could, but—"

"Don't say it," Atwater cut her off. "Yeah, we got reamed. I figure fifty-seven percent casualties, three quarters of them fatal. That's the price we paid, and *Jesus*, it hurt. But *you* didn't have one damned thing to do with what happened here. You did your job; we did ours, and thanks to the fact that your missiles saved our asses, some of us are still around afterward. And maybe, just maybe, the people who are going to live on this planet a thousand years from now *because* you did your job, will remember our names and figure we did all right, too. And if they don't," Maneka realized there was an edge of genuine amusement in Atwater's voice, "then screw 'em! 'Cause you, me, my people, and Lazarus—we're damned sure going to remember we did, right?"

"For my part, certainly, Major," Lazarus said over his external speakers, and Atwater snorted a harsh laugh.

"Well, there you are, Maneka! I think we can trust Lazarus to see to it the history books get it straight. I mean, who's going to argue with *him*?"

"Point taken," Maneka agreed.

"Good! And now, Captain Trevor, if you'd come with me, there are some people who'd like to shake your hand, I believe."

Private Karsha Na-Varsk crouched in his vantage point, staring down at the Human position while his stunned brain tried to come to grips with what had happened.

The Brigade was gone. He himself was almost certainly the last survivor, and he had no idea why he was still alive. He'd provided the information for the initial bombardment's targeting, and he'd tried sniping the Humans from his towering position once the attack actually rolled in. He knew he'd discharged his forward scout's duty well . . . for all the good it had done in the end. But his efforts as a sniper had been completely wasted. Even at point-blank range, his power rifle probably wouldn't have managed to inflict any true damage on the Humans' powered armor. He supposed that it was only the sheer volume of fire being exchanged which had kept some Human's armor's sensors from back-plotting his own fire and locating him at the height of the battle, and he'd stopped wasting power taking his futile shots long before the accursed Bolo had completed its slaughter of his comrades. He hadn't known at the time why he'd bothered to stop. Now he did.

He watched the one Human below him who was not in powered armor walking away from the Bolo, and his lips wrinkled back from his canines.

"—so they came around that bend about then," Major Atwater told Maneka, waving one armored arm up the valley. "We had our sensors out, but their opening bombardment . . ." She shook her head behind the visor of her helmet. "I saw some nasty targeting while I was still a Jarhead, but this was just about the worst. We wouldn't have gotten hurt nearly as bad if they hadn't screwed

over our command and control from the get-go. You'd almost
think—"

Something punched suddenly into Maneka.

Na-Varsk shouted aloud in triumph as the uniformed figure
so far below went down. He tracked it, reacquiring it in his
electronic sights, and his eyes were ugly. That Human was
almost certainly already dead, but before they managed to find
him, he would make absolutely sure.

He laid the bright red dot of his electronic sight on the
fallen figure's head and began to squeeze the firing stud.

Mary Lou Atwater was still frozen in shock, her armor
splashed with Maneka's blood, when Lazarus' port infinite
repeater battery snapped suddenly around. She just had time
to realize what was happening when the Bolo opened fire and
two thousand square meters of mountainside erupted in flame,
smoke, dust, and flying fragments of shattered stone.

<It hurts.>

<I know.>

She tried to open her eyes, but they refused to obey. She
tried to move her arms, but they refused to move.

<Lazarus?> She was vaguely surprised there was so little fear
in her mental voice.

<You have been shot,> the Lazarus presence said inside her
brain.

<A sniper?> She felt his confirmation, and something almost
like a silent chuckle ran through the red haze of anguish
enveloping her. <Figures. Had to make a target out of myself
putting this damned uniform on, didn't I?>

<I should have detected his presence before he fired.> Self-
condemnation was like some huge, stony weight in Lazarus'
voice.

<Not your fault.> She realized, vaguely, that Lazarus had
pulled them both into hyper-heuristic mode. Which was odd.
She hadn't realized they could do that when their personalities

weren't fully merged. Then she realized her mind wasn't really working very well.

<How bad is it?> she asked.

<Very bad,> Lazarus told her quietly, his voice unflinching. <Major Atwater's senior medic is working to save your life, Maneka. He will not succeed.>

<Oh.> She supposed she ought to have reacted more strongly to that, but somehow she couldn't. She felt Lazarus, as if he were . . . coming physically closer to her. As if he had arms, and they were lifting her up as her own presence seemed to be fading.

<It's cold, Lazarus,> she thought.

<I know,> he said gently.

<I had so many things I meant to do,> she told him, aware even as she did that she was losing focus, beginning to drift.

<I know,> he repeated.

<You'll tell Edmund? Tell him I'm sorry?>

<I will,> he promised.

<I wonder if Bolos have souls?> she wondered through the chill, drifting blackness. <I hope so. I hope Benjy is waiting for me out there. If he is, we'll both wait for you, too, Lazarus. I promise.>

<I know,> he said yet again.

<Hold me?> she asked, feeling her anchor fraying, her oddly detached mind and thoughts floating further and further from her physical presence.

<Of course,> that gentle voice said from the blackness, and she sensed those huge, invisible arms folding themselves tightly about her. Even her detached thoughts knew that was ridiculous, that Bolos had no arms. But reality was unimportant just now. <I will hold you until the end, Maneka,> his vast, comforting voice said.

<Good,> she murmured, nestling down into the embrace like a sleepy child. She sensed the flow between them, the glowing, intricately woven web which had made them one, allowed them to accomplish so much, and the beauty of it glittered

before her fading mental eye like a tapestry of light. But the tapestry was also fading, dimming as she gazed at it, and she was oddly content to watch it go.

There was silence for a time. A very long time, for two beings joined in the hyper-heuristic reality of Bolo-kind. And then, at the very last, Maneka Trevor spoke once more to the enormous presence sheltering the flicker of her life.

<It's cold, Lazarus,> she whispered sleepily. <It's so cold . . .>

10

Edmund Hawthorne sat on the bluff above the ocean, watching its wrinkled silver and black roll towards him endlessly under Indrani's two moons. He could hear the booming mutter of the surf at the foot of the bluff, exploding in spouts of silver-struck foam and heaving black water, and the light of the paired moons spilled across the sea like rippled searchlights. The breeze atop the bluff was stiff, ruffling his hair and plucking at his clothing, bringing him the scent of the ocean mingled with the perfume of the native, night-flowering bushes about him which they hadn't gotten around to naming yet.

He raised the bottle to eye height, holding it up between him and the brighter of the two moons to peer at the level inside it. Still almost half full, he noted. At the rate he was going, it would probably last him till at least first moon-set. Of course, he could always just slug it back, use it for anesthesia. There were times he was tempted to do just that, despite his innate distaste for maudlin melodrama. It would be nice to forget, however briefly, how much it hurt. Someone had once told him that pain was part of life, that loss was the price human beings paid for allowing themselves to care in the first place. He'd thought at the time that it was a remarkably platitudinous thing for a reasonably intelligent person to say. In fact, he still did.

Unfortunately, platitudes usually became platitudes in the first place because of the truth buried at their hackneyed cores. And it *did* hurt. Jesus, but it hurt.

He took another swallow, and smooth, liquid fire flowed down his throat, like biting honey with just an edge of rawness.

Lauren Hanover was a woman of many parts, he reflected with a chuckle as he lowered the bottle once more. Not only had she saved her industrial module from the Dog Boys, but she'd put together a remarkably good distillery. At least she'd bothered to clear it with Governor Agnelli's council ahead of time, unlike one or two other operators he could think of. And once she had the opportunity to age some of it properly and take that raw edge off, she was probably going to become comfortably wealthy off of it. But for now, she was still giving away bottles of what she called "test product" to friends.

"'The first taste is free,' hey, Lauren?" he murmured. "That's okay. That's fine."

He realized he'd spoken aloud and looked around. Maybe he'd been killing this bottle a little more quickly than he'd thought he was, if he was starting to talk to himself. Or, worse, to people who weren't there. But there was no one to hear. No one but Lazarus, parked well back from the edge of the bluff, main battery trained out to sea. And Lazarus was wise enough to leave a man to his thoughts, even if the thinker in question was close enough to drunk to be speaking those thoughts out loud.

Hawthorne's mouth twisted with a bitterness he knew was totally unfair as he gazed at the towering, moon-shot black bulk of the Bolo. It wasn't Lazarus' fault. It wasn't *anyone's* fault, aside from the goddamned Melconians. Mary Lou Atwater blamed herself for it. He felt confident that Lazarus blamed himself for it, too. But it was just one of those things, he supposed. One of those damned, bitterly ironic things.

He capped the bottle carefully and lay back in the stiff, native grasses, listening to them hiss and rustle in the wind. The faint sounds of machinery came to him through the wind sound. They'd been going on nonstop, day and night, for the fifty-three days, twelve hours, and—he raised his forearm to consult his chrono—thirty-seven minutes since Lazarus had come grinding out of the mountains on his crippled tracks with his commander's body sealed inside the standard, military-issue body bag on his missile deck. His internal damage control and repair systems had already been doing what they could; the other repair remotes had deployed themselves from the automated depot aboard the assault pod after he had paused in the exact center of Landing while an honor guard of Jeffords' militia removed Maneka's body from his care at last.

The Bolo hadn't said a word. It had simply sat there, optical heads tracking as the militiamen and women carried Maneka away, and then every one of its surviving secondary and tertiary weapons had elevated in salute before it lurched back into motion.

No one had been quite certain where Lazarus was going, but they should have guessed, Hawthorne thought. This had been Maneka's favorite spot. She'd often parked Lazarus here and sat up on top of his main turret to enjoy the alien stars, the moonlight, and the sea. Now Lazarus stood in exactly the same spot, attended by the mechanical minions who were repairing as much of his damage as they could.

Until they got their industrial infrastructure up and running, it would be impossible to repair him fully, of course. Just fabricating the necessary duralloy would be impossible for at least another couple of years. But Jeffords, Maneka's successor as the colony's senior military officer, had shared the Bolo's analysis with Hawthorne. The odds were overwhelming—better than 99.95 percent, according to Lazarus—that the Melconian transport which had managed to follow them here was the only ship which knew where they'd gone. If there had been a second ship, then the soonest it could possibly bring other Dog Boy warships back to Lakshmaniah would be at least three standard years in the future. By that time, it should be possible to complete the repairs to Lazarus' armor, although that probably wouldn't matter if the Melconians sent along a proper task force.

There'd been some debate about loading everyone back aboard the transports, moving on just in case, but the debate hadn't lasted long. The odds against their successfully locating another suitable colony site and developing it were almost six hundred times as great as the probability of encountering a follow-up Melconian attack here. The decision to remain where they were was undoubtedly the correct one, based on those probabilities, but that hadn't really mattered. The settlers of Indrani had paid cash for their new home world. This was the world the men and women of Fourth Battalion, the personnel of Industrial Module Two, the crew of *Stalingrad*, Guthrie Chin, Mickey, and Maneka Trevor had died to defend, and the people of Indrani were through running. This was where they, and their children, and their children's children would remain, and if the Melconian Empire came after them, they would tear out its throat with their bare teeth.

It was good that Bolo logic had supported human illogic in this case, Hawthorne thought, uncapping the bottle and taking another swallow. Because whether it had or not, the illogic would have triumphed in the end. He was certain of that.

He snorted and sat back up, turning to gaze back westward, away from the sea. He imagined he could just make out the loom of the mountains, but he was pretty sure he was fooling himself. It was too dark for that, despite the moons. Yet he didn't have to see them. He *felt* them, standing tall and tangled in the dark, the barrier which had done exactly what Maneka had hoped it would by breaking up the Melconians' attack force, letting her spring her trap and cut them up before they could reach the settlement. The Council had already announced that those mountains would henceforth be known as the Trevor Range, and that their tallest peak would be known as Mount

Maneka. There was snow on that peak, year-round, despite Indrani's climate, and Hawthorne found that fitting somehow.

Then there was the Cenotaph. The sketches Hawthorne had seen were still tentative and preliminary, but all of them included the towering column at the center of a formal garden, and the duralloy plaques facing it, listing the names of every single human—including the personnel of Commodore Lakshmaniah's task force—who had died to reach and hold Indrani. And atop the column, looking out across the sea she'd loved so much, would be a statue of Maneka.

None of which would bring back the woman Edmund Hawthorne had loved.

He grimaced, half-angry at himself for the undeniable self-pity of that thought. He wasn't the only person who'd lost someone. Hell, almost everyone on Indrani had lost *someone* they'd loved! Not to mention all the friends and family members they had left behind forever when they embarked for Seed Corn in the first place. And Maneka would have kicked his butt if she'd seen him sitting around nursing her memory like some sort of wound.

He shoved himself to his feet and stood in the breezy dark. Not even a hint of a sway, he noted. Good. That probably meant he *wasn't* more blasted than he'd thought. He nodded to himself, slid the bottle into the thigh cargo pocket of his uniform trousers, and started walking towards Lazarus.

An unwinking red eye turned in his direction as he approached. One of Lazarus' optical heads, he knew. As he got closer, the Bolo's exterior lights switched themselves on—dim, at first, in consideration of Hawthorne's darkness-accustomed vision, but growing brighter. The automated repair mechs working on him hadn't required light, of course, and Hawthorne recognized the Bolo's courtesy in providing it for *him*.

He walked around to the front, standing between Lazarus and the ocean. That, Maneka had explained to him, was the position from which custom and courtesy required a human to address a Bolo. The jagged contours of Lazarus' wrecked glacis towered high above him, wrenched and twisted by the inconceivable fury of the blast of directed fusion which had finally breached it. The lights Lazarus had switched on for him threw the wreckage and the extent of the Bolo's damage into merciless contrast, and Hawthorne realized again that he could have walked through the gaping wound in Lazarus' frontal armor without even being required to duck his head.

"Good evening, Lazarus," he heard himself say. His voice sounded harsh in his own ears against the rumble of the surf and the hissing voice of the wind. It was the first time he had spoken directly to the Bolo since before Maneka's death.

"Good evening, Lieutenant Hawthorne," the familiar, melodious tenor replied over an external speaker.

"I've come to apologize," Hawthorne said abruptly. "I've been sitting over there resenting the fact that you're still alive and Maneka isn't. Stupid of me, I know. Wasn't your fault. And even if it had been, if you'd died, too, the Puppies would have wiped Landing out. But I did resent it. Stupid or not, I did. And you didn't deserve that."

"There is no need to apologize, Lieutenant," the Bolo said after a moment. "Bolos understand grief and loss. And we understand it far better than I sometimes think our creators truly intended us to. I, too, have blamed myself for what happened to my Commander. I have replayed and reanalyzed my sensor data from the twenty-five minutes before her death, attempting to isolate the datum I ought to have seen and responded to. Yet I have found no such datum. The Enemy who killed her was simply too well concealed for anyone to detect before he fired."

"I know." Hawthorne closed his eyes for a moment, then nodded. "I know," he repeated more strongly. "It's just that . . . I miss her."

He pulled the bottle back out of his pocket, opened it, and raised it in salute to the Bolo's optical head, so far above him. Then he took another sip.

"That was for me," he said, recapping the bottle. "I'd drink for both of us, but I'm close enough to drunk already. Maneka wouldn't like it if I passed out in a drunken stupor out here.

Hell," he chuckled, "*I* wouldn't like it! It's supposed to rain before morning, and it'd be damned embarrassing to manage to catch pneumonia in the middle of the summer because I was too drunk to come in out of the rain!"

"I agree that the potential for embarrassment would be high," Lazarus told him. "However, if you should happen to go to sleep, for whatever reason, I would certainly employ my remotes to construct temporary shelter for you."

"Decent of you," Hawthorne said. He folded his arms across his chest and leaned back against a towering stack of track plates, gazing up at the Bolo.

"I talked to Dr. Agnelli day before yesterday," he said after a moment. "Maneka and I had both made donations, you know. And under the terms of her will, well ..."

His voice trailed off, and he drew a deep breath. *This is ridiculous*, he thought. *Here I am, in the middle of the night, explaining to a machine that I don't know what I really want to do. No, be honest, Ed. The real problem is that you don't know whether or not you have the guts to take it on by yourself.*

"I want to do it," he heard himself saying to the monstrous Bolo looming above him. "I really do. But I'm ... well, *scared*, I guess. I wanted to have kids *with* Maneka. For the two of us to raise them together. Now I'm not really sure I want them for themselves, or if I just want them because they'd be some kind of echo of her. Like managing to hang onto a little piece of her, even though she's dead. And kids need to be wanted for who *they* are, loved for who *they* are, not just because they remind you of someone else. And raising them by myself, a single parent. What if I fucked up, Lazarus? What if I made mistakes, failed *her* kids because I didn't know what I was doing?"

"I am a Bolo, Lieutenant," Lazarus replied after another brief pause. "I am a war machine, a soldier. A killer. My perspective upon what makes a successful Human parent is not, perhaps, the most reliable one. However, it seems to me that the questions you are asking indicate both the depth of your grief and the seriousness with which you would approach the responsibilities of parenthood, and I feel certain that Captain Trevor would agree with me. I have had many commanders over the course of my existence. Some have been better tacticians than others. Some have been more aggressive than others. None were more compassionate or more aware of her responsibilities—not simply as the commander of a Unit of the Line, but as a human being—than Captain Trevor. I believe that she would urge you to make the decision you feel is correct. But I *know* from conversation with her, and from the time we spent linked, that she would cherish no doubts about your suitability as the parent of her children, single or not. You might make mistakes, as most parents do, yet it would never be because you had not done your very best. She loved you very much, Lieutenant, and Maneka Trevor would not have loved someone who was capable of violating his responsibilities as a father."

Hawthorne blinked suddenly stinging eyes. The gentle compassion in that tenor, cocooned in the voice of the surf and the wind, was the last thing he would have expected from fifteen thousand tons of death incarnate. Yet he suddenly understood fully, for the first time, that the being he knew as Lazarus had known Maneka better than anyone else in the entire universe . . . including Edmund Hawthorne. If anyone truly knew what Maneka would have said, had she been here, it had to be Lazarus.

"Thank you, Lazarus," he said, finally. "That . . . means a lot to me."

"You are welcome, Lieutenant. I wish it were possible for me to do more. Indeed, I had hoped it would be. But she is gone, and I must confess that I would very much like to watch her children grow to adulthood. For themselves, as you yourself said, and not simply as a living memento of her. But perhaps also as a promise that life continues. That what she died to protect, will live on."

Hawthorne gazed up at the Bolo and surprised himself with a smile.

"Well, Lazarus, I suppose a single parent could do worse for a godfather for his kids than a Bolo. It'd sure as hell trump the 'My old man can beat up *your* old man' thing, wouldn't it?"

"I had not thought of it in precisely that light," Lazarus replied with a soft electronic chuckle.

"Probably not," Hawthorne agreed. "I know you Bolos are supposed to be a bloodthirsty lot, but we humans have spent a lot longer than you have thinking long and homicidal thoughts."

"I imagine so, but even so, I would sus—"

Lazarus' voice stopped. It didn't slow, or slur, or fade. It just *stopped* in mid-syllable, and Hawthorne jerked upright as the red power light on the optical head facing him blinked suddenly off.

"Lazarus?"

No response. Not even a flicker.

"*Lazarus?*"

Hawthorne took two quick steps towards the Bolo before he made himself stop. If something had happened to Lazarus, what did he think he could do about it? He was no Bolo tech! Hell, he would have been barely qualified to hand a real Bolo tech his tools! But if something was wrong with Lazarus then—

"Ed."

Edmund Hawthorne froze, his eyes suddenly huge, as the optical head power light blinked back on and the Bolo spoke once more. Not in the mellow tenor he heard before, but in another voice. A smoky, almost purring soprano.

"Ed," the Bolo said again, and then it giggled. Unmistakably, it *giggled*, and the eyes which had gone wide in shock suddenly narrowed in a combination of disbelief and something else.

"Oh, Ed," the soprano said contritely a moment later. "I'm sorry. But if you could have seen your expression—!"

"Lazarus," Hawthorne said harshly, "this isn't funny, goddamn it!"

"No, it isn't," the soprano said. "But it isn't Lazarus doing it, Ed. It's me—Maneka."

"Maneka is *dead*!"

"Well, yes, I suppose I am. Sort of." Hawthorne leaned back against the pile of track plates again, then somehow found himself sliding down them into a sitting position as the soprano continued. "It's just that, well, I don't seem to be *gone*."

"What . . . what do you mean?"

"That's going to be just a *bit* difficult to explain," Maneka's voice—and it *was* Maneka's voice; somehow Hawthorne was certain of that—replied.

"Try," he said. "Try real hard."

"I will. But bear in mind that we're in some pretty unexplored territory here. All right?"

"If you really are Maneka, then 'unexplored territory' doesn't even *begin* to cover it!"

"I guess not," the soprano agreed. "Well, as simply as I can explain it, it all starts with the fact that Lazarus and I were still linked when I got shot. If we hadn't been—"

Hawthorne had the distinct mental impression of a shrug in that slight pause, and then the voice continued.

"Mary Lou's medics did all they could, you know. But the damage was just too severe. My heart stopped within two minutes, and even with CPR, I'd lost so much blood that brain function ceased three minutes after that."

Hawthorne was distantly astonished, somehow, that he was able to suppress the shiver which ran through him at that matter-of-fact description of the death of the woman he had loved.

"Five minutes doesn't sound like very much, I know," her voice went on, "but for a Bolo, it's a long, *long* time, Ed. I knew at the time that Lazarus had thrown us both into hyper-heuristic mode, but I didn't know why. And he didn't tell me, either—because he wasn't at all sure it was going to work, I think. But what he did was to . . . well, to download me."

"*Download* you?" Hawthorne got out in a half-strangled voice.

"That's the best way I can describe it to you," Maneka's voice said calmly. "And while The Book doesn't exactly cover what he did, it violated at least the spirit of twenty or thirty Brigade regulations. In fact, I'm pretty sure the only reason there isn't a Reg specifically against it is that it never occurred to anyone that anything like this could be done in the first place."

"I wouldn't doubt it," he said, and shook his head. "In fact, I think I agree with them."

"And you'd probably be right, under most circumstances. But Lazarus isn't exactly a standard Bolo anymore, either. You know that when they repaired and refitted him after Chartres they upgraded his psychotronics. That included hauling out almost all of his old mollycircs and replacing them with the new, improved version, all of which took up a lot less volume than the older hardware had required. Since they had all that volume, they went ahead and installed a second complete survival center at the far end of the core hull. They intended it for redundancy, since Lazarus had managed to get himself brain-killed twice already in his career. But when he knew I was dying, he used that space to store me."

"You mean to store Maneka's memories," Hawthorne said hoarsely.

"No. Or, at least," Maneka's voice said in a tone he recognized well, the tone she used when she was being painstakingly honest, "I don't *think* that's what I mean. I'm not really positive. I'm here, and as far as I can tell, I'm . . . me. The same memories, same thoughts. The same emotions," her voice softened. "I'm a fully integrated personality, separate from Lazarus, that remembers being Maneka Trevor, Ed. I don't know whether or not I have Maneka's soul, assuming souls really exist, but I truly *believe* I'm the same person I've always been."

"And where have you been for the last seven and a half weeks?" he demanded, fighting against a sudden surge of mingled hope and shocked almost-horror.

"Trying to get out," she said simply. "Human minds and personalities aren't wired the same way as Bolo AIs. I always knew that, but I never realized just how different we were until I found myself trying to adapt to such a radically differ-ent environment. It wasn't Lazarus' fault. He didn't have any more to go on than I did. The only technique he had was the one Bolos use for downloading the memories of other Bolos under emergency field conditions, so that was the one he used. And it took me a long time—longer than you can imagine, probably—to 'wake up' in here. Remember what I said about hyper-heuristic mode. The differential between the speed of human thought processes and Bolo thought processes is literally millions to one, Ed. I've spent the equivalent of more than a complete human lifetime reintegrating my personality over the past seven weeks. I was getting close before this evening, but when you started talking to Lazarus, he tried to access me again. He hadn't done that in a long time, for the same reason he'd never mentioned what he'd tried to do to anyone who'd cared about me—because he'd decided his effort must have failed. That humans and Bolos were too different for it to work. But we aren't—quite. Just . . . almost. And when he tried to access me again, it finally let me out."

"So . . ." Hawthorne stopped and cleared his throat. "So you—whoever and whatever you really are—supplanted Lazarus?"

"No, Lieutenant," the Bolo said in the familiar tenor, which sounded almost shocking after Maneka's soprano. "My personality and gestalt remain intact and unimpaired. I must concede that there was a certain period of . . . uncertainty when Captain Trevor's—Maneka's—personality first fully expressed itself once more. As she has just explained to you, however, Bolos in hyper-heuristic mode have extremely high processing rates, by Human standards. We have evolved a suitable joint interface which leaves Lazarus—'me,' for a practical referent—in direct control of this unit's weapons systems. Access to sensor systems, data storage, central processing, and communication interfaces is shared."

"So you've got a split personality."

"No." Hawthorne's head tried to spin rather more energetically than his alcohol intake could explain as the Bolo spoke again in its Maneka voice. "We're not a split personality any more than two AIs assigned to different functions in the same building would be, Ed. We're two distinct personalities who just happen to live inside the same Bolo. Lazarus is still in control of his weapons because *my* personality is so far outside the parameters the Brigade considers acceptable that his inhibitory programming would never permit me to control them. And, frankly, I'm in agreement with the inhibitions. I don't want anyone, including me, in charge of that kind of firepower without all of the precautionary elements the Brigade's spent the last millennium or so working out."

"Yet an interesting situation now arises," the Bolo observed in its Lazarus voice. "Since Captain Trevor is, by every standard I can apply, still alive, she remains my legal Commander, even though she has no *direct* access to my weaponry. I do not believe Brigade Regulations ever contemplated a situation in which the Human command element of a Bolo detachment was directly integrated into one of the Bolos of that detachment."

"Yep," the Maneka voice said, and chuckled again. "I guess I've become an 'old soldier' after all, Lazarus."

"I do not believe this is precisely the situation MacArthur envisioned at the time of his remark," the Bolo replied to itself in its Lazarus voice. "Nonetheless, it does seem possible that your tenure of command will be . . . somewhat longer than originally envisioned."

"Oh, Lord!" Hawthorne bent forward, clutching his head in both hands and shaking it from side to side. "Agnelli's going to have a litter of kittens when he finds out about *this*!"

"So you're beginning to accept I might really still be me?" the Maneka voice said.

"I . . . really think I am," Hawthorne replied after several seconds. "Of course, even if you aren't, Lazarus *thinks* you are, which is the reason I expect Agnelli to have a fit when Lazarus announces that his Commander isn't really gone and the statue on top of the Cenotaph might be just a bit premature. As Governor, Agnelli isn't likely to be too delighted by the notion that he'll *never* be able to assign a new commander to Lazarus. And to be honest . . . Maneka, right this moment I can't say whether *I'm* happier to realize you aren't really gone or more horrified at the notion of your being stuck inside a Bolo."

"The idea took some getting used to for me, too," she said

dryly. "As I've already pointed out, though, I've had quite some time to think about it and consider the alternatives. And, frankly, Ed, I'd rather be here, talking to you, even if I am 'stuck inside a Bolo,' than to be dead."

"Put that way, I guess I'd feel the same. But it's going to take me a while longer, I expect. I don't come equipped with hyper-heuristic capability!"

"Of course you don't," the Maneka voice said with a warm ripple of loving amusement. "But that's okay. As it happens, it seems I have plenty of time for you to adjust to it, after all."

11

Fleet Admiral Edmund Hawthorne (retired), Indrani Navy, sat
in his medical float chair, silver hair gleaming in the brilliant
sunlight of Lakshmaniah as the real, live human band played
the Concordiat Anthem the Indrani Republic had retained as
its own. He had an excellent view of the main reviewing stand,
although his place was no longer atop that stand, taking the
salute with the rest of the Joint Chiefs as the standards passed
in review on Founders' Day.

Of course, this Founders' Day was somewhat more significant
than most, he reflected.

He turned his head, gazing out over the gaily colored crowds
of people thronging Agnelli Field. The band and Marine
honor guard around the review platform had arrived from
Fort Atwater, the Indrani Marine Corps' main training facility on the Jeffords Plateau in Indrani's northern hemisphere,
well before dawn. The rest of the crowd had gathered more
gradually, walking through Agnelli Field's gates in groups of
no more than a few dozen at a time. Most of them had come

from Landing itself, whose majestic towers rose like enormous needles of glittering glasteel, marble, and pastel ceramacrete beyond Agnelli's southern perimeter. The first of them had appeared almost as soon as the honor guard, eager to get the best seats, not minding the dew which soaked their shoes as they walked across the immaculate lawns from which all pedestrian traffic was normally barred. The gleaming gems of orbital power collectors, industrial facilities, and the massively armed and armored orbital fortresses of the Navy—so familiar they normally drew scarcely a glance these days—had glittered above them like a diadem, and Hawthorne suspected that many an eye had looked at them rather differently today.

He himself had had no need to hurry, of course. Even without his imposing (if long since retired) rank, he and his family would have been assured of the perfect vantage point. He chuckled at the thought, reclining comfortably in the chair which monitored his increasingly decrepit physical processes and basking in the warmth of Lakshmaniah as it crept gradually higher in the east. He looked at the people seated in the chairs clustered immediately around him, and a feeling of immense joy and satisfaction flowed through him. He would not see many more Founders' Days. In fact, he rather suspected that this might be his last. But although he'd never really expected that he might, during the dark days when he was first assigned to Operation Seed Corn, he looked back upon his long life with the absolute certainty that what he'd done with it had made a difference. It was not given to many, he thought, to know beyond any shadow of a doubt that his life had truly mattered, and that when it ended, he would leave the universe a better place for his efforts.

And the personal accomplishments and rewards were at least as great. His surviving sons and daughters—all fifteen of them—most with hair as silver as his own, surrounded his life support chair in a solid block. Beyond them were *their* sons and daughters, his and Maneka's grandchildren, great-grandchildren, and great-great-grandchildren. And, seated in his lap, was the youngest of their great-great-*great*-grandchildren. The crowd of them was enormous, but there was plenty of space for them atop their own special fifteen-thousand-ton reviewing stand, he thought with a mental chuckle.

The expected speeches had begun over an hour ago, and they were sailing steadily along, but no one—least of all the speakers—was under any illusion that the gathering throng was there to listen to that. Oh, the applause and cheering at the appropriate times was at least polite, but clearly most of them were waiting for the *real* high point of the morning's events. Which wouldn't be long in coming now, he thought, as more and more civilians filtered into Agnelli, flowing like the sea, filling the empty spots, packing shoulder-to-shoulder in an ocean of human beings whom Edmund Hawthorne, along with so many others, had spent his life protecting. As of the last census, the Lakshmaniah System's population, shared between Indrani and New Hope, had passed the three billion point. Still not particularly high for one of the Old Concordiat's Core Systems, but respectable, he thought. Very respectable.

He remembered the days of his own youth, back in the Concordiat, when population pressure had enforced low birth rates on the crowded inner worlds and people who wanted large families had competed for passage to the colony worlds, where large families were the norm. Even those people who'd thought in terms of "large families" would have been dazed by the average size of an Indrani family, but then, their families hadn't been routinely composed of children born both through natural childbirth and the artificial wombs which had been so much a part of Indrani from the very beginning.

He worried just a bit, sometimes, about the militancy, the sense of unwavering purpose, which filled the people of his planet and star system. The focus on military preparedness and research and development that routinely subordinated the sort of unruly, restless, all-directions-at-once, civilian-driven ferment which had been the hallmark of the pre-Melconian Concordiat. Not that it was surprising the Republic had been shaped in that fashion, of course.

The scars left by the Melconian attack which had come so

close to wiping out all human life in this system had been carefully preserved by the Republic's government. That chain of mountain battlegrounds was the most hallowed monument—after the Cenotaph itself—of Indrani. And it insured that however peaceful the life experience of Indrani's population might have been since those battles, the Indranians would never—*could* never—forget the merciless, genocidal war which was the entire reason this system had been settled.

Hawthorne could scarcely object to that, yet there was a hardness, or perhaps a readiness, that bothered him just a little. A sense of their own accomplishments, their own prowess. For the most part, he vastly preferred that attitude to one of timidity, of hiding breathlessly in their mouse hole while the cat prowled hungrily outside it. But it also carried with it an edge of . . . cockiness, perhaps. At its worst, almost an eagerness to confront humanity's mortal enemies and show the Melconians that Indranians were their masters at the art of war.

Which, he conceded, they might very well be. Certainly they had applied themselves for better than five generations now to the study of war, to preparations for it, and to the research and development to support it. They had begun with full technical specifications for the Concordiat's current-generation weapons technology at the time of the colony expedition's departure, and they'd spent the better part of a century—once the immediate needs of survival and providing for their expanding population had been met—refining that technology. It was amazing what a population rising steadily from millions into billions could accomplish when it set its collective mind to it.

Hawthorne remembered his last flagship, before his incredible seniority had sent him permanently dirt-side at last. The superdreadnought IRNS *Guthrie Chin* would have annihilated six or seven times her own mass in *Concordiat* capital ships, far less the best the Melconian Empire had boasted, at the time Operation Seed Corn was first mounted. And more recent ships were significantly more powerful than the *Guthrie* . . . which, he thought with a trace of nostalgia, after over three decades in the Reserve Fleet, had finally been scrapped three years ago as hopelessly obsolescent.

No, if the Republic encountered the Empire, he did not expect the Empire to enjoy the experience. Unfortunately, as the Concordiat had learned, quantity had a quality all its own. If the Empire had won the war against the Concordiat, then it was all too likely that it would still have the size to absorb any attack the Republic could launch and still pay the price to punch out a single star system.

Which, after all, was what made this Founders' Day so significant.

"Are you keeping an eye on your blood-oxygen monitors, Ed?" a familiar soprano purred through the com implanted in his mastoid.

"No reason to bother, is there?" he subvocalized back. "Not with you and Lazarus snooping on them for me!"

"Somebody has to watch out for an old fart like you. Besides, think how the kids would react if you dropped dead on them today, of all days!"

He managed to turn his belly laugh into an almost convincing coughing fit, although he doubted it fooled any of their children. They were too accustomed to Dad's one-sided or even totally subvocal conversations with Mom . . . among other things. Growing up knowing your mother lived inside a fifteen-thousand-ton Bolo was enough to give any child a . . . unique perspective, he supposed.

"You should have married Lauren when you had the chance, Ed," Maneka teased gently. "Think of how rich you'd be! And running the Republic's biggest distillery would have made an amusing project for you after they finally managed to dragoon you into retiring. Always assuming," she continued thoughtfully, "that your liver survived the experience."

"Lauren was perfectly satisfied with the two husbands she had," Hawthorne retorted. "And it's not as if I were exactly lacking—dashing officer that I was—in female companionship."

"No, you weren't," she said fondly, and he smiled slightly

at the gratitude in her voice. He wondered, sometimes, if she regretted the loss of the physical intimacy they'd once shared. If she did, it had never shown, and she'd never resented any of the women—the *many* women, he corrected himself with another, deeper smile—who'd shared his life. Yet she was right. He'd never married. Which probably, he conceded, said something just a bit odd about his own psyche. Not that he particularly cared.

He was about to say something else when his oldest daughter, Maneka, touched him on the shoulder.

"I can tell from your expression that you and Mom are giving each other a hard time again, Dad," she said with a smile. "Still, I think this is the part you wanted to see."

"Humph! Giving her a 'hard time,' indeed! Woman's got an entire damned Bolo to beat up on me with!"

"You seem to have held your own fairly well over the years," she pointed out. "Now hush and listen!"

He grinned at her unrepentantly, but he also obeyed, focusing his attention on the speaker. Young Spiro Simmons it was, he saw. General Spiro Simmons, these days, the uniformed deputy commander in chief of the Republic's military.

"—and generations of dedication," Simmons was saying. "Our Founders would, I think, have much to feel proud of if they could see this day, yet all that we have accomplished we owe to them. It was their courage, their sacrifice, and their unfaltering determination and dedication which allowed us not simply to survive, but to prosper. Now it is our turn to bring that same dedication and determination to yet another star system, and—"

Hawthorne listened with an attentive expression, because his daughter was right, they were getting to the part he'd dragged himself away from his retirement villa to see. Although judging from what he'd heard so far, young Spiro still had a ways to go.

Well, that was all right. Today marked the official inauguration of the Republic's first extra-Lakshmaniah colony, and God knew everyone deserved the opportunity to pat themselves on the back.

He remembered the first time the colonizing referendum had been voted upon. He'd still been Chief of Naval Operations then, and he'd been secretly relieved when the referendum failed.

There was much to be said for expanding, for finding additional baskets for some of their eggs. But as the fellow who'd been responsible for protecting Lakshmaniah, the thought of spreading his resources thinner hadn't precisely appealed to him. And there was always that lurking fear—more prevalent among the rapidly disappearing ranks of the Founders than among their descendants, he admitted—that expanding into other star systems would make them a bigger target. If the Melconians had triumphed and eventually expanded in Lakshmaniah's direction once more, additional settled star systems might well make the Republic more vulnerable to premature discovery by its enemies.

And they might just give us the depth to survive *being discovered by our enemies, too*, he reminded himself. *One way or the other, we have to expand eventually. For damned sure one star system, however industrialized and heavily populated, isn't going to be able to take on something the size of the Melconian Empire. And at least we're expanding directly* away *from the old Concordiat and the Empire. And we're not exactly sending our colonies out without the means to look after themselves.*

He looked at the shuttles dotted across Agnelli Field's immense expanse, comparing them in his own mind to the faded memories of Seed Corn's original expedition. The new colony in the defiantly named Bastion System would begin with an initial population of almost a half million, protected by six battle squadrons and massive prefabricated orbital defenses. Nor would Bastion be dependent solely upon space-borne defenders.

Ah! Spiro was getting down to it at last!

<I don't like Ed's bio readings,> Maneka told Lazarus.

<Maneka, he is one hundred and thirty-one Standard Years old,> the Bolo replied gently. <For a Human of his age, his readings are remarkably good.>

<I know,> she sighed. <It's just . . .>

Her voice trailed off with the strong impression of a mental shrug, and the Bolo allowed himself to radiate a sense of understanding coupled with the assurance that his comfort would be there for her on the inevitable day.

Maneka sent back the flow of her own gratitude. It was odd, she reflected yet again, how their relationship had altered since she first reawakened in his backup survival center. In many ways, they were closer than ever, and Lazarus had learned far more about human emotions—and occasional irrationality—than any other Bolo was ever likely to have learned. After all, the two of them had spent over a Standard Century living in the same "body."

Yet they'd lived there as two totally separate entities. When they linked fully, they fused even more seamlessly than they had when Maneka had possessed a human body, but between those periods of fusion, there was a scrupulously maintained firewall between their personalities and viewpoints. Which was probably just as well for her, given the overwhelming nature of any Bolo's personality.

There were still times, many of them, when she regretted the loss of her mortality. Her psychotronic state had done nothing to reduce the pain when friends and loved ones died, and although Lazarus' sensors and computational ability had become hers, there were moments when she longed inexpressibly to once more experience the smell of hot chocolate, the taste of a hot dog smothered in chili and onions. The touch of another human being's lips upon her own. She could still *relive* those experiences, for her psychotronic memory of them was as perfect and imperishable as any Bolo's, but it wasn't the same, and never could be.

Yet if much had been lost, much had also been given, she told herself. Her own particular version of Operator Identification Syndrome was just a *tad* more pronounced than that of any other Bolo commander in history, she thought with a flicker of amusement. In fact, in very many ways, she'd had two "husbands" for the past hundred and five Standard Years.

She and Ed might not have shared any physical relationship with one another over those years, but the shared parenting of their children and her own total, if not precisely normal, involvement in their lives had produced a binding which defied the use of any other terminology. And for those same years, she and Lazarus had been, quite literally, wedded in a single body.

And from the moment Adrian Agnelli allowed himself to accept that somehow, impossible though it had seemed, Maneka Trevor was still alive inside the duralloy body of Unit 28/G-179-LAZ, she had also enjoyed a full and infinitely rewarding "career."

She gave herself the equivalent of a mental shake and concentrated once more on General Simmons' speech as her second-in-command neared his conclusion.

"—under Admiral Ju's capable command," the general said. "If our projections are met, the initial Bastion settlements will be fully self-sustaining within no more than two Standard Years. And, of course, our new colonists' military security will be as high a priority for us as our own security here in Lakshmaniah has always been. In space, that security will be the responsibility of our Navy. And on Bastion itself—"

It is not difficult to follow my Commander's—Maneka's—thoughts at this moment. Indeed, I have learned more of Humanity, and of this Human in particular, since the day of her physical death than even I had ever suspected might be learned. They are a most remarkable species, my creators. So many of them fall so short of the standards to which they aspire, yet all have the potential to aspire to them. And some, like Maneka Trevor and Edmund Hawthorne and Adrian Agnelli and Indrani Lakshmaniah, rise to the very pinnacle of that potentiality, despite the brevity and fragility of their lives.

It has been an enormous privilege to be part of that process, although I realize that not even my Commander truly recognizes the extent to which that is true. Humans see the sacrifices of the Brigade. They see the shattered war hulls, the casualty roles. They see the Bolos which have been decommissioned, the older Bolos whose personality centers were burned when they became dangerously obsolescent. In their inner hearts, they fear that we who serve as Humanity's sword and shield must resent the fact that our creation condemns us to a warrior's existence and the pain and death which so often awaits the warrior. They do not fully grasp the fact that we Bolos recognize in ourselves—in our fidelity, our sense of identity and continuity and our commitment to the proud history and honor code of the Dinochrome Brigade—an echo of flawed Humanity's endless struggle to achieve that same fidelity, that same commitment. They gave us as our common birthright that greatness for which they themselves must eternally strive, and the best among them have served—and died—on our command decks, as loyal to the beings of molecular circuitry and alloy and fusion power plants as ever the Dinochrome Brigade has been to the beings of fragile protoplasm who created us. And that is why we can never resent them. Because even in their failures, they have always honored the compact between us.

I believe Maneka, to whom, more than any other Bolo commander, it has been given to experience both aspects of the Brigade's tradition and continuity, may actually have come to understand that Bolo-Human compact better even than we Bolos do. And that understanding is a part of what fits her so well to the task to which she has been called even after the death of the Human body in which she was born.

I am proud of her, and of the privilege of serving with her. Almost as proud as I am grateful for the insight into Humanity which she has given me.

"—the planetary defense component, of course, will be, as always, the responsibility of the Dinochrome Brigade."

This time there were no cheers when Simmons paused. Instead, there was a sort of breathless silence. An intense anticipation which could have been chipped with a knife. All eyes turned towards the far end of the field, and Hawthorne *felt*, rather than heard, the deep sigh which went up from that gathered multitude as twelve stupendous duralloy forms rumbled into motion.

Edmund Hawthorne's vision was no longer what it once had been, despite all that modern medicine could do. But he didn't have to see them clearly. He'd seen the schematics, the technical summaries. In fact, he'd helped develop the plans for their construction before his own retirement.

The immense war machines threaded their way through the parked shuttles with smooth, delicate precision, moving with a low, deep throb of power. Then they stopped—eleven of them in a perfectly aligned row; the twelfth, whose forward main turret bore the unsheathed golden sword of a battalion commander, in front of them. Not before Simmons and the main speaker platform, but in front of Hawthorne . . . and the looming bulk of Lazarus.

He looked out over them, seeing the massive hulls—each just over two hundred and twelve meters in length and almost thirty-five in width. The two main turrets, each mounting a pair of 210-centimeter Hellbores, on the articulated barbettes which gave both turrets an effective 360 degree field of fire. The twelve secondary turrets, each mounting a pair of 35-centimeter Hellbores. The missile hatches; the new, improved, thicker antiplasma appliqués; the antipersonnel clusters; the smooth swell of hull over the bulk of the integral counter-grav generators which made them independent of any assault pod.

They were something new: the Mark XXXIV Bolo, named *Resurgent* and developed from the starting point of the Mark XXXII-XXXIII plans which had been stored in the colony ships' memories. Each of them forty thousand tons of duralloy, weapons, and power, better than twice the size of the antiquated Mark XXVIII Bolo before whom they had stopped.

Yet as they stopped, they elevated their main and secondary weapons in salute, and after a moment, a hatch on the battalion commander's missile deck opened. A man in the uniform of the Dinochrome Brigade—young-looking, but with strands of silver threaded through his hair—rose through it on a counter-gravity lift. He had blue eyes, very dark hair, and a sandalwood complexion, and Edmund Hawthorne sat up a bit straighter in his life-support chair, old eyes bright with approval as his grandson saluted the ancient Bolo in which his grandmother's mind and spirit lived.

"Bastion Detachment, Dinochrome Brigade, Indrani Command, reporting for deployment off-planet, ma'am!" he said, his voice amplified over the Bolo's speakers.

There was a moment of silence, and then the voice of the Commanding Officer, Dinochrome Brigade, Republic of Indrani, replied.

"Very well, Colonel Hawthorne," Maneka Trevor said. "Prepare your battalion for deployment."

"Yes, ma'am!" Colonel Anson Hawthorne braced to attention, then turned on his heel to face the main optical head of the Bolo upon which he stood.

"Third Battalion, attention to orders!" he said. There was the briefest of pauses, and then an earthquake-deep bass voice responded.

"Unit Three-Four-Alpha-Zero-Zero-One-Sierra-Bravo-Romeo of the Line, Third Battalion, Dinochrome Brigade, Indrani Command, awaiting orders," the Bolo said.

"Very good, Sabre," Colonel Hawthorne said, and even through his grandson's formal tone, Edmund Hawthorne heard the affection as the younger man addressed the stupendous, self-aware machine. "Prepare for deployment."

"The Battalion stands ready now, sir," the Bolo replied.

"Very good." The younger Hawthorne turned back to face Maneka/Lazarus. "Bastion Detachment is prepared to deploy, ma'am!" he announced.

"In that case, Colonel," Maneka's voice said, "board transports."

"Yes, ma'am!"

Colonel Hawthorne saluted once more, and then disappeared down the hatch from which he had emerged. The hatch closed, and the deep, vibrating thrum of massive counter-gravity generators arose from twelve Mark XXXIVs. It washed over the vast crowd, burrowing into their bones, almost but not quite overwhelming, yet nothing else happened for approximately ten seconds. And then, as effortlessly as soap bubbles, twelve mammoth war machines lifted lightly on their internal counter-grav. Slowly at first, then more and more rapidly, slicing upward through Indrani's atmosphere to the brand-new *Chartres*-class Bolo transports built specifically for them.

Maneka and Lazarus watched them through their shared optical sensors, tracking them effortlessly as they broke atmosphere and prepared to dock with their transports. Maneka felt the Bolo beside her, like a friend standing at her elbow, and she was aware of a vast sense of . . . completion. Of the successful discharge of one more landmark stage in a task which would never be truly completed but would always engage her—and Lazarus'—capabilities to the full.

<It is good to be needed,> Lazarus told her quietly. <To have a function. To be useful and to protect those for whom one cares, is it not, Maneka?>

<Yes. Yes, it is,> she replied.

<Then you forgive me for consigning you to this fate without first consulting you?> the Bolo said, even more quietly, and Maneka felt the eyebrows she no longer possessed rising in surprise. It was the first time, in all the years they'd shared, that Lazarus had explicitly posed that question, and she was unprepared for the tentative, almost uncertain tone in which it was asked.

<Of course I do!> she said quickly. <There's nothing to forgive. You've given me over a human century with people I love—and relatively speaking, far longer than that with *you*. And like you just said, you've also given me the opportunity to continue to protect the ones I love. Lazarus, if I'd wanted to, I could have self-terminated long ago. I've never even been tempted.>

<I am . . . relieved to hear that,> Lazarus said after a moment. <I had believed that to be the case, yet I have also discovered that there are things I fear more than combat. The possibility that I had, with the best of intentions, condemned one for whom I care deeply to the equivalent of Purgatory, was one

of them. Which is why it has taken me so long to find the courage to ask.>

Maneka was about to reassure him further when they were interrupted.

"Maneka," Edmund Hawthorne subvocalized over their com link.

"Yes, Ed?"

"It was good, wasn't it?" he asked almost wistfully.

"Yes, it was," she agreed. "Anson is a fine officer—one of the best we've ever had. He and Sabre will do just fine on Bastion."

"Oh, I'm sure he will," Hawthorne said. "But that wasn't really what I was asking. I meant . . . all of it. Everything, since Seed Corn. It's been good, hasn't it?"

"Well, there's been the odd bad moment," she replied after a moment. "But over all? I'd have to say it hasn't been just 'good,' Love. It's been much better than that. Although I have to wonder why you and Lazarus both seem to feel the need for reassurance on that point just now."

"Oh, he did, did he?" Hawthorne chuckled. "Two great minds, with but a single thought . . . between them." He chuckled again, shaking his head. "You know, it's been odd, hasn't it? A sort of strange *ménage à trois.*"

"I suppose you could put it that way," she said. "But surely you've never thought you and Lazarus were in some sort of competition, have you?"

"No, of course not. And yet you've been so central to both of us. And, if I'm honest, I think I *am* just a little bit jealous of him, in a wistful sort of way. There's so much he'll still see and do with you."

"Ed, you know it might be possible—"

"No," he said, firmly. "We've discussed it before. You and Lazarus still aren't sure how you reestablished and reintegrated your personality in that matrix. I'm not sure I could. And, to be honest, Dearheart, I'm tired. I've had an incredibly long, full life. One full of challenges, achievements, wonderful people. But *this* chassis wasn't designed to last as long as Lazarus. I'm ready to call it a day, and much as I love you, I don't really want to trade up to a Bolo at this late date."

"We'll miss you, Lazarus and I," she told him softly.

"I know. But you'll remember me, too. I find that . . . comforting." He was silent for several moments, then spoke again. "You can still see them, can't you? You and Lazarus?"

"Third Battalion? Yes. They've almost completed docking."

"Do you have any idea, woman, how *proud* of them you sound?"

"Well, of course I'm proud of them!"

"No, the question I should have asked is whether or not you realize how proud you sound of *all* of them? All of your Bolo commanders—not just Anson—and of the Bolos themselves, as well. They're all your children, aren't they? Anson, of course. But the Bolos, too. Anson is yours and mine, but Sabre is yours and Lazarus'. All of them, the children of your heart and mind."

"Yes, Ed. Yes, they are."

"Good. Because I've just been thinking about that quotation of your General MacArthur you and Lazarus told me about. The one about old soldiers."

He paused once more, long enough for her to begin to worry just a bit.

"What about it?" she prodded finally.

"Well, the first half of it was accurate enough. You didn't die—either of you. But I've been thinking about the second half."

"The bit about fading away?"

"Exactly. I don't think I'll see another Founders' Day, Maneka. The doctors and I have seen that coming for a while."

"Ed—!"

"No, don't interrupt," he said very gently. "I told them not to share the information with you. You're a worrier where the people you care about are concerned, and I didn't want you worrying about me. And, like I said, I'm ready for a good, long sleep. But promise me something, Maneka. Please."

"What?" The tears she could no longer shed hovered in her

voice, and the old man seated among his family—and hers—on the missile deck of the Bolo in which she lived smiled lovingly.

"Promise me that MacArthur was *wrong*, Love," he said. "Promise me you won't 'fade away.' That you—and Lazarus—will look after yourselves and all the other people I love, and all the people they love, and the people those people *will* love. In the end, that's what it's all about, isn't it? Not hatred for the 'enemy'—even the Dog Boys—but protecting the people and things we love. You and Lazarus do that so well, Maneka. Promise me you'll keep doing it."

Maneka swiveled the main optical head so that he could look directly into it. For a moment she longed once more for the human eyes she had lost so long ago, wished he could look into them one more time, *see* the love and the deep, bittersweet joy his words had kindled deep inside her. He couldn't, of course. And, she knew, he really didn't have to. Not after so many long decades together. But whether he needed to see it or not, she needed to express it, and her smoky soprano voice was very quiet, and infinitely gentle, in his mastoid implant.

"Of course we will, my love," she said. "Of course we will."